OCT 2022

THE
KILLING
CODE

THE KILLING CODE

ELLIE MARNEY

(L)(B)

LITTLE, BROWN AND COMPANY

New York Boston

Copyright © 2022 by Ellie Marney

Cover art copyright © 2022 by Mojo Wang. Cover design by Jenny Kimura.
Cover copyright © 2022 by Hachette Book Group, Inc.

Little, Brown and Company
Hachette Book Group
1290 Avenue of the Americas, New York, NY 10104
Visit us at LBYR.com

First Edition: September 2022

Little, Brown and Company is a division of Hachette Book Group, Inc. The Little, Brown name and logo are trademarks of Hachette Book Group, Inc.

The publisher is not responsible for websites (or their content) that are not owned by the publisher.

Quotes on pages 30 and 360 from Elizebeth Friedman's diary, April 22, 1913, box 21, folder 1, ESF Collection, used with the permission of the George C. Marshall Foundation Library.
Quote on page 45 from the poem "1918" (1920) by Phyllis Lewis, published by The Specialty Press.
Quotes on pages 60, 221, and 300 from *An Introduction to Methods for the Solution of Ciphers* (1918) by William F. Friedman, published by Riverbank Laboratories.
Quote on page 89 from "A Few Words on Secret Writing" (1918) by Edgar Allan Poe.
Quotes on pages 112 and 346 from *And I Was There* by Rear Admiral Edwin T. Layton with Capt. Roger Pineau and John Costello. Copyright © 1985 by Estate of Edwin T. Layton and Capt. Roger Pineau and John Costello. Used by permission of HarperCollins Publishers.
Quote on page 121 from the unpublished essay "Intelligent Machinery" (1948) by Alan Turing, used with the permission of the National Physical Laboratory, UK.
Quote on page 129 from *Manual for the Solution of Military Ciphers* (1916) by Colonel Parker Hitt.
Quote on page 141 from Ann Caracristi's October 2011 interview with Veterans History Project, used with the permission of the Library of Congress.
Quote on page 191 from the Espionage Act of 1917: 18 U.S.C. ch37.
Quote on page 203 from Lewis Carroll's letter to Edith Rix (1888).
Quote on page 229 from "The Friedman Lectures" (1958) by William F. Friedman, publicly released June 1977 with the permission of the National Security Agency.
Quotes on pages 245, 262, and 338 from Oral History Interview (1982) by Wilma Davis (née Berryman), publicly released May 2016 with the permission of the National Security Agency.
Quote on page 277 from *Where Is Science Going?* (1933) by Max Planck.
Quote on page 295 from Eleanor Roosevelt's syndicated newspaper column (1957).

Interior art: Blood spatter © Mrspopman1985/Shutterstock.com

Library of Congress Cataloging-in-Publication Data
Names: Marney, Ellie, author.
Title: The killing code / Ellie Marney.
Description: First edition. | New York : Little, Brown and Company, 2022. |
Audience: Ages 14 & up. | Summary: Kit Sutherland moves to Washington, DC, to work as a codebreaker at Arlington Hall, but when she stumbles onto a bloody homicide scene, she joins forces with other female codebreakers to find the person killing government girls.
Identifiers: LCCN 2021051358 | ISBN 9780316339582 (hardcover) | ISBN 9780316340069 (ebook)
Subjects: CYAC: Serial murderers—Fiction. | Cryptography—Fiction. | World War, 1939–1945—Fiction. | Washington (D.C.)—Fiction. | Mystery and detective stories. | LCGFT: Novels.
Classification: LCC PZ7.M34593 Ki 2022 | DDC [Fic]—dc23
LC record available at https://lccn.loc.gov/2021051358

ISBNs: 978-0-316-33958-2 (hardcover), 978-0-316-34006-9 (ebook)

Printed in the United States of America

LSC-C

Printing 1, 2022

This book is dedicated to the tens of thousands of women who worked at signal intelligence facilities like Arlington Hall during World War II—and to every woman who has ever had to hide her light under a bushel.

1

We knew, from our training, about
cryptographic continuity—how these new
codes were based on old codes, and
some of the old elements were bound to
show up again.

                    —BRIGID GLADWELL

June 1942

This is the story of a murderer and about the fast friendship between girls.

Of course, the Great Murderer was the war, in which young men were dashed to pieces while their mothers cried for them back home and millions of innocents were killed by hate in the terrible ovens of Europe. It was not enough merely to love and to hope that the world could be changed by loving. Change would come only with gunshots and battle stations and bomb blasts—love and hope were insufficient.

But it was love and hope that created an immense change of fortune in a third-story room in the mansion schoolhouse of Arlington Hall during the summer of 1942, where Katherine Sutherland lay dying.

Katherine had been dying for most of her life. She had been a sickly infant and a sickly child, sent in her time to more doctors than she could count. Now she was a dying young woman, counting each gasping breath. She'd fought to be allowed to come to this finishing school, where the hunt course and the riding arena and the hockey fields were largely out of her reach. She'd fought to complete her classes in deportment and literature and astronomy and botany and good homemaking. She would never make a good home with some handsome smiling man returned from the war, but it comforted her to know that in a different world, in a different, healthy body, she might have had the option.

Options were the thing. Katherine fought to die in her own way and on her own terms. Mainly that meant fighting to stay where she was happy even at her worst, on the grounds of the school, rather than returning to the clammy embrace of her parents in Pennsylvania, who had long ago realized that nothing they or the doctors did was going to help, that she was never going to make a match or improve the family fortunes. Katherine knew she was a lemon.

Lemon girls, forced to be brave, get to set their own terms.

So Katherine stayed. As the schoolgirls in other rooms packed up for their summer break—a break from which they'd never return, as it happened—she lay on her bed in her nightgown, with the big window open. She looked through it to the cherry trees outside and held the hand of a girl beneath notice because she wore a maid's uniform. This was Kathleen Hopper, and she was Katherine's companion.

Companion and nurse and lady's maid, Kathleen had been hired four years previously because she wasn't Black (Katherine's mother had insisted on a white girl). And a sickly girl needed someone to help her dress, read with her, fix and carry her meals, walk at her pace while others ran.

If it was a confinement for Kathleen—a little like she was slowly dying herself—then that was just the price you paid to hold down a good job. With five siblings back in Scott's Run, she was lucky to *have* a job. But the daily routine of Katherine's life had been the entire existence of Kathleen's for so long that the barriers between employer and domestic had thoroughly broken down, which is why they held hands.

Maybe that wasn't the only reason they held hands.

Now here they are—two lemon girls, lives and minds so intertwined they can't imagine one without the other. Kathleen truly believes that Katherine is only alive because of her. Not in a practical sense, but in a soul sense, like she's easing some of her own energy into Katherine's body. But things have started to change for the worse. She's given and she's given, but it hasn't been enough, and there's nothing Kathleen can do about it.

They've kept pace with each other over these long summer days, reading Austen and Euclid aloud, talking about the way the stars turn in their glimmering constellations and which horse in the stables has the nicest nose for patting. Kathleen has fed Katherine possets and mopped the floors to keep off the dust, and now the windows are open on a glorious soft afternoon.

Katherine folds both their hands into a tented arch and speaks in her breathless voice. "Did you ever think about it, the way our names are so similar? I mean, the day you first came, I said—"

"I know what you said." Kathleen adjusts her seat on the bed. "I was there. I remember."

Katherine isn't deterred. "I said, *Oh my, we're like name twins*. That was the best day."

Kathleen remembers that day's terrors: whether her new employers would like her, whether they'd be awful or take advantage, like her mother had told her sometimes happens. Pressed into service at fourteen, Kathleen was dismayed to find herself in charge of the daily care of a girl her own age. At first it had felt as if she and Katherine were gasping for the same air. But then it became normal and easier, like they were breathing together.

Now Kathleen says nothing in reply, and Katherine, who can least afford to speak, goes on.

"Have you thought about what you're going to do in the fall? When all this is over?"

Kathleen shakes her head, because *all this* is too big, and she doesn't know, she doesn't know what she's going to do. Katherine is her *all this* and has been for some time.

"*I've* been thinking," Katherine says, then pauses to draw breath. Each breath is like shrapnel in her lungs. She leans forward for help with a sip of honey tea, settles her back against the pillows. "I've been thinking, and I've decided. But you have to decide, too."

Kathleen, who knows her decisions mostly mean nothing in this world, plays along. "What have you decided? And don't tell me to start giving away your jewelry again, because you know that's stupid and I won't do it."

Katherine smiles because she can't laugh, but then her smile sobers. "I'm not talking about the jewelry, Katie."

Katherine is Katherine and Kathleen is Katie, so other people can keep them straight. But in the night, they are only Kitty and Katie, which is just how it is when you're cuddled together in solace. Four years, and Kathleen is praying for four more, although she can tell it isn't going to happen.

"Shut up," she whispers, but Katherine will not shut up.

"Listen, and listen good." Katherine's tone is dangerous now. "When all this is over, they'll tell you to go back to West Virginia. A girl like you, with a head full of geometry and piano playing and crossword puzzles and the Latin names of plants—"

"—and how to steam iron and lay a tea tray and light a fire in the grate," Kathleen says, ever practical.

Katherine shakes their joined hands. "You know that's not enough. It'll never be enough. Not anymore."

"It doesn't matter," Kathleen says, but her throat is thick.

"This is the last thing, okay?" Katherine looks out the window, looks back. "It's the best thing I can give you to make up for all the coughing and the bad days." She waves to the foot of the bed. Her trunks are arranged there, and Kathleen always keeps them neat. "Listen to me—listen. I'll go, and then everything will need to be packed up. Sent home."

"No," Kathleen says.

"That's right. No." Katherine has fine blue eyes, and at the moment, they're clear and hot. She clutches both hands of her best friend in all the world. "I want you to take my big trunk, Katie. It has everything in it you'll need. Clothes. Papers. References. Not the jewelry, because someone would make a fuss about that, but money, yes, that they don't know about. Enough to set you on your way. Enough to launch you."

It's like she's talking about a boat setting sail. She's giving Kathleen a boat. Kathleen's heart is pounding. What the hell will she do with a boat?

What will she do without one?

"Someone will notice," Kathleen says, urgent. She doesn't want to think about this. The idea of going back to her parents' tiny shack in Scott's Run—back to copperheads and coal dust and bitter wind whisking up through the plank floor—fills her head with a rushing, panicked sound. But she doesn't want to think of launching into the unknown, alone.

"Nope." Katherine shakes her head. "They'll notice me and what a trouble I am. And they'll probably take what they can carry—the little trunk, my blue handbag. But the big trunk will need to be packed up, and the rugs and blankets and everything will need to be cleared out, and you'll be here to do that."

She coughs again. More honey tea. A respite in her breathing. "I heard from Miss Grey—they've sold Arlington Hall. It's going to the War Department or some such, and you know how muddled everything is with the trains and the gas rations. It could be weeks before anyone notices the trunk has been mislaid. You could take it to Union Station.

You could take it anywhere. It's just dresses to them. No one will care."

"I will care," Kathleen says. Her tears are so well trained they stay on her cheeks without falling.

"You've always cared," Katherine says, then gently, "and this is how I can care back. It's all I can offer, but I give it to you. You can be me to be you. Say you'll take it, Katie. Say you'll live, even when I can't."

Promises are made and kept between girls all the time, but this one means more. Terrified, Kathleen nods her assent because it seems Katherine won't rest easy without it. Their two heads bow together. Impossible to know what other words pass between them, and then the moment is gone and it's evening.

Katherine Sutherland dies in the night, still holding Kathleen's hand.

————

Next morning, everything happens exactly as Katherine predicted. Kathleen is numb. Still in her maid's uniform, she helps wrap the body. She answers questions from the headmistress and accepts a handclasp from Miss Grey. Arrangements are made.

Katherine is taken away, which is the hardest part, but the school is largely empty, and there are no other girls to see the stretcher with the white-wrapped figure carried down the stairs to the mortuary van. The authorities take the blue handbag and the little trunk, all the jewelry in the rosewood box on the dresser.

Of course Kathleen will stay to pack the rest and clear the room; of course she will do this last duty for her mistress. The military trucks are already at the gate, so she will have to make haste. All that remains, the headmistress explains with her gloves in hand, is to finish the last packing, and only a few kitchen staff are left behind. She pats Kathleen's shoulder before departing. After receiving these final instructions, Kathleen is largely forgotten.

Kathleen closes the door, then walks across the room and opens the window wide on the cherry tree view, clutches the white frame with both hands. She has to decide now whether to step into the boat and sail. But all she feels is a sadness so profound it's like dying.

Katherine is the one who died, though. She would be telling you not to be a nincompoop. Step into the boat.

Step into the boat, or stand alone at the dock as the boat pushes off. Either way, she is alone.

She can hear Katherine's voice so clearly. *You can be me to be you. Say you'll live, even when I can't.*

Kathleen remembers her promise. Not allowing herself to think too hard, she steps back from the window and reaches both hands behind her. Cold fingers as she pulls the tie on her apron, unravels the string, slips the apron straps off her shoulders, and eases the garment away. She folds it and lays it on the dresser, because she's accustomed to folding.

She kneels down on the rug and opens the big trunk.

It's familiar, in the way of things she's handled and laid straight a thousand times. But it's also more than she expected. Among the clothes, a folder of papers—references attesting to Miss Katherine Sutherland's good character, the quality of her family. A series of grade reports from Arlington Hall and from other schools, assuring her qualifications and abilities in typing and French and so on. Identity documents and—God bless—a birth certificate, all filigreed along the side. An envelope of cash, which Kathleen is too scared to count, but it looks like a lot. It looks like enough.

How did Katherine put all this together, right under her nose? There's no time to ponder the mystery of it.

Kathleen undoes all the buttons of her black shirtwaist dress and takes off her oxford pumps. She strips off her hose and her brassiere, leaving only her panties. She folds the apron and the dress and everything else into a bundle, which she tucks down inside the trunk.

Then she dresses herself in Katherine's clothes. First the corselette, tucking herself in with the many hooks and eyes. She draws on Katherine's stockings and fixes them in place, eases the slip over her head, smooths it over her thighs. She takes out the traveling suit and puts it on: the navy skirt, the patterned blouse, the navy jacket with the peplum waist. Katherine was winnowed by illness and Kathleen by hard work, so they are of a size. She finds the accompanying shoes, with the continental heel.

She puts everything on, everything she used to put on her mistress. Then she turns to the mirror and faces herself, and what she sees...She doesn't have time for that right now. As she knots the tie of the blouse with shaking fingers, her heartbeat seems very loud.

Her hair is wrong. She unpins her cap and releases her

hair out of its tight, tiny bun at the nape of her neck. Brushes it with Katherine's hairbrush, left in the bowerbird nest on the dresser, along with the other personal items: Katherine's enamel combs, the hairpins and rats, the compact and lipstick, plus the newspaper folded to the last crossword they worked on together. There's a photo of Katherine's family. A dried rose in a bud vase.

Quick, trembling hands as Kathleen rolls and pins her auburn hair in place. Her hair is thick and shorter than is fashionable. She tucks the cap away in the trunk, digs further for another handbag—the soft brown vinyl—and a small brown hat. She pins the hat over her hair, opens the bag, and finds a pair of dark brown gloves. Before she dons the gloves, she powders her face and uses the lipstick. She takes ten dollars—a week's wages—from the envelope and slips it into an inside pocket of the handbag.

Now, in the mirror, she looks more like the girl she's pretending to be. The powder does not disguise her freckles, but freckles are fine—lots of girls have them. Freckles do not give her away. Kathleen adjusts the handbag and buttons the jacket. She practices a few short gestures. Hands like this. Posture upright. She is being Katherine, but not Katherine. She has to erase the Katherine she knew, overwrite her with this new version, the version who is herself.

Kathleen closes her eyes for a moment. The whole thing is disorienting and terrifying.

When her eyes open, the detritus on the dresser seems suddenly, impossibly sad. She can't bear to see it lying there, so she sweeps it all into her handbag—everything but the vase. Then she closes and locks the trunk, clips it upright onto the metal frame with the little wheels, and grabs the handle.

Stepping into the hall makes her breath halt in her throat, but there's no one around—no one at all. Kathleen tries to walk the way Katherine walked, but she's not used to her shoes. After a few feet, she realizes she can't do it like this: She can't *impersonate* Katherine. That will give her away. She straightens and walks with her normal gait, which feels better.

The trunk is a heavy weight. She takes it to the dumbwaiter, but it won't fit. *Dammit*. She takes it to the stairs and begins the long descent.

On the second floor, a young man.

There is both the shock of seeing someone in the empty corridors and the fact that it's a *man*. Typically, the only men on the grounds of the school are the janitor and the groundsman and the kitchen delivery boy.

This man is in uniform, with a rifle on his shoulder.

No, not a rifle. A sawed-off broom handle.

"Can I help you?" Stupid words, servant words. My god, she's blown it the first time she opened her mouth.

But the young man seems just as shocked as she. Or maybe embarrassed, because of the broom handle. Must be that rifles are in short supply. "Uh, no. No, ma'am. We're just clearing the building. We were told all the residents had gone."

It's his manner, perhaps, that allows her to smile. This boy is a servant, just like her. A servant of the War Department.

11

"Yes, I think I'm the only one left," she says brightly.

"Would you like a hand with that trunk, ma'am?"

This is a new concept. "Uh, yes. Thank you, I'd appreciate it."

He wheels the trunk to the next set of stairs. Kathleen has to prevent herself from snatching it back. *Just concentrate on the stairs.* Left foot, right foot, gloved hands on the banister. It's good her hands are gloved—she has the short nails and calluses of a maid.

On the ground floor, the elegant front foyer with the administration desk facing the outside. Parquet under her heels as she directs the soldier to set the trunk just inside the grand entrance door. The door is open, and through it she can see vehicles parked in front of the green hump of the turning circle: vans in wartime drab, plus a black car.

The soldier gives her a brisk salute as he heads back up the stairs.

Now what? She returns to the administration desk and sets her handbag there, pulls out the newspaper and a comb to find the ten dollars. Nervous about losing the money, she slips it into the pocket of her jacket. Then back to the door, to check the clips on the trunk. Sweat on the nape of her neck.

The sound of chatter, and she startles as two young women walk in together from the auditorium off the foyer.

"Oh my. Well, hi there." The taller of the two, black-haired and, shockingly, wearing pants. "Are you one of the girls from the school?"

"Yes." Both true and untrue. She has to think quickly now. She cannot be Katherine and she cannot be Kathleen—she must be an amalgamation of both. She extends a hand, the cotton of her glove soaking up the dampness in her palm. "Kit Sutherland, hi."

"Moya Kershaw." The young woman's handshake is warm, firm, not the limp-fingered polite shake of the upper classes. She looks only a year or so older than Kit herself. "And this here is Dottie. Are you waiting on a cab?"

"Yes." Kit wets her lips. "I mean, I called a cab, but it hasn't arrived."

"It might've been stopped at the gate," Dottie suggests. Dottie is sweet-faced, with blond curls and a pleasing round figure.

Kit acts appropriately flummoxed. "There are soldiers at the gate?"

"Afraid so." Moya leans on the administration desk and takes a cigarette out of a slim pocket case. "The whole building has been appropriated. You didn't hear?"

"I heard," Kit says. "But everything... Well, everything has been a bit of a rush."

"No kidding." Dottie smiles. "Sorry about the cab. Where are you headed?"

"Union Station." It's the first place Kit can think of, and the most obvious. "I guess I'll walk down to the road and wait for the bus."

"Do you need some help with your luggage?" Dottie asks.

"Thanks, but I should be okay." Kit shoulders her handbag

and walks to the trunk. She can do this. She can just walk out the door and keep on walking.

"Miss Sutherland?" Moya's voice. The speculative tone of it turns Kit around.

Her whole face feels stiff. "Yes?"

Moya has lit her cigarette. Her lipstick is fire-engine red. She's tall for a girl, angular and sharp-cornered at hips, shoulders, cheeks. She's holding up the folded newspaper in her other hand. "Is this your crossword puzzle?"

Will a crossword puzzle give her away? Kit thinks for a moment, decides she's being paranoid. "Yes. Sorry, that's mine."

Moya exchanges a glance with Dottie, like they're sharing a secret. "You like puzzles?"

Kit feels perspiration pop at her hairline. But she's too far in to back out now. "I do them in my spare time."

"And you studied here...." Moya cants her head. "What were your favorite subjects?"

The handbag is slipping down Kit's shoulder, but she doesn't want to adjust it. Her throat is very dry. "Literature. Botany. French. I liked the astronomy classes, too." She tries to make it all sound natural. These are the classes she helped Katherine with. "It was better than typing."

Again, the glance between the two other women.

"Do you have family waiting for you? Or a fiancé?" Dottie's cheeks are pink.

Kit feels her answering blush. "Family, yes. Fiancé, no."

Moya steps closer, holding out the folded paper. The red curve of her lipstick is like a lamp in the night. "Miss

Sutherland...what would you say if I told you I might be able to offer you a job helping the war effort?"

Kit stands completely still, except for the round O of her mouth.

I'm stepping into the boat, Katherine. God help me, I'm stepping into the boat.

She takes a single, considered pace toward Moya and Dottie. "I'd say tell me more."

2

cryptology (n.): secret or occult language; from *kruptos* (Gr.), "secret, hidden," and *logos* (Gr.), "word, reason."
From 1945 as "science of secret charac-
ters or codes."

March 1943

"Comin' through! More pencils comin' through! Hey, Kitty-
Kat, I've got the erasers you said you needed." Dottie shim-
mies her way between the rows of chairs and tables in the
workroom, a small cardboard box under her arm. She's a
flash of peach sweater under the new fluorescent lights.

Kit doesn't hear her, too engrossed in the typed numbers on
the index cards laid out on the wooden table in front. She holds
a pencil, and like every other girl at one of the large tables in
Arlington Hall, she is wearing knitted gloves with the fingers
cut off and extra socks. Out the window, the grounds of the
school look quite lovely in the early spring: The cherry trees
that Katherine enjoyed so much have all blossomed. The outside air is getting warmer, a welcome relief after the punish-
ing winter, but the upper floors of the schoolhouse are much
cooler than outside, and conditions are close to icebox.

The workroom hums with low conversation, the scratch of pencils, and the clack of typewriters on the next floor down. In her white cotton blouse and blue sweater and warm skirt and socks, Kit sits forward on her hard wooden chair and counts under her breath. "One, two, and three... And one, and two, and... *there*. Opal, are you seeing that?"

"Show me." Opal Jenks, who usually sits closer to the window, is sitting beside Kit and peering over her shoulder. "One, and two, and three... I'm not seeing it in the first group."

"Next line down." Kit points at a set of numbers on her index card with the pencil's tip. "Wait, I need an eraser—"

"Got you covered," Dottie says, grabbing one from the cardboard box and handing it over.

"Thanks, Dot." Kit's smile is a flash of gratitude before she returns to the cards and makes the correction. She's trying not to get excited. "Okay, here. Do you see it? Next line— here again."

Opal bites her bottom lip, staring at the numbers. "Okay, maybe."

"I don't know." Kit sets down her pencil, leans back, and chafes her fingers together. "Maybe I'm forcing it."

"Show me." Brigid Gladwell pushes back her chair and takes up position on Kit's other side. In every workroom, there is one girl who keeps things running smoothly, and right now, Brigid is it.

Kit angles her cards and points to the number groupings. "Am I imagining things?"

Brigid frowns. "If you are, we're imagining them together."

17

The workroom is packed full of tables and girls: girls in winter coats, girls with victory rolls, girls between the ages of eighteen and twenty-five. A few girls with pencils behind their ears get up and move closer to Kit's table. There's a frisson as everyone senses that something is happening.

"Write it out again." Brigid pushes a notepad over. "Do we have the crib? Rose?"

"One second." Rose, the overlapper, hurries to collect the correct sheet from her table. "Got it!"

"Pass it here." Kit raises a hand, and a little bucket-brigade of girls sends the crib sheet her way.

Kit is on the third floor of the schoolhouse. It's the same floor she left in such a hurry in June last year. But since that time, most of the dorm rooms have been transformed: curtains taken down and replaced, beds dismantled, lush carpets rolled. The bathtubs were too hard to remove. They're all full of intercepts now.

Far away in the Pacific, the Imperial Japanese Army is shooting young American soldiers, with the occasional pause to send a message. Kit works on the messages sent in the pause. Her job is to take a card from the wire basket in front of her, skim each four-digit number, strip out the encryption used by the local operator to forward the numbers to Arlington Hall, then start looking for patterns. Like every other girl in the room, Kit circles four-digit repetitions, two-digit repetitions, subtracts one number group from another, tries a dozen other techniques with slide rule and graph paper to find anything that matches up. Although the numbers on the cards often just look like a garbled string of digits, Kit knows there are words in there somewhere—romanized Japanese words like *dan* and *tuki* and *maru*.

The hum of the radiator by the wall is like a burr inside her brain, the soundtrack of the buzzing intellectual focus that permeates the room.

Kit has become part of a great hive mind.

The work of the hive is breaking enemy codes.

With trembling fingers, she and Opal slide the crib sheet underneath the cards and the rewritten number groupings, to do a comparison.

Other girls have stopped working to observe and make whispered suggestions. "Give 'em more light!" Edith says, and a girl repositions a table lamp.

"Check it against the crib," Brigid instructs them.

Kit's pencil is already tracking along the lines. "I'm checking—"

"Kit, I think I've got one," Opal says, her voice suddenly an octave higher. A hum skitters through the room. "Holy mackerel, Kit—"

"That's one," Kit says, nodding. "And here—"

"I'm calling upstairs," Brigid says decisively, and she starts for the black Bakelite telephone near the door.

Dottie waves a hand. "Moya's on her way down!"

Moya Kershaw walks into the doorway from the corridor. "I'm here already, what's going on?"

Kit glances up, suddenly distracted. Moya's pants are divine and her blouse is silk—which means it's old. Everything is rayon now that Japanese silk is frowned upon.

"Possible break," Brigid says. "Come see."

19

Moya slides between chairs and girls, and Kit puts her head down so nobody will notice her cheeks going pink. She turns back to the hunt for number repetitions.

"I've got one," Opal says, her pencil flying now. "And Kit's got one—"

"I've got two," Kit says. She circles the places where pairs of numbers come together, from the crib and the card. "Here. And here."

Moya plants her palm on Kit's side of the table and leans closer. Kit registers Moya's presence the way she registers the sound of the radiator: like the low buzz of a powerful magnet.

Moya scans the cards, frowning, and everyone holds their breath. Then she says, "That's it. You've got it," and tension breaks as girls all over the room cheer.

Dottie and Rose whoop, embracing, and Opal lets out a ragged hoot. "Kit, we got it!"

"Thank God." Kit huffs out a laugh of relief and pleasure as Opal drags her in for a hug. "I've been seeing those numbers in my dreams."

"Heck yes." Opal rubs her eyes. "That run of code was busting our chops."

"Not anymore." Brigid is grinning. "Great job, girls."

"Yep—well done." Moya is still leaning over the crib sheets. She grabs a loose pencil on the desk and circles another number pair. "But keep pushing. You've got another one here."

Kit blinks at the new pair. "How did I not see that?"

Moya gives her a sphinx smile, straightens. "Congratulations, ladies. You saved some lives today." She looks around. "And now we can save more lives by getting back to work—let's get shakin', the war won't wait."

Her attention is snagged by the sight of a young man in a brown suit standing at the door. Kit recognizes him. Emil Ferrars—Kit can only think of him as Mr. Ferrars—is a twenty-two-year-old math genius who studied at Princeton. Now he works with the legendary Miss Caracristi on some of the most advanced attacks on Imperial Army codes in the Hall.

Mr. Ferrars waves. "Moya? Do you have a minute?"

Dottie notices Mr. Ferrars, too, and immediately straightens her shoulders and smooths a hand down her skirt. Kit hides a smile. Emil Ferrars is tall and slim and attractive, and sometimes, when he is walking around in the cafeteria, he leaves pencils tucked behind his ears or forgets to take off his reading glasses. Dottie has mentioned more than once how she finds this adorable.

Dottie has also mentioned that Mr. Ferrars gets debilitating tension headaches. With his headaches and his brain power, he has a dispensation from the War Department to be at Arlington Hall, instead of on the fighting front, and according to Dottie, he sometimes feels embarrassed about this. Kit thinks that anyone who wants to put Mr. Ferrars in a GI uniform and give him a rifle and push him out to fight Japanese and Germans is obviously a complete idiot. It would be a shocking waste of a first-rate mind.

Moya acknowledges Mr. Ferrars with a nod before turning back. "Okay, duty calls. Dottie, are you done here? They want you back in traffic."

21

"On my way." Dottie gives her hair a little flip as Moya meets Mr. Ferrars at the door and the two of them exit together. Then she leans down to give Kit a sideways squeeze. "You champ. Is that three breaks this month?"

"Just two." Kit smiles, relaxed and happy.

" 'Just two,' she says. Hey, let's celebrate in the cafeteria later—Carol said there's crullers." Dottie straightens her sweater. "And did you hear the latest gossip? There's *English guys* coming to visit."

Kit frowns. "Why?"

"To watch our magic pencils work, I guess." Dottie waggles her eyebrows. "I hope they look like Joel McCrea and sound like Cary Grant."

Kit rolls her eyes. "They're probably all sixty years old, with hair coming out their ears."

"Ew, get away, you." Dottie stands. "Cafeteria at four?"

"For sure. Okay, go on now, before Moya rolls around again." Dottie gives her a cheeky salute and heads for the door.

"All right, ladies, fun's over," Brigid announces as girls find their seats again. "Let's get focused."

Opal lifts her chin at Dottie's retreating figure. "English guys are visiting Arlington Hall?"

Kit's still feeling a hazy glow of euphoria from vanquishing the code. "If you believe the rumors. I suppose that'll mean more security."

Opal rolls her eyes. "We've already got ID badges and military police on duty and steel-mesh fences all over the compound. What are they gonna do, check our panty girdles?"

Kit snorts in reply. But she's thinking about it.

She settles herself in her chair and tries to shift her concentration back to the card in front of her. The numbers on it are a disguise, and it's her job to strip that disguise away.

The irony is not lost on her.

She and Opal look for more repetitions until the shift change at four, when all the girls put down their pencils and tidy their workstations and their hair, ease off their gloves, and head for the door. They join the hallway rush of girls exiting from other rooms, and a half dozen streams of girls all meet in a great girl river that flows down the left side of the corridor. On the right side, flowing up, more girls arrive for the 4:00 PM till midnight shift.

Kit diverges near the banister to slip into her dorm room. Only six rooms on Floor Three are dorms, with another six rooms on the floor below and a handful on One. There are many more girls than rooms, so the bulk of the workforce is housed off-site.

She removes her gloves and hangs her coat, feeling cooler but more comfortable, and takes off her shoes. Then she sits on her made bed, waiting for the shifting numbers in her head to dissipate.

The room itself is tiny, with dark dado panels and twin beds on either side of a window. A wardrobe with an attached mirror stands between the bed and the door on Dottie's side, and on Kit's side, a dresser. If she straightens her legs, her toes will touch the metal frame of Dottie's bed. But Kit doesn't mind; it's a long way from the room she grew up in, with newspapers glued to the walls, the barrel stove with the hot water jug on top, an enamel plate warming leftover cornbread.

Underneath her bed is the trunk—Katherine's trunk—with all the elements she requires to perpetuate her facade.

The window view shows the familiar genteel green quad of the school grounds. Past the western edge of the schoolhouse lies the forested part of the property. Somewhere among those trees, the old stables. A mile or so beyond the forest are more steel-mesh fences, but Kit can't see them from here.

Past the quad lawn, behind the schoolhouse, lies the former administration cottage. Farther back, construction has ripped a gash in the green as War Department workers complete a new storehouse on the sloping land behind. It's a shame to wreck the lovely area at the north of the grounds, but God knows they need the space. Where on earth will they put the English visitors?

Nine months ago, Kit was given an opportunity. Once the interview and paper checks were over, she simply became another girl. There are girls everywhere now: girls in the streets, girls in uniform, girls in the newly completed Pentagon building three miles away. Girls are crammed into every available space in the capital, hot-bedding it in billet bunkhouses, lining the counters at drugstores and train stations, sitting three abreast on buses. Newspaper editorials complain about the lipstick brigade, but that's just how it is while the boys are overseas.

Another government girl swelling the ranks of the Signal Intelligence Service and Washington, DC, in general...Kit is hiding in a forest, just one more tree. She's been counting on that anonymity. She has her trunk, her handbag, her shared room with Dottie, and her photo ID badge with the color of her clearance plainly marked. She stays low to the ground. She does her work.

Arlington Hall has been her refuge.

But foreign emissaries coming to the Hall might change the routine.

Kit recognizes the light flutter of fear in her chest, assuages it by watching the leaves shift in the trees outside. The oaks remind her of childhood, of lugging bundles of oak bark down from the mountain—her mother used to sell the bark to the tannery at one cent per pound. Kit puts that old memory firmly aside; thinking too much about who she was, who she became, and who she is now makes her head ache. She concentrates instead on simply absorbing the quiet in the room.

When the door of the room opens, Kit's first reaction is disappointment.

"You forgot, didn't you?" Dottie says, bustling in. "I had a feeling you'd forget."

Kit bites her lip. "The cafeteria—"

"Don't worry about it, hon." Dottie grins. She's wearing the cutest gingham shirt, the collar peeking over the neck of her peach sweater, and her blond curls are bouncing. "I just came down from Four myself. Emil Ferrars had a little headache episode, so I stayed to help Moya."

"Is Mr. Ferrars okay?"

"He'll be okay. It's just the pace—you think it's busy here on Three, it's goddamn frantic in the attic."

"He should move offices, so he's closer to the infirmary," Kit suggests.

"It'll never happen." Dottie warms her legs by the radiator. "They'd never move the high-classification stuff to a lower floor—too much foot traffic. And there's no available offices down on One anyway. This whole place is like a warren crammed with rabbits."

Kit wonders if asking about the English visitors would seem suspicious. The transition from maid to upper middle class has her constantly watching how she presents. For the last nine months she has checked herself: Is her question too nosy? Is it something she should already know? Is her accent or phrasing too coarse?

At least with Dottie she doesn't have to worry too much. Dorothy Crockford comes from Baltimore, where her father runs a grocery, and she acts the same whether she's talking to kitchen staff or debutantes. Kit has learned a lot, spending time with Dottie, and not just about the Hall gossip. "So what's the story with the English guys?" Kit prompts her.

"I don't know much," Dottie admits, stripping off her sweater and hanging it in the wardrobe. "Just what I've overheard while I'm collecting transcripts, and it's not for repeating, okay? But they're arriving sometime in the next two weeks."

Two weeks. "What are they coming here for?"

"Picking up tips, maybe?" Dottie takes off her shirt, shivering, and settles it over the rail at the foot of her bed. She retrieves a pink utility dress out of the wardrobe. "According to Moya, they have their own unit in England, doing all the same stuff we're doing. They got started before we did, she says."

Kit kicks her legs gently. "So it could be us picking up tips."

"You think?" Dottie's expression says she finds this doubtful as she unbuttons her skirt. "But why would they come here if they didn't need help with something?"

"Exchange of ideas?" Kit suggests.

"I'll 'exchange ideas' with English boys any day of the week." Dottie gives Kit a flirty wink as she steps out of her skirt. "Are you coming with me to Arlington Farms tonight?"

That would be a no. But Kit can't explain what keeps her tethered to the Hall. "I'm thinking about it."

Dottie shakes her head. "That's what you always say. Well, don't think too long, I'm leaving at five thirty."

"My brain is beat." Kit makes it sound like a confession. "I don't know that I'll be much good for conversation."

"Good-looking soldiers and music playing—who needs conversation?" Dottie puts away her skirt and shirt. Her voice turns wheedling as she wiggles her way into the utility dress and ties the belt. "Come on, Kitty-Kat, I'll do your hair and let you borrow my lipstick...."

Kit smiles at the idea of someone doing *her* hair, instead of the other way around. "I'd be more tempted if my feet and back weren't so darned sore. But I'll help you draw on your stocking seams, how about that?"

"I'd take your company over a stocking seam, but sure. If your feet are already hurting, then a dance won't be much fun." Dottie pulls a new sweater over her dress and finesses her collar. "If you're not coming out, at least walk down with me to the cafeteria. Come on, I know you missed lunch."

"Do you think anyone in the cafeteria would notice if I showed up in my slippers?" Kit sees Dottie's expression. "Oh, all right then."

Kit shoves her shoes back on and follows Dottie out. The shoes are still bothering her; Katherine was half a size smaller. Kit's had plans to buy new ones, even has a ration card for them, but who has the time? The schedule is seven days on and one day off. On her day off, she mostly wants to sleep.

And if she's a little nervous about leaving the known quantity of Arlington Hall, braving the wider world, then that's understandable, too.

She accompanies Dottie downstairs and through the first-floor hallway to the cafeteria—what used to be the old concert auditorium—where they find trays and collect dishes of meatloaf and coleslaw, with a side of Jell-O. The crullers are already gone, which is a shame. The kitchen only gets a limited ration of butter and sugar, so it might be a while until they get more.

Half an hour later, Kit is drawing Dottie's stocking seams on. Dottie stands on two big dictionaries—one German, one Japanese—that she's borrowed from the transcribing room. "You're going with Edith and Carol?" Kit asks.

"And Libby. And Betty from Two said she might come along." Dottie holds her skirt hem high above her knees. "What will you do here tonight, all on your own?"

"Mm...don't know. Maybe join in Moya's poker game?"

28

"Since when have you ever—and *don't*, she'll fleece you blind!" Dottie laughs, twists around to see. "Hey, I'll be catching the last bus home, so don't wait up."

"Okay," Kit says. "Now hold still."

"I'm holding still! But listen, I meant what I said—you oughta get out more, Kitty. Throw care to the wind a little!"

"Next time," Kit says, knowing there won't be a next time, trailing the eyebrow pencil down the back of Dottie's leg with a steady hand.

3

Kit does not go to the poker game. Time alone is such a rarity, and only when she's alone can she truly relax. She gets hot chocolate from the cafeteria and reads in bed—an old copy of *Emma*, a book that always made Katherine laugh—and then at about ten o'clock, she turns off her lamp and goes to sleep.

At 1:00 AM, she wakes up.

She knows it's 1:00 AM because the hands of the bedside alarm clock glow faintly in the dark. The curtains are open. Through the frosted window, Kit can see the stars wheeling high in the night above the trees.

A glimmer catches on the tight folds of the bed opposite.

Kit turns on the lamp. Dottie's bed is empty, still neatly made. For a second, Kit's head is foggy. She looks at the bed, then the clock. Back to the bed.

She reaches for her robe.

As she scuffs on her slippers, she runs through the possibilities: Dottie went to the Farms. She could have missed the last bus. The dance might have run late.

But Kit's pretty sure that the matrons who run these things would want everything packed up by midnight. Folks have to go home, get some sleep, go to work the next day. All the girls at Arlington Farms are government girls.

The bus might have broken down....Kit rules that out quickly. *Think now.* What are the other options? Dottie could have met someone. That isn't unlikely, but it's unlike Dottie. She's not really a "stay the night on the first date" kind of gal.

Kit considers more ideas, discards them. The room is cold with the curtains open. Kit bites her lip for a moment, then exits to the corridor.

She goes down one floor. It feels peculiar, walking around the Hall in her slippers and pajamas when other girls are working at the tables just one corridor away.

The door Kit arrives at is made of dark wood, like the dado on the walls. Kit raises her fist, hesitates.

Moya is her colleague. Dottie's friend and therefore *her* friend. But Moya is also the Floor Three supervisor—essentially, her boss. She bats away the other concern, that Moya is sharp-cornered and glamorous in a way that makes Kit a little tongue-tied. Moya has a cool, steely center that's a little intimidating.

And Kit doesn't want to get Dottie into trouble. But maybe Dottie is already in trouble.

Kit raps sharply. "Moya, it's me."

Muffled sound of movement. Moments later, the door opens inward. Moya is in a men's dressing gown, her typically sleek hair tousled. She's holding a silver lighter and there's a cigarette stuck between her teeth.

"Dottie hasn't come home," Kit says.

Moya rubs her forehead with the back of her hand. "It's one in the morning."

31

"Yes. And Dottie hasn't come home."

There's a pause.

"Shit." Moya lights the cigarette. "One minute." She shuts the door in Kit's face.

Kit waits in the cold corridor, shifting on her feet. Someone could come by. Girls from the typing rooms nearby could come out to the bathroom and see her standing here in her slippers and robe—

The door opens again, and Moya is wearing brown twill trousers and a white button-up shirt. She's pulled a jacket on, too—a leather jacket, with a shearling collar. She's still smoking the cigarette, and she's wearing soft boots. She has a dark blue scarf in her hand. "Dottie went to the Farms? To the dance tonight?" Moya closes her dorm room behind herself.

Kit steps back as Moya locks her door. "Yes."

"Right." Moya starts walking back to the stairs.

Kit realizes she's supposed to follow. "She said she was catching the last bus home."

"*That* obviously didn't happen." Moya ties the blue scarf around her hair as they take the stairs to Three, to Kit's room. Moya waves a hand. "Get dressed. You're still in your pajamas."

Flustered, Kit realizes this is true. She goes into her room and quickly dispenses with her robe and nightwear to throw on a corduroy skirt, warm shirt, long socks, a sweater, her brown coat.

Moya talks to her through the door. "Was Dottie meeting anyone at the Farms?"

"No," Kit says back to the wood. She makes a face as she

puts on a different pair of shoes: her old oxfords, with the Cuban heel. They give her all kinds of weird feelings, but they're definitely more practical in this situation. "Actually—I don't know. She went with some other people. Betty from Two. Libby. Edith. Carol."

"Carol from Hagerstown?"

"Carol from New Jersey."

"Oh, okay." The smell of Moya's cigarette is seeping under the door. "And they're all back now?"

"I don't know," Kit says. She opens the door.

Moya is leaning against the door jamb, looking down the hall. "I can ask Beverley Gaskin to check. She's on nights. Is Dottie involved with anyone at Arlington Farms?"

Kit is confused by the question. Arlington Farms is a brand-new facility. It's only three and a half miles northeast of the Hall and a short bus ride away from DC proper, which makes it popular accommodation for government girls. It's also an all-female dormitory residence.

"The—what?"

"Is she *involved* with anyone at Arlington Farms?" Moya makes a face. "Kit, please don't be dense."

"No. Um." Kit blushes, because she really isn't dense. It's just surprising that Moya is so casual about it. "You know Dottie. If she missed the bus, she would have caught a cab. She knows breaking curfew isn't worth it."

"All right." Moya starts walking again. "Let's go find Emil."

Kit trots to keep up, pulling at her sweater sleeves under her coat. "Why Mr. Ferrars?"

"Because we need a ride and he owes me a favor."

They stop near the workrooms so Moya can ask Beverley Gaskin who's come back from the dance. Betty and Edith and Carol have all returned. Libby works elsewhere, in intercept logging, but she's reliable; she's probably back. Moya thanks Beverley and gives Kit a significant look.

They take the stairs again, up to Four. This is not a part of the schoolhouse that Kit is typically allowed to visit. The attic corridor is brightly lit, and the sounds of conversation and movement come from rooms on each side. As she and Moya pass an open door, Kit sees two girls, both in their twenties and working at typewriters. Kit wonders if any of the Hall codebreaking superstars are on shift—Miss Berryman, maybe, or Mr. Kullback.

It's warmer up here than on Three. They arrive at a door at the far end that's in a dim alcove. Kit remembers this room—it was originally used for storing field hockey equipment, when Arlington Hall was still a school.

Moya raps on the door.

After a moment, the sound of a polite voice. "Yes?"

"Emil, open up," Moya says.

The door obliges, and Emil Ferrars stands barefoot in trousers and a long-sleeved undershirt. Kit's first thought is that Dottie would probably prefer to be the one seeing Mr. Ferrars in his undershirt.

"What's happening?" Mr. Ferrars says, blinking.

Moya blows smoke above his head. "One of my girls is AWOL at Arlington Farms, and I want her back without a lot of fuss."

"Moya, it's one in the morning."

"She's a good girl, Emil."

Mr. Ferrars sighs and pulls his braces up onto his shoulders. "I'll get my coat."

He comes out straight after putting on a shirt and a sweater, carrying his shoes—he pulls them on in the corridor—and hands Moya his coat. "The keys are in my coat pocket." He leans on the wall to tie his shoelaces. "Inside left."

"Will you be okay to drive, after this afternoon?" Moya is being cryptic, but Kit knows Mr. Ferrars usually needs to rest after an episode of his illness.

"I'll be fine," he says calmly.

The typewriting women don't even blink as they walk past again. Mr. Ferrars has slightly longer strides. Moya has long legs, but Kit has to double her pace to keep up.

"You'll owe me big time after this, Moya," Mr. Ferrars says.

Moya laughs. "That's what you always say."

"My head just hit the pillow."

Kit knows what that's like, and she feels bad for him. "I'm sorry."

"Oh, it's not your fault." He glances over. He has nice brown eyes. "Let's just hope your young lady's all right."

Kit isn't sure what to say to that, because it strikes a very solemn chord inside her.

The remaining trip downstairs is very quick. They don't go out the main door on One; instead, Moya and Mr. Ferrars veer left and walk past rooms—including some quiet dorm rooms—to the far end of the carpeted corridor, where they turn left again and go under the stairs.

They exit through a rear door and come out on the concrete steps. To the right is a parking area with a few black-domed vehicles. Mr. Ferrars and Moya head straight for the parking area. Kit pulls her coat closer and rubs her arms: The night outside is way colder than the schoolhouse, and her breath steams up in front of her.

"Have you got enough gas?" Moya isn't talking to Kit.

"Yes." Mr. Ferrars jogs to the nearest sedan—a very nice black Chrysler—and unlocks the driver's side, gets in, and leans across to unlock the passenger side. "Although I was hoping to save some for a midweek trip to town."

"Sorry, Emil." Moya seems sincere this time. She flicks away her cigarette butt, then slides into the passenger seat and waves Kit over. "Come on, let's move."

After a brief hesitation, Kit gets in the back. She's never ridden in a personal car before. She's taken the train and the bus, and twice she's been in cabs. The leather seat is freezing under her palms, and she's glad she wore corduroy.

Emil Ferrars starts the engine, backs the car out of its parking spot, and they coast down the moonlit curve of driveway to the security gate, where they're waved out by the MP on duty.

Kit feels like she's in the middle of some bizarre dream. Driving along Arlington Boulevard at this time of night is slow and strange, and there are few other cars on the road. The streetlights are off, and everyone is driving with dimmed headlights because of blackout rules. The moon is an advantage, but Mr. Ferrars is still not going more than fifteen miles an hour. It's weirdly lonely, being out in the Virginia night like this.

Moya turns to look at her. "Do you know where Dottie might be? Idaho hall?"

"I think so." Kit's not sure, but that's where the jitterbug dances are usually held.

"Let's start there and work our way around." Moya rubs her hands together to warm them. "I'd prefer not to wake up half the Farms residents unless I have to."

Arlington Farms is colloquially known as Twenty-Eight Acres of Girls. Dances there attract servicemen from all over, and Dottie has said that some of the men are nice and some of them are dull, and many of them are overeager. The matrons keep an eye on things, but Kit knows that it's very easy for social situations to get out of hand. Sometimes it's hard for polite girls to say no. She looks out at the moonlit oaks going past the window of Mr. Ferrars's car and hopes Dottie is okay.

They turn a sharp corner off South Washington Boulevard onto Arlington Ridge Road and then into the driveway. The Farms are still finishing construction—pretty much everything war-related is still finishing construction—and the landscape is dusty once they get past the main gate. Kit is reminded again of her past: black walnuts in the fall, water from the spring down the hill, red clay dirt in the yard. There's a lot of dirt and concrete at Arlington Farms, and not much grass. Some of the piping is exposed, yet to be disguised under gardens. In the dark, all the boxy two-story buildings look like so much warehousing, with the occasional big tree.

Midnight shifts started nearly two hours ago, and the

place is ghostly quiet. There are no pedestrians. Everyone who can sleep is sleeping.

Mr. Ferrars pulls up right outside the front entrance of a prefab building with a large, high portico and lots of windows. The sign on the front reads IDAHO. Across the street, an INFIRMARY. Moya jumps out straightaway.

"Do you want me to come in?" Emil Ferrars asks through the open car window.

"Not for this." Moya's walking backward. "Stay here. Hopefully we'll be right back." She glances at Kit. "Come on, what you waiting for?"

Kit isn't sure why Moya needs *her*, if she doesn't need Mr. Ferrars. But Moya's voice is commanding, so Kit opens her door and follows Moya into the building.

The lobby is a large, wood-floored open space with a round pedestal couch at its center. On the right, an unoccupied desk. On the left, a long counter stands in front of a wall of mail slots. There's a WAVES reservist on duty, but she's reading a newspaper.

She looks up as they come in. "Bit early, isn't it?"

Moya's voice loses its tone of authority, becomes polite and casual. "We're looking for a friend. She came out to the jitterbug dance tonight, but she hasn't made it home yet."

"Maybe she stayed on with a resident, if she missed the bus," the reservist says.

"It's possible, but she's breaking curfew." Moya takes her case of cigarettes out of her jacket pocket, opens it, and offers one. "We're trying to save her a headache come sunup."

The WAVES reservist considers, takes a cigarette. "I've had that headache from time to time."

"Dottie Crockford." Moya's lighter is already in her hand. "About yea high, blond curls..." Moya turns to Kit. "What was she wearing?"

Kit steps forward. "Uh, a pink dress with a red sweater. And saddle shoes. She didn't take a coat."

Moya pockets her lighter once the cigarette is lit. "She was here with four other girls from the Hall."

At the mention of "the Hall," the WAVES reservist straightens, blows smoke upward. "Well, my duty shift only started at midnight, but I haven't seen her."

"She might've sat down somewhere for a rest and fallen asleep."

"You could check the kitchen and the bathrooms? I don't know where else she might be, if she isn't in one of the dorm rooms. The service shop's been closed since eight. Everything else is closed, too."

"What about the infirmary?" Kit asks suddenly. She catches Moya's fast, approving glance.

The reservist doesn't seem convinced. "Was she feeling poorly?"

"Not when she left. But she might've gotten dizzy from the jitterbugging." *Or if she had a drink.* Kit knows she doesn't have to say this last out loud.

"Is there someone on duty at the infirmary?" Moya asks.

"Yes, ma'am." The WAVES reservist holds her cigarette politely under the counter.

Moya turns to Kit again. "You go across the street and check. I'm gonna look here."

Kit walks out the way she came in, as Moya and the servicewoman negotiate whether the reservist can leave her post to help Moya search. Kit exits the building and hurries past the car.

Emil Ferrars is leaning out the window. "Need a hand?"

"Give us another minute."

"Happy to wait."

She takes the path to the infirmary, another building with the same portico but lower set. There's a warm-looking lamp on in the foyer and a nurses' station with an older lady—in her thirties—on duty. Kit outlines their search and asks the question.

The woman shakes her head. "Not that I know of, dear. We've only got two beds occupied right now, and those girls are both residents."

Dammit. Kit's anxiety bubbles inside her. "Well, thanks anyway."

"You could try the back lounge of Idaho, or Ohio next door." When Kit looks mystified, the nurse explains. "There's a little seat out the back door of each residence, for girls who want to sit and smoke."

Kit grabs onto that spark of hope. "Thank you, that's really helpful."

"You're welcome." The nurse smiles. "I hope you find your friend."

Kit backtracks across the dark street. But instead of going into the Idaho lobby, she follows the concrete path left, toward the back of the residence. It's a little walk—about ten rooms long, according to the window count.

At the rear of the building, it's just like the nurse said: A set of steps leads from dirt at ground level up to a shadowed backdoor porch. A wooden bench seat is knocked together there, decorated with an ashtray. Two empty glasses sit on the railing. No Dottie.

Oh Dottie, honey, where are you?

As Kit bites her lip, a light comes on at the kitchen window and the back door opens. It's Moya, alone.

"Anything?" When Kit shakes her head, Moya deflates a little. "I got nothing, either."

"Give me a minute to check next door," Kit says. She's not leaving until they've exhausted all possibilities.

"I'll come with." Moya flicks off the light and descends the steps. "I can check the kitchen and the lobby in Ohio."

They follow another concrete path in the dark. Kit doesn't want to say she's worried about more than Dottie breaking curfew, but Moya confronts those fears head-on. "Would she have gotten into a serviceman's vehicle?"

Kit is relieved she's not the only one thinking about this. "Not if she was sober."

"Well, there's no guarantee of that."

"I know. But Dottie's not stupid. You know how she is— she acts frothy and she's outgoing, but she keeps her head."

There are two buildings at the end of the split path: Ohio hall on the left and a much smaller Cemesto structure on the right, maybe a laundry.

"You go right, I'll go left," Moya says.

41

Kit takes the right path, but she's only made it a few paces before she hears Moya's shout. She returns at a run.

Dottie's on the cushioned rattan couch on the back porch of Ohio, a blanket over her shoulders. Moya is sitting beside her, giving her a squeeze. Dottie's face is pale and her hair is curling all over. She's still got her shoes on.

"...thought I'd lie down just for a minute. What time is it?"

"Late," Kit says, taking the steps. "But that doesn't matter—are you okay?"

"I'm fine." Dottie's hand pushes through her hair. She looks disoriented. "Just cold, and a little woozy. But I only had punch all night, I swear."

Moya leans in to check her eyes. "You take a glass from one of the boys?"

"One or two..." Dottie's blush isn't visible in the shadows.

"Sounds like someone mickeyed your drink, honey."

Dottie bursts into tears.

Moya hugs her gently. "You don't look mussed—you must've made it out here before anything happened."

Kit's relief is coursing through her like a gush of warm water. She kneels, chafing Dottie's hands. "How did you end up out here, Dot?"

"Oh, Kit!" Dottie reaches out, silver on her face in the moonlight. "I don't even remember!"

"It's okay. It's all right." Kit lets her cling. "Dottie, I'm so glad we found you. Are you okay to walk?"

"I think I can walk," Dottie says, voice muddy. "Let me try."

"We've got a car. Mr. Ferrars—"

"Hey!" An angry female voice comes from somewhere in the building behind them. *"Folks tryna sleep here!"*

Moya eyes Kit. "Let's go."

They help Dottie stand and start walking the path back toward Idaho. Dottie really is woozy—they have to direct her steps.

Now that the anxiety and adrenaline have faded, Kit is returning back to her body. She feels an urgency that didn't even register before. She looks at Moya. "Can you take her? I need the bathroom."

"I wouldn't go back into Ohio, if I were you," Moya warns. "Let me try the laundry."

Kit quick-steps back along the path, follows the right-hand turning to the little prefab concrete-and-asbestos laundry. Outside, there's another bench seat and the familiar portico, but even smaller scale.

Inside, it's dark as hell. Kit can't locate the light switch. Moonlight through the windows reveals steel and concrete tubs along the left wall and folded drying racks leaning together like a monkey puzzle. At the end of the room, a door labeled in glowing white: BATHROOM.

Thank God. Kit walks past the tubs and pushes the bathroom door enough to see another door for the nearest stall. She hurries in. Blessed relief.

She has to find the toilet paper by feeling along the wall of the cubicle. The sounds of her fumbles for the flush echo strangely in the enclosed concrete space. She hits her fingers on the cistern—dammit. No, she's got it. The plumbing is loud, and Kit thinks guiltily of the women trying to rest in the dorms nearby.

She comes out to wash her hands. It's pitch-black and freezing, and the concrete under her shoes feels tacky. She follows the glint of a mirror, but takes only two steps before she trips over something. When her hands go down, they don't connect with cold concrete. Her left hand lands in a puddle, and her right hand—

It's something she recognizes by touch. Fabric, and the soft give of flesh.

There's someone in here, lying on the floor.

Kit pitches back, shuffles away quickly on her butt, breath hitching, mouth open, overcome by a prickly sub-terranean sense of wrong. It rises in her like steam, melds with the tang of concrete and iron in the air. A miasmic terror that builds and builds inside her until it reaches an overpowering peak.

When her back hits the wall near the door, she reaches with one hand for the light switch that must be here, it *must* be—

She finds it. Flicks up hard.

Her left hand is painted a bright, violent red against the white wall in the stark light.

Kit looks back.

Starts screaming.

4

Oh God, is there no light,
And no release from grief?
—PHYLLIS LEWIS

Moya hears the screams while she's tucking Dottie into the backseat of the Chrysler.

Dottie startles. "What *is* that?"

That's Kit's voice. Moya turns to Emil, who is holding the door of the car. "Take her. Look after her."

"It's all right, Miss Crockford, don't you worry." Emil kneels beside Dottie and holds her hand, glancing up. "Moya—"

"Stay with Dottie!"

Moya runs back along the path in the dark. Her mind contracts on the idea that she's running toward Kit—a girl she's noticed, a girl she's been careful to maintain distance from because she can't afford that kind of distraction. And the guy who drugged Dottie could still be here, could have been hiding while they—

A shape barrels out of the night, slams into her.

It's Kit, hands lifted. "Oh *Jesus.* Oh *God*—"

"Kit." Moya stumbles back, then catches the girl by the shoulders. "What are you—"

Kit sags in Moya's grip for a second, her body warm. Then she jerks sideways and is messily sick onto the dirt.

Moya manages to catch her around the waist before she keels over. Kit heaves again; the noises coming out of her are vile and lost and deeply human. There is something terribly wrong. Kit is not given to fits of the vapors. She comes from money, yet she is not the typical snob. She's guarded, and tense for reasons Moya cannot fathom, but she's one of the best recruits they've taken on. She's highly intelligent, quietly dependable.

"Kit." Moya moves a hand to keep Kit's hair back. Kit's shaking like a leaf. "Honey, tell me what's—"

"There's a girl in the laundry and she's dead," Kit gasps, still bent over.

Moya freezes.

Kit heaves once more. Spits and makes a groan. "There's a girl in there, and she's—" Her next indrawn breath is a sob. "Oh *God*, I never…Oh *God*!"

Moya exhales as dread unfurls inside her. She pulls her scarf free from her hair. "Wipe your face. Let me go see."

"No!" Kit grabs her hand with the proffered scarf. "You don't want to see. You don't want to—"

"But I have to," Moya says. "That's the first thing I have to do, Kit."

To confirm. She already knows that what Kit's saying must be true. Beyond her observations of Kit's reliability, Moya grew up in New York City. She was raised blue collar, and she's seen things; she has heard women cry like this before.

Moya looks over. There's a glimmer through the windows of the dark laundry building, from the light Kit must have left on.

"I can't go back in there," Kit blurts, her pale face glowing in the night.

"It's okay." Moya didn't expect help. It's her job to be tough when others can't be.

Kit looks apologetic and horrified and messed up all at once. Suddenly another brighter light cuts across her face—someone has switched on a lamp in Idaho. Moya has to act fast.

"Stay here," she commands. "Don't move until I come back."

Moya turns toward the laundry. Before Arlington Hall, she spent six months working in the Notifications Office, typing up messages about sons and husbands and brothers killed or missing in action. It gave her a hide like a rhinoceros—it was that or cry at work every day.

"Wait," Kit says. "It's not okay. You shouldn't go in there alone. I'll...I'll come with you."

Moya turns back, blinks: Nobody has ever volunteered to do the tough stuff with her before, and it clearly took a lot for Kit to make the offer. But she needs to stay focused. "Are you gonna throw up again?"

"No." Kit straightens, stuffs the scarf in her coat pocket. "I don't think so."

She's close enough that Moya can still feel her warmth, or maybe it's just the warmth of her support. "All right, then. Come on."

They walk to the building together. The door is shadowed by the portico and cold to the touch. Moya doesn't consciously steel herself, but she switches over to her work-self, her "just get the job done" self. The part of her that's used to reading transcribed intercepts reporting the deaths of men lost at sea, men fallen in battle. She leverages every bit of that work-self now as she opens the laundry door.

Kit's voice is a whisper. "She's in the bathroom at the end."

Moya feels her breathing ratchet higher, controls it. She and Kit walk close to each other, moving past the dark shapes of washing tubs and a spider-tangle of drying racks to the bathroom door. It's edged all around with light.

Kit's teeth are chattering. Moya puts out a hand—maybe she thinks she's urging Kit behind her, but instead she finds her hand clasped, Kit's fever-hot fingers in her own.

Moya hasn't held hands with a girl for a long time, and the contact brings a jolt. Her voice comes out low and rusty. "You can stand behind me if you want."

Kit's grip tightens. "Not for this."

"Okay." There's a fluster in Moya's head that makes her glad they're both facing forward. "Are you ready?"

"No. But go ahead."

Moya reaches with her free hand and pushes the bathroom door gently open.

Oh.

Oh, oh.

Moya's breath escapes in a sharp huff of air. The first sight of it is like an assault—stark white, attacking red. Like she's been slapped. She should've braced more: Kit held her hand and she got distracted, but this is not...this is not...

This is a girl on the white-painted concrete floor of the bathroom. She is dead—no one can lose so much blood without dying.

Oh my god, there is blood *everywhere*: on the floor, under the girl, on the white sink, on the wall. Moya feels like her eyelids have peeled back to take it all in.

The girl's delicate body is splayed obscenely. Her skirt is hiked up, her face turned away. She's lying on her back, and there are glistening mauve loops on her torso that look like flowers until Moya recognizes them for what they are. For a moment, she's light-headed. Then Kit's brutal grip on her hand registers and her senses return, and she remembers to inhale. "What...what is it?"

"Oh no." Kit has tears on her cheeks. "I think...I think that's Libby Armstrong. The brunette hair and the pink skirt—"

"No," Moya whispers, denying it instinctively.

Kit nods. "It's her."

And suddenly it's as if the entire scene before them has been flipped upside down, because this is Libby Armstrong lying on the laundry floor. Moya saw Libby yesterday in the log room on Three. Now that girl with the shy smile is here, in a pool of blood, unrecognizable except for her skirt and—

"Shoes," Moya says, her lips numb. "She's wearing those brown pumps with the little bows."

"Yeah," Kit says, voice hitching.

One pump is loose, like Libby's about to slip it off. Oh *God*.

Moya closes her eyes for a moment, but then she realizes—she has to record this. She has to hold it all in her head, in order to give a proper account. It will keep her and Kit in control of their emotions. It will be necessary for the police.

And it's necessary for Libby, so there's a witness. It might help somehow, in some way—

In what way? This girl is dead. No one is coming to bring her back to life—

Shut up, shut up.

Moya swallows. "Kit, hold the door." God, her voice is so hoarse! But it feels good to be issuing orders.

Kit doesn't seem to mind receiving them. She props the door open with her foot. "What are you—"

"Help me." Not an order. Too trembling to be an order. Moya clutches Kit's hand tight. "What else do you see?"

"Her...her stockings are torn." Kit's voice is faint.

"She's got pink nail polish," Moya says. A sickening cold sweat pops on her forehead, down her neck. "A gray blouse."

"Yeah. And she—" Kit gulps audibly. "No purse. I don't see a purse."

"Or a coat." Moya presses her lips. "Are those footprints?"

"I think they're mine." Kit sounds ill.

"No. Your footprints are over there."

"And that's my handprint on the wall. . . . Moya, let's go. I want to go."

"Okay. Let me just..." Moya takes one unsteady step farther in, over the threshold. She makes herself look. Trails her eyes over everything, from left to right and back again. Draws in the scent of the bathroom. The feel of the space. The way the harsh light falls, and on what. "There are glasses on the sink," she says. And it's true: A pair of spectacles sits on the flat ceramic spot where the soap is supposed to be.

"Libby doesn't wear glasses," Kit says.

"I know."

"Moya." Kit pulls on her hand, radiating a keening energy. Moya nods, steps back as Kit releases the door. The vision of hell is gone. It's just them again, in the dark. They are clutching each other's hands, each other's arms.

Moya grew up hard. Her ability to compartmentalize didn't come from nowhere—it's a product of childhood and circumstance. Her public face is shielded, all cool glamour and aloofness. Here, in the freezing black laundry, she has to work very hard to maintain that shield.

She has always believed God is a woman. But she herself is a woman, and Kit is a woman, and Libby Armstrong, lying there utterly beyond reach behind the door, is a woman, too—

"Let's go," Kit whispers, and she's leading Moya now as they make for the laundry door.

Outside again, Moya feels the cold air on her forehead and cheeks as a relief. Then there are sounds, and a flashlight shining right in her face.

"I spoke to the gentleman in the car out front," the WAVES reservist says, from a little away, "and he said there was some commotion?"

"Could you lower that flashlight, ma'am?" Kit releases one of Moya's hands to cover her own eyes.

Moya recovers her shield fully, pulls it around herself like a cloak. She lets go of Kit and steps into the circle of white from the reservist's flashlight.

"Call your petty officer." Her words are hard, her face a stone. "And then call the police. A girl's been murdered in your laundry."

5

Oh, heck no, it wasn't magic! We never
thought of it like that. But we under-
stood that codebreaking was about seeing things in a different way.
                        —OPAL BUKOWSKI

"D'you think it'll be much longer?" Dottie moans.

"Not much longer now, honey," Kit says, which is the
same reply she's been giving for the past four hours. Her
shoulders are sore with tension, her eyes are gritty, there's
a headache throbbing inside her skull, and she wishes more
than anything they were all back in the Hall.

The police questioned them first near the Chrysler, in
the glare of flashing blue strobes and the hubbub of dark-
uniformed officers dashing back and forth. Kit was still in
shock at that point, working hard to keep from weeping as
she sat in the Chrysler with the door open, her feet on the
edge of the sidewalk.

Then Emil Ferrars was sent home to Arlington Hall with
the car, and Kit, Moya, and Dottie were moved to the foyer of
Idaho hall, where they were questioned again by a more senior
officer. Kit had herself together enough to feel nervous about
answering when the questions turned to personal identification.

They were moved to the infirmary when Dottie suffered a crying jag, and they've spent an hour in the tiny guest lounge. Dottie is tucked into one corner of the sofa with Kit beside her. Moya paces near the window. The best the nurse could offer them was a glass of Coca-Cola each, and for Dottie, an Alka-Seltzer.

Now it's dawn, sunlight blushing over the bare dirt and Cemesto walls of Arlington Farms. Moya flicks back the chintz curtains occasionally to check on progress outside. Her face is a sharp, furious mask. She's puffing through her last cigarette, and the vulnerability that Kit saw in her when they were in the laundry is gone. This sere, controlled version of Moya is the version she's most used to, and the idea that there might be a more unraveled version underneath is strangely unsettling. But this is the Moya she knows—the Moya who has handled the exchanges with police, ensured that none of them was questioned alone, made a point of stressing that they're needed back at Arlington Hall as part of the war effort. She was able to provide a much more detailed and succinct description of the horrific discovery in the laundry than Kit, which was another good thing.

The last thing Kit needs is to be the focus of police interest.

Simmering hot in the back of Kit's mind is the worry that this police investigation is attention she doesn't want. She feels guilty, because she knows it's callous to think in such a way. But Libby Armstrong is dead and has nothing left to lose. Kit, on the hand, is very much alive.

"Oh, why won't they just let us go *home*?" Dottie whimpers.

Kit pats her hand gently. "They will, Dot. They're just making sure they've got everything they need."

To balance out the responsibilities Moya has assumed in dealing with the police, Kit has taken charge of Dottie. Hearing that Libby was the murder victim nearly sent Dot over the edge into hysteria, and whatever was slipped into her drink at the dance has left her with a shocking migraine. One of the officers questioning them made a comment about Dottie being lucky she only had her drink spiked, and Kit wasn't at all surprised when Dottie threw up on his shoes.

"You'd think they might have had enough of me being sick all over the place," Dottie says, cheeks flushed.

"Hey, I threw up, too." Kit hears her voice turn astringent. "And that'll teach them not to be jerks. As if you need to hear that you're lucky not to be murdered, after everything else. What a thing to say."

"She was, though," Moya says. She flicks the curtains back into place and steps away from the window. "She was damn lucky." Moya has shrugged out of her jacket—it's around Dottie's shoulders right now—and she's rubbing her neck with the hand not holding the cigarette. "She came in the same group as Libby, and she was right there. That's why they're racing around so hard. It's driving them nuts that there was a witness to what happened lying barely twenty feet away."

"She wasn't even conscious!"

"I know that. But like I said, it's driving the police nuts. And they're trying to figure out if the guy who spiked Dottie's drink was the same guy who killed Libby."

"How can they be sure it was a guy?" Dottie looks up plaintively.

"It was a guy," Moya says without elaborating.

Kit swallows and nods, not meeting Dottie's eyes. "It was a guy."

"But—" Dottie looks between them, then looks ill. "Oh."

Moya has smoked her cigarette all the way down to the filter. She stubs out what's left in the ashtray on a side table. "The police are looking into the details of Libby's movements. She's not a boarder at Arlington Hall; she only stayed late after work to go to the dance with the other girls. And she wasn't a Farms resident. She lived in DC, like half the other attendees."

Kit forces her brain to function. "Do the Farms staff have a record of who attended? Like, do they keep names from ticket sales or something?"

"It's not like that," Dottie says. "Folks just walk on in. This isn't a military base with MPs at the gate. Sure, they have WAVES on duty, but there are WAVES residents, so that's just... What's the word?"

"Expedient?" Kit offers.

"Expedient, yeah."

"So the guy might not have come here for the dance," Moya points out. "He might've been here for some other reason—he might be a deliveryman, or just a regular visitor. He might not even have gone into Idaho."

"He might not be a serviceman," Kit says, staring toward the curtains. "Dot, you described the men you met to the police officers, right?"

55

"I did—I mean, I tried. But there was so much I couldn't remember, and the officers said some things behind their hands, and it was…well, it was embarrassing. And there were so many guys at the dance.…" Dottie rubs her temples. "Ow, my head."

"You're doing great, hon," Kit reassures her. "It surely can't be long now."

"Dot, are you warm enough?" Moya asks. "Can I take my jacket back?"

Dottie nods, so Kit hands the jacket over. "You're going out there again?"

"Yep." Moya pulls the jacket's lambskin collar high. "I'm gonna see if I can get some cigarettes and information off one of the officers. This girl is one of ours, and they can't ignore that."

"Ask them when they're letting us go," Dottie suggests. "It's not fair that we're still here."

Kit knows that Moya's interest doesn't only lie with poking around about the time of their release. "What are you trying to find out?"

"The footprints," Moya says. "And the glasses. They weren't Libby's, but they looked like girls' glasses to me."

Kit's not sure she likes the direction of Moya's mind. "It's not our job to investigate this. The police know what they're doing."

"Do they?"

The look Moya gives her is level, and Kit shies away from it. Moya wants justice for Libby: *One of ours* really means *one of mine.* The commitment Moya feels to the Hall girls in

56

her care doesn't just cover their work at the tables; it extends to their health, their comfort, and their future prospects. It's why she's one of the youngest supervisors in the Hall and the most effective. It's why Kit went to knock on her door at one in the morning.

But Moya isn't the one living a lie. She can stick her nose into other people's business without fear of exposure. Kit doesn't have that luxury. "I'm sure they're doing the best they can," Kit offers, but even to her ears it sounds unconvincing.

"Well, I'm going to see what exactly 'the best they can' means," Moya says, and she walks out of the lounge.

"I don't know how she does it." Dottie leans her head on Kit's shoulder, leaking tears. "I don't want to talk about this awful stuff anymore. I just want to go home, take a bath and some aspirin, and try to sleep. Oh, Libby."

"Dot..." Kit isn't sure if she wants to ask her question. But the feeling she got in the laundry won't dissipate: not the shock she felt at the sight of Libby's body, although that was horrifying, too, but the fear she experienced before she switched on the light. Kit's never felt a fear so all-consuming, even while stepping out the door with a new identity. It was huge, paralyzing—and Libby Armstrong would have endured that.

What would it be like, to feel such absolute terror in the moments before death? Kit is appalled by it.

"Dottie, you told the police you talked to a lot of guys," she starts. "A lot of servicemen. Did any of them stand out to you? Any that seemed weird, or...I don't know...."

"Did one of them have a big flashing sign above his head reading 'murderer'?" Dottie looks washed-out and wan, but if she's still managing sarcasm, she'll probably be fine. "No, Kit. They all just seemed like...regular guys."

"Maybe that's what he looks like. A regular guy." Kit bites her lip.

"Maybe. That probably makes catching him harder, right?" Dottie tucks back her hair. "Anyway, there were lots of other girls around. We were all talking and hanging out and dancing...."

"Everything just seemed normal," Kit prompts Dottie when she trails off.

"That's right. And then I woke up on the couch outside the dorm."

Kit's gaze snaps to her. "One of the girls must've helped you out there. Someone put a blanket over you."

Dot makes a face. "They didn't bring me inside, though."

"They probably just thought you needed some air, and you'd go back to Idaho...." Kit shuffles closer to Dottie on the couch. "Dottie, whoever that girl was, we need to talk to her. The police need to talk to her."

"About Libby's murder?"

Kit nods. "She might've seen something. The laundry is between Ohio and Idaho." She reaches for Dottie's hand. "But not just that. A girl was killed. But what happened to you was a crime, too."

"The police don't seem to be much concerned about that right now," Dottie says sadly.

"Which is stupid. If the guy who did this to you isn't the killer, that still means there's another man coming to these dances and trying to prey on girls. Drugging them."

58

Dottie squeezes Kit's hand. "I guess Moya was right—I *was* lucky."

Kit swallows hard. "Dorothy Crockford, don't you say that. We're the lucky ones. We're lucky you're okay. Oh, Dottie…"

She leans in to give Dottie a hug, and Dottie's solidity and warmth give her some relief. The way Dottie squeezes back suggests she's glad for the hug—for all the hugs. They're still embracing when Moya walks back into the room trailed by the scent of cigarette smoke and early morning air, to say the police are releasing them.

6

Deciphering is not a process for a
one-cylinder mind.

       —ELIZEBETH FRIEDMAN

They take a cab back to the Hall, and once they get through the clamoring reporters outside the gates of Arlington Farms, the ride feels short: Kit finds it astounding that, all this time, coffee and a bath and the comfort of her own bed were only three and a half miles away. She's never been so happy to see the white columns of the schoolhouse, the crisp green of the grounds.

They pile out near the watch gate, navigate the MP at the gate guard house—thankfully, they all have their badges—and trudge wearily up the drive to the house. Dottie carries her shoes.

Past the big front door, it's clear that the world hasn't altered: Work is going on as usual, peppered by the sound of typewriters. It's only nine in the morning.

Moya starts issuing orders. "Kit, help Dottie upstairs and put her to bed. I'll tell the kitchen staff to lay out a tray, if you wouldn't mind fetching it. I'm going up to Four."

Kit looks at Moya's pointed face and enormous gray eyes. Her black hair is limp, her skin so pale it's almost translucent over her cheekbones. "Tell me you're not going straight back to work."

"I have to brief admin and break the news to the girls in Libby's workroom." Moya shakes her head at the idea. "And I'm supposed to be on shift." She combs back her hair with her fingers. "The war's still on, Kit. I won't be the first soldier to go back into the fight on no sleep."

"Then I should—"

"No. You look after Dot." Before Kit can say more, Moya's tone softens. "If I need you, I'll send for you."

The idea of being needed by Moya, being sent for, reassures Kit somewhat as Moya splits off and heads for the kitchen. Kit turns back to Dottie, trying to keep her voice upbeat. "Okay, hon, just a few stairs and we're there. Let me take those shoes."

Kit helps Dottie change clothes and get into bed. Then she returns to One to fetch the tray. She passes through the cafeteria to the kitchen, where the mostly Black staff is working hard on lunch preparations. At the far end of the long kitchen bench, near the back door, a young Black girl in a sweater and a dark purple skirt is collecting a tray with a coffee service. She glances up, does a hard blink, and meets Kit's eyes—but Kit doesn't have the energy to do more than stare vacantly back.

Is her hair disheveled? Is her face drawn? She doesn't have the energy to care, and it's all she can do to concentrate as an older matron gives Kit a tray—there's an extra glass of orange juice, Kit's relieved to see—and instructions on how to balance it. Kit nods along, as though she needs these instructions.

She takes the tray back upstairs. Everything feels off-kilter: She's wearing her old maid's pumps and carrying a tray. Maybe someone will see her and notice how competent she is in this role. Kit has to push the thought away.

Once Dottie has the tray, she encourages Kit to get some shut-eye. Kit drinks her orange juice, changes back into her pajamas—discarded on her unmade bed—and tumbles onto the mattress. She's conked out before she can think anymore.

When she wakes again, from restless sleep, it's to hear a gentle tapping on the door. The room is darkened with the curtains drawn, and Dottie is snoring gently in the other bed. Kit rubs her eyes and pulls on her robe.

It's Rose Haskell at the door, looking tentative. "Hey. I'm sorry to wake you. Are you okay?"

"I'm fine," Kit says in a low voice. From the way Rose's eyes roam toward Dottie, Kit can tell that news has already made the rounds. "We're both fine. Does Moya need us?"

"Only you," Rose whispers. "You have to go up to Four, to make a report."

"What time is it?"

"Noon." Rose shifts on her feet. "I heard about the... well, about what happened—"

"Sure," Kit says. She doesn't want to get into it now. "Tell Moya I have to change, but I'll be right up." She closes the door before Rose can say any more and leans against the wood. Her dreams were full of gore and terror, and she doesn't feel rested. Her eyes are aching and her teeth feel fuzzy, and the idea of getting back into her clothes makes her want to groan. These are the most dangerous times: when she's tired, when she can't maintain her accent so well, when the little mannerisms and points of etiquette desert her, leave her exposed. She probably shouldn't have closed the door in Rose's face.

Okay. To work.

Kit pushes off the door and collects fresh clothes. Her skirt is the one she wore yesterday, not the corduroy from last night. She puts on her uncomfortable shoes. Then she visits the bathroom to splash water on her face, brush her teeth, apply powder, lipstick. Her hair is being awkward, so she tucks it under a scarf. Moya's blue scarf is still in the pocket of her coat, she remembers. She pinches her cheeks in front of the mirror and whispers to herself, "Come on, now. That's it."

Leaving Dottie to snore on, she takes the stairs to Four. Disappointingly, Moya is not there. An older woman with her hair in a French roll gives Kit instructions: She is to write out her report and submit it for typing.

Kit sits on a wooden chair in the corner of the office— there is no desk space to speak of—with notepaper on a hard clipboard balanced on her knee. She writes out the entire account in pencil. At certain times during the recollection, her hand shakes; nobody seems to notice.

When she returns the report to the woman with the French roll, she is told to get some lunch.

"And then what?"

The woman doesn't seem to know. She waves a hand. "Just report to your usual table on Three, I guess."

You guess? Kit closes her mouth and begins the long trek back down to the cafeteria. But when she arrives at the bottom of the stairs, something in her just refuses to budge. Kit presses a palm to her forehead. She needs... God, what does she need? She needs Libby not to be dead. She needs the image of Libby in the bathroom to stop rolling back into her mind, unbidden.

She needs some peace.

Without thinking about it, Kit crosses the parquet and starts down the corridor, following the carpet runner. Last night, she and Moya and Mr. Ferrars turned left here to get to the back door. Now she passes that exit and continues all the way to a door in the wall.

Back when Arlington Hall was a school, this was the door to a library. Kit is very familiar with it, because Katherine was an avid reader but didn't have the strength to come here herself. As she turns the knob and pushes open the door, Kit's relieved to see the space largely unchanged. Art studios and deportment rooms are unnecessary in the new Arlington Hall, but libraries are still important.

Thick curtains cover the tall windows. Walls are shelved high with books. It's not a big room, but there's a chesterfield sofa and two club chairs. Kit's always had the feeling—maybe because of the club chairs—that this room was designed by a man. The smell of dark wood and aged leather reinforces that impression now.

It's a quiet sanctuary. She should have come here sooner.

Kit walks to the shelves on the left and lets her fingers wander over the spines of the books. Many of them she's read, or read aloud for Katherine. She carefully pulls a book of poetry off the shelf, opens the cover, and breathes deep.

She can just stand here for a minute and read. Just for a little while. Then, when her mind is settled, she'll go back upstairs, find her chair at the tables on Three. But just for now, a respite.

Kit stands by the shelves for a good ten minutes before she feels the hairs on the back of her neck prickle. When she turns her head, the young Black girl she saw in the kitchen is standing in the doorway. She has large eyes and a small, clever face. Her purple skirt is distinctive against the wine-red and rich teak colors in the library room. She has curly hair, controlled by a snood.

Kit blinks. "Can I help you?"

The girl looks her dead in the eye. "I saw you in the kitchen. They said you saw a murder."

"Uh, yes," Kit says. "But it wasn't—"

"They said your name is Kit Sutherland," the girl says. "Katherine Sutherland."

Kit feels a strange discomfort, low in her stomach. She closes the book in her hands. "That's right."

"Well." The girl crosses her arms. "I think we both know that's not true."

7

A lot of the ciphers we worked on were substitutions, where some or all of the letters in the message were replaced by different letters or figures. You just had to work out how to spot them.
—BEVERLEY GASKIN

Kit always thought that when the time came, when someone figured it out, she'd go quietly.

Instead, she finds herself putting her shoulders back, her heart slamming in her chest. "I don't think I know what you mean."

The girl just looks at her for moment. Then she closes the library door. Now it's only the two of them. An electric tension under Kit's skin makes her breaths climb into her throat.

"You're not Katherine Sutherland," the girl says. "You look kinda like her, but you're not her."

Kit hears a rushing sound in her head, like the wings of a hundred crows. "I don't think—"

"Your hair's the wrong color, for starters." The girl takes a step closer. "And then there's the fact that Katherine Sutherland is dead."

Kit can barely swallow. Her fingers have gone ice-cold.

The girl cocks her head. "Katherine had a maid, a little

white girl with a frilled apron.... That's you, isn't it? You're the maid."

The poetry book slides out of Kit's grip and lands on the carpet with a dull thunk. She has to bear down hard to get words out of her mouth. "Who are you?"

"Violet DuLac." The girl comes forward with her hand extended. When Kit doesn't take it, her expression changes. "What's the matter—you don't shake hands with Black girls?"

"That's not—" There was never much call for hand shaking when Kit was a maid. She blinks, and understanding comes. "You worked here before. Here in the Hall."

"That's right." Violet pulls her hand back, sets it on her hip. Her lips quirk on one side of her mouth. "Kitchen staff. But Mr. Coffee pulled me out of there once he realized I could figure and had a brain."

"Mr. Coffee?"

"William Coffee, head of the Black unit." Violet straightens when she talks about it. A point of pride.

"There's a Black unit?" Kit blurts.

"Over in the old administration cottage." Violet seems amused at Kit's ignorance. "We do commercial codes. Make sure nobody's slipping anything through Mitsubishi channels and so on. You'd be surprised what we pick up. But I'm getting ahead of myself now—where'd you get the clothes? And don't try to tell me you bought a society wardrobe on a maid's salary."

It's a little like jumping off a cliff, Kit realizes. Only this fall will send her crashing onto the rocks. Everything she's

67

worked so hard to maintain over these long months will be lost. All the daily anxious moments, the constant self-checking, the time she's spent suppressing her accent, the blisters from these damn shoes...

But it's too late. She's already fallen. If this girl knows, there's no way Kit will be able to keep her real identity a secret anymore.

"Katherine." She lets out a breath—one she has been holding for way too long—and the name comes out with the rush of air. "She gave me her trunk before she passed."

"You didn't put a pillow over her head to hustle things along?" Violet grins. Her expression changes quickly once she realizes she's overstepped. "Ah, okay. I'm sorry. She meant something to you."

"She was my friend." Kit draws herself up. This life, this blessed life of numbers and teak and leather, was never hers to begin with. She can't begrudge its loss now. And she can't start crying—she doesn't have time for that. "Well. Thanks for talking to me, Miss DuLac. It was nice to meet you."

She passes Violet as she walks toward the door. Her knees are unsteady, her chest tight and hollow. She's reaching for the doorknob when Violet's voice sounds behind her.

"Where are you going?"

"I..." Kit turns back, running her palms down her skirt. Trying to hold on to her dignity. Trying not to look pleading. "Let me have an hour. I can leave the trunk and the papers. I'll take ten dollars as wages, but you can have the rest of the money. If that'll buy me an hour—"

"Excuse me?" Violet's nose is scrunched up.

"Just one hour." Kit's chin wobbles. She abandons the idea of not pleading. "That'll give me enough time. I can be on the bus and halfway to Union Station by then, I swear—"

"Now, hold on a minute." Violet raises a pale palm. "Just hold on right there."

"Half an hour, even," Kit says, desperate.

"I don't want your money." Violet rolls her eyes. "Lord. Listen to me, okay? I don't want your money, and I don't have any plans to talk about this. I'm not gonna *tell* anybody." She makes a little twist of her mouth. "Not yet, anyway."

"You—" Kit feels her own mouth open and close. The rushing sound in her head recedes. "Why?"

"Because there's something I need." Violet grips the edge of the chesterfield sofa. "That girl who died at Arlington Farms last night, she was a Hall girl, right? A government girl?"

"I don't..." Kit gets a jolting sense of whiplash. She was steeling herself to run; now she has no idea where all this is going. "Yes. Libby Armstrong. She worked in logging on Three."

"That's what I said, a government girl." Violet's face is much more serious now. "Well, she wasn't the only one."

"What are you talking about?"

"There was another girl killed, is what I'm talking about. Three weeks ago, in Downtown."

"What?" Kit does a double take. "The police didn't say anything about another murder."

Violet's tone is caustic. "Well, they wouldn't, would they."

That's all it takes for Kit to work it out. "She was Black."

Violet lifts her chin. "The police, they don't care if it's just a colored girl. But Dinah was..." She seems haunted for a second, before letting herself sink down onto the arm of the chesterfield. "She was my friend."

Kit finds it jarring, hearing her words repeated back. "You don't think they'll investigate her murder."

"I *know* they won't. Which means some madman out there has killed two Washington girls in less than a month, but the cases won't be examined properly because the police are too bigoted to see the pattern...." Violet slumps on the arm of the sofa, gaze turned away. "I mean, I guess there's a pattern. I won't know until I get the details from you."

"Excuse me?"

"Look, I'm offering you a good deal." Violet squints at her. "A trade. You tell me what you know, and I keep my mouth shut about how you're an impostor."

Kit's mind does a large, unhurried revolution, disorienting enough that she wants to sit down. If she's revealed as an impostor, there'll be no avoiding a court martial and a return to Scott's Run.

But Violet's offering a lifeline.

Kit clenches her fingers, hesitant. "I can tell you what I saw. I don't know if it'll be much comfort. But I can tell you what the police told us."

Violet considers. "Who's *us*?"

"Me. Dottie Crockford, from Three. Moya Kershaw, from Four."

"Moya Kershaw..." Violet angles her head. "Tall white girl, wears pants?"

70

Kit nods. "She saw it all, too. And there are reports. I can maybe get you copies."

"That would be useful." Violet's sitting straighter now. "It would help with putting the pieces together."

Suddenly Kit understands what's going on. "You're planning to investigate this yourself, aren't you?"

"That's right." Violet's expression is set and stubborn.

"That's crazy," Kit blurts out.

"You see anybody else willing to do it?" Violet's hands go out as she gestures around the room. "It's me or nobody. So are you going to help or not?"

"I don't..." Kit falters. Violet has the same look in her eye that Moya had this morning, when she went to talk to the police at Arlington Farms: like she's on a mission. A mission for justice.

And Kit shouldn't get involved. Justice is a luxury she can't afford with her Arlington Hall identity at risk.

So you're just going to stay silent, do nothing? She hears the words in Libby's voice.

Kit swallows hard. She's an impostor, a fake. There've been so many times questions were asked of her, and she said and did nothing, was complicit in her silence. Worse than that—she's lied. Over and over. She's woven a mask out of falsehoods to cover her true face, and now she can hardly tell the mask from the reality.

She works with Opal and Brigid and Moya and Dottie every day, and they don't really know anything about her that isn't a lie. She's supposed to be a trusted colleague. But she won't even stand up for a dead girl, lying on the cold floor in a laundry bathroom in her pink skirt and her brown shoes with the little bows. . . .

Dammit. *Dammit.*

"Okay," she says. The words feel thick in her mouth. "Okay, I'll help. I can talk to Dottie and Moya and get you the information you need."

Violet stands up slowly. "I'll take that help. And you can stay being Kit Sutherland, I guess."

"You guess?"

"You're more useful if you're not a maid." Violet grins, extends her hand again. She has fashionably full lips and unfashionable dimples. "Nice doing business with you."

Kit shakes Violet's hand. Queasy at the chance she's taking. She's taken chances before, and they've paid off: She hopes to God this will be the same.

As Violet passes by her for the door, something—an image—falls into Kit's brain. She turns and speaks on instinct. "Violet, this is going to sound strange, but . . . did Dinah wear glasses?"

Violet pulls up short. She looks over her shoulder, an eye-crinkling grin dying on her face.

"Okay," she says. "No kidding around now. Tell me how you knew that."

8

Gosh, the transcripts. You'd come back
to your desk and there'd be a pile up
to the ceiling. There were always more
than you could keep up with.
                                    —BETTY JOHNSON

Moya feels that vacant buzz she associates with staying up all night and smoking too many cigarettes.

She spent a long time up on Four, debriefing with Colonel Corderman and Sheila Kelly from Human Resources. They're collecting statements from everyone involved. The final report will go to Mr. Kullback, and there will be ripples; aside from the horrifying tragedy of Libby's death, which affects every girl in the Hall, there are War Department issues to consider. Questions about whether Libby might have been targeted because she was a keeper of government secrets. Colonel Corderman has briefed the police, using vague references to "matters of national security."

Moya imagines there's a way to ensure the details of Libby's work remain classified, but the circumstances of her murder have already made the news. Girls all over DC will be locking their doors at night, and strident commentators will use it as another excuse to argue that women shouldn't be employed in war roles.

As an added complication, the authorities at the Hall

now have to recruit another codebreaker. But she can't even think about that now. She's only had an hour's sleep in the last twenty-nine, and her weariness is making her light-headed. She went downstairs to eat, poked at her serving of potato and hot dog salad until she noticed the headline in the newspaper broadsheets stacked near the door: "Horror at Arlington Farms." Nearby that headline was an article called "How to Defend Yourself Against a Rapist." Combined with her memories of last night, it made her push her plate aside. She grabbed a mug of strong black coffee and trudged back upstairs to Four.

Now it's 3:00 PM, and she feels like she's floating. She glances into one of the workrooms on Three as she passes by and sees...

"Kit?"

Kit's sitting on one of the chairs nearer the door, her hair tidied back with a mint-green scarf that contrasts with her burnt-orange sweater. A spill of auburn fringe escapes from the scarf to fall over her eyes, large with exhaustion. Her cheeks are pale and the collar of her shirt is slightly askew, but she's working.

She looks vulnerable, but she's strong. And everybody knows she's strong. How does she do that? "I thought you were resting." Moya takes a deep drag on her cigarette, hears the paper burn. "Your dedication is admirable, but go back to bed. You look like you're falling asleep at the table."

Kit stands. "Can I talk with you a minute?"

Moya thinks of the way she and Kit held hands in the laundry. She presses her lips together and scans the room, checking that everyone is on task. Checking to see if anyone notices her and Kit talking. No, it's fine if people see them talking. They'll assume that she and Kit are talking about what happened at the Farms. Nobody is looking, anyway.

God, she's overanalyzing. She really needs some sleep.

"Sure." She steps out of the doorway into the corridor, trying to seem nonchalant, and Kit follows.

There are no empty rooms on this floor of the Hall—they go to the end of the corridor to talk. Their footsteps are deadened by the dark red carpet runner. As they reach a private corner, Kit's voice emerges, warm and low. "The glasses in the laundry. They were girls' glasses."

Moya hears the absolute certainty in Kit's tone. She glances down the corridor, keeping her expression neutral, before fixing her eyes on Kit's face. "Yes. The police told me. How did you know that?"

"Because I just met a girl who was a friend of the girl who owned them." Kit's words are level. Her eyes are urgent. "Those glasses came from another murder victim. A girl who was killed just three weeks ago. Her name was Dinah Shaw. Dinah was stabbed to death in Downtown. She was a Black typewriter with the Munitions Board—another government girl."

Moya has kept herself busy since they arrived back in the Hall, and the weight of her tiredness is oppressive. But now she remembers what she was feeling this morning, what's been wearing on her all day: She's *angry*. Angry at the way Libby died—one of her girls, violated in a bathroom, slaughtered like an animal.

Now Kit's saying it's happened before.

"I can't believe this." Moya releases a breath, inhales the next one through her cigarette. "So another girl has been killed this way, and the police didn't say a word about it."

"That's right."

"God *damn* the cops. God *damn* them." Moya cups a hand under her elbow, looks away. "I can't stop thinking about it. About what we saw."

"I...I dreamed about it," Kit confesses.

The clash of anger and exhaustion inside makes Moya feel brittle. When she registers a light touch on her shoulder, she jerks.

Kit pulls her fingers back. She looks startled, apologetic. "Your...your hair is coming loose from your bun."

Moya sways a little on her feet. With one gentle gesture, Kit has almost undone her. The last fifteen hours have been a kind of nightmare, but Kit is close and warm and real, her face upturned, expression open.

Moya smooths a hand down the front of her sapphire-blue blouse and tries to find some equilibrium. Some professionalism. "You...you said you met someone—Dinah's friend. I'd like to talk with her."

"Now?" Kit plucks at the hem of her sweater, eyes suddenly wide.

"Not now." Moya snorts, stubs out her cigarette into a nearby ashtray stand. "I think I should have at least ten hours of sleep before our next complicated conversation. Tomorrow."

"Violet said she works at the cottage." Kit bites her lip,

thinking. "But she collects coffee from the kitchen around nine thirty."

"I'll leave a message for her," Moya says. "We'll meet at eleven, someplace downstairs."

"I know a place," Kit says. "The old library on One."

"Okay." Movement down the corridor—Moya's attention splits. It's Edith, sobbing quietly, being led out of the workroom by Brigid. This mess is hurting everyone, and Moya wants to see an end to it. "Okay, that's a plan. Now for God's sake, Kit, go back to bed."

"All right." Kit nods. "Is it bad manners if I tell the boss to take her own advice? You look as tired as I feel."

"I'm the supervisor, not the boss." Moya feels something loosen inside her, though.

"Uh-huh." Kit smiles gently. "Get some rest, Miss Supervisor. You'll need some gas in the tank for tomorrow."

Moya controls a shiver. This morning there was one murder, and now there are two.

Tomorrow, anything could happen.

9

So long as you had a good volume of
traffic, you'd get a break. The more
depth you had, the easier a code was
to break.

—BRIGID GLADWELL

Kit runs her pencil across the rows of digits on her card, trying to keep her nerves in check. Trying to look busy while
surreptitiously checking the clock.

Her official day off isn't until Wednesday. Today's Sunday, which is only a day of rest outside of wartime. All the
girls are back at work. Kit's sitting near Opal and Brigid at
the tables. A decent night's sleep has made a huge difference to her state of mind, and she's attacked code groups
typed on green cards with renewed vigor. But no amount
of vigor is going to provide reassurance that this upcoming
meeting with Violet and the other girls won't expose her
real identity.

She taps the end of her pencil against her bottom lip,
ignoring the urge to chew on it. She's worked twice as hard,
squashed down all her memories of her past, done everything she can to fight for her own survival—it still may
not be enough. And the idea of what Dottie and Moya will
say, the looks on their faces if they find out the truth...Kit
presses a hand to her stomach, fighting queasiness.

At ten to eleven, Dottie appears in the doorway and waves. "Kitty-Kat? They need you for a minute."

Kit feels eyes on her as she stands and tidies her workstation.

Opal glances up from her cards. "You're not in trouble, are you?"

"No, no. It's probably something to do with yesterday."

"God—Libby." Opal shudders. "It's awful. Awful. I still can't get my mind around it."

"Me either." Kit tries to keep her hands steady. "Okay, I'll be back soon."

Dottie ushers her out the door and down the corridor toward the stairs. "This is a tricky time for a meeting."

"Violet lives off-site," Kit points out, "and we don't know if she can stay after four, so it's work time or no time at all."

"Well, fingers crossed we can make it quick."

"You've got color in your face this morning," Kit says approvingly.

"The sleep was good for me." Dottie still looks a little washed out and worried, but her blond curls have regained their bounce. "I'm just nervous about Moya. She wasn't happy when she heard I was coming along."

"What? Why?" Kit grips the banister.

"I don't know." Dottie shrugs. "It's Moya—you can't always tell."

"You're as much a part of this as anyone else," Kit says. She checks Dottie's face. "I mean, if you want to be. You might not want to get caught up in—"

"I was there." Dottie pauses on the stairs. Her expression

is uncharacteristically serious. "I was *right there*, Kit. It could've been me instead of Libby in that laundry."

"Dottie, don't think that way—"

"Libby was my friend, and it's like you said." Dottie's shoulders straighten. "I'm as much a part of this as anyone else."

Kit gives her a squeeze, until Dottie hustles them both onward down the stairs to One.

Dottie has never been to the library in the Hall. When Kit opens the door, Dottie says, "Huh. Books," and gives the space a cursory glance.

"You don't like books?" Kit finds the idea hard to comprehend. Just entering the library has given her a measure of peace.

"Sure. Books are okay," Dottie says, wandering into the room. "You like 'em, though. Every night before lights out, you've got your nose stuck in one."

"I could actually sit in here and read all day," Kit admits.

"Eh, I'm not that big a reader." Dottie waves a hand. "But maybe you could do this, after the war."

"Do what? Read all day?"

"Become a librarian, silly." Dottie grins. "I can see you behind the counter, looking all proper in your tidy little outfits. Telling everyone to hush."

"Okay, yeah—I'd kinda like that." Kit looks at the books, her smile sneaking out. The idea holds a lot of appeal. "And what do *you* want to do, after the war?"

"Oh, I don't know." Dottie trails a finger across the shelved spines. "Go back to Baltimore, finally become a schoolteacher,

I guess. Or maybe help out at home with the grocery store until I get married. I know it's not very ambitious, but I never really thought much beyond that."

"Give yourself a couple of years, you'll be running your own store," Kit suggests.

"Maybe I'll build a grocery empire." Dottie laughs, glances over. "Hey, Moya, what are you gonna do when the war is over?"

Kit looks behind her to see Moya walking through the doorway.

"The war's going to be over?" Moya settles herself in a club chair and picks up a small, leather-bound tome she finds on a nearby table. "Now there's an idea."

She blends comfortably with the academic background in her brown trousers and a cream blouse under a tweed waist-coat. Her sense of containment and self-possession seems recovered today, and her hair is a crown of neat black rolls. There's a pale pink brightness in her cheeks. Her eyes seem brighter, too—less bleary.

"You look better," Kit blurts. She feels herself blush. "I mean, you look like you got some sleep."

"I feel better." Moya stretches her shoulders back, then returns the book to the table. "I'm out of cigarettes, but I got some rest, so it's swings and roundabouts, I guess."

"You didn't answer the question," Dottie chides her. "What are you gonna do after the war is over?"

Before Moya can answer, a voice pipes up.

"She'll go into business for herself." Violet stands grinning in the doorway. "She'll get hired by companies who need someone to boss the CEO around," Violet suggests. "Am I right?"

Violet is wearing the snood again, but this time her button-up sweater is blue and her skirt is brown. She looks radiant, her cheeks smooth and her big eyes sparking. She's younger than Kit realized, maybe seventeen at most. For a seventeen-year-old, Violet's sure got a lot of moxie.

"Hi. Close the door." If Moya is surprised, she doesn't give it away. She stands and walks forward, hand extended. "Moya Kershaw."

"Violet DuLac." Violet shakes with the hand not pushing the door closed. "Thanks for the message."

"Thanks for meeting with us."

Dottie steps over quickly and clasps Violet's hand. "Hi, I'm Dottie Crockford."

"Pleased to meet you." Violet lifts her chin as they drop hands. "Is that a Baltimore accent?"

"You got me." Dottie grins. "You already know Kit."

Kit makes a tight wave.

"Indeed, I do," Violet says. Her eyes say a few things that Kit alone can decipher. "So. Here we are."

"Here we are—and I don't imagine any of us has a lot of time, so it's probably best if we cut to the chase." Moya returns to her club chair. "Kit told us about your friend Dinah. I'm sorry for your loss."

"Appreciated." Violet finds a place on the seat of the chesterfield. "Kit probably also told you I want to look into it some more."

"She did." Moya's eyes flick toward Kit. "And we'll get to

82

that in a minute. First, do you want to tell us about what happened to Dinah?"

Kit realizes she can't continue hovering by the bookshelves. Violet's not poisonous, and if she doesn't keep her word—to hold on to Kit's secret—it won't matter where Kit's standing. She drifts closer, all the way over, to perch on an arm of the chesterfield.

"Dinah lives…" Violet's fingers twine together as she glances down. "Lived. Dinah lived on Lowell Street with her family, same as me. We used to catch the bus together. I mean, we knew each other before that, when we both lived in Queen City."

"Queen City." Moya's eyes narrow. "That whole area was cleared out when they built the Pentagon, right?"

"That's right." Violet's gaze gets a little steely. "It was the only town in the state with history going back to free Black folks in slavery times. Funny how they picked just that spot to clear for the new building. They evicted every Black family in the space of a month. Dinah's family and mine both moved into places in Green Valley. She got a job with Munitions the same week I was transferred out of the kitchen here."

"Kit said you work with the segregated unit now." Moya laces her fingers loosely in her lap. "I've heard about the unit—I heard you do good work. But I've never seen it."

"I didn't even know there *was* a segregated unit." Dottie claims the other club chair.

The look Violet gives her is mild. "You took the pledge, right? Signal Intelligence is supposed to be secret. Seems we're just better at keeping secrets than some others."

Kit takes some consolation from that, and from Violet's surreptitious glance in her direction.

Moya redirects the conversation. "When did you learn about Dinah's murder?"

"Same day it happened, three weeks ago." Violet runs her palms down the brown fabric of her skirt, over her knees. Her voice goes somber. "Dinah went to work in the morning and never came home. She used to work late a lot, so her parents didn't think anything of it until nearly midnight. About a half hour later, the police came knocking—that was when we all heard."

"And how did she die?" Kit asks softly. It's the first time she's let herself speak.

"Dinah was..." Violet sucks her back teeth, stares down. "She was in an alley. She'd been stabbed, brutalized. We thought it was some random act, y'know? Or maybe the KKK."

Dottie frowns. "Are they active in Washington?"

Now Violet's look is less mild. "Girl, they're active *everywhere*—everywhere Black folks are trying to exist." She lets out a sigh. "Anyway, I just knew the police wouldn't chase it too hard. If it was the Klan, they'd write it off. If it wasn't, they'd say it was some crazy man they'd never catch. Then I heard about what happened at the Farms."

Kit lifts her head. "Which is why you made contact with me."

"You got it."

Dottie is still playing catchup. "So...how do you even know the murders are connected?"

"Because two government girls murdered in less than a month is significant. And because of what Kit and I saw in the laundry on Friday night." Moya's like a cat, sunk in the club chair in a state of poised stillness until she speaks. "Libby was in the laundry bathroom. A pair of glasses was set on the wash basin. The police said they were girls' glasses, something left behind from the dance. But the way they looked, how they were placed...Something just seemed off."

"Moya's right." Kit has to clear her throat. "They kind of...stuck out. Everything else was such a mess, and the glasses were set away. Like they didn't belong."

"Dinah wore horn-rimmed frames." Violet's hands sketch in the air before her face. "Round, with thick lenses. She couldn't see a yard in front of her face without her glasses."

"That's what I saw," Moya says, nodding. "Kit, do you remember?"

"Yeah." Kit's answer is slow and sad. "I remember the frames were dark and round."

"But what does that mean, then?" Dottie leans forward in her chair, elbows on the cushioned leather arms. "That the killer at Arlington Farms left a—God, I can hardly say it—a *souvenir* of the last girl he killed at the scene of Libby's murder? Why would he do a thing like that?"

"Why kill a girl in the first place?" Violet counters. "Crazy is crazy. How did you get caught up in this anyway?"

"I was there." Dottie pales under Violet's stare, but continues. "I went to the dance with Libby and some other girls. But someone slipped something into my drink....I passed out on the porch outside Ohio hall, twenty feet from the laundry where Libby was killed. And I was wearing the same color dress."

The reminder hits Kit with a wallop. If it had been Dottie in that laundry, Kit would want justice as badly as Violet. She'd feel less constrained by the accumulated weight of her own lies. She'd want to find this killer, whoever he is, and—

Wait.

Kit joins the dots in her own mind, and the realization comes, fast and clear. *I know this man. He's an impostor, too—pretending to be normal. He's in disguise, eluding the authorities, and I understand exactly what that's like....*

Maybe she can put that understanding to good use. "There's a lot we still don't know," Kit says, unprompted. "We're not even completely sure if the glasses in the bathroom were Dinah's. So that's our first step—get more information."

"There are steps?" Dottie asks.

"There are." Moya looks at Kit, her gaze curious. "If we decide to look into the murders ourselves."

"Is that something we want to do?" Dottie looks concerned but nervous.

"It's something *I* want to do." Violet stands, her chin set. "Whether you folks decide to join in or not—"

"We are," Moya says, placating. "Joining in, I mean. But Violet, you've been burning this torch for weeks—me and Kit and Dottie are only just catching up. Give us a minute to get things straight in our minds, okay?"

Moya's calm candor seems to make an impression. Violet

sits back down. "Okay. But I need to know now. Today. I've already wasted too much time."

"That's fair. But let's work out what we can do. And what will make a difference."

"I think..." Kit steadies herself on the arm of the sofa. "I think there's information out there that we can use to solve this. Or at least make some suggestions for the police to follow up on."

"Whatever we find, we'll have to be thorough—I don't trust the police to investigate this right." Moya's eyes are hard and dark. "We *can* solve this. But we'd all have to commit to it. This isn't a game."

"It's not a game to me," Violet says flatly. "Dinah deserves more than that."

Dottie chews her bottom lip. "Where would we even start?"

"With getting more data." Kit has been thinking about this. "The men at the jitterbug dance. What was left behind in the bathroom. The details of both murders." She feels the other girls' eyes on her, opens out her hands. "I don't know where we'd get all that."

"I could go back and talk to the police again," Moya suggests.

Dottie nods. "And I can go back to the Farms and find the girl who took me outside. Maybe talk to some other girls, too."

"I have a friend working at DC General." Violet shoves a stray curl of her hair behind her ear. "It's where they took Dinah's body—they might have taken Libby Armstrong there."

"Do you think..." Dottie swallows, eyes wide. "Do you think there might be more girls? More than just Dinah and Libby?"

Everyone takes that idea in for a moment, horrified.

"We'd have to tackle this like we'd tackle a code." Kit feels compelled to speak. "The easiest way to break a code is to find more depth. The more messages you have in that code, the better." She looks at Violet, at Dottie and Moya. "The more information we can find out about this, the more we'll understand. We'll be able to create links. Develop a plausible chain of ideas."

Moya is nodding slowly. "And looking into two murders will give us a lot of depth."

Dottie looks intrigued now. "We'll be able to see if this killer's doing the same things each time."

"Repeating a pattern," Violet agrees.

"And...what happens if we find a pattern?"

"We stop him." Kit straightens her shoulders, feels her expression harden. "We stop him from killing more girls."

10

It may be roundly asserted that human
ingenuity cannot concoct a cipher
which human ingenuity cannot resolve.
                        —EDGAR ALLAN POE

"Hello, excuse me, everybody." Captain John Cathcart
is standing in the doorway of the workroom. "Can I have
everyone's attention, please? Thank you."

It's Monday, and Moya's day off. On these days, Captain
Cathcart takes over her role. He's a beanpole of a guy in a
khaki uniform, serious and soft-spoken. Kit knows Cathcart
is twenty-four, which isn't so old, but he's survived battle
and it has aged him. A jagged, ugly line runs from his temple
to the top of his lip on the left, and he walks with a limp.

Dottie has said that Cathcart is single—and how it's a
shame that he'll have a tough time getting hitched, with
his scars. The girls in the workroom are always teasing him,
though, doing their best to draw him out.

"He-*llo*, Captain Cathcart!" Carol from New Jersey calls
out enticingly.

Cathcart brushes back his dirty-blond hair with his fingers and clears his throat. "Yes, hello. I'm sorry to interrupt,
but I have an announcement."

Public service announcements happen periodically. Kit's already listened to dozens of announcements about the timing of the girls' breaks, when supplies of stationery are due to arrive, how to report "unwanted attentions" on public transport, and what to do if there's an air raid siren. But this is about something else.

"Security badges are being reviewed and renewed these coming weeks," Cathcart says. "You'll be called alphabetically, and you'll have to go down to the old gymnasium to have your clearance verified, or reissued if necessary."

A small flurry of murmurs.

"Why're they doing that now?" Brigid asks. "We were told badges would be valid for a year."

Cathcart nods. "Yes, they were originally due to be renewed in three months, but circumstances have changed."

Rose pipes up. "What circumstances?"

"Uh, that's not a...I don't have the information on that. Sorry. I've just been told to pass on the announcement."

Kit hears Dottie's voice in her head. *There's English guys coming to visit.*

Opal leans over toward Kit, her words quiet. "They've been canceling extended leave, too. I thought it was a rumor, but mine got canned yesterday. I mean, I don't want to see my baby sister get married to some goofy guy from Omaha anyway, but I feel bad that I'm not gonna be there."

There's a buzz of talk in the workroom. Cathcart is gamely trying to answer queries from all corners. "Uh, no, sorry, I can't tell you when. But clearance will be reissued on the spot once your review checks out."

Kit is hoping someone else will ask her question. There's a query from Edith about whether they need to take paperwork down to the gymnasium.

"Uh, yes," Cathcart says. "Just your current badge and your identity documentation—your birth certificate, if you have it."

Nobody is asking the question.

Kit forces her hand into the air. "Excuse me, Captain, but what does the review process involve?"

"Oh, um, it's not complicated." Cathcart consults a paper he's holding. "For those of you who've already been interviewed and gone through background checks—which should be almost everyone here—it's just a rubber stamp."

"Oh," Kit says, relief flooding through her veins. "Okay."

"For those of you who haven't had an extensive background check," Cathcart goes on, "administration will be making inquiries during the interview. It's just phone calls, mainly," Cathcart explains. "We'll be calling families, or in some cases, institutions, to make sure everything in your documentation is in order."

Kit's whole body goes ice-cold.

She looks out the window to focus. The scene outside is idyllic. The grass below Arlington Hall still glistens with dew this early in the morning.

Think, Kit.

But there's nothing to think about. This review will mean the end of her fake identity. Her papers won't stand up to direct scrutiny. If the interviewers call her references, the whole story will come out.

She swallows down a burble of laughter. She's avoided one crisis with Violet, only to fall into another.

Breathe now. You're in the workroom. Act normal.

With an enormous effort, Kit pulls the threads of her awareness back together. Starlings chirp in the trees outside, competing with nearer sounds: the radiator's hum, the murmur of low conversation, a phone ringing somewhere down the corridor.

"All right," Cathcart says finally. "If you have further questions, there'll be a notice in the break room with more information. Thank you. That's it."

Kit looks up as Cathcart leaves and another figure takes his place. It's Dottie, wearing a lovely red polka-dotted utility dress that is probably too cool for the current weather. "Everybody all right?" She rubs her arms against the chill in the room. "We okay for pencils?"

"Pencils are fine," Brigid replies. "But we could do with some more graph paper."

Dottie grimaces. "Sorry, but we're waiting on a new shipment. At least you're not waiting on typewriter ribbon, like the girls on Two. Kit, d'you want to collect the tray from downstairs? Kitchen says it's ready." Dottie looks meaningfully between Kit and the wall clock, which reads 9:20 AM.

Kit's been waiting for this summons—she has to deliver a message—but now her head is a mess. She fumbles to stand and push her chair in.

"You want me to take that pile to the overlapper?" Opal asks.

"Um—sure. Thanks."

Dottie touches her arm as she passes by. "Hey. You okay? You look like you saw a ghost."

"Oh, I'm fine," Kit answers. "Just a little tired." She needs to get out of here, away from other people. She needs time to process, but the only time she has is during this walk down to the kitchen. Her brain churns over the problem as she descends the stairs.

They're going alphabetically, which means it could be days. Maybe so long as a week. I could say I'm going out for the afternoon. Going shopping. Or...to visit my sister. That way I could pack a bag and take it with me and nobody would be any the wiser—

She pauses on the landing. She can't spiral now. She has a week's grace. It'll be okay. She'll figure it out.

Kit arrives in the kitchen right at nine thirty, and there are two trays waiting, one for the third floor and one for the cottage. Violet's tray, with a stack of mugs and a pot of fresh-brewed coffee, looks better. The tray for Three only holds saltines and the standard plate of graham crackers.

Violet stands by her tray, rubbing her palms together. She's wearing fingerless knitted gloves and is waiting for the kitchen server to fill up a pot of hot water. Kit has to wait for more saltines.

Kit sidles up so they're side by side. "Cold where you're located?"

"You bet." Violet blows on her fingers and keeps her eyes averted, just like Kit. She nods at Kit's tray. "That for upstairs?"

"Yep." Kit rearranges the plates for better balance. "We're meeting at Moya's at six tomorrow night. Second floor, room seven."

Violet gives a small nod of acknowledgment. "I've called the hospital. My friend Ruth will have the files ready for me by four tomorrow."

"It'll be tight. Are you catching the bus?"

"Yes. I'll make it. Did you hear about the review?"

"I heard." Violet receives her pot of hot water, lifts her load, and gives Kit a wry glance. "Don't spill your tray."

Kit snorts. "I've had plenty of practice with trays."

"And don't let the review rattle you." Violet's gaze is concerned. "I mean it. We'll figure it out—it'll be okay."

"Thanks," Kit stammers.

It's kind of Violet to reassure her. *We'll figure it out.* Kit hopes with all her heart that those words come true.

11

The first job was always logging, and
then after a message was logged and
typed, you had to strip out the local
transfer code before you passed it on.
—CAROL ANN WHITE

"It's nearly six," Dottie says. "Kitty, stop fussing with your hair."

"These combs keep falling out." Kit throws up her hands. She's standing in the middle of the room, facing the mirror on Dottie's wardrobe, in just her bra and panty girdle and brown skirt. She survived yesterday's bombshell about the review, but these combs will be the death of her.

"Show me." Dot—who had today off and seems to have benefitted from it—pushes Kit's fingers away. In about ten seconds, she's figured out the problem and fixed the combs in place. "There. It's not like you have to worry, hon, it's just us girls."

Kit refrains from commenting. They're meeting at Moya's, and for reasons she doesn't want to examine too closely, she wants to look nice. She pulls on a white shirt, fastens and tucks it in, and slips a sage-green cardigan over the top. Since Dottie pointed it out, it seems impossible for Kit not to notice that she *does* look like a librarian. Well, that's fine. Librarians are competent and knowledgeable.

Except Kit doesn't think she's as competent and knowledgeable as the image implies—once again, she's faking. Should she change? There's no time for that, and these are all the clothes she has. Dammit.

Get yourself together. It's just clothes. It's just a meeting.

There's so much mental effort involved in maintaining this facade she's constructed, and the peculiar, swirling feelings she experiences when she's around Moya—even *thinking* about Moya—are making concentration hard. She steps into her uncomfortable shoes and grabs her handbag. "Okay, let's go. Don't forget your notes."

Dottie comes closer, so they're together in the mirror. "We don't look like we're going to a poker night."

"Sure we do." Kit has no idea what proper poker night attire consists of. Two weeks ago, if anyone had told her she'd be going to secret meetings in Moya Kershaw's dorm room, Kit would've said they were wisecracking. "Okay, come on."

Dottie closes the door behind them, and they head for the stairs. The hall runners on every floor are identical, but there's one surefire way to know that they've reached Two. "Jeebers," Dottie says, "I can never figure out how Moya sleeps with all the typewriting going on down here."

"Earplugs?"

"I guess."

They've arrived at the right door. Kit tugs her bag higher, raises her hand, and knocks. The door opens, and she immediately realizes she's overdressed.

Moya is in socks, her hair down and natural. It's cut off

blunt at her collarbones, and there's very little wave there—
she must work hard to wrangle it into rolls. She's wearing
soft navy lounge pants and a loose white shirt underneath a
flowing black satin robe. This is not like her men's dressing
gown. The robe is elaborately embroidered with a red Chi-
nese dragon that climbs up one lapel and curls its tail over
Moya's shoulder to trail down the other side in a slither of
sparkling fire.

Kit tries not to act dazzled.

"Nice cardigan," Moya says. "Welcome. It's five past six."
But she doesn't look worried about punctuality. She's holding a burning cigarette in one hand and a glass of whiskey in
the other. Music is playing somewhere, down low.

Dottie stands patiently with her notes. "Kit was fussing
with her hair."

"Was she?" Moya's eyes light on Kit, flit away. Her lips are
faintly upturned. "Oh well, come on in."

Moya's room is unique in a number of ways. First, that
she has it, when space in the Hall is at a premium. Second, that it's big enough to hold more than one resident, yet
Moya has hung on to her single-occupant status.

Third, the decor is a major surprise.

Kit's always assumed that Moya's room would be a
reflection of her usual public persona: elegantly utilitarian,
ordered, and reserved. But this room is not like that. It's . . .
messy. The interior is dark-paneled, like every other place
in the schoolhouse, but tall lamps with fringed opalescent
shades cast a rosy glow. A framed art nouveau print of the
Folies-Bergère occupies one wall. Just to the right of the

doorway is a large lacquered armoire. Nearer to Kit, on the left, a round baize-topped card table is set tightly around with chairs. Past the card table, deep in the left-hand corner, Moya's bed is framed by long, blue velvet drapes. Kit sees a white pillow, a dark red duvet tumbled together with scarves and clothes, and a number of jewel-colored cushions, before she quickly looks away.

Moya is still holding the door, amused by Kit's reaction. "In or out?"

"Oh. Sorry. In." Kit steps over the threshold.

Moya closes the door and walks over to a small bookcase hidden on the other side of the armoire. The bottom shelf contains a pile of books, and on the middle shelf, a compact Philco wireless provides the music; Kit recognizes Anne Shelton's swaying rendition of "A Nightingale Sang in Berkley Square." The top shelf holds a tray of glasses and bottles.

"Drink?" Moya looks over. "Dottie, your usual?"

"You're a gem." Dottie dumps her notes on the card table and flops on Moya's bed.

"Kit?" Moya's robe swirls as she turns to look over her shoulder. "I have gin, whiskey, brandy, and soda."

"Uh, just..." Kit decides she needs to hold on to her wits. "Soda. Soda is fine."

Moya raises her eyebrows, shrugs. "Find a seat. Dottie, don't put your feet on my bed."

"I've already taken my shoes off," Dottie counters. "Moya, I like the new cushion."

"I found it in a bathtub on One. Here's your brandy." Moya hands Dottie her glass, then moves closer to pass one

98

to Kit. "Most of the furniture is stolen. I grabbed everything I could before they stripped all the good stuff out of the Hall. I had to bribe two privates with a pitcher of beer to carry in the armoire."

"Are those drapes from the old auditorium?" Kit sets her handbag on the floor. She sips her drink—plain soda over ice, with a slice of lemon—and eases a chair out from the arrangement at the card table for herself.

"Good eye." Moya stubs out her cigarette in a glass ashtray on the table. "They were going to throw them out. I should stop saying 'stolen' and start saying 'rescued.'"

"How do you keep this all to yourself?" Kit blurts out.

Moya touches the side of her nose. "Connections. Actually, it's because I'm a supervisor. Also because no one else wants to sleep so close to the typewriters."

"Oh." Even inside the room, with the door closed and music playing, Kit can hear the *tap-tappity-tap-tap-ping!* from across the corridor.

"I don't mind the noise." Moya cants her head. "Kinda like it, to be honest. After a while, it's like listening to rain on the roof."

Moya's lips turn up again gently. Kit wonders what Moya's full-blown smile would look like. The idea makes her heart speed its rhythm, and she digs in her handbag for a distraction. "Oh, I have your scarf. I washed it after...well, you know."

"Thank you." Moya accepts the slip of blue cloth. "Ironed, too. You didn't have to do that."

"It's too nice *not* to iron." Kit feels her face heat as she

99

closes up the bag. She sips her drink. "Uh, Violet said she's getting files from the hospital, then catching the bus. She might be a little late."

Moya nods. "Then let's talk about other information. Dot, did you end up going to the Farms today?"

"Yep." Dottie's feet are tucked under her. She clutches her drink in one hand and cuddles a cushion with the other. "It was very weird, going back there, but everything went okay. I didn't get to talk to everybody, though. Some of the girls were at work."

Kit sits up straighter. "The girl who helped you—did you find her?"

"She was—" Dottie stops when a knock comes at the door.

It's Violet, clutching a thick bunch of papers. Her hooded coat is sparkling with crystal drops of rain. She ditches her paperwork on the table and pushes back her hood. "It's drizzling out there. I'm lucky the bus was early. And look, it's great to meet, but we might have to find somewhere else to do it."

"Why's that?" Kit stands and helps her hang the coat over the back of a chair to dry.

"Don't know if you've noticed, but Black staff only work in and out of One." Violet dabs at her face with a handkerchief. "I stick out a mile walking up to Two."

"Damn, I should've thought of that." Moya frowns. "All right, let me figure out a solution. Want a drink?"

"Anything that isn't alcoholic." Violet looks around. "Wow, this place is real nice."

"Thanks. It's more private than the library, at least. But, Violet, if getting you up to Two is going to be a problem, we'll find another place."

"Great." Violet settles herself in the chair with the coat. "You gals get started without me?"

"Not really." Dottie's propped herself up with the cushion, and now she's leaning back with her glass of brandy. "I just launched into what I heard at the Farms today. Was it your day off, too?"

"Nope. I went to the hospital after work." Violet accepts her glass of soda. "So what did you find?"

Dottie beckons to Kit to pass her the folder of notes. "Okay, first I tried to remember anything more about the guys from the dance—but honestly, my memories are just a blur. When I went back to the Farms, though, I managed to find five girls who were there last Friday. Two of them said they saw Libby, but only in passing. One of the girls said she thought she saw Libby talking to someone, but she couldn't see who because of the crowd."

"Not very helpful," Violet notes.

"You got it. Anyway, the girl who helped me out to the back of Ohio hall? She's with the Bank Commission, and her name is Mildred Gregory. She thought I was 'feeling delicate,' so she took me out for some air and gave me the blanket. That was about eleven thirty Friday night."

"She didn't notice you'd been drugged?" Kit finds the idea appalling.

"No—she thought I'd had too much to drink. She went

to bed once she settled me on the back porch. She didn't notice any guys lurking around Ohio or the laundry."

"Doesn't sound like Mildred is the most observant person, though."

"You'd be right about that. And she wasn't keen to talk. The notion of someone being killed so close to her dorm has put her in a spin. She mentioned that she might move out of Arlington Farms, if she can find a cheap place closer to the center of town."

Moya rolls her eyes. "Good luck with that. I know girls near the Capitol building who're paying rent to sleep on the couch in a shared room. Dottie, did you leave your contact details? So Mildred can tell you where she's going if she changes her address?"

Dottie nods. "You bet. But honestly, I think she's a dead end. She didn't see anything, didn't hear anything. Said she sleeps with a beauty mask and earplugs because of her roommate's snoring."

"Huh." Moya ties the belt of her robe and pulls out a chair to sit down near Violet. "I got better information at the police station. I had to wear a dress, but it was worth it."

"Who did you talk to?" Kit reaches again for her handbag and withdraws a small stack of cream-colored index cards and a pencil. She jots down Dottie's information—*Mildred Gregory, Bank C, no insights, Arlington Farms/Ohio hall, address to change?*—and starts a new card for Moya.

"Detective Sergeant Brendan Whitty." Moya sips her drink. "He'll be the guy I go back to if I need to know more."

"Why? Was he nice?" Dottie asks hopefully.

"Nice? No. He took off his wedding ring when he thought I wasn't looking." Moya's tone is dry, her voice roughened with the whiskey. "But it seems like he'll talk to anything in a skirt, and once he starts it's hard to shut him up, which is good for us."

Kit looks up from her cards. "What did you find out?"

"Well, after he finished complaining about how DC is being taken over by young women and what a pain that is for the police, he was quite cooperative. He's been briefed by Colonel Corderman, so that helped. He gave me some details from the police file. Hold on." Moya walks to the armoire and opens the doors wide.

Kit manages to repress a gasp, but only just. The inside of the armoire is a paradise of clothes, all in rich, crisp colors. Now she understands how Moya always manages to look so well put together. Moya rummages in the pocket of a burgundy trench coat and finds what she's after. She lays a photograph on the green baize of the card table. "I stole a picture out of the file while Whitty was going on. Violet, this is Libby Armstrong. She was nineteen years old."

Violet leans forward, and Dottie comes over from the bed to look, too. But Kit hardly needs the picture—she remembers Libby. A petite-featured brunette, Libby wore whimsical shoes and white blouses with Peter Pan collars. She's smiling hopefully in the photo, in a way that Kit finds sad. Libby went to the dance for company, or maybe to find someone who would love her for who she was. Instead, she met a man who didn't care about her personhood. Who violated and killed her in the most brutal way imaginable.

Kit has seen this girl laid out like bloodied meat on a bathroom floor. The juxtaposition of that remembered image with this image on the table—of Libby Armstrong as she was in life—is hard to bear.

"She's…" Dottie tears up. "I still can't believe she's gone. I was talking to her on the bus, on the way to the Farms. She was telling me about her little brother and how her mother was hoping they'd meet up for Easter…. God. This whole thing makes me feel sick."

"According to Whitty, there were no witnesses," Moya explains in the solemn quiet. "Nobody saw Libby leave the dance, much less caught sight of who she might have left with. The police seem to be taking the angle that she had a beau who saw her with another man on the night of the dance, and then when she left Idaho, her 'beau' killed her in a fury."

Violet makes a face. "What a crock."

"They've got no evidence of any beau or boyfriend." Moya's hand goes into the pocket of her robe, pulls out her slim silver case. She removes a cigarette but holds it without lighting it, like her fingers need something to do. "Libby lived with two other girls in Foggy Bottom, and they both said she wasn't romantically involved with anyone. But the police need their theories."

Kit takes in Moya's scornful expression. "What about the other case? Dinah's case?"

"When I said I'd heard in the papers that another girl was

killed recently, Whitty told me that was something different. Not related."

"My lord, the police are unbelievable," Violet says.

Kit nods in agreement. "Either they don't know, or they don't want to link the two cases publicly, or they're deliberately ignoring the circumstances."

"But if they keep doing that, more girls will *die*." Dottie's voice is hot as she thumps her glass down on the table. "Any man who does this, commits crimes like this... He's not just going to stop. He's going to keep killing."

Kit looks again at Moya. "Did they check out the footprints? And what about fingerprints?"

"No fingerprints. They think he wore gloves." Moya angles her cigarette like she's smoking it, one elbow cupped. "From the footprints, they figure the killer is about six feet tall. They're chasing down men who knew Libby—friends, and friends of friends."

"That's just going to get a lot of boys who did nothing wrong in a whole heap of trouble." Violet picks up the photo by the edges for closer examination. "Poor girl. What about the glasses? Did the police have anything to say about that?"

"When I mentioned them, Whitty just said someone from the Farms must've left them behind in the laundry bathroom."

"Wow," Violet says. "They're really not giving Dinah's case any energy at all, are they?"

"Did you really expect them to?" Moya asks quietly.

Violet shakes her head, wordless.

Kit is writing it all on cards—Whitty's name, the police

theory. Another card for Libby Armstrong and her details. There's more information coming, and she wants to get it all down, lay it out like the pieces of a puzzle.

Or a code.

"We're going to have to strip it back," she says, pencil moving. "Like the work upstairs, or in the cottage."

"What do you mean?" Moya's expression is speculative.

"When you get a new code message, you strip out the transfer code first." Kit adds more details to the card, looks up. "We're going to have to do the same thing here. The police have biases—they don't believe there's a link between the two murders, they don't believe that Libby had no boyfriend because they can't imagine a girl without one, and they're ignoring Dinah's case because she's Black. They have a . . . a screwed-up way of thinking that clouds their reasoning."

"Which means every theory they come up with will be tainted," Violet says.

Kit nods. "We have to strip that out. Strip out the bias and the prejudice, just look at the information. The unvarnished truth."

"Just look at the evidence." Dottie pushes her curls back behind her ears and settles in the seat next to Kit.

"That's right." Kit selects another card. "I'm going to try to make notes of every little piece of information that we get. We strip out anything that looks like transfer bias. Then we'll have enough raw data to start putting things together."

"Well, I've got plenty more data here." Violet pulls her pile of paperwork closer. "This is all from Ruth Freeman—after she

106

got laid off during the UVA Hospital Black nurses' walkout in January, she got a job at DC General. This paperwork is only a loan; I have to get it back to her by Sunday. I asked her to get me anything she could find on Dinah and Libby's deaths."

"Libby *did* go to General," Kit says.

"Yes."

"You look at this yet?" Moya resumes her seat, takes the top piece of paper off the pile.

"I wasn't game to look at it on the way home," Violet admits. "I...I was worried I might start crying on the bus."

Dottie reaches across the table and squeezes Violet's hand. "You want us to look at this without you?"

"No," Violet says, her eyes hard. "No way. You can look at Libby's information; I can look at Dinah's. I want to know everything. I want the unvarnished truth."

She splits the papers into three piles and hands one to Moya and one to Dottie. Kit acts as compiler. For the next ten minutes they dive into reading. The only sounds Kit hears are the whisk of papers being shuffled, the low, lonely saxophone music drifting from the radio, and the distant ping of typewriters.

Moya smokes as she scans the pages and sips her drink. Dottie strips off her sweater. The room is warm, and Kit registers the other girls' soft breathing—sometimes the noise of breath catching as one of them reads something particularly heinous.

Once Kit has the last details of the police theories written and her cards in order, she looks up, pencil ready. "Okay, what've we got?"

"Rape," Moya says bluntly. "Of both girls."

"That's disgusting." Dottie's expression is pale. "Look here, though. Both girls had bruises around their necks, but it says something about...some kind of bone. That it wasn't broken."

"Let me see?" Kit accepts pages from Dottie. "The hyoid bone. It's in the throat, near the voice box."

"How do you know that?"

"I read a lot, remember?" Kit returns the pages. She doesn't want to say she stood at attention for more medical examinations about Katherine's respiratory issues than she cares to count.

"What does it mean, if that bone wasn't broken?" Moya asks. "Is that important?"

"Here." Violet lifts her chin at the page in her hand. "I've got a note here that says both girls were strangled, but they didn't *die* of strangulation."

"Maybe he subdues them by partially strangling them," Kit suggests.

"Looks like," Violet says. "But both girls died of blood loss. They were both stabbed."

"There was sure enough blood in the laundry to convince me of that." Moya taps the tip of her cigarette against the ashtray.

"Lord." Violet lets out a shaky breath.

"I'm sorry." Kit rests her forearms on the table. "This must be hard for you to hear."

"Yeah." Violet takes a swig of her soda water. "Harder for you to witness it, though. And I said I want the truth. Okay, so he throttles them, assaults them, stabs them..."

108

"It says here that Libby had 'defensive wounds,'" Dottie says. "Cuts on her hands and arms. So she tried to defend herself at first."

Violet nods. "Dinah, too."

"What kind of knife did he use?" Kit's pencil is moving fast as she takes everything down.

"They haven't figured that out yet. Something long and sharp—not a pocketknife."

"But there was no knife found in the laundry," Moya says. "No murder weapon, according to Detective Whitty. We don't have the police file on Dinah's case—so, Kit, you might want to include this under speculation—but I'm guessing there was no knife found in Downtown, either."

"The killer must've planned this," Dottie says suddenly. "He brought a knife, then he took it away again at the end. He knew what he was doing."

Kit straightens in her chair. "And Whitty said there were no fingerprints, that the killer wore gloves. That's another clue he planned this in advance."

"But there must've been a hell of a mess when it was over," Violet says. "A big knife, and his clothes must've been covered with blood... How did he escape without anyone noticing?"

Moya looks up. "He must have a car. He can't have caught a cab or ridden the bus."

"Kit, are you getting this down?" Dottie asks.

"Yes." Kit finishes a note, shakes out her hand. "Is there anything else? He took Dinah's glasses—what did he take from Libby?"

There's a moment of silence as everyone searches through their pages. Moya gets up to pour herself a soda.

"I can't find anything," Dottie announces at last. "Libby's roommates might have known what she took with her to the dance, but there's nothing in this report. Only what she arrived with at the morgue."

"She didn't have her purse—Kit and I both noticed that—but she might not have taken one." Moya is leaning against the armoire, swirling the ice in her glass and staring at the Folies-Bergère print on the opposite wall. "The item might have been something small and personal. Hair combs, or keys, or something that wouldn't be missed right away..."

A sudden, sharp gasp from Violet makes them all look over.

"What is it?" Moya asks.

"He...he..." Violet has found a picture in the notes. Now she pushes it away from herself. "Oh, Lord Jesus."

"What is it, hon?" Dottie takes the picture. Then she, too, gasps in shock. "Oh my god."

Kit has seen and heard a lot of things in the last few days that she wishes she'd never encountered. But that doesn't stop her from reaching over to take the photo. It's a photograph of Libby's body, post-autopsy. And Kit can see the cause of Violet and Dottie's horror straightaway, sewn in with garish black stitches.

She feels the blood drain out of her face as she looks over at Moya. "I'm sorry, but you need to see this."

Moya sets her drink down and steps closer, takes the photo. Her expression goes hard and cold. "Did he cut them both like that?"

Violet has turned away, and Dottie is holding her. Kit is the one who has to sift through pages until she finds the other picture they need.

"Yes." She swallows as she takes the first autopsy photo from Moya, places both photographs together on the table. They sit there like a stain in the middle of the green baize.

"He cut that disgusting antisemitic symbol into their stomachs." Moya exhales slowly. "So the killer we're looking for... He's probably American, if he goes to dances at Arlington Farms. He might even be a serviceman. But he's a Nazi, through and through."

12

The reason you're not getting anywhere
is because this is a new code.
                    —AGNES MEYER DRISCOLL

That night, Kit dreams of home.

She's outside her parents' house in Scott's Run in the late afternoon, beside the iron-green water pump near the knockabout porch. She's wearing the navy travel suit, clutching the brown vinyl handbag. Looking up at the house, a feeling rises in her—the same dread and burgeoning horror she felt in the laundry at Arlington Farms.

Her feet hurt. When she peers down, blood is staining her stockings, oozing from the edges of her too-tight shoes. But her body moves without volition, taking the first step onto the porch, and the next, until she's standing on the battered boards, looking in the dark open doorway.

"Ma? Papa?"

Her soft voice is whisked away in the flat, chill breeze. Kit can see the chipped whitewash on the front of the house, the metal pail for fireplace ash. The broken-down easy chair, where her father sits to smoke in the evening after he gets home from the mine, creaks softly as it rocks. Farther away, the dirt road, empty of people.

When she looks back, Libby Armstrong is standing in the doorway.

Libby's hair is bedraggled and her lips are blue. She's wearing the pink skirt. The front of her blouse is open, exposing the soft gray pucker of her skin. A black caterpillar track of stitches keeps her symbolically marked stomach together.

The terror that Kit felt a whisper of before is now an urgent throb pulsing in her veins.

Libby's eyes are milky in death. Her pale lips move like she's trying to speak. She takes a step closer, lifts a hand.

Kit knows that if Libby touches her with those cold, dead fingers, her heart will seize in her chest. She has to run, she has to—

She steps back, misses her footing on the stairs. Then she's flailing, *falling*...

"*Kit.*"

A gasp, a pounding sense of wrong, and her vision clears. Dottie's face is above her; Dottie's hand is on her arm.

"*I can't.*..." Kit tries to get her breathing under control. "I can't...."

"Shh, honey, it's okay." Dottie sits on the edge of the bed, rubs Kit's shoulder gently. "You had a bad dream, that's all. And no wonder, after all that grisly stuff last night."

"What time is it?" Sweat in her hairline: Kit blots at it with the cuff of her pajama sleeve.

"Nearly eight. I'm about to go on shift." Dottie smooths her skirt over her hips. "Are you gonna be okay?"

"Yeah." Kit clears her throat. "Yes. I'll be fine."

"Get some coffee and breakfast—you'll feel better after that. It's your day off, remember? Sorry to hug you and run—"

"Don't be silly," Kit says. "Go, go. You don't wanna be late."

Once Dottie has left for her shift, Kit sits on the bed and scrubs a hand over her face. It's Wednesday—her day off. Right. She reaches for her handbag and pulls out the cream-colored index cards with all the information they gathered last night. She lays the cards out on the bed, trying to see how they all link together. But the blankets on her bed are mussed, and the cards all just seem like random, jumbled noise....

She needs to get herself together. She doesn't want her rest day infused with this post-bad-dream sourness.

It's hard, though: Her brain won't switch off. While she's taking a long hot shower, washing her hair, tidying up her dresser, having breakfast, she thinks about the identity review. While she's ironing her clothes for the week, completing other chores before lunch, she thinks about the murders.

She's still tired. Normally, she'd take a nap, but the prospect of having another nightmare is unappealing. Kit hangs her washing, then puts on her coat and goes for a walk.

The quad at the rear of the schoolhouse has park-style benches but feels too exposed, so she turns left and walks into the trees. She's not actually sure how far into the forested grounds she's allowed to go. There was a PSA about it, but unfortunately she didn't pay a lot of attention.

The rough-barked trees are comforting, with their vibrant new leaves. Administration is talking about razing part of this forest for a parking lot, which Kit thinks is sad. Everything here smells of green. The grass is thick, dampening her shoes, but Kit strolls on, and before she knows it, she's reached the little school gazebo. Cream-painted, open-walled, just the place for sitting.

Kit settles on the wooden bench inside, watches the birds flitting around. Listens. It feels a world away from the close, cramped rooms of the Hall, with the ever-present noise of typing and girls' voices. The air is cool on her cheeks.

"Weather's still kinda cold to be sitting in the shade, don't you think?"

Kit's head jerks around. Violet is standing beside the gazebo. The girl's face is hot with color from the brisk air, and she has a brown cable-knit cardigan wrapped tight around her. Her hair is a soft dark cloud, held back with an Alice band. The blue of her skirt is rich against the all-around green.

"I guess." Kit looks back at the trees. "It's quiet. It's nice. Aren't you on shift?"

"I'm on break." Violet walks up the step, into the gazebo. She nods her chin toward someplace over Kit's shoulder, beyond the tree line. "But the cottage is just over there, and I saw you out the window. Would you prefer to be on your own?"

Kit shakes her head. "It's fine. Have a seat."

"Do the woods remind you of home?" Violet asks suddenly.

"Kind of." Kit doesn't allow her accent to shift. If she relaxes once, it's harder to suppress again later. "Kind of not. There's woods where I grew up, but it's mostly just...dirt."

Violet's expression softens. "Where are you from? Like, really?"

"West Virginia." Kit finds the words hard to get out.

"If it makes you feel better, I wouldn't have guessed if I didn't already know," Violet says.

Kit isn't sure how to respond to that. She settles for a neutral nod. "Well...thanks. I guess everyone will know soon anyway, with the review."

"Have you thought about what you're gonna do?"

"No." Kit kicks her crossed ankles forward and back gently. "I'm just not sure. I mean, I know I'll have to run, but I'm not sure how, or where to go."

"You don't want to go home," Violet says, with a touch of surprise.

Kit says nothing. Just kicks her legs. Then she thinks of something, a way of framing it. "It's kind of like pickles. You know the taste of pickles? You either love it or you hate it—there's no in-between."

"You're comparing going home to pickles?" Violet's lips turn up gradually, until she's grinning.

"Yep." Kit finds herself grinning back. She looks at her feet, feeling the need to explain a little. "Maybe I'm wrong, but you seem like you come from a family that's getting by?"

"We get by," Violet says, nodding slowly.

"Yeah." Kit bites her lip, still looking down. "That's not how I grew up. We were never getting by. My papa worked the mine, and my brothers trapped muskrats in the creek to sell the hides. I stripped tobacco or helped my ma collect May apple roots in tow sacks for lye money. I never owned a pair of shoes until I was twelve—we used to wrap our feet in newspaper tied with string, then go dig stove coal from the mine tailings."

Violet's face is serious again. "That's a hard, heavy life."

"I didn't even know how poor we were until I got a job as a maid. The Sutherlands had indoor plumbing. I had regular meals, a nice apron, two pairs of stockings, a pair of shoes...."

"Riches," Violet says softly.

"I was fourteen, and I'd never had those things before. I thought I was in heaven, y'know?" Kit shakes her head at herself. "But I was still a maid. Then I started thinking about it and realized that I was paying off those nice aprons and those stockings and shoes. I got a job and room and board, and my folks got a flat rate on their loan."

"They sold you into service," Violet says bluntly. "That's how it works. It just doesn't happen to whites so often."

"Yeah, I guess." Kit nods. "I have five siblings, so I understand why—it was a good deal for them. But...it left a sour taste. So no, I don't want to go home. But it doesn't matter. Everybody's got their own troubles. You've got your own troubles—I'm a poor white girl, but I'm still a white girl."

Violet is staring away contemplatively. "That's the truth. You've got a chance to rise. You don't want to go back home—well, I can't go back to the kitchen. Not after working in the cottage with Mr. Coffee."

"You want something more."

Violet presses her lips. "I know there's nothing wrong with being kitchen staff. My mother worked in kitchens— it's honest work, and it pays twenty-five cents an hour. But I can't do it anymore. And I don't know where that leaves me. Once the war is over, service jobs are about all that a Black girl can hope for, even with a college education."

Kit's kicking her legs still. "The world is not fair."

"That's the world," Violet reminds her.

Kit feels that. "Would you go to college, if you could?"

"I've got the application for Howard University," Violet confesses. "But I haven't submitted it."

Kit's breath huffs out with surprise. "For *Howard*? Excuse me, but *damn*, Violet. What's holding you back?"

Violet looks down, frowning. "I'm in two minds about it. College would be great, but there's the cost. I don't want my folks to carry that."

"You should still do it," Kit insists. "Any chance, you should take it."

"At my family's expense?" Violet looks at Kit sideways. "And what's the use if I'm only gonna be the best-educated girl in the laundry room?"

"You won't end up in the laundry room," Kit says firmly. "You're too smart for that, and people have noticed. It's true the world's not fair, but there's a war on, and the world is changing."

"Not fast enough," Violet whispers. "I don't want to sacrifice my family for college. Years of study and expense…What if it all comes to nothing?"

"What if it all comes to *something*? You could lift your family up, as well as yourself." Kit nods toward the trees. "You've got to have hope, Violet. Hope's all we've got. And education. Education is part of it. I honestly believe that."

Violet scuffs at the boards of the gazebo with the toe of her shoe. "You got any education?"

"Nope." Kit shakes her head slowly. "My ma taught me to read and write and to figure. All the education I had after that was because of Katherine. Once she found out I had some basic skills but nothing else, she made sure I took lessons with her. Told her parents it was boring to have a companion with no learning. She made it her job to smart me up. Got me reading French and studying poetry and history and geometry..." Kit trails off, wistful.

Violet is looking at her. "She sounds like a good person."

"She was. I miss her so much." Kit bites her lip over a sad smile. "But it's a double-edged sword—now I've got some learning, it's ruined me as a maid."

"Makes you a handy little codebreaker, though." Violet grins.

"I guess." Kit snorts. "But hey—*Howard*. I swear, Violet, if you fill out that application, I'll take it to the post office myself."

Violet presses her lips primly. "Lord, hear you. I can post my own application, thank you."

"Then do it!" Kit figures Violet's break must be well over by now. She pushes off the seat, extends a hand to help Violet up. "Listen, I've been thinking about the information we've got on the murders."

119

"Well, that's a change of subject," Violet says as she stands, brushing off her skirt. "But okay, go on."

"There's a lot of data now," Kit says, re-buttoning her coat, "some of it useful and some of it not. If I had a photographic memory, I could sort it all in my head. But I don't have a photographic memory, so..."

"We need to lay it out," Violet says. She wraps her cardigan more firmly around herself. "We need to *see* it all laid out. Like when you have a bunch of messages in the same code group."

Kit catches on. "Right—you need to spread them out and then find the repetitions before you can make sense of it."

"Can we do that?" Violet asks. "Can we lay out the cards you made somewhere?"

Kit feels her expression change with the new concept.

"That," she says, "is a very good idea."

13

It's 7:00 PM on Floor Two, and Moya is reading about Beryl Markham's airplane-flying exploits in Africa when Kit's quiet voice comes from the corridor.

"Moya." A gentle knock on the door. "Moya, open up."

Kit.

There's the immediate physical reaction: heartrate speeding up, sweet tension in her muscles. Moya takes a moment to breathe. She slowly and deliberately rests her cigarette in the ashtray beside her, turns her book over, and gets off her bed.

She makes it halfway to the door before realizing she still has a towel on her head. She yanks the towel off, tosses it over the back of a chair, checks herself in the full-length mirror inside one of the armoire doors. Her black shirt has the sleeves rolled up, the hem untucked over brown trousers. She rakes back her fresh-washed hair. No makeup—it means she looks about sixteen, but she'll have to live with that.

She stares at her reflection. *What are you doing? This is Kit. Just because you held hands once when you were both under stress doesn't mean—*

Another gentle knock. "Moya?"

"Coming!" She closes the armoire and turns down the swing music on the Philco before answering the door. "Hi."

"Hi." Kit hitches up her handbag. She's wearing the same sage-green cardigan as the other night, over a peacock-blue utility dress cinched at the waist with a thin white belt. Her auburn hair is getting longer—she's keeping it back with little clips. Her freckles are lovely. "So...can I come in for a second?"

"Oh." Moya forces herself to focus. "I mean, of course."

Moya's suddenly aware of the state of the room. There's a jacket hanging off the back of one of the chairs and the damp towel dumped on another. Her books are piled next to the bed, and there's a scattering of shoes. Only her reading lamp is on, the dim light making everything seem dingy. And dammit, the cigarette—Moya goes to rescue it as the soft sound of "Begin the Beguine" drifts from the Philco.

"I had an idea." Kit doesn't seem bothered by the bohemian mess. She sets her handbag on the baize card table. "Actually, Violet had the idea, but she gave it to me. We need to lay out the information cards in a permanent way. We need a corkboard, or a chart, maybe. So we can see everything arranged in order."

Moya blinks for a moment before catching up. "Like an overlapper's table."

"Yes. I wanted to do it on the wall of my room, but Dottie wouldn't let me."

"Too gruesome?"

"Yes." Kit winces. "So I thought maybe you might have space here."

"Right." Moya tries to think. "I don't have a corkboard."

"The card table?"

"Yeah, that won't work on poker nights."

Kit lists things on her fingers. "The library's not private. Nowhere else is private. I know Violet can't come here, but—"

"That's not going to be a problem." Moya waves her hand with the cigarette. "I've made an arrangement so Violet can come onto Two."

"Great. Then here. But...where?"

They stand there, thinking. The table is out; the wall is too visible. The back of the Folies-Bergère print might work, but it's probably too small. That just leaves the bed, the bookcase, and...

"Oh—okay." Moya smiles, gratified that her brain is still working.

Kit blinks. "What's okay?"

Moya doesn't answer, because she wants to enjoy Kit's reaction. She stubs out her smoke, then opens her armoire. The armoire has a heavy base, and it's big enough that she would fit inside comfortably if she were playing hide-and-seek.

"What are you—" Kit stops talking when Moya takes a bunch of clothes on hangers and dumps them into her arms. "You want me to...hold the clothes?"

"Put them on the bed." Moya shoos Kit with one hand. "Go ahead, it's fine."

Another armful of clothes later, Moya separates the remaining hangers to frame the inside rear of the armoire. "How's that?"

"Ingenious." Kit's expression is all wonder.

It's exactly the reaction Moya was hoping for, and she enjoys it immensely. "When we don't want it seen, we can just draw the hangers back in front."

"Perfect." Kit grabs her handbag. "I brought thumbtacks."

While Kit tacks all the cards up inside the armoire, Moya shoves the excess clothes into a trunk under the bed that she uses for storage. Having gained momentum, she also puts away her ashtray and tidies her bedlinens and books. Bundles up a ravel of scarves. Kicks her shoes into a pile. The damp towel goes on a hook behind the front door.

"You don't have to tidy for me, you know." Kit's half inside the armoire, so her voice is slightly muffled.

"It's fine." Moya brushes crumbs off the card table. "It needed doing."

"I have to be honest with you." Kit steps out of the armoire, dusting her hands. "I'm a little jealous of your room."

"*Jealous.*" Moya snorts. This girl never ceases to surprise her. "Of what? The mess?"

"The privacy." Kit bites her lip. "I mean, my room is great. And I don't want to sound resentful of Dottie—she's a great roommate. The best. But sometimes it's just nice to have a little..."

"Alone time?" Moya props herself back against the table on her hands.

"I know I'm lucky—there are worse places to be living than in the Hall." Kit's cheeks go a delicate shade of pink as she rests against the table, too. "It seems rude to complain."

"You're not complaining. Everybody needs privacy from time to time."

"Sometimes my head gets full up," Kit blurts out. "And then I just need...I don't know. Some distance."

"Thinking time," Moya suggests. "Personal time."

"That's right," Kit agrees. "Personal time."

Kit has turned her head and their faces are close. Propped together like this on the card table, in front of the armoire, Moya is acutely aware of the place where her shoulder touches Kit's shoulder. That place is very warm and comfortable.

Moya looks at the constellation of pale freckles wheeling across Kit's cheeks, the bridge of her nose, and acknowledges that they are fascinating. Maybe that's what's got her so hypnotized. A heady thrill shivers under Moya's skin like glitter. And it's so tempting to be unguarded. It's something Moya hasn't had for a long time.

But some things you just don't say out loud, and sometimes you can't trust your instincts. She's been wrong before, to her cost.

Better to redirect the conversation onto safer territory. "So, uh, it must be a big adjustment living in cramped quarters, after the way you grew up."

"The way I grew up?" Kit looks confused.

"Your family's from the Philadelphia Main Line, right? You probably had a big room to yourself and acres of land...."

125

"Oh. Right." Kit's blush from a moment before fades into white. She looks away. "Yeah, I guess. Although I've been living here at the school a while. Years in student dorms."

"Right." What just happened? Kit closed up like a Venus flytrap.

Now Kit stands, lifts her chin at the armoire. "Anyway— it's done."

Moya steps closer to see. Kit has tacked up about a dozen index cards in a way that shows the links between them. She's also put up photos of Libby and Dinah as they were in life and some drawings of the layout of the laundry.

Moya's eyes narrow, taking everything in. "There it all is."

"Not all." Kit rubs the pad of her thumb, which must've gotten a workout with the tacks. "We need more. So much more. There must be newspaper reports—"

"There are," Moya confirms. "Have you seen the latest in the papers? Lots of 'Be careful, ladies!' articles."

"Well, we can leave that stuff, but we should get copies of everything directly related to the murders. And I still want to get as much information from the hospital file as I can, before Violet takes it back. And some of the cards are just a title waiting for fill-in detail—the killer's car, the kind of knife..."

"But now we can see what we're missing," Moya points out.

"I'm worried that we won't get enough information." Kit's words come out in a rush. "That we won't gain any insights before there's another murder. I don't want us to be waiting for the next girl to die to make progress."

"Hey, listen." Moya turns toward her. "We can do this. Do you know why we can do this? Because it's a team job."

Kit fixes one hair clip back in place. "What do you mean?"

"It's like working at the tables. Codes are never broken by a single person." Moya puts up a hand when Kit opens her mouth, anticipating her objections. "Yes, there are some standout people, like Ann Caracristi and Emil Ferrars and Solomon Kullback. Those people are important. But the largest percentage of code is broken by a group of people working together. It's the power of a collective bunch of brains. That's why Arlington Hall was set up this way."

Kit's shoulders straighten. "That's why so many girls are working in the same room."

"Right. Because *you* might get a partial break, and Carol from New Jersey might get another part of it, and then the overlapper—"

"Rose."

"And then Rose puts everything together and makes another break. That's how it's done. It's a group effort." Moya looks back at the murder board in the armoire. "And between me and you and Violet and Dottie, we have enough brain power to figure this out."

"You think?"

"I know."

"I wish I had your confidence." But Kit's grinning.

Moya's pleased to see it. She moves toward the bookshelf. "Relax—I've got plenty to share around. So we're done with the murder board. D'you want a drink?"

"Uh, I..." Kit's color has returned. She shifts on her feet. "I told Dottie I wouldn't be long."

"Oh." Moya notices Kit glance toward the door and is reminded once again why she doesn't let her instincts rule her. "Okay."

"So...maybe just a little one?"

Moya pauses in the act of reaching for a glass. She looks over her shoulder, trying to seem nonchalant. "Soda? Or a real drink?"

Kit wets her lips. "Whiskey."

"One shot of whiskey, coming right up."

Moya's abashed that the fine trembling in her hands is pinpointed by the clink of the decanter on the glasses as she pours. *Settle down, girl.* Moya pushes down hard through the soles of her feet, makes herself breathe normally.

The tremble is gone by the time she extends Kit's glass. "Here you go."

"Thanks." Kit takes it with both hands.

"Here's to..." Moya contemplates the murder board in her armoire. "What are we drinking to?"

"Catching this guy?" Kit frowns, puts one hand on her hip as she lifts her glass with the other. "No, wait. He shouldn't be the focus of anything. Let's say...to group effort."

"All right, then. To group effort."

They touch glasses, and the crystal makes a chiming ring.

14

There is an old miner's proverb: *Gold
is where you find it.*
—COLONEL PARKER HITT

"My turn," Edith Faber says quietly. She collects her handbag with all her identity papers. The other girls in the room
give Edith a nod or a wave.

Kit watches her go. Progress on the reviews has been slow
but steady. Every day this week, different girls have left the
room with alphabetical precision to go down to the gymnasium, and every day, Kit has felt her ribs clamp tighter. It's
like waiting for the arrival of creeping death.

She exhales, focuses back on what she's doing. She and
Opal and Brigid are currently swapping cards back and
forth, working on the message system's sum check. The
sum check is meant to guard transmissions against message
garble, but it's sometimes a weak spot they can use to find a
way in. They've spent the last two days chaining the numbers, looking for the same additive repeated, but that didn't
seem to go anywhere.

Now it's Saturday, and things are getting busy. More and
more messages are arriving, and cards are flooding in. Dottie
is being run off her feet—Kit's glad *she's* not the one to-ing
and fro-ing from logging and traffic analysis, because she'd

be crippled by her own shoes after a single shift. The volume of traffic is disconcerting, because they haven't been told that any of this is urgent. It's all marked "routine," which suggests that action is heating up in little Pacific islands far away.

On the plus side, increased volume means more depth. Kit hunches over her cards, pencil moving, and after a while she forgets about the identity review, doesn't notice the time passing, until Brigid taps her on the shoulder.

"Kit? It's four o'clock."

Kit looks up, distracted. "But there's only one more row."

"Let it go, hon," Brigid says, smiling gently. "Shift's over. The girls in the corridor are waiting for their chairs. Don't you have somewhere else to be?"

She does, Kit remembers. She grabs her coat and moves.

A half-hour stop at her room, to give her feet a break. She's been trying to alternate the continental-heel pumps with an old pair of Katherine's wedge-heeled sandals, but if anything, they're worse, and she has to wear thicker socks with the sandals. She changes her shoes and her shirt, gathers her things.

Walking around the schoolhouse carrying her handbag looks odd, but everyone's doing it at the moment, because of the review. If Kit makes it past the review, she'll have to figure out another discreet way to transport paperwork: Carrying around a folder of papers inside the Hall looks like a breach of security.

But she currently has no strategy to make it past the review. Kit looks in the mirror and smooths her hair. *One thing at a time.*

She leaves the dorm room and closes the door. She's not waiting for Dottie; at the start of shift, Dottie said that she had to fetch something before the meeting. And Kit isn't sure if Violet finishes her shift at the cottage at the same time as the girls finish in the Hall. Which means that Kit might get to Moya's before everybody else.

She and Moya will get a moment to talk together. Alone.

Kit feels a hot, sweet fizz inside her chest. *What is this?* She isn't sure. She's always admired Moya from a safe distance. Moya is intellectually sharp, but she also knows her own mind; she knows who she is. She steers her own ship, and that's admirable. Kit's always appreciated Moya's sense of controlled composure—but something has changed. Now Kit's started thinking about how much she'd like to see that control slip....

And she feels less intimidated, somehow. Maybe it was the experience they had together at Arlington Farms. Or maybe it was because of that first visit to Moya's room, when Kit realized that the unraveled, messy Moya behind the glamour is actually the real Moya.

Hardest to ignore is that time a few days ago, when they last talked. They were leaning on the table together, and there was a...a *feeling* between them. Kit's not sure how to describe it. But she's sure she wasn't the only one feeling it.

And now here she is, walking downstairs to Moya's again.

This anticipation and delight and pleasant nervousness isn't something she experienced with Katherine. But she and Katherine grew up together, to some extent. The progress of their friendship felt natural, almost preordained. And she and Katherine were very alike. So alike that Kit's found

131

slipping into Katherine's identity to be fairly easy. Much like the shoes, the fit isn't exact, but it's close enough that the difference is largely unnoticeable to outsiders.

Moya is another case altogether.

It's a little terrifying—Kit can't afford to have feelings like this. Her whole life is a web of subterfuge. She doesn't want to get hurt, or hurt someone else. And then there's the need for discretion. Nothing has happened or been said that might reveal her interest, or Moya's reciprocation. Kit doesn't even know how that might work, and speaking plainly is always risky.

But—but!—some taut thread inside her thrums in Moya's presence. Soon she might *have* to speak, or she'll fly apart with the tension.

Kit smooths her sweater at her hips as she steps off the stairs onto Two and is immediately distracted by the sight of someone—a particular someone—walking along the corridor toward her. Moya's wearing a white collared shirt, severely buttoned, with a sharp black tie. She's also wearing a black pencil skirt, which is a surprise because skirts are not her usual style. Carrying her own folder of paperwork and a jacket over one arm, she looks very official. Her hair is caught up in elegant rolls, pinned at each side. She almost looks like one of the WAVES girls.

Kit allows herself a moment of shivery appreciation. *Wow.*

"We're in the library," Moya says quietly as she arrives. "I needed to make an excuse to get Violet onto Two, so I said we've started a crossword puzzle appreciation society. Come on."

Kit follows her to the next set of stairs. "You said we're doing *crossword* club?"

"Well, we're solving a puzzle, aren't we?" Moya's glance is amused. "We won't be able to use your murder board in the armoire today, but after this first 'club meeting' I'll just say we're continuing in my room. How does that sound?"

"Plausible," Kit admits. She gives Moya an amused glance of her own as they traverse the stairs. "Nice skirt."

Moya rolls her eyes. "I had to give a formal committee report with Colonel Corderman, and there was no time to change. Come and help me get set up."

When they push open the library's nondescript door, Violet has already arrived. She's in a smart berry-colored skirt and a white shirt with a pointed collar and a low-line gray jacket. Her eyes are shining, and Kit thinks it's likely she's just hurried over from the cottage: Her shoes are damp, and she has a fresh, outside look about her.

"Hi." She slips the book she's been perusing back into its space on the bookshelf. "Moya, in that getup, you look like you're about to give me a salute."

"Don't tempt me." Moya unloads her paperwork onto the knee-high coffee table near one of the club chairs. "I'm glad you could make it. Did you have any trouble getting away?"

"Nope." Violet's lips quirk. "I finish at four, same as all of you. So I told my parents I'm catching the later bus and Mr. Coffee approves. If Mr. Coffee approves, my daddy and momma think that's just fine."

"What did you tell Mr. Coffee?"

"Same thing I told everyone else—that it's a crossword

puzzle club. Mr. Coffee encourages us to take a hobby away from work. And he's happy I'm mixing with other girls from the schoolhouse because for one, he's all for desegregation, and for two, I'm the youngest codebreaker he's got."

Moya's forehead puckers. "He seems like a good guy. I'm sorry you have to lie to him."

"He *is* a good guy, but it has to be done." Violet shrugs, grins. "And you know I love those crosswords."

Between the three of them, it's short work to rearrange the coffee table to a spot between the club chairs and the chesterfield sofa. They don't have any refreshments to suggest a club meeting, but Moya's brought a short stack of newspaper puzzles, and Violet collects a few dictionaries and an old thesaurus off the shelves. Kit wishes their gathering really *was* about something as innocuous as crosswords.

"Oh, I've got the hospital file." She pulls the thick file out of her handbag and finds a place to sit on the sofa beside Violet.

Violet takes the file. "Thanks. I'll return it to Ruth tomorrow afternoon."

"And I've written out the notes from my meeting with Detective Whitty," Moya says, teasing the papers from her pile. "Plus, here's copies of the Arlington Farms reports— Dottie's and Kit's and mine."

It's quiet as they sort through both the new and old paperwork. Kit can hear a car being started up in the parking area outside, beyond the library window. The room is cold, and Kit's glad for her stockings and sweater. Moya pulls on her jacket, gaze abstracted as she pores through notes.

134

"So the way I see it," Violet says, pushing up her cuffs, "we've got two main aims. Develop an idea of who the killer is targeting, and a picture of the killer himself."

"He targets government girls." Moya taps her pencil on her knee. "Young, pretty. He's not fussy about race."

"We need more on the victims. For the killer, we already know a lot." Kit rummages for blank cards. "He's six feet tall. He's a Nazi sympathizer."

"We should check old files on membership of the German American Bund," Violet says, making a note. "There'll be something at the Treasury Department."

"That's a good idea," Kit agrees. "The other thing we know about this guy is that he's smart."

"Smart—because of the gloves?" Moya asks.

"Yes. He's a planner—that means he's intelligent."

"And you know, he's probably good-looking," Violet says.

Moya's pencil tapping stops. "What makes you say that?"

"Think about it. The police assumed that the killer followed Libby out of Idaho to the laundry. But we already know that a lot of what the police assumed was wrong. What if the killer coaxed her out?"

"He has to be good-looking for that?" Kit asks.

"It sure helps."

"It's possible," Kit agrees, nodding. "I'll put it down as speculation, but actually, it reminds me of something Dottie said—that all the guys at the dance just seemed like regular guys."

"Yeah, he's just a regular, all-American guy...," Moya muses.

135

"He's probably white." Violet takes in the other girls' stares. "I mean, you know the dances at Arlington Farms are segregated, right?"

"No, I didn't know that," Kit says, taken aback. She reaches for another card.

"And correct me if I'm wrong," Violet continues, "but Libby seemed pretty square. A girl like Libby probably wouldn't go with a Black man, even if he were in uniform."

"A six-foot-tall, intelligent, good-looking white man..." Kit frowns, shakes her head. "He must've seemed like a real catch."

"Not to mention—he's rich," Dottie says from the doorway. She looks like a curvy, blond Rita Hayworth. She's wearing her red polka-dot dress again, but bolstered this time with sensible warm stockings, a cozy cream sweater, and a long coat. Her hair is done up with a sassy red ribbon, and she's carrying a book of crossword puzzles and a box of pencils. She closes the door behind her. "Sorry I'm late."

"We only just got started," Violet says. "I like your dress."

"Thanks!" Dottie smiles. After pulling a club chair closer, she tucks her skirts under to sit and eases a folded piece of heavy paper out of the puzzle book. "Moya, is this what you needed?"

Dot dumps the puzzle book to one side, opens up the paper, and Kit can see what it is.

"*A Map of Washington, DC, and Surrounds*," Kit reads from the legend on one side. "This is clever."

"Yes, that's perfect. Lay it down here." Moya makes room for the map on the coffee table.

"Go back a little," Violet says. "How is this guy rich?"

Dottie pulls her arms out of her coat, bundles it behind her. "Private car because he'd be covered in blood, remember? Most of the boys come to the Farms by bus or cab—some even come by bicycle, but I can't see our killer doing that. Guys who drive their own cars are usually ritzy. The only other vehicles are service cars, which usually carry groups, or delivery vans."

"Makes sense," Violet concedes. "What's with the map?"

"We need to keep track of locations. There was a spare copy, so...I borrowed it."

"Will they miss it upstairs?" Kit asks.

"I doubt it—they're mainly interested in maps of North Africa and the Philippines right now." Dottie takes a red colored pencil out of the box she arrived with and makes a circle on the map. "Here's Arlington Farms. Look, there's one thing that's bothering me. Violet, you said Dinah was killed in Downtown—can you show me where?"

Violet takes the pencil, examines the area in question, makes a circle. "Here—in Embassy Row."

"That's not too far from where the union protests about women's wages were held." Dottie retrieves the pencil, tilts her head. "Are you sure that's where she was found?"

"Yes. That's what the police told her parents."

"But you said Dinah worked in Munitions, and she caught the bus home." Dottie points on the map with the tip of the red pencil. "The Munitions Building is here, on Constitution Avenue. Moya and I both know that building—it's where Signal Intelligence was housed before the US Army offices got too crowded and the War Department set us up here at the Hall. The bus to Arlington goes right along Constitution Avenue."

"Yeah, that's weird." Moya loosens the knot of her tie and the top button of her shirt. Her attention is still on the map. "Dinah could have caught that bus right outside the door of Munitions and been home in half an hour. If she was found in Embassy Row, she was way off her normal route."

"So...how did Dinah end up in Downtown?" Kit asks.

Violet chews the end of her pencil. "I just assumed she went up to Second Baptist for service."

Kit measures the distances with her finger. "Would she go all that way for service so late? Do they even *hold* a service there that late?"

Violet squints. "To be honest, I don't know."

"I'm sure we can find out," Dottie reassures.

Violet rubs her temples. "It's like every piece of information we get creates new questions."

"No—that's good." Kit looks over at her. "We *want* new questions. Because the answers to those questions will be new data. It'll be a way in. There's always a way in. Remember Captain Hitt's requirements for codebreaking?"

Violet nods. It's one of the first things new code girls are encouraged to learn during their induction. "Hitt's first requirement for codebreaking success—careful analysis of the data."

"Second—perseverance," Dottie adds.

"Intuition," Moya pronounces.

"And luck," Kit finishes. "All these things in combination

give us the greatest opportunity for success. We have the intuition and the perseverance. We'll make our own luck. And careful analysis of the data... That just means we need more data."

"I think we need the police information on Dinah's case," Moya says. "Which is an obstacle. I could go back to see Detective Whitty, but he's not going to let me take a copy of that report."

Dottie frowns. "And he doesn't even think the two cases are related."

"Then we need another source." Moya has a steely expression, as if she's focused on a particularly knotty code problem. "Kit, you mentioned something—you suggested finding out what was said about the murders in the newspapers."

Kit nods. "I know there's been a lot of sensational articles, but if we could find some that provide more facts, it'd be useful, yes. Everything's useful."

"I might know someone who could help with that."

Dottie's eyebrows lift. "Someone in Archives?"

"No." Moya shakes her head. "A reporter."

"You know a *reporter*?"

Violet looks up, hopeful. "Reporters get information out of the police that we can't get."

"And this reporter has connections." Moya bites her lip. "If he's still working the crime beat, he'll know."

"He?" Kit tries not to sound too prying.

"Raffi." Moya's gaze turns inward. "But it's been years...." She snaps out of it. "I'll try to get a message to him."

"Which paper does he work for?" Violet asks.

"The *Washington Star*—that's where he interned, at least."

"Would he be interested in meeting with us?"

"Maybe." Moya considers. "If he's still in DC. And if he thought there was a story in it, for sure."

A story. Kit feels a sickening lurch, looks up quickly. "We'd have to keep our names out of the papers."

"Absolutely," Moya affirms. "That's the last thing anyone from the Hall wants." Still thinking, she pulls away the tie at her neck. "I think he'd meet with us, though. Not here— somewhere in the city. Give me forty-eight hours to find out."

Dottie grins. "So...looks like the Crossword Puzzle Appreciation Society is going on a field trip."

15

Well, we did lots of things. We played
tennis. We went to the theatre. . . . Kully—
Colonel Kullback—was a great enthusiast
about softball, and he used to sponsor
softball tournaments. . . . There was a lot
of social activity.

—ANN CARACRISTI

From the moment Moya told them the meeting with the reporter was going ahead to now, standing in the aisle of a municipal bus on a Monday night, Kit hates the field trip.

"Kit, cheer up," Dottie whispers. "You look like you're going to a funeral, not out for a night on the town."

"Okay." Kit clings to the edge of the nearest seat back and reaches with her other hand to adjust her hem.

"And leave your hem alone or you'll mess up the stocking seams I drew."

"Sorry."

"And stop apologizing!" Dottie angles so their heads are closer together. "Oh, hon, you're really having a hard time with this, aren't you? Is it the crowd?"

There's barely room for shrugging, but Kit lifts and lowers one shoulder. The bus is definitely crowded. Nowadays there are no spare seats, so she and Dottie are crammed in with strangers on every side. Girls are going out for the evening, going to their jobs on factory ready-lines, going home. Young servicemen josh each other about evening plans. There's a low hum of conversation, the air smells of hair oil and gasoline, and somewhere near the back, a baby is crying. But Kit's not anxious because of the crowd.

She just doesn't like leaving the Hall.

Arlington Hall is safe. Kit knows everybody there, and her identity is firmly fixed in people's minds. The world outside is a completely different ball game. Kit's unfamiliar with DC streets, and she has no idea where she's going, what she's doing, how to behave. Someone will be sure to look at her and realize, *This girl is faking it*. It's the culmination of countless nightmare scenarios in which she's exposed for what she really is: a fraud, an identity thief, a monster.

She braces her legs for balance as the bus jolts over the concrete of Arlington Memorial Bridge. Night has descended on Washington, DC. They're meeting Moya and Violet at a hotel bar at 7:30 PM.

Kit blots her forehead with the wrist of her glove. "It's hot in here. Are you hot?"

"It's a little warm, sure." Dottie bites her lip, her expression concerned. "Can you see out the window? We'll go past the Lincoln Memorial soon. Does it help to look at the view?"

It helps a little. Out the obscured windows, dark scenery trundles by: the city lights reflecting on the water of the Potomac, the hulking shadows of buildings.

Dottie—pink-cheeked, her eyes sparkling at the prospect of a night on the town—pats Kit's shoulder for encouragement.

"At least you've got some great clothes for going out. You look swell."

Kit had to raid the lower levels of Katherine's trunk for a midnight-blue cocktail dress with matching accessories. The neckline is cut square across her collarbones and pinned tight at the waist, with a little satin bow at her décolletage. There's another midnight-blue bow for her hair, plus a white clutch and white gloves and strappy white sandals.

Dottie fussed for hours, putting their outfits together, and Kit was grateful for that help. "You too," she offers. "You look great in that color."

"Aw, thank you!" Dottie beams.

Dottie does look lovely in her kelly-green dress, the fabric draped in a vee from the collar down across the bodice, the skirt swirly and soft, emphasizing Dot's curves. A gorgeous brooch in the shape of a black cat is pinned beside her generous bosom. With her honeyed curls down and her lipstick bright, she's a knockout.

Kit hangs on to the bus seat and her clutch purse as the bus corners. This is normal. Normal girls go out and enjoy themselves. Maybe normal girls don't meet reporters for drinks to find out about horrifying murder cases, but at least she and Dottie have classy outfits.

But Dottie's right: There'll come a day—maybe sooner than Kit expected, with the review coming—when she'll have to break out on her own. This trip into the city is good practice.

The bus lumbers up Seventeenth Street NW, and Dottie forges a path to the door so they can exit at the next stop.

When they finally manage to alight from the bus onto the pavement, Kit finds she can breathe a little easier. The night breeze is crisp, and the city doesn't smell particularly clean, but the mix of scents is intriguing: the tang of exhaust, the iron smell of asphalt, the faint whiff of garbage, the lilt of women's perfume.

Kit sets her clothes to rights. "How do we get to the Hay-Adams from here?"

"Okay, that's H Street." Dottie points. "We go right and it's two blocks thatta way."

"You know your way around the city."

Dottie grins. "I borrowed that map, remember? Come on."

She leads forward, demonstrating how to navigate the sidewalk and the city traffic crisscrossing nearby. There are plenty of people around: WAVES girls, groups of dressed-up matrons, older men in suits. The concrete underfoot is damp from an earlier sprinkle of rain, and the streetlamps and hoardings are glittering in the dark. Evening DC is a kingdom of dreams, and Kit takes it all in. But there's the occasional flash of reality: old posters with drawings of angry male workers raising their fists and the slogan FIRE WOMEN—HIRE MEN blare right next to other posters exhorting MAN THE GUNS—JOIN THE NAVY!

Kit follows Dot determinedly, ignoring the bite in her feet from the sandal straps. "Who do you think this reporter is, the one we're meeting?"

"Now that *is* a mystery," Dottie says. "Maybe Moya knew him from when she worked in Notifications or something?"

Kit remembers Moya's soft, reflective murmur in the

library on Saturday—*But it's been years....* "Somehow I don't think so."

"Then he must be an old friend of Moya's." Dottie gestures to encourage Kit to cross over near Lafayette Square so they're not walking in an unlit area. "I guess we'll find out."

Another half a block, then the great white edifice of the hotel is rising up from among the other buildings, grand and imposing. Before they reach the corner of Sixteenth Street, Kit spots the illuminated entry to the hotel's basement. A discreet golden plaque reveals that the bar is called Off the Record: a thoroughly appropriate name for a place where they're meeting a reporter.

A smartly dressed couple goes down the stairs. Murmurs and music exit in the backwash of the door being opened and closed. "Do we just go on in?" Kit scans the street. "Or do we wait for Violet?"

"I don't know." Dottie pulls her shawl wrap closer; she and Kit both have wraps against the evening chill. "I think we go in. Violet might've already arrived. And it's freezing out here." They pinch their cheeks for color and descend the stairs.

Behind a red-painted door, the rest of the low-ceilinged bar is also done up in red: mahogany walls, banquette seats with red velvet upholstery, small dark tables with little lamps. Music is playing, sensuous and quiet. The whole place smells of expensive alcohol, cigarettes, and style.

Kit fights a surge of panic. Never in her life has she thought she would get to frequent a place as sophisticated as this. She could imagine being an employee behind the bar, maybe, or a cleaner after hours, but not a *customer.*

Then she sees Moya standing by a table, beckoning them over and signaling to the bartender. She looks like a vision: Her blouse is a clinging, silky gold, with a low vee in front, and her wide-leg trousers are a rich caramel brown. Her hair is rolled in a glossy black chignon. A dark fur stole slips elegantly off one of her shoulders.

All other thoughts flee Kit's head immediately. She wets her lips and tries to dim her smile to a more acceptable wattage as they head in Moya's direction.

"I've bought you martinis," Moya says, by way of greeting, as they reach the table. "Where's Violet?"

Dottie slides off her black velvet wrap as she sits. "We thought she was already with you."

"Not yet. More to the point—where's Raffi?" Moya checks her watch. "He was supposed to be here a quarter hour ago. Damn, that boy never could be punctual."

Kit finds a seat beside Dottie in the banquette, takes off her gloves and her white satin wrap, settles her clutch on her lap. If she watches what the other girls do, copies them to the letter, there's a chance she might pull this off.

The bartender delivers two martinis to complement the one already in front of Moya—she hands him a dollar from her purse as Dottie finishes talking about the route they took to get here.

"...by the time we found the place. Do you know if Violet took a bus or a cab?"

"No idea, but I guess she'll show up soon," Moya says, lifting her half-finished martini. "Drink up, ladies."

Kit watches how Dottie and Moya hold their glasses. She

146

lifts her own carefully and takes a sip. The liquid is strong, with an oily tartness, and freezing cold; her fingertips tingle and her face warms as her first taste of martini slips down her throat.

Dottie licks her lips. "This is the kind of field trip I could get used to."

Which is wrong, Kit thinks. They're here because two girls were murdered. It seems almost repugnant for her to be enjoying herself.

"This bar might be stuffy," Moya says, "but they make a mean martini. Oh, hold up—there she is. Violet!"

She rises to gesture to their youngest team member. Kit cranes her head and sees a small figure hesitating just inside the door. Then Violet's face lights up and she walks over. "I wasn't sure whether to come straight in," Violet says. "Wow, you gals clean up pretty good."

"Same to you," Dottie says. "Gosh, you look super!"

"Why, thank you." Violet looks pleased. She's wearing a lavender dress with a full skirt and a matching bolero jacket with white piping. The material of the dress has a soft sheen, and with her hair rolled, she looks elegant, older than seventeen. "Where can I get a chair around here?"

"I'll find you a chair," Moya says. "And a drink—virgin cocktail, right?"

"You got it," Violet says, but before she can take her seat, the bartender arrives and begins speaking in a quiet voice to Moya.

Moya, still standing, makes a face back at him. "Excuse me? D'you want to repeat that, because I don't think I heard you right."

Kit sees Violet's expression change and knows there's going to be trouble. She rises from her place on the banquette and leans toward Violet. "He doesn't want to serve you?"

Violet shrugs a little, her mouth set in a grim line. "Oh, there's plenty of places like that in the city. They say they're open, but what they mean is, they're only open to whites."

Dottie looks bewildered. "What's going on?"

Moya says, "Listen, mister...," and Kit barely has time to think *This could get ugly*, when a new person appears between the bartender and Violet. He's a tall, lanky young man, olive-complexioned, in a wide-shouldered suit. He's got the shoulders to wear it, too.

"Ladies, good to see you." His fedora sits at a rakish angle over his dark hair, and his smile is broad. "Are we having a little problem here?"

"Raf?" Moya's eyes go wide for a moment, before she turns her head to glower at the bartender. "I'm not the one with the problem."

"Don't worry about it," the young man says. "Did you already pay for those drinks? Great. Then down 'em quick—let's go."

"We're leaving the bar?" Dottie laments.

"Relax, honey—I know a better one." When the young man grins, twin dimples pop on his cheeks. "Great dress, by the way. Lots of va-voom. Ladies, shall we?"

It's a whirlwind, Kit thinks, a whirlwind of dynamic male. But, in under a minute, their martini glasses are drained and they're all outside on the dark sidewalk as "Raf" hails a cab, which quickly pulls up at the curb. "It's gonna be a squish, but we're not going far," he says.

He's right—it *is* a squish with all five of them in the car, and the cab driver grumbles.

"Five minutes," Raf counters, "and I'll make it worth your while. Take us all the way up Sixteenth and make a right— corner of U Street and Eleventh."

"The Caverns?" the cabbie asks.

"You got it." Raf turns from his position next to the driver and extends a hand to Kit in the back seat. "Raffi Ramale, *Washington Star*, nice to make your acquaintance."

Kit's still feeling the warm purr in her stomach from the martini, and she can't help but laugh at his cocky expression as she shakes his hand. "Kit Sutherland. Hi."

"You're a redhead," Raffi says, his smile lighting further. He turns to look at Moya, crammed near the window on the front bench seat beside him. "You didn't tell me you had a redhead in your girl gang!"

"I didn't tell you much of anything, except where to meet us," Moya drawls, but her lips are raised at the corners.

"It's great to see you, Moya," Raffi says. "And excuse my French, but damn, you look gorgeous. Why didn't you marry me, back in the day?"

"Why didn't I marry you?" Moya's defined eyebrow arches. "Probably because you were thirteen and I was twelve, and your mother thought I was hell in a handbasket."

"But look how you've shaped up. . . ." Raffi grins again and kisses her cheek, before turning back to introduce himself to Dottie. "Va-voom! It's nice to meet you properly."

"It is." Dottie laughs, shaking his hand. "Dottie Crockford."

"A pleasure, Dottie." He reaches across to Violet. "And hi—I'd apologize for stealing you from that bar, but you didn't want mediocre drinks and bad service anyway."

"Indeed I did not," Violet says, as they shake. "Violet DuLac."

"A Violet wearing violet—touché," Raffi says, touching the brim of his hat, but he's immediately distracted by the cab driver pulling the car over. "Just a little farther down? Near the old Industrial Savings Bank...That's it—good man. Ladies, this is our stop."

Raffi pays the cabbie, and they pile out onto a very different street—one with wide lanes and crowds of nightlife. Young women in their finest, men in suits and men in blue jeans, kids running on the pavement, matrons in fox fur... They're all picked out under the lights of shimmering bulbs and neon.

Kit doesn't know the city, and this area is very different to the formal-looking streets near the Hay-Adams. There are drugstores and beauty salons and chili restaurants and groceries all crowded into the same few blocks, and a theater marquee is lit up nearby. The asphalt is crowded with cars and cabs.

Kit scans the scene in confusion. "Where are we?"

"In the beating heart of Cardozo." Raffi gives her a wink as he directs them along the sidewalk. "This whole block is full of juke joints and cabarets and bars."

"And which one are we going to?" Dottie asks, trying to keep up.

"Over here."

Raffi ushers them across Eleventh Street to a curious corner building with winking bulbs on the facade. He gets a wave from someone at the door as they miraculously bypass the line outside, and he shakes hands with people on the way in. Then there's a set of stairs going down, and they arrive at a round sculpted entrance. Kit can hear crowd noise and music. Raffi extends a palm. "Ladies first."

Kit follows Moya through the entrance, looks around in wonder. The cabbie said "the Caverns" and she thought it was just a fancy name, but it's like a proper *cave* in here. The walls are chipped out of stone, stalactites hanging from the ceiling. While a cave would be cold, this one is warm, crammed with people and white-clothed tables.

A band is playing on the stage: A man in snappy trousers and suspenders is swinging in front of the microphone. Silhouettes flicker in the glow of candles, women's dresses sparkle like rainbow jewels, and a few couples are dancing on the tiny floor. There's the hubbub of conversation, the flare of laughter, the smell of booze. And it's a mixed crowd, Kit notes: White and Black and brown faces are intermingled, everyone just here to enjoy the music and the atmosphere.

Violet's expression is rapt. "I've heard about this place."

"How does it stack up?" Raffi asks.

She grins. "It holds its own so far."

"Excellent—now all we have to do is wrangle a table."

They find a place when Moya notices a small group leaving; she hurries forward, weaving through the crowd and the tables, to claim their spot before anyone else can steal

151

it. A waiter comes for their drinks order as they're taking their seats. Raffi recommends the margaritas as he slips off his suit jacket and hangs it from the back of his chair. He assures the waiter that everyone is of drinking age, winks at Kit as the waiter leaves. Violet is laughing at the antics of the band, exchanging comments with Dottie. Even Moya seems more relaxed.

Kit tucks her clutch and her wrap in her lap, bumping knees with Moya under the table. Conditions here are more cramped than at Off the Record, and they have to talk louder over the music, but this feels more comfortable somehow. She's less worried about watching her p's and q's.

Raffi Ramale leans his lanky frame back in his chair. "Look at me," he says, beaming around at them all, "sitting in Club Caverns with four beautiful women. I'm officially the luckiest guy in DC."

As Kit watches, Raffi's smile changes in subtle ways—his eyes squinting, his grin flattening at the corners. There's a new diamond-hardness in his face. Suddenly she remembers: Raffi is not just a guy having a fun evening out on the town with friends. He's a reporter. His charm is part of his journalistic technique.

"Now we're all here," he says, "maybe you lovely ladies would like to tell me how you ended up researching a pair of brutal murders. Moya, what the hell have you gotten yourself into?"

16

No, we weren't allowed to say anything.
We signed a pledge, you know. Fiancés,
parents, friends, family—we couldn't
tell anybody what we were doing for
the war effort.

—ROSE OVERTON-MITCHELL

"Let me see if I've got this straight." Raffi uses his hands when he's speaking, pointing at Violet, Dottie, Kit, and Moya in turn. "*You're* the best friend of the girl who was murdered in Downtown. And *you* were at Arlington Farms the night of the last murder. And *you two* walked into the crime scene at the Farms."

"That's right," Moya says. She sips her drink calmly.

"And now you've all decided to do a little Nancy Drew number on this...." Raffi grimaces, like the sight of the four of them is hurting his head. "I know girls can do anything these days, but it still seems kinda far-fetched. What do you already know about these cases anyway?"

"A lot." Kit speaks up because they *need* this; they need him to understand. "We know that whoever killed these girls is a tall, wealthy, good-looking white man. We know he drives his own car. We know he leaves a souvenir of his last murder at the site of his most recent one. We know he rapes the girls—"

"Jesus," Raffi says, glancing away and back at her candor.

"We know he wears gloves, takes a knife to the scene, and then takes it away with him, which means he's smart and careful."

"We know he's a Nazi sympathizer," Violet says.

"The symbol he cut into them." Raffi's expression is flat. "I saw the morgue photos."

"And we know he plans in advance," Dottie says. "Which means he's going to kill more girls if nobody catches him in time."

There's a lull in the music and the audience applauds.

Raffi shakes his head. "You know that this...this *investigation*, or whatever you want to call it, is bananas, right?"

Violet angles forward and talks as if he hasn't spoken. "What we need is more information about the victims— who they knew, where they went, what routes they took. I can fill in some of the details about Dinah, but there were obviously things about her, and about her murder, that even I don't know."

Moya nods. "The police won't release the details of Dinah Shaw's murder to us—"

"Well, of course they won't," Raffi scoffs, leaning over his crossed arms on the table.

"And they claim it's unrelated," Moya continues. "But that's simply not true. So we need more information about that crime scene. We need to dig out potential connections to the old German American Bund, or even the America First Committee. And we need to know what's been said about the murders in the press, what's been suppressed— and if there are any more cases we've missed."

"Which would be where I come in." Raffi squints at her. "And I should tell you what I know because...?"

"Because we can give you a lead on a big case that is currently getting a lot of attention." Moya smiles sweetly as she sips her margarita, before becoming more serious. "Because you're a good man, Rafael. And you don't want any more young women to be assaulted and killed."

He's sitting straighter after being called a good man. "What makes you think you can do a better job of figuring this out than the DC police department?"

"We're not like the police," Kit says. "We're not clouded by prejudice. We care about these girls, and about catching the man who's doing this. And because...it's what we do. We solve puzzles, make breaks—"

Moya gives her a quelling glance.

Raffi rolls his brown eyes. "Look, you don't have to be delicate with me, okay? I wouldn't be any kind of decent reporter if I didn't know that there's something war-code-related going on at Signal Intelligence in Arlington Hall."

Moya inclines her head. "But like you said, Raf, you're a reporter—and there are things we can't talk about."

"That's fair." He blows out a breath as the band starts a new number. "So first, you need the press reports on the murders."

"Did anything make it into the press that we don't already know?" Dottie asks, taking the toothpick, with its speared maraschino cherry, out of her Mary Pickford.

"Not that I'm aware. You ladies seem to have it pretty well covered. But I can get clippings of those stories sent to you by mail." He frowns and considers. "And I can probably

155

sniff around a little about DC folks connected to the Bund. Then you need to know if there are other cases."

"Have there been other cases?" Kit asks. The temptation to reach into her clutch and draw out index cards and a pencil is nearly overwhelming. She stalls the urge by sipping at her margarita—she likes it better than the martini.

"Well, I work the crime beat, and I haven't seen anything." Raffi pulls the edge of his bottom lip between his teeth. "There was one case, about two months ago, of a girl who drowned. But that's not what you're looking for, right?"

"Drowning?" Dottie shakes her head. "That doesn't sound like our guy."

"Was she a government girl?" Kit asks impulsively.

"Yeah," Raffi admits. "She worked in clerical at some department."

"Send that one along, too." Kit looks around at the others. "Another government girl death—we should check before we rule it out."

"What about the police report on Dinah Shaw's murder?" Moya draws her silver cigarette case out of her pants pocket.

"A little harder, but I can probably get you that." Raf leans to light her smoke. "I have a few connections in the DCPD, and some of them work the Downtown beat...."

Violet frowns, toys with the stem of her glass. "We still don't know how Dinah ended up in Downtown, when she worked in Munitions. It's been driving me crazy."

"You don't know?" Raffi looks at her. "Well, I can't be one hundred percent certain, but I can hazard a guess. Lots of government girls are on short shifts, and since the Revenue

Act came in, money's tight. So they supplement their income with side hustles like busing tables, to make rent."

"Or to help their families make rent." Violet's expression is regretful. "She never told me."

"Maybe she didn't want you worrying, if her family was behind," Raffi suggests. "But there was a big-time swanky party at the Fairfax in Dupont Circle on the night of Dinah's murder. I'm betting she was probably coming back from her moonlight job as waitstaff."

Kit takes a breath: *This could be it.* This could be the information they need.

Moya's expression has gone sharp, too. "A party? What kind of party?"

"There's some shindig in this town every other week." Raffi shrugs. "PAC soirees, war fundraisers, society gatherings—take your pick. Old money attends, and the nouveau riche, plus political candidates and their wives. Throw in a few merchant bankers and industry chairmen, add some high-profile players, like media bosses and actors and the rest of the glitterati…"

"Sounds like a recipe for a good time," Moya says, her eyes narrowing.

"I've been to a few—they serve free drinks. In fact, I'm going to one this Friday night." He frowns when he sees Moya's expression, but she's looking over at Kit.

"A tall, wealthy, good-looking white man."

"He could have seen her there," Dottie suggests.

"And followed her home," Violet agrees.

"A party," Kit says quietly. "Like the event at Arlington Farms."

"That's right," Moya says, nodding. "I think we need to check it out."

Kit's not sure. "All of us?"

"Absolutely. We're a team, aren't we?" Dottie says, taking a sip of her Mary Pickford.

"And if something happens, there's safety in numbers," Violet reminds.

Moya grins at them all, then turns to Raffi with a coy look. "Raffi..."

"What?" He looks from one face to another. Does a double take. "No. No way."

"Raf, we need to see it," Moya insists.

"Moya, you know I love you, but that's nuts. I'm not a social manager. I don't know how I can get you into—"

"You can," she interrupts. "You said *how* you can get us in, not *if.*" She smiles and sits back. "Come on, Raffi. That's why you brought us here, isn't it?"

"I brought us here to dance!" he counters.

"Sure, but it's more than that, right? I saw you shaking hands on the way in—showing us what a big player you are, showing us your local connections. Now we're asking you to use those connections for the greater good."

Raffi just sits there, his mouth opening and closing like a fresh-caught trout's. There's a blast of trumpet as the band starts a new number, and Violet stands. "Okay," she says, looking at Raf. "You came here to dance? Let's dance."

"Now?"

"Hey, I didn't get all dressed up in my finest and come to the best club in DC just to sit on the sidelines." She extends a hand. "Come on. You can think about getting us party invitations while we're out on the floor."

Raffi sighs and pulls himself up, as if looking at them all makes him tired. Violet just grins and tugs him away into the crowd.

"Oh, I want to dance, too!" Dottie exclaims.

"You can dance with me," Moya suggests, with an impish smile. She stubs out her cigarette and stands. "Kit, would you mind—"

"I don't mind," Kit says quickly. She's thinking of her shoes and the fact that she has no idea how to dance. "I'll just watch."

There's not a lot of room to swing out on the floor; the space is just too tiny. But Raffi and Violet seem to do okay. Raffi clearly likes to dance and he handles himself well, even giving Violet a few spins. She says something that makes him laugh.

Nearby, Moya grins as Dottie swirls her green skirts and encourages them both into a dip. Nobody bats an eye at two girls dancing together—not these days, when there aren't enough boys to go around. The two of them have an easiness that Kit envies. True, Dot has known Moya for longer. They worked together in the pool of girls at Munitions, after all. But it's more than that: Dottie isn't tense around Moya the way Kit is. This tension in Kit's body whenever Moya's nearby is something she can't seem to shake. But she still hasn't worked up the courage to do anything about it.

She sighs and takes another sip of her margarita, tasting salt.

The night seems to stretch after that. Raffi takes each of them out on the floor—everyone but Kit, who keeps demurring—and by nine thirty, they're all a little tipsy. Violet says she needs to get home, and Moya herds them all to the exit. Climbing the stairs and leaving Club Caverns, arriving back onto the cold street, is like emerging from Wonderland.

"You never danced with me," Raffi points out. He's walking with Kit, a little behind the others, as they head for the taxi stand.

Kit's noticed that his cheeks are pink and his words are looser, but he's steady on his feet. He's very good at giving the appearance of drunkenness while not actually being completely intoxicated. It must be a handy skill to have as a reporter.

"I'm kind of particular about my dance partners," Kit replies with a grin. "Don't take it personally."

"Ah." Raffi nods over this piece of information. "So, it's not because of your shoes? Your shoes are too tight."

Kit stiffens. "My shoes are fine."

"You're interesting," Raffi declares. "You don't give much away. I find that interesting in a girl."

"Don't get too interested," Kit mutters under her breath.

He screws up his eyes. "You really want to go to this party on Friday night?"

"I don't really want to go to any party," Kit says. "But I want to find out more about who's murdering these girls. And the party is a good place to do that."

"Well, I think you're all out of your minds, but I respect what you're trying to do." He hiccups a little, pulls his wallet from his jacket pocket, and takes out a card, presents it to Kit with a smiling flourish. "This is my number. Call anytime, if you need anything for the case. Or, y'know, if you want to ditch those too-tight shoes and come dancing."

17

Certainly, some single ladies lived
together as "dear friends" or "longtime
companions." Those were the euphemisms
everyone used, even for years-long
committed partnerships.
                                    —BRIGID GLADWELL

The party invitations arrive by mail on Thursday, along with press clippings about the murders.

"Raffi's a good egg." Moya pulls the paperwork out of its envelope and onto the baize table in her room on Thursday evening. "He's a bloodhound, but it's his job to be. Ohmigod, these newspaper columns are getting hysterical; every woman in DC will be terrified....But look, here's the report about the other government girl, the one who drowned."

"Let me see?" Kit's been waiting for this. She reaches across the table for the scrap of paper, then scans it, frowning.

"What's it say?" Dottie turns from the open armoire. In her white shirt and red pencil skirt, she's perusing the murder board and adding small details to Kit's cards.

"Her name was Margaret Wishart. She was a twenty-year-old clerical assistant transferred to a consular office—"

"That means the American Foreign Service," Moya notes.

"Well, she was transferred from the Department of Commerce. She was found floating at the edge of the water near the ferry port, just off Maine Avenue Southwest, on January seventeenth...." Kit glances to her right. "Violet, could you pass me a card?"

Dottie looks crestfallen. "So you think she's another victim? Oh, that poor girl."

"I don't know yet," Kit counters, still reading. Yes, this case is different, but something about it pings strangely in her mind.

"Any mention of objects found with her?" Violet digs out another cream-colored index card and hands it over, along with a pencil.

Kit skims the newsprint. "Not that I can make out. They may not have noticed anything, if she was down among the pillars. I'm going to make a note, though. She's a government girl and the right age. There's no mention of rape, but it says she wasn't found for two days. I imagine that the physical evidence might have been lost in the water."

"But was she cut?" Violet insists.

"No," Kit admits, looking up. "Okay, the case is still a question mark. But we should try to find out a little more, if we can. This might have been how he got started."

"We've got the news reports on Dinah and Libby, at least." Dottie picks them out of the pile. "I'm going to tack these up, along with the Downtown bus schedules."

"Let me get details from the article about Dinah." Violet pushes up the sleeves of her blue cardigan and extends a hand for the clipping Dottie passes her.

"Tack this one up, too, when I'm done," Kit says, jotting onto a card. "We're getting there. We're getting more data."

"That's the good news," Moya says. "Do you want to hear the bad news? There are only two party invitations."

Violet looks up as she collects a pencil. "What's the party for, anyway?"

"It's a political fundraiser—Harry Hopkins is delivering a speech to invited guests." Moya fishes a remaining slip of paper out of the envelope everything came in. Kit notices how her collarbones are exposed with her dark green jersey blouse loosened in front, her sleeves rolled up to the elbow. "Raf's also sent us the name and number of the catering company that's serving the night of the fundraiser. Two of us can use the invites, and two of us can attend as waitstaff."

"Guess I'm spending the night in a maid's uniform," Violet says in a resigned voice.

Dottie tucks her own pencil behind her ear. "What? Why?"

"How many Black attendees d'you think they get at these things? I'll stand out like a sore thumb if I arrive as a guest."

"They must have *some* Black guests on the register?"

"It's not gonna be a long list of those, I can tell you." Violet eases her shoulders back. "And they'll all know each other—everyone knows who's who in the local community. I'm not a 'who.' It'll be way less obvious if I go as waitstaff."

"Well, that's not fair! You shouldn't have to go to every party as the maid."

"You keep thinking that." Violet snorts. "If more folks start believing it, one of these days we'll see some change."

Kit shifts in her chair. There's a maid uniform stuffed in the trunk in her room, just one floor above. She could attend the party as a maid: It would be easy. The idea of donning her black uniform again, tying on her apron, makes her throat go dry. She swallows hard and opens her mouth—but Dottie beats her to it.

"In that case, I'm going as waitstaff, too," Dottie declares.

Kit blinks, bewildered. "Dot, you don't have to—I can go as a maid."

"Don't be silly, hon." Dottie gives her an amused look. "I'm the daughter of a grocer. I've had *way* more experience serving the public than you."

"But—"

"Nope, I've decided." Dottie tosses her curls over one shoulder. "Me and Violet will be the undercover servers. We'll probably hear lots more gossip that way, in any case—and we'll get to talk to the kitchen staff, who might know more. You and Moya will be our glamorous contacts."

"That all sounds great," Moya drawls, "and I hate to bust your bubble, but where are we getting staff uniforms?"

"The kitchen," Violet says. "They have a stack of uniforms down there in the pantry in case of spills, or for folks who get changed when they arrive at work. Aprons, too."

"Problem solved." Moya inclines her head in acknowledgment.

Dottie gathers some thumbtacks. "What about Kit?"

"What *about* Kit?" Violet asks, stacking their notepaper into piles.

"Well, she only has skirts and such for school, I think." Dottie turns back to the armoire, speaking to Kit over her shoulder. "What will you wear? The same cocktail outfit you wore to Club Caverns?"

"She can't." Moya waves the invitation card, on its thick paper stock, and takes a sip of soda as she catches Kit's eye. "You can't—it's formal wear. Black and white for the boys, gowns for the ladies."

Kit hadn't considered that. "I might have to check my wardrobe...."

"Check mine," Moya says blithely, papers fluttering as she turns her wrist to check her watch. "Oh, goddammit, it's quarter to nine. Ladies, I call this meeting over."

"Quarter to nine? Heck, I need to scramble or I'll miss the bus home." Violet rises from the table, grabbing for her handbag.

"And I have to make this place presentable for poker night." Moya is already sweeping clippings and papers and pencils into a pile, ferrying glasses back to the drinks tray. She uses her glass to point at Kit. "Don't go anywhere yet."

Dottie is helping Violet with her jacket. "Talk to me tomorrow about uniforms, okay?"

"You'll need shoes." Kit, standing, looks at them both and bites her lip. "I mean, you'll probably be on your feet a lot."

"We'll talk about shoes," Violet says, nodding at Kit and Dottie both, then hitching her bag and pushing back her hair. "And uniforms. Gotta go!"

"Go, go!" Dottie sees Violet out the door as Moya marches around, throwing folders into the armoire and doing a general tidy-up. Dottie gives Kit an apologetic smile. "I'm sorry. You probably would've preferred to stay in the background as a maid at the party. I know how you hate crowds."

Kit shrugs, not sure how she feels about it. "I'm sure it'll be fine."

165

"I really have had plenty of experience dealing with Joe Public, though."

"Kit—a second?" Moya is kicking shoes into corners and hanging towels out of sight.

Dottie slips on her cardigan and gathers the remaining folders before giving Kit's arm a squeeze. "I'm going to take all our paperwork back upstairs. Looks like you and Moya are raiding her clothes stash."

"We are?" Kit says.

"See you upstairs in a bit." Dottie grins. "Unless you decide to stay for poker night."

She sweeps out the door as Moya sweeps forward, dusting off her hands and doing a last visual check of the space. "Looks all right. Nobody cares if a few scarves are still lying around." She turns to Kit, who's setting her handbag on the cleared-off table. "We have about forty minutes, and you need something fancy to wear."

"I don't know what I need." Kit suddenly realizes that she and Moya are alone. For only a short time before the poker group arrives, but still. She smooths her hands down her front, trying to allay her nerves. "I mean, I don't know if I have anything more fancy than the dark blue dress. Most of the clothes I have from home are more . . . day wear. Practical."

Moya cocks her head. "You never had formal dinners here?"

Kit hesitates. There were formal dinners, but she never attended them. Their number was also reduced in the year before Katherine's death. "Not since the war got busy."

"Fair." Moya steps back and turns the full force of her

stare on Kit, looking her over from head to toe. "Okay, nothing too form-fitting."

"You're slimmer than me," Kit points out.

"And taller," Moya agrees. "Our measurements won't match up. But I *have* got a few things that might work...." She moves to her bed, pulls out the trunk from underneath it, lifts the lid.

As Moya draws piles of jewel-colored fabric out of the trunk, Kit thinks about what going to a formal event will mean. Will she know how to behave? She was able to successfully fit in at Club Caverns, but this may be a different order of operations. Her fingertips have gone cold at the idea. Opening her handbag to tidy away her pencils is the nearest diversion. "D'you think this is going to work?"

"The fundraiser? I guess." Kneeling on the rug, in front of the trunk, Moya throws clothes on her bed with careless abandon, as if her recent tidying has given her license to make a mess again. "It's as good a lead as anything we've got so far."

Digging in her handbag, Kit spots the card with the *Washington Star* logo. She really needs to tack that up on the murder board. It reminds her of something else, too. How well do they really know Rafael Ramale?

She doesn't want to insult Moya's friend right in front of her, but she can't be quiet, either. "Do you trust Raffi? I mean, completely trust him? He's followed the murder cases, he has the run of the city, he's got police and DC political connections who might protect him.... For all we know, *he* could be the guy we're looking for."

"Kit!" Moya chides.

"I can't help it!" Kit throws her hands up. "It feels like every man I meet lately is a potential suspect."

"Sure," Moya says gently. "But not Raffi—never Raffi. Does he really strike you as someone with Nazi sympathies? No. And I *do* trust him." She hesitates before continuing. "I trust him because we grew up together. In a place called Mott Haven in New York City."

"I didn't know that," Kit says quietly. It's the first time Moya's revealed anything personal about her background, and she can't help but want more. "What was it like?"

Moya leans over the trunk, the loose tie of her blouse trailing in front, her soft navy lounge pants creasing at the knees. Slippery swathes of fabric spill through her hands— shining yellow, brilliant magenta—and Kit waits, knowing Moya needs to feel comfortable.

"It was a tough area, full of migrant families." Moya keeps her hands busy and her eyes on the contents of the trunk as she speaks. "The Ramales lived across the street from my family. Raffi's father worked at a printmaker's. Mine worked as a bookkeeper at a garment factory. We were tenement kids, playing stickball in the street." Moya's lips quirk. "I was a hellion."

Kit feels her own expression soften. "You? No."

Moya smiles further at the joke, but then her face saddens. "My father got laid off the year I turned thirteen. He started drinking more. It was a bad time for my family. Things got rough. My father...got rough."

Kit understands. "I'm sorry."

Moya waves the sentiment away with a swatch of taffeta. "Raffi's family was there for me when I needed a break.

168

They didn't make it into a big deal. Raffi was about my age, but he didn't bite back when I lashed out. I was angry at a lot of things then."

Her chin lowers. Black tendrils of her hair drift down in gentle waves as she digs in the trunk. Kit thinks Moya's searching has become a distraction, and she feels a yearning sympathy for the young girl who suffered back then—the girl who's turned into the Moya she knows now.

"What happened?" Kit asks gently.

Moya shrugs. "Oh, you know. My father got another job, we moved upstate. Things got better. Raffi and I kept in touch, here and there."

Kit knows the enduring loyalty you feel to those who've been faithful through hard times. And it's raised Raffi higher in her estimation. "He always wanted to be a newspaperman?"

Moya nods. "He would've enlisted, except the newsreels are part of the war effort now. I know he'd prefer to be interviewing soldiers and generals closer to Japan, but he's useful in Washington."

"I never thought of journalists that way before," Kit muses. "As part of the war effort, I mean."

Moya shrugs. "FDR and the rest of the government still need political news about the war to run. The public still needs to feel like things are happening—that all this is going to end someday. Someday soon, I hope."

"We all hope."

Moya straightens and looks over, her gray eyes large. "That's why I trust Raffi. Because of a bunch of old memories and some shared purpose."

"To see the war end." Kit spells it out clearly.

"Yes. I signed up to work at Signal Intelligence to help it end sooner."

There's a pause, in which they look at each other and the Philco lilts out a low, swaying tune. Moya's so guarded, she so rarely gives away private information; Kit knows she's just been entrusted with something precious. She's honored by it. More than anything, she wishes she could share herself with the same honesty... but if she did that, this moment would turn to ashes.

She can't stand here and say nothing, though. "Now here you are," she blurts out, "sorting information in another kind of war."

"I'm starting to get the feeling that wars *don't* end," Moya says fiercely. "That they just change shape. Thin out and infest homes, families. Plant a seed in some man's heart that the best expression for his hate is to target young women in this awful, awful way..."

"We can stop him." Kit believes that's true.

"Someday soon, I hope." Moya breaks the eye contact. She eases herself to standing and comes closer, a swathe of colors draped over one arm. "But now we have to dress you for a party."

Kit pushes against a trill of butterflies in her stomach at Moya's sudden nearness. "Ugh, I hate parties." At least she can be honest about that.

"I know you do. Shut up." One side of Moya's mouth lifts. She holds up a gown of brilliant red velvet, still on its hanger, and makes a face. "That's going to be way too long for you."

"Won't they all be?"

"Maybe." Moya tosses the red dress back onto the bed and picks through the pile draped over her arm. She holds a kingfisher-blue scarf up beside Kit's face. "Another reason to work with Raffi—he's good at sniffing out information, and he'll be there at the fundraiser to introduce us to people." She throws the scarf aside, tries another one in sunset orange that smells of heady perfume. "Dottie's right, though. She and Violet will probably get more behind-the-scenes gossip than we will."

Kit winces. "I still have to get dressed up, though, huh?"

"Yep." Moya smirks, looks down to sort through her armful. "Okay, let's try this."

She holds up a dress composed of draped, toga-like layers of liquid gold. Kit eyes it suspiciously. She can't see where one end of it starts and the other end begins.

"It's too long."

"It's adjustable. Just try it."

"I'll have to, um..." Kit glances around for a private place to change. "Maybe the bathroom down the hall—"

"Kit." Moya rolls her eyes, turns her back, returns to the trunk. "Go behind the door of the armoire. I promise not to look."

Feeling her face flame, Kit scoots over to the corner of the room between the armoire and the door. Hands shaking a little, she strips off her sweater, steps out of her shoes. Moya is kneeling again by the trunk, fussing over escaping fronds of ostrich feather and loose strands of tulle. Kit's pretty sure she's not glancing back.

171

Kit unbuttons her shirt and skirt. Finally down to her underthings, she isn't certain if it would really bother her if Moya looked, or how to put on the dress, or if she can get her heart's rhythms to settle. "Is it supposed to...Is there a zip?"

"It wraps around you," Moya calls, a grin in her voice.

Kit staggers to the table, feeling like she's drowning under masses of gold chiffon. "I'm not sure if I can...Um, help?"

Moya stands and comes back to the table, wearing a fond frown. "How did you get this tangled up?"

"I don't know!" Kit wails. "It's not that easy to get into!"

"Wait, wait—let me fix it." Moya moves Kit's hands aside gently. She circles to the back and lifts Kit's hair, adjusting the sequined straps and excess fabric of the dress. They are standing close together, the two of them, and Kit is acutely aware of it. Of the stutter in her own breathing. Of the warmth emanating from Moya's body and the way her own body responds, the blood rising hot in her cheeks.

Moya's hands are careful, unwinding and rearranging the fabric. Her thumbs graze the sensitive nape of Kit's neck, and Kit is too conscious of the closeness between them to move even a muscle. If she moves, this moment might disappear.

"I think you made a mistake." Her voice sounds shockingly husky. "I think this is two dresses."

"It's not two dresses." Moya's words are soft, too. "Hold still."

Kit lets her head drop forward. "I'm very...I'm very still."

Moya's fingertips trail down Kit's back, along with a spill of chiffon. The sensations create a trail of fire that makes her shiver.

"You won't be able to wear a corselette or a brassiere with this," Moya says. "The straps will show."

Kit finds all these sensations going straight to her head. "Then I'll go without."

Moya pauses. Audibly clears her throat. "Lift your arms a little." Moya's hands tuck and smooth and pleat. She revolves around Kit like a star, circling back until they are eye to eye once more. She reaches around Kit's waist to tie a length of amber fabric in front. "I might have to hem it a little." Moya's voice is throaty. "Just here."

Moya looks up. Now their faces are nearer together than Kit has ever dreamed possible.

This is not a mistake, she realizes. This is not an accident. Moya is not a person who does things without purpose.

Kit's throat has gone magnificently dry.

"Long skirts." She tries to swallow. "Now I understand why you prefer trousers."

"Trousers give me freedom of movement." Moya's breath smells faintly of cigarettes and whiskey. She pulls a sheer length of gold over Kit's head, slides it slowly down her shoulder. "You should try it."

Kit feels it in her bones when she decides to commit. She holds Moya's gaze. "I might."

"All the girls are wearing trousers these days." Moya's gray eyes are sparking in the low light.

"Not all the girls," Kit says softly.

"Some girls." Moya adjusts the fabric descending at Kit's sides, skirting light fingers over her hip without breaking eye contact. "Certain girls."

Kit finally manages to swallow. "Certain girls."

There is only a fingertip between their lips now. When Kit lifts off her heels and closes the gap, it's simple, like breathing.

Moya's lips are soft as clouds. She makes a delightful tiny noise, a sigh, as their lips meet. She sighs again as the kiss deepens.

Kit has been thinking of this moment for so long, and now she doesn't know where to put her hands, until they settle naturally, rightly, on the curves of Moya's waist. There is hard muscle under the soft jersey, and Moya makes a little flinch and whimper. Kit strokes her hand gently over Moya's hip to soothe her until Moya is relaxing, easing into the kiss, coming undone with the kiss. Until they are both gasping, their hands rising, cupping cheeks, fingers tunneling through each other's hair.

They kiss until things start to spiral. When they break apart, it's not to separate but to rest their foreheads together. Kit is breathing heavy, feeling the heat and languor in all her limbs. Her arms are tangled with Moya's, the taste of Moya's lips is rich on her tongue, and her heart is thrumming like a timpani.

Moya's face is flushed. "I didn't know . . . I wasn't sure . . ."

Kit says, "I've never been surer," and Moya kisses her again for that, until it's time to come apart and take off the dress, with much slower movements than before. Then, when Kit is only in her corselette, there is the wall of Moya's room to lean against.

"Are you still shy?" Moya asks, teasing her fingers along Kit's collarbone.

Kit laughs and Moya smiles, a full-blown smile. Kit can only bask in the radiance. *I knew—I knew it would be like this. Look at that smile.*

"Thank you," she says softly. "For choosing me a dress… For choosing me."

"We chose each other," Moya says, her eyes bright. She runs a hand lightly down the side of Kit's arm. "This… is going to make it tough to keep my mind on what we're doing tomorrow night."

Kit grins. She can't stop leaning in to inhale the smell of Moya's hair at that silky spot just behind her ear. "We're not going to be doing much. Just listening. Watching the guests. Keeping an eye on any tall, good-looking, rich, white men in the room."

"There'll be plenty of those, I can guarantee." Moya glances down to where their hands are entwined. "There's another factor about the killer. He's younger. No older than thirty."

"What makes you say that?" Kit frowns, before realizing. "The Farms."

"Yep." Moya looks up. "Older gentlemen don't go to jitterbug dances."

"That narrows things down again," Kit says, the idea clicking in her head. She starts toward the table to find a pencil.

"Wait." Moya drags her back with their joined hands. "Do you understand what it means, Kit? We'll be at the party. We're government girls. We fit the age profile."

"Oh." Kit understands now. She wets her lips.

"Yes." Moya lets the idea sit out in front of them for a moment. "We're bait."

18

That was the main thing we did—looking
for repetitions. Because sure as God
made little apples, at some point something would repeat.

—EDITH YOUNG

Champagne corks pop in the Grand Ballroom of the Mayflower Hotel, and Moya startles. She tries not to let it show,
but her glass of bubbles sloshes a little.

"Oops—you okay?" Kit asks.

"Fine," Moya says. "Just jumpy. I don't know what's wrong
with me tonight." But that's not true—she knows. Her head
has been a riot since she and Kit kissed last night, and she's
been running on that nervous energy all day.

It doesn't help that operations between Three and Four
were so busy she hardly had time to sit down. Breaks suddenly
started appearing everywhere today. Sometimes it's like that:
There'll be nothing for weeks and then *bam*, everything comes
clear at once. Moya was run off her feet; consulting with Emil
Ferrars, notifying the women in traffic analysis, liaising with
the overlappers, trying to make it all make sense in time to
create an order of battle for the Pentagon report, so the information would do some good in the field.

Overlaid on top of the heart-cranking pace was the sensation on her skin, the awareness of Kit—Kit at her chair, Kit

with the sun behind her, Kit with a pencil over her ear...
Just exchanging an innocent look with Kit in the workroom
was enough to leave Moya feeling like she was an exploding
star.

Now they're standing together in a ballroom on a Friday
night, and Moya can hardly believe her luck. Kit's auburn
hair is raked back and braided in a Grecian style—in her
draped dress, she looks like a tiny, perfect golden idol. Her
dress descends from her bare shoulders on thin, glittering
straps that meet the bodice of gold chiffon. Yards of copper
cloth, twisted into cord, wrap the loose folds of the dress
at her breasts, her waist, her hips, where the material falls
free at last, all the way to the floor. Behind, twin lengths of
burnished chiffon float down from each of Kit's shoulders,
meeting in a soft scoop of fabric at the small of her back.

She looks over and smiles, and Moya is appalled to find
her hands shaking. She's never this uncontrolled. But right
now, it's all she can do not to take Kit's champagne glass
along with her own, toss them in one of the enormous potted palms gracing each glorious ballroom colonnade, and
find a quiet alcove somewhere she and Kit can kiss each
other in private.

Slow down there, girl. Moya tries to concentrate on her
breathing and take in the view of the Mayflower ballroom,
which is spectacular. Beneath the high, arched ceiling and
lavish chandeliers, the long room is filled with the crème
de la crème of DC society. It's literally packed to the raf-
ters: The mezzanine level is crowded with men in tuxedos
or dress uniform, women dripping jewelry, the low roar of

conversation and laughter competing with the swing band on the first floor stage near where she and Kit are standing.

An immense Stars and Stripes is suspended from the mezzanine balcony, and red-white-and-blue bunting swags through the gilt-edged colonnades. Girls in black uniforms and white aprons circulate with trays of glasses. The noise, the glittering lights, and the heat in the ballroom are almost overpowering. Moya chose a high-collared black velvet gown to wear tonight, and now she's sweating in it.

Kit leans in to make herself heard. "What do we do now?"

"Enjoy more drinks from the silver platters?" Moya shrugs, pitching her voice over the band. "Raffi's going to arrive soon and meet us."

"We're just supposed to stand here and wait?"

Moya grins and sips her drink. "I think we're supposed to mingle."

"God, I am *so* bad at that." Kit's frown is worried. "I should have just been a maid."

"I need you where I can keep an eye on you." Moya gives her a flashing look, then softens. "You really like the quiet life, huh?"

"I really like not being the focus of attention," Kit says firmly, "and not having to talk to total strangers."

Moya snorts. "You're a disgrace to society maidens everywhere. How come you went to Arlington Hall, anyway?"

Kit stiffens—not a lot, but it's noticeable. "Why wouldn't I go to Arlington Hall?"

Moya gestures with her glass. "Uh, because you could've gone to Bryn Mawr?"

Kit looks, unseeing, at the crowd. "I...I didn't want to be so close to my parents."

"I understand that." Moya scans the faces of the serving staff, but she doesn't spot Dottie or Violet yet. Raffi still isn't here, but it's time to get to work. "Well, if you don't want to mingle, relax and help *me* mingle. These people could be an important source of information. We should get farther away from the band. Take a turn around the floor with me?"

"Sure." Kit looks back and gives her a shy smile that makes Moya goosebump all over.

They slip behind a potted palm and dodge guests until they reach the area under the mezzanine. It's dimmer and quieter here—still busy, but not shoulder-to-shoulder. The ballroom is a long rectangle, with one grand entrance off the Mayflower's promenade foyer and another smaller one far down on this west side. Twin staircases on the east side take guests to the balcony area above. The main floor is a seething mass of people, but this understory is all fancy carpets and resting couches, where older matrons chat with standing guests and cool themselves with ostrich feather fans.

Kit is holding her champagne glass like a prop, watching the dance floor. Moya calculates the likelihood of people noticing if she put her arm around Kit's waist.

"How many people are here, d'you think?" Kit seems dazzled by it all.

"Maybe six hundred?" It's easier to talk now they don't have to shout. "But it's still early—they'll probably squeeze more in before the end of the night. Looks like everyone who's everyone has turned out for Harry Hopkins's speech."

179

Peering over her shoulder, Moya sees the band members playing against a backdrop of silver velvet curtains. On either side of the stage, more silver velvet conceals the doors to back-of-house, where the servers are entering and exiting, laden with trays.

She looks back around when Kit tugs on her hand. "There's Violet."

"Time for more champagne," Moya says as they head in her direction.

Violet meets them halfway. Her hair is pulled back, appropriately neat, with a white cap pinned over it. She looks trim but anonymous in a black cotton uniform, and not entirely thrilled to be waiting on a crowd of white folks again.

Moya can't blame her. "How're you holding up?"

"Oh, fine." Violet sucks her teeth. "Is it loud enough in here, d'you think?"

"Loud and busy," Kit says. "I was worried we'd miss you in this crush. Is Dottie here?"

"You haven't seen her yet?" Violet hoists her half-full tray of glasses with a long-suffering air. "She's doing the rounds. Probably better than me, to be honest—I always was a terrible server in the kitchen at the Hall."

"Is it frantic in the kitchen here?" Kit asks.

Violet nods. "It's next level down, which means we're all going up and down the stairwells like worker ants."

"Hear anything juicy so far?" Moya swaps out her empty glass for a full one on Violet's tray.

"It's been too busy to gossip," Violet admits. "But once

things settle down, we might hear more. Okay, I've gotta look like I'm circulating—I'll check in again later."

"Keep your ears open," Moya says, "and don't go off into any dark corners on your own. Stay safe."

"I hear that," Violet says fervently, and she whisks away.

Kit angles to watch her leave. "You really think we should be on alert while we're here? Dinah wasn't killed until she left for home."

"And Libby was killed while people were dancing in the building next door," Moya reminds her. "Yes, I think it's smart to be cautious. Goddamn, where's Raffi?"

Kit's lips quirk. "You said he hates to be punctual."

"It's his major character flaw." Moya sighs, craning her neck to look toward the main entrance again.

"It's hard to remember that we're here to investigate a murder," Kit says wistfully. Her voice softens further. "I told you that you look beautiful, right?"

Moya's eyes snap back, some of the tension leaving her body in a rush. "About a dozen times before we got in the cab, yes."

"Well, it's still true." Kit smiles, her cheeks going pink. Moya can see her freckles through the face powder like a dusting of gold flecks. "Would people notice if I kissed you right now, d'you think?"

"Probably," Moya says with a grin, although she's been thinking the exact same thing. The sight of Kit's lips reminds her of the taste of ginger wine. She eases closer so they're brushing together, black velvet purring against gold chiffon.

Kit's eyes darken. "Seems a waste of all these fancy clothes, if I can't do anything to show how I appreciate you in them."

"We'll still be wearing them when we get home."

"Something to look forward to, then." Kit lifts her champagne flute to her lips, her face flushed and radiant.

Moya watches Kit swallow, and bright waves of desire ripple up and down her spine. This is the part of wooing that she loves: the magnetic push and pull of it, the flirty banter and riposte that curls her toes, the electricity under her skin that edges all her feelings higher. Knowing she's not the only one affected by it adds to the thrill, but she tears her eyes away before she self-combusts. "Oh—Raffi's here!"

She grabs Kit's hand and moves them both toward the colonnade closest to the band as Raffi closes in on them. No fedora tonight, but he's dressed in his finest, his sharp cheekbones complemented by an even sharper tux.

"You like?" After kissing their cheeks in turn, he holds out his hands for admiration. "I've rented this one so often, the lady adjusted the cuffs for me. You two both look gorgeous. Who've you chatted with so far?"

"Nobody," Moya says, smiling. She snags a glass from a passing tray and hands it to him. "Figured you'd have a better idea of the lay of the land."

Raffi's dimples pop as he grins and rolls his eyes. "Fine, let me see...." He sips his drink, scanning the crowd. "Ah, okay. Come this way and let me introduce you to my good friend, Bob Pepper...."

For the next hour, Raffi moves them around the crowd like a chess master, nodding at people here, laughing with people there, exchanging pleasantries and bestowing compliments. He explains to everyone that Moya is "one of my oldest friends from New York" and that she and Kit are now "working for the State Department," a handy euphemism that covers everything from secretarial typing to foreign diplomacy.

Mining magnates and state senators fall for it, pressing business cards into Moya's palm with champagne-sticky fingers. By 10:00 PM, she and Kit have made light conversation with industrialists' sons and bombing engineers and ranking servicemen, including at least a few young men who fit the profile.

During a break, she and Kit stand by a refreshment table stacked with a tower of canapés while Raffi disappears into the crowd to find them both glasses of water. "I never thought this would be the night when I'd learn everything I wanted to know about manufacturing nylon," Kit says, attempting to fan herself with a fabrication magnate's business card.

"The parachute factory guy?"

"Yeah—he didn't seem like a potential suspect." Kit collects her third glass of bubbles from a passing server.

"Have to agree," Moya says. "Hey, slow down there. Wait for the water. Eat something—those canapés look good."

"I don't think the men we're talking to are young enough."

"I'll tell Raf." Moya is distracted by something over near the ballroom stage. It's Dottie, who makes a swell-looking server, shimmying her way through the crowd.

"There's Dot," Kit says, surprised.

As Moya watches, Dottie hands a glass to an older man in a Great War uniform, then turns when she's hailed by another man in uniform—it's Captain John Cathcart from

Arlington Hall. Dottie smiles winningly and inclines her head, nodding at something he's said.

"I didn't know there would be folks from the Hall here tonight," Kit says. She sounds unnerved.

"It's not just John," Moya says. "Look, Emil's with him. I didn't even know Emil owned a tux."

What else don't I know about Emil? For the briefest moment, Moya looks at her co-worker in a different light. *And he has a car....* She shoves those thoughts aside. Kit's tendency to view every man as a potential suspect hasn't shifted her own lens on the world quite *that* far.

Kit lifts her chin to look around. "I wonder if Miss Caracristi and Mr. Kullback are here, too?"

But Moya is thinking hard. "That's how he knew."

"Pardon?"

Moya turns to face Kit. "That's how he knew. I've been wondering all night—how did the killer know that Dinah was a government girl when she was at the Fairfax party in a server's uniform? But that's how he knew. Because someone from her work was there—"

"And the killer heard them say hello to her out on the floor," Kit finishes. "I think you're right."

"I know I'm right," Moya says firmly.

Kit is gazing into the air above the heads of the party-goers. "That changes our theory about the killer's process, though. We know he plans and brings his equipment in advance. But if he's not stalking his victims, if he's targeting girls he meets by chance, then he must have his equipment with him every time he comes out to an event...."

"He's always prepared," Moya suggests.

"He's always *carrying evidence*," Kit counters, staring back. "Even if he washes his gloves, washes the knife, there'll be traces of blood left behind. If we can find him, that evidence will be with him. It'll be enough to convict him."

"We could give the police more than just a bunch of theories...." Moya is catching on.

"We might be able to give them enough to catch the killer *and* the evidence to put him behind bars." Kit's eyes are alight.

"Damn, Kit." Moya takes a breath. Being so close to Kit's combination of beauty and intelligence is intoxicating. "Would people notice if I kissed you right now, d'you think?"

Kit grins. "Probably."

The buzz under Moya's skin is so intense, she's only saved from throwing care to the wind when Raffi arrives. His arms are lifted to protect the two sweating glasses of chilled water he's carrying as he edges through the crowd.

"Okay, here you go." He deposits a glass with each of them. "There's champagne aplenty, but d'you know how hard it is to get water around here? I had to search high and low." He shakes droplets off his hands, then spins to survey the party. "Who's next? You want politicians' sons or an old-money landowner?"

"You make it sound like we're at a grocery store," Moya says, snorting. "Canned beans or canned corn?"

Kit looks like she's trying not to laugh. "Moya can choose. Give me a minute—I'm going to visit the powder room."

She hands Moya her glass before weaving through the

multitudes. Moya doesn't even realize she's tracking Kit's movement until Raffi taps her on the arm.

"You like her, huh?" He looks a little mournful.

Moya does a double take. "Don't tell me you thought you had a chance with her?"

"Pshaw, no way." Raffi flaps a hand, all nonchalance.

"You *did*." Moya huffs a laugh, presses her lips together as she sets both glasses on the refreshment table. "Sorry to disappoint you, Raf, but you've been barking up the wrong tree there."

"Makes sense." His expression is rueful, then settles into a smile. "Well, good for you—for both of you. Just don't let her break your heart, you hear?"

"I'll do my best," Moya says, chuckling. But part of her is wondering how she seems to have fallen so hard, so fast. That's not her usual modus operandi. Being around Kit has broken through some wall inside. She's beginning to suspect that wall was a confinement rather than a protection.

"Okay, come on," she urges Raf, to change the subject. "Landowner or politician? You decide. Anyone with rumored connections to the Bund would be useful. But let's see if we can find some younger guys—venerable gentlemen aren't our target range."

"Landowner, then," Raffi says. "He's old, but the men he's with are whippersnappers."

He extends his elbow so she can thread her hand onto his arm and leads them both away from the refreshments toward a group of four men gathered closer to the silver-velvet stage. "Why, is that... Howard! Great to see you again!" Raffi exclaims as they make an "accidental" bump into the group. "Gosh, it's been an age. Have you met Moya Kershaw?"

"I don't believe I've had the pleasure," Howard says. He's a man in his late fifties, of the type Moya's seen before: well-dressed, slope-shouldered, with a commanding eye.

"Moya's a longtime friend from New York," Raffi explains, "and I had no idea she was working with the State Department in DC until we met up again just last week. Moya, this is Howard Lascar, he's working with...is it still the Department of Agriculture?"

"Yes, indeed," Howard Lascar intones, pressing Moya's proffered hand. "Delighted to meet you, Miss Kershaw. One moment, and when there's a break in the music, I'll introduce my colleague Richard Kingett and his sons."

"I didn't realize you'd come down from Pennsylvania for this shindig," Raffi says, before a discordant blast of trumpets from the stage drowns out all hope of conversation. Raffi squints and casts around. "Hold on, I think there's something happening—it might be Harry Hopkins. I'll go find out and return with a report. Howard, take care of Miss Kershaw for me? I'll be back in just a minute."

As Raffi dashes away, Moya sees Howard Lascar watch him go, bemused. "Good lad—bit flighty, but he's got some brains. Shame he's chained to the *Star*. He'd be an asset in the field."

Moya's not convinced that Raffi Ramale is suited for the grime and horror of the front lines, but it's probably best not to mention that to him or Lascar. "You're not usually a resident of the capital, then, Mr. Lascar?"

"Howard—please, I insist." The man has a broad, gruff face. "No, I'm usually busy touring farms in the north, but I'm an admirer of Hopkins, and I thought I'd like to see his speech in person."

"Oh, if you're from the north, you might—" But whatever Moya was going to say is interrupted when Kit arrives, pink-cheeked and breathless, with Dottie in tow.

"I'm glad you didn't wander too far," Kit says. "I thought I'd get lost in here! I asked Dottie to show me the way—" She notices Lascar. "Oh, excuse me, I didn't mean to interrupt."

"No interruption at all," Lascar says smoothly. He takes a glass of champagne from Dottie's tray. "Thank you, my dear."

"Certainly, sir," Dottie says, biting back a grin.

Moya straightens. "Mr. Lascar—"

"Howard."

"Howard, of course. Let me introduce my friend and colleague Katherine Sutherland."

Lascar's eyes narrow with confusion. "I beg your pardon?"

"Kit," Kit says, hand extended with a smile, angelic in her golden finery. "That is, I'm Katherine Sutherland, but everyone calls me Kit."

"Katherine Sutherland?" Lascar seems flummoxed.

"Yes." Kit's smile dims a fraction as her hand hovers in mid-air.

"Are you..." Lascar shakes his head. "You're one of the Grand Rapids Sutherlands?"

"Uh, no, I'm..." Kit seems to be losing her glow. Her hand slowly lowers. "My family's from Pennsylvania. Robert and Charlotte Sutherland, from Bryn Mawr? I don't know if you're familiar—"

"I *am* familiar, and if this is a joke, it's in very poor taste." Lascar's white eyebrows are furrowed and the cast of his face is harsh.

"Excuse me?" Moya feels a strange current shift in the air between their group: Kit beside her, getting paler by the second; Dottie hovering and concerned, with her laden tray; Howard Lascar's stony visage. "Mr. Lascar, you said you're from Pennsylvania, so you must know—"

"I *do* know the Sutherlands," Lascar says sharply, "and I received word of their bereavement in June of last year."

"Bereavement?" Moya finds her head turning back and forth, between Lascar and Kit.

"Of their only daughter, Katherine." He turns his glare directly on Kit. "Young lady, I don't know *who you are*, but this is an insult to Robert and Charlotte's grief. I don't know why you'd be using Katherine Sutherland's name, except for some nefarious purpose—"

"What?" Dottie's smile and her tray are both sagging lower now.

Moya looks between the two major players in this scene with a sense of fracture, as if she's tipped into some kind of alternate reality. "Mr. Lascar, I'm sure there's some mistake. I've known Kit for nine months, and she—Kit?"

But Kit is still. Silent. Absolutely white. Staring at Lascar, lips parted, it's like she's turned to wax. With a seemingly gargantuan effort, she closes her mouth. Opens it again to speak. "I'm sorry," she says hoarsely.

Moya feels an abrupt shearing sensation, like the floor has dropped away from her feet.

"I'm so, so..." Kit's eyes are bright and hot as she turns from Lascar, toward Moya. "I didn't want to...Moya, I'm so sorry."

Moya can only gape, all breath sucked out of her chest.

"It wasn't supposed to be like..." Kit trembles, her hand coming to her mouth, head starting to shake. "I can't...I'm sorry."

And she turns and walks away, into the crowd.

"What do you mean *bereavement?*" Dottie wails. "What is going *on?*"

Lascar is saying something, but Moya can't hear him. The guests in the ballroom close behind Kit's wake, as if she never existed. Moya hears a fierce roaring sound, like a maelstrom in her head, and then the maelstrom is clanging loud, and she realizes it's screaming.

Someone is screaming in the ballroom.

The noise is coming from nearby. A hand grabs her arm, and Raf is there. Moya feels his presence as a warmth, a solidity, which is a relief after what just...what just...

"What just happened?" she asks him plaintively.

"Moya." His face is serious, his eyes dark and searching. "They found another girl."

19

The Espionage Act of 1917:
It is a crime to convey false reports
or false statements with intent to
interfere with the operation or success of the military or naval forces
of the United States or to promote the
success of its enemies when the United
States is at war, to cause or attempt
to cause insubordination, disloyalty,
mutiny, refusal of duty, in the military or naval forces of the United
States, or to wilfully obstruct the
recruiting or enlistment service of
the United States.

—18 U.S.C. CH37

When Kit walks away, it's like she's walking away from any kind of future.

She pushes, unseeing, through the crowd, and she's trying—trying so hard!—to stay grounded. But the voice in her head berates her. *What did you think would happen? Did you really imagine it was going to last?*

Her ears are ringing, and her heart is tearing, tearing. Feelings rise up in a black, drowning wave, drag her under, make her gasp, until she finally pushes clear of all the bodies in the ballroom and she's out the doorway, in the promenade.

Someone is calling her name.

"*Kit!*"

When she turns around, it's Violet standing there, the door swinging closed behind her. Violet's black cotton uniform still looks crisp, and she's ditched her tray somewhere. The sight of the maid uniform is enough to make Kit groan.

"Kit?" Violet comes closer. "Kit, you need to come back, there's a—"

"*Moya knows.*" Kit's shocked to hear how strangled her own voice sounds. But now she's said it, made it real, words come easier. "There was... there was a man from Katherine's home state. He knew her family, and he knew I wasn't... that I wasn't..."

Violet's mouth opens.

She clasps Kit's arm. "Okay. It's gonna be okay."

Kit can only stand there, shaking.

Violet lets go, reaches up and unpins her cap, unties her apron. She folds both of them into a square, which she pockets, before grabbing hold of Kit's arm again. "Your coat is in the cloakroom, right? Come on."

They retrieve their coats from the cloakroom, then walk back to the opposite end of the promenade. Kit finds herself ushered to where an older man in Mayflower livery opens the outer doors. Quaint lampposts provide illumination against the night, but it's a much plainer area than the front of the hotel. They're in a service driveway. "Staff entrance," Violet explains.

Kit knows she should pull her coat tighter against the chill wind, but she can't make her fingers work. The man in livery hails them a cab off Seventeenth Street; it eases to a stop before them in the driveway. Once they're in the cab, it's warmer. Violet gives the driver directions.

"Where are we going?" Kit whispers.

"Home," Violet says. The cab begins to move, and she turns to Kit. In the back of the car, they are just two girls in coats, one in a maid uniform, one with golden combs in her hair. "So it's out. Moya knows. What about Dottie?"

"Yes." Kit still feels numb. "She was right there."

"Okay. You have money? You have your Hall badge?"

"Yes."

Violet's expression is set. "You get back into the Hall, you get your things. You make the cab wait, and he'll bring you to this address." Violet has taken a pencil and a card— a cream-colored index card, Kit notes—out of her other pocket. By the light of passing street lamps, she scrawls on the card, passes it to Kit.

"What…Where is this?" Kit asks.

"It's my place. My parents' house, on Lowell Street. You can get yourself together there, then catch the bus to Union."

The card in Kit's hand is trembling. She clutches it tight. "I have to run."

"Yes." Violet grasps Kit's arm. "I'm sorry. I know this isn't what you wanted—"

"I don't think I've ever known what I wanted," Kit whispers. *Except for Moya.* But the things she might have wanted are immaterial now. Maybe they always have been.

"Look, I know this is bad, but you still have a chance to get away." Violet snatches a glance at the cab driver, lowers her voice. "You made plans, right? Maybe you don't know where you're going, but you had a plan to get to Union and get free. You can still do that, if you move fast."

Kit looks out the window. The city is a rain-drizzled blur of twinkling lights and shadowed buildings. "Why did you leave the ballroom?"

For the first time, Violet's face loses its "take charge" expression, looks hollow and sad. "They found a girl. She was in back-of-house, in a storage room near the stairwell—"

"Another girl?" Kit's head whips back. "You mean there was another *murder?*"

"Yes." Violet takes in Kit's look. "I wasn't there, okay? I didn't see it, I just heard the screaming, and—"

"We need to turn around." Kit sits up straighter. "We need to go back, we can—"

"No." Violet looks almost angry. "Lord, girl, are you *crazy?* This is your only chance! I know it hurts, and I know you want to do right by these girls—I love Dinah, and I want to do right by them, too. But you've got to think about getting *away."*

Kit covers her face with her hands, talks through her fingers. "Violet, I can't. This is wrong, this is all—"

"Listen to me." Violet's hand goes to Kit's shoulder, gives a little shake. Her voice is low and serious. "This isn't just about how you *feel.* You lied on government documents."

"Yes, and I knew there would be repercussions," Kit insists. "A court martial, a fine—"

"It's way worse than that. This is wartime. You breached the Espionage Act—that's *treason,* Kit. For Pete's sake, they sentenced that Detroit tavernkeeper to hang just for giving an escaped German POW a cup of coffee!"

Treason. Espionage. Hanging.

Kit remembers the words of the loyalty oath she signed, right on the little wooden desk after her interview: It said that she took the oath freely, "without any mental reservation or purpose of evasion." She remembers that the pen she picked up to sign had run out of ink, so the interviewer allowed her to use his own pen from his breast pocket....

She feels sick.

"I know..." Violet catches her breath, lets her hand drop. "I know this must feel like everything is crumbling right now. And you want to save those girls, get justice for them. I get it. But you have to think about saving yourself, too."

Kit looks at Violet, her eyes hot. Violet's blinking fast, her brow furrowed. All Kit can do is nod her assent. Then Violet is reaching for her, pulling her into a hug.

"Save yourself, Kit," Violet whispers. "Before it's too late."

20

Sometimes there'd be a schedule for the
blackouts. But sometimes the sirens
would go off, and that was that—you
couldn't move.

—CAROL ANN WHITE

Out front of Arlington Hall, the girls share another hug; then Violet instructs the driver to take her home and return to the same location to collect Kit in a half hour. It's just before midnight, and the soft dark around the base is deeply quiet, disturbed only by the distant hum of traffic and the crunch of the gritty asphalt as Kit walks up to the boom gate. She digs in her coat pocket for her badge.

At the guardhouse, a GI is sharing a smoke with the duty officer. The MP on duty gives her a nod. "Have a nice night?"

"Yes," Kit lies, and it takes a gargantuan effort not to say *Yes, sir*. She used to struggle with that a lot when she first assumed Katherine's identity, but this is the first time in a while she's had to suppress the habit.

"Right, well…"

The MP inspects her badge closely. Kit feels her heart's arrythmia grow. But then he simply hands the badge back, waves her on through. Kit presses her lips together to smile her thanks, allows the breath she's been holding to trickle out as she takes the driveway road to the schoolhouse.

Inside the dim foyer, the tap of her heels on the glossy parquet echoes the tap of typewriters on the floor above. She takes the stairs up to Three, trying not to appear as if she's rushing.

You lied on government documents.... You breached the Espionage Act—that's treason, *Kit.*

The words echo around and around in her head. A girl in a navy skirt and a smart twinset comes down on the other side of the staircase. Kit controls her breathing, makes sure to meet the girl's eyes and nod, like normal. Finally, the last step onto the landing of Three. Kit walks down the corridor and slips into her room, closes the door, leans against it.

Breathes.

Her chin is quivering, but she doesn't have time to cry. "Come on, now," she whispers. She flicks on the light.

First, the trunk. She unpacks enough clothes to expose a dark blue carpetbag, which was not part of the original contents of the trunk—it's something Kit acquired about six months ago, from a girl on Two who was giving it away. The carpetbag is large enough to hold essentials and clothes. Most crucially, it doesn't look like a suitcase.

Kit wonders why she has never, until this moment, packed for her escape. It's not as if she hasn't had plenty of forewarning. And it's not that she thought she'd never get caught—it's that she didn't want to think about leaving. She packs her bag quickly and efficiently, adding toiletries, underwear and stockings, a change of skirt, another shirt, a utility dress, a cardigan, plus the reference papers and the envelope of money. The rest she leaves where it is.

Now for the hardest part.

Kit stands up and takes off her coat. She turns to the full-length mirror on Dottie's wardrobe and looks at herself: the golden dress, the sparkling sheen of the combs against her hair, the lovely borrowed shoes. Kit thinks of the way Moya gazed at her in the ballroom—like she was a natural wonder. Like she was an aurora borealis.

Kit's final sight of herself in the dress is clouded by tears, but she looks one last time. A painful memory is still one worth preserving.

She steps out of the shoes, unties the fabric cord in front, unwinds it all, slips off the glittering straps. She suspends the dress on a hanger, slips it into Dottie's wardrobe, along with the shoes. She takes the combs out of her hair and sets them on the dresser.

Everything after that is methodical: brassiere, girdle, warm stockings, blue shirt, gray sweater, blue skirt. She puts on her oxford shoes for faster movement. She fills the brown vinyl handbag with a comb, her lipstick and powder compact, the copy of *Emma* from her nightstand, an envelope with ten dollars in it. She pins a gray beret over her hair and puts her coat back on. She shoulders the handbag and picks up the carpetbag by its bamboo handle.

There's a moment to survey the room—this room, where she lived and read and slept, where she talked with Dottie about everything imaginable, where they laughed and ate treats they snuck out of the cafeteria and tried on each other's clothes and fussed with their hair, and gossiped and confided and stayed up too late.... This room where she felt free for the first time, a girl with a life of her own. A girl who set sail on a boat, so long ago, and arrived on the distant shore of a new way of being.

Kit turns out the light.

Back in the corridor, she checks to make sure the coast is clear before heading back to the stairs, descending on quiet feet. It's easier in these shoes. Although the sound of typewriters and murmurs and shuffling paper comes from rooms on other floors, no other girls appear to ask Kit what she is doing, going downstairs in traveling clothes so close to curfew.

She reaches the first floor without incident and is mentally composing the lie she will tell the MP at the gate so she can exit the compound: She received bad news—her mother is ill, gravely so. This is a mercy dash. The guards don't know who she is, can't tell one girl from another, so she can say she is only going to Bethesda, and no one will be the wiser. Kit rehearses the lie as she walks over the floor toward the main entrance, hitches her handbag higher to reach out and grab the door pull—

A siren goes off, pealing through the building.

Kit drops her carpetbag. Her body flattens itself against the wall. The clamor in her mind competes with the foghorn of the siren, and she has to clench her fists hard to focus, to realize that this alarm is not going off because she's touched the door pull, or because they've figured out she's trying to leave.

It's the air raid siren.

It's an air raid.

A flurry of movement—a girl dashes across the foyer, heading for the auditorium. Lights go on in the hallway on the floor above and are just as quickly snapped off. Kit hears the hubbub of girls' voices carrying from this floor and on Two as floor supervisors marshal their charges. In a moment, this front entrance area will be crowded with girls as Signal Intelligence employees hurry to the air raid shelter.

Kit has to move.

She reaches down for her carpetbag. The air raid siren is still making its dreadful *aaaooooowwwooo*, and she's trembling so hard, breaths coming fast and panicked, that it takes her two tries before she can grab the handle again.

She could join the crowd of girls about to descend and take cover in the basement. No, that's the last place she wants to be—stuck in the claustrophobic basement with everyone else, with no chance to get away. But there's absolutely no chance she'll be allowed through the gate during an active air raid.

Dammit.

She can't go back to her room—heading upstairs, against the flow of traffic, will draw notice, and they'll be checking dorm room to dorm room to ensure that no one has been left behind.

The library.

Kit seizes on this idea as the building lights go out, plunging the schoolhouse into darkness. Little screams from girls on the floor above are quickly smothered.

Kit knows her way in the dark.

The siren wails throughout the Hall. She clutches her bag

200

to her chest, against the front flaps of her coat. She walks briskly to the right-hand corridor off the foyer, jumps as a girl exits her room into the carpeted corridor and heads toward the main entrance. Kit quickens her pace in the other direction.

A few more steps and she's there.

The door to the library opens soundlessly. Kit closes it quickly behind her. No lamps illuminate the room, and the thick curtains keep out even the light of the moon. There's the smell of cold furniture polish in the dark.

Kit holds her bags with one hand and gropes for the chesterfield. The noise of the siren is lessened in here, at least. Kit sinks down onto the chair, recoils—the leather is freezing. She fumbles further and finds the edge of one of the wingback club chairs, its fabric upholstery more friendly. She angles the chair so it's facing away from the doorway. If someone enters, it won't be immediately obvious the room is occupied. Then she settles her bags on the floor, behind the curtain, and sits down.

She slips off her shoes and tucks her feet underneath her. She's not going anywhere, that much is for certain. Even if she made it out onto the street, she'd be pulled up by air raid marshals. No vehicles will be moving in the blackout. Her cab is now out of the question.

She's stuck.

A mohair lap blanket is draped over the back of the chair; Kit unfolds it over herself. She unpins the beret and lays it on her knee. Impossible to know what time it is, but it's late.

The air raid siren abruptly goes silent.

Kit sits there in the dark, tucked into the club chair, thinking about Moya. Tense with worry that someone will come in and find her. Anxious for her friends, anxious about a court martial, heartsick at how everything has gone so badly wrong.

She sits and listens and waits.

But after more than an hour of listening and waiting, the tension and anxiety and heartache wear her down. Closing her eyes is no different from sitting in darkness. Kit clutches the mohair blanket. Lets her body sink back into the chair. Counts her breaths.

Falls asleep.

21

When you have made a thorough and rea-
sonably long effort to understand a
thing, and still feel puzzled by it,
stop. You will only hurt yourself by
going on.

—LEWIS CARROLL

Moya looks out the window of the cab as they turn onto Arlington Boulevard, wondering when she will start to feel again.

There's been no time for feeling. Last night was a mess even before the air raid siren that confined everyone to the Mayflower Hotel. Police had only just arrived to cordon off the crime scene in the ballroom stairwell when the sirens began screaming. Staff quickly arranged for the fundraiser guests to seek shelter or find beds once it became clear that everyone was stuck in place.

All night, Moya thought about the expression on Kit's face when she said *I'm sorry* and ran out of the ballroom.

Now it's early Saturday morning, and Moya's been thinking for hours, and still no emotion registers. It's as if the events of last night have scoured her completely clean; there's no energy inside her to dredge up anxiety or upset anymore. Maybe this is just how she's going to react to everything now—with this hollow, emotionless calm. That might actually be a good thing.

"Moya, your badge?"

She realizes she's on the sidewalk near the guardhouse in front of the Hall with no memory of getting out of the cab. The outside air is crisp. A crowd of girls swirls around the guardhouse, everyone trying to get in at once. Dottie is speaking to her.

"You've got your badge, right?" The lapels of Dottie's coat are limp. Her mascara is smeared and her hair is down, and she looks exhausted.

"Oh—yeah. Right here." Moya fumbles in the pocket of her dress for her ID.

The MP waits with ill-concealed annoyance but finally lets them through. Moya thinks they must look like quite a pair: her in the black velvet gown with the high collar and the tight sleeves, Dottie in her bedraggled maid's uniform and coat. Together they trudge up the driveway to the grand entrance of the Hall.

When they make it inside to the foyer, the idea of walking up even one flight of stairs to get to her room leaves Moya completely enervated.

"Do you think Kit came back?" Dottie asks, her voice low.

"I don't know." Moya closes her eyes and stands on the parquet, almost swaying with tiredness. "I just want to sit down."

"The cafeteria?" Dottie suggests.

Moya thinks of the harsh, unforgiving fluorescent light bouncing off the white walls and cafeteria bench seats, shakes her head. "The library."

"Okay." Dottie turns in that direction. "I can maybe get us some coffee?"

"Sounds good," Moya intones as she follows, hearing the lack of color in her voice.

At the end of the corridor, the library door. Beyond the door, a world of warm teak and dark drapes and—

"Moya!" Dottie waves a hand wildly.

Kit is tucked in the chair between the chesterfield sofa and a window. A mohair blanket is spread over her knees, the blanket edge clutched in her hand, along with a gray beret. Under her coat, she's wearing a gray sweater and a blue traveling skirt; a handbag and a carpet bag are tucked beneath the curtain hem nearby. By the crease of washed-out light along the wall, Moya can see that Kit's asleep; her cheeks are pale, and her head is turned into her shoulder like a baby bird's.

A diamond-sharp sting of pain unrolls in Moya's chest, makes her breath catch. She's feeling again.

Kit's eyelids flutter.

"She's waking up." Dottie's voice is all hard particles.

It's pathetic, but the sight of Kit slowly opening her eyes brings a little spark of gladness. Kit's face gains color. She blinks up at them, strangely calm. "You broke curfew," she says softly.

For a moment, it's as if Moya forgets how to speak, how to move. Then she swallows, her throat unglues, and the sense of being in her body returns. "The air raid." She scrapes a shaky hand through her hair. "No one could go anywhere. Dottie and I spent the night on couches in the Mayflower ballroom."

"You're leaving." Dottie's chin is trembling faintly as she glares at Kit, her face wan and accusing.

Kit doesn't answer. She unfolds from her awkward position in the wingback; Moya can almost hear her muscles creaking. "What time is it?"

"It's seven in the morning," Moya says. Then she asks the most important question, the one that's been bursting to come out: "Who *are* you?"

Kit rubs her biceps through her coat, sits forward in the chair. "Kathleen." She seems almost serene, saying it. There's even a different accent slipping through in her voice. "I'm Kathleen Hopper, from Scott's Run, West Virginia. I was Katherine Sutherland's maid."

Dottie seems aghast. "You're a *maid*?"

"Maid. Companion. Nurse." Kit looks between both girls. "Katherine grew up sick. I helped her bathe, helped her dress, helped her with her lessons. We were...very close." Kit's chin drops. "She died the night before the War Department took over the school."

Dottie is even more aggrieved. "And you stole her papers?"

"I didn't *steal* anything." Kit's lips purse, then release, perhaps recognizing that Dottie has made a reasonable assumption. "I didn't take anything except a name. Katherine gave me her trunk and her papers the afternoon before she passed. She encouraged me to go. And I was all ready to...until I met the both of you in the foyer."

Moya wets her lips, remembering. "And we offered you a job."

206

"Why didn't you tell us?" Dottie says. "Why didn't you *say* something?"

"What could I say?" Kit stares up now with more fire. "Would you have given me this job if I'd said I was a maid? A girl with no references, no education to speak of? Would you have taken me in the way you did if I'd told you the truth? I'd already introduced myself as Katherine, I was…" She swallows. "I was scared. I'm still scared. That's why I'm leaving."

There's a long silence. Moya presses a palm to her stomach, over the velvet. The pressure is good—it keeps her centered. She looks over at Dottie, making her voice quiet but firm. "Dot, could you get us something to drink from the kitchen? Coffee…I don't know—anything, so long as it's hot."

"I can't stay for coffee," Kit starts. "I've stayed too long already—"

"One cup of coffee," Moya says, raising a hand. "It's only seven—there's time before the shift change."

Dottie frowns, but—after a long look at Kit—she turns and leaves the library, shutting the door after herself. Kit watches her go.

Moya feels as if all her strings have been cut. She's still standing, but only through force of will. Before her, Kit's pale face is lit with high dots of color. Her hair is an autumn fire, contrasting with the blues and grays of her outfit. Beautiful Kit—tough, smart Kit. Moya can hardly fathom how a girl this smart could be so damn foolish.

But Moya knows she's the one who was the fool. "I can't believe you lied to me," she whispers.

207

Suddenly Kit's entire soul seems to show in her eyes. "You were the person I least wanted to lie to. But I'd already been Katherine for too long to go back. And I had too much to lose."

"Kit..." Moya feels a sharp, glassy pain in her chest. She can't do this anymore. She sinks slowly onto the chesterfield, fingers over her face. "I don't even know whether to call you Kit or Kathleen."

"I'm Kit. Just like I've always been."

Moya doesn't know what to believe. She hardly trusts herself to speak. She lets the pause grow until Kit changes tack gently.

"What happened at the Mayflower last night?"

Moya drops her hands, gathering all the broken pieces of herself to reply. "They found a girl just off the stairwell. Young, pretty." She feels her expression contort, shakes it off. "I never got close enough to see. Raffi told me some of the details."

"Was she one of the servers?"

"No. She was a guest. A stenographer with the War Department, in Procurement."

Kit's frustration and anxiety sneak through in her tone. "Violet and Dottie were going up and down those stairs all night."

"I know it."

"I nearly came back," Kit confesses. "Violet talked me out of it in the back of the cab."

Moya feels another stabbing pain, can't help how her voice turns fierce. "*Violet* knows?"

Kit nods. "She used to work in the kitchen. She recognized me the morning we got back from the Farms."

"She kept your secret, all this time...." Moya wonders if Kit knows what all this means. "Did she tell you that what you've done—faking your identity on official documents—is a federal crime?"

"Yes," Kit acknowledges simply.

Moya just gazes at her, thunderstruck. "Kit, do you have any idea how much danger you're in?"

Kit seems calm about it, which is terrifying. "Yes. My papers, my references... They all belong to someone who no longer exists. I got through the recruitment interview, but I'm not going to make it through the security review." She makes a sad snort. "If I leave now, at least I'll have a head start."

"You should've left a week ago." It's a comment designed to hurt, and Moya is glad to see Kit flinch; maybe she'll start taking this seriously.

The library door opens, and Dottie walks back in with a tray—and Violet, hard on her heels. Violet's dressed warm in a camel trench coat, a green woolen dress with long sleeves, and a brown cardigan. She brings cold air into the room, and Moya's glad to see her: Maybe, between the two of them, they can make Kit see sense.

"I just got back into the compound," Violet says, shucking her coat and throwing it on the sofa arm, tugging off her gloves. "They kept all the Black unit members out front of the gate for a half hour, double-checking badges like they don't know we belong inside." She glares at Kit, on the club chair. "You didn't arrive at my house last night. What the heck are you still doing here?"

"I couldn't leave." Kit shrugs. "The air raid—"

"Was *last night*. You should be twenty miles away by now!"

"I fell asleep."

"You're *insane*," Violet says, shaking her head.

Dottie finally sets her tray on the low table between the wingback and the chesterfield. "Coffee." Her face is still sour, but she also looks very tired. "I made it myself—the kitchen staff haven't been allowed back in the building yet."

"And I stayed for coffee," Kit says to Violet, but it sounds feeble.

"You stayed to give your apologies, is what this is, and you're risking your *life*." Violet turns to Moya and Dottie. "Look, I know she's not the real Katherine Sutherland, and maybe that ruffles your skirts. But she's just another girl trying to get by, like all of us. And right now, she should be as far away from Signal Intelligence as she can possibly be. If they catch her—"

"*Stop*. Just...wait and let me think." Moya's fingers curl into fists, which she puts at her forehead for a moment. But it's going to take more than a moment to sort out this mess. She releases her hands, reaches for the coffee pot, pours a little of the milky-looking brew into three cups—there's only three on the tray. She passes a cup to Violet. "Drink that and give me a second."

Kit reaches for a cup to hand to Dottie on automatic, falters when she realizes that Dottie is just staring at her. But then Dottie's fatigue seems to overcome her indignation. She takes the cup and settles herself on the couch.

Violet only takes one sip before the quiet seems to bug her. "You know she can't stay—"

"But she can't leave, either," Moya interrupts. She drums her fingers on her velvet-napped knee, still thinking hard. "Day shift is about to start."

"It's berserk out there," Violet says. "All the girls who were on swing, who got stuck during the air raid, plus girls from the graveyard shift calling to ask if they should've been here, plus the girls coming in to start at eight. It's a good time to make a break for it."

"But she doesn't have to go *yet*," Moya insists, her heart beating a furious tattoo against her ribs.

"What if the guy from the ballroom reports her? The one who knows her family?"

"I never told Lascar where she worked, so he wouldn't know who to call." Moya worries her thumbnail with her teeth. "If she got in last night, her badge is still good, and the security review hasn't made it to the end of the alphabet."

"She should go while she's able," Violet points out, "not cut it fine."

Moya knows Violet's idea won't run. "That sounds sensible, but it's not. She'll draw more attention if she doesn't show up for work. She'll be reported to Human Resources."

Kit opens her mouth; then she seems to change her mind. She says nothing, sips her coffee. Wise choice.

Dottie, forlorn, warms her hands on her cup. "I can't believe this is all happening on my day off."

That's it. Moya looks up. "Dot, you're right. Kit should leave on her day off. That's only a few days away—Wednesday, right?" Moya checks Kit's nod. "Then we aim for Wednesday. Until then, we act like normal. Me and Kit and Violet go to work. Dottie takes her off day to rest. I'll make some arrangements so if Kit leaves Wednesday, they won't expect her back until late—that'll throw them off her scent for a few extra hours."

"She's an *impostor*!" Dottie's voice is raised, and she bangs her cup on the tray. "How are we supposed to act *normal*?"

"Be *quiet*," Moya hisses. "Do you want her to *hang*?" Her body shakes with the effort required to regain control, but she bears down. "This is the best way to do it."

"I think it's crazy to wait so long," Violet blurts out. "But if this is how you want to play it..."

Kit's eyes are darting between them all. "You're forgetting something. What about the murder? What about the girl at the Mayflower—"

Dottie stands and whirls away, throwing up her hands.

"Oh, hon." Violet shakes her head tiredly. "That's not your concern anymore."

"But that girl—"

"Kit." Moya gives her the hardest stare, trying to make her understand. "Don't fight me on this. I'm trying to help you get away."

"Moya—"

"*Please.*" Moya feels the tension in all her muscles. Her voice, without permission, turns ragged. "I can only save the life of one girl at a time."

212

22

No, the codes weren't like a crossword puzzle or an anagram—codes aren't
meant to be solvable. Some codes we
never solved. We kept trying, though.
                          —BRIGID GLADWELL

They leave the coffee tray in the library. Dottie says she'll
return and pick it up later, but that right now, she just
wants to get out of her maid uniform. Moya leaves for
her own room, to step out of black velvet and into work
clothes—Kit hates to see her leave. Violet heads onward to
the cottage.

Kit slips her coat off to cover the carpetbag as she trudges
up the stairs. She's still peculiarly numb. It occurs to her
that she's tried to escape Arlington Hall twice, only to turn
back at the door.

At least she can wear her own shoes, now.

Today. Tomorrow. Two days after.

That's all the time she has left. She has to put thoughts of
Dinah Shaw and Libby Armstrong and this new girl aside.
She needs to focus on maintaining her disguise for another
four days and maybe—just maybe—find a way to make
amends with Moya and Dottie. If that's even possible.

Kit hangs up her coat and handbag behind the door in
her room. She has to go to the workroom, but what will she

say to the other girls there? How can she make conversation now? In four days, she will be gone.

She takes her toiletries out of the carpetbag. Hasn't this whole nine months been one long process of leaving? Didn't she know in her heart that one day she would just have to disappear?

With a sigh, she slides the carpetbag under her bed, next to the trunk. There's no point unpacking the rest of it. She thinks of the lies she's told, to maintain her fake identity, to keep herself safe.... Is that why she's so compelled to find justice for the girls who were killed? Has she been trying to balance out her everyday lies and betrayal with dogged gestures of moral decency and virtue?

Or is it because she has fought hard to *have* a life, and Dinah and Libby and this new girl—Kit doesn't even know her name—never had the same chance?

Kit growls at herself, opens the door.

Down the hall and around the corner, in the workroom, everything is quiet paper rustlings, pencil scratchings, and the smell of rose talcum powder.

Opal shifts her cards off Kit's desk space. "Sorry! I didn't know if you were going to show—"

"I overslept after the raid," Kit says. Another lie—my god, she's full of them. She clears her throat as she takes her place at the table. "Is everything back to normal now? Were there any news reports about it?"

"Just the usual," Carol says, poking her head up as she reaches for another card. "A cab ran into a ditch. A bunch of government girls said they were denied entry to an air raid shelter at Catholic University by the man at the door. Oh, and a lady fell onto the railway track at Union."

"Was she all right?"

Carol shrugs. "They didn't say."

"But was it a drill or an actual raid?"

"Nobody seems to know."

"Great," Kit sighs. Then her gaze lights on the new bundles of cards. "Blue cards, now?"

"Yep," Brigid says, from the other side of the table. She rolls her eyes. "And you're gonna *love* them."

That usually means the code is hard. Kit selects a card from the top of her wire tray and examines it. The first thing she notices is that the message seems abbreviated. It's only a few lines of digits, and there's no obvious address code.

The address code is usually at the start of every message, and it's distinct because that code is different from the code of the message itself. The address specifies who the message is from, who it's going to, and where those units are located—which is interesting enough on its own—and it's usually a good place to try first, because there are almost always repetitions of things like greetings and acknowledgments and honorifics.

"Where's the address?" She shuffles through the other blue cards in her tray. "None of them have addresses?"

Opal shakes her head, her expression grave. She holds up the bundle in her hand. "Look at this—all the cards left over from last night."

"But that's—"

215

Kit stops, stands, and looks up and down the table. In every tray, there are twice as many bundles as usual. Edith, at the end of the row, has an empty basket for the overlapper. *An empty basket.*

Kit turns back to Opal. "No breaks? Nothing?"

"A whole room full of dead ducks," Opal confirms mournfully. She throws up a hand. "I mean, sure. The girls on graveyard got held up with the raid. But this stuff is just... really tough."

"Okay, let me see." Kit picks up her pencil and begins her first card. Her initial impression is that Opal and Brigid are right—there won't be a simple solution to this code. It won't be like yesterday, when they had their big haul of breaks: Someone has figured out that the previous cipher was too easy to read, or maybe the Japanese have just changed to a fresh codebook. Sometimes it's like that, a rash of tricky messages when the codebook first changes over. "I guess you've tried all the obvious attacks." Kit runs her pencil down the rows. "These are all stripped?"

"That pile, yup." Opal passes her an eraser. "Edith said she might've found a repetition in one of her cards, but she's nowhere near a break."

"Can I see?"

There's a moment of consultation with Edith, and some of the other girls crowd around. Kit thinks Edith's math is sound. Carol makes a suggestion, and they try a few of the more advanced techniques on the message on Kit's card. But the numbers that come out the other end make no sense whatsoever.

"This isn't working," Opal notes. "Has anyone tried chaining differences?"

"I tried that." Another girl, Florence, from the other side of the room. "It was a bust."

"Well, there's got to be *something* we can do to get in," Kit says, and the girls all agree to try different strategies. Edith and Carol make up copies of two cards—one of Kit's and one of Brigid's—and everyone sets to attacking the same two messages from different angles.

By lunch, there's still no result. Some of the girls are getting frustrated, and Opal has to cheer them along. "Remember, ladies, this isn't flower arranging." She fans herself with the cards in her hand. "You have to be prepared to work at it and fail—then pick yourself back up and work at it again."

But it's tough when you keep getting thrown down over and over. It's especially hard when the girls know that without a code break, boys in the field are going to be left wide open and vulnerable. Without these breaks, American boys will die.

By the end of the shift, Kit's head is aching and she's sure hers is not the only one. She takes the stairs down to the cafeteria, her shoes clumping heavily with each step. Over a dinner of franks and beans, she tries to encourage the numbers to dribble out of her head. But that doesn't leave much behind except a renewed sense of loneliness: Neither Moya nor Dottie have crossed her path all day, and Violet will have finished her shift and gone home.

Kit goes for a walk on the grounds, then to the library to collect a book before heading back to her room. After a shower, she tidies her things and reads in bed. Dottie still hasn't returned.

Kit finds her mind straying from the words on the page every time she hears footsteps in the corridor. Finally, as she's about to turn off her light and have an early night, another set of footsteps, and the doorknob turns.

Dottie bustles in, with two paper shopping bags in one hand and her handbag over her other arm. She goes straight to the wardrobe to put her things away, and she does not look at Kit.

"Did you go shopping in the city?" Kit asks.

The doors of the wardrobe are open, and Dottie doesn't answer. Kit can see herself, in her pajamas, reflected in the mirror on the wardrobe door.

Kit tries again. "Did you have a nice day off?"

Dottie still doesn't answer. She collects her towel and toiletries and pajamas. Leaves the room.

Kit sighs. She sets her book aside, lies back on her pillow, and thinks of Opal's speech to the girls in the workroom. *You have to be prepared to work at it and fail—then pick yourself back up and work at it again.*

When Dottie comes back into the room, she turns off the light and gets into bed.

It's very quiet for a while, there in the dark.

"I didn't want to lie to you," Kit says to the room. "It wasn't that I didn't trust you. You're my best friend. I just… didn't know how to say it."

The sound of Dottie turning over in bed, to face the wall.

"I'm sorry," Kit says.

She waits, hoping. But there's no reply. After a while, she hears Dottie's breathing level out.

Kit dashes the sleeve of her pajama shirt against her damp eyes. *Dammit.*

But there's still a chance. She has three more days.

She pushes the blankets down to her chest, feeling stifled. All she has is words—*I'm sorry, I didn't mean to hurt you, please forgive me*—and maybe that's not enough. Maybe she needs more. If she could show Moya and Dottie somehow...

But show them what? That she's still trustworthy? How are they ever going to believe that? If she were in their place, she'd find it hard to believe.

She turns the problem over and over in her mind, without result, then tries to put it out of her head. There's nothing else to think about except the numbers on the blue cards in the workroom. The lack of an address on the blue cards makes no sense and makes everything harder, because the beginning is the best place to open up the message.

She mentally adds and subtracts from the numbers in the first row of her sample card—she spent so many hours working over it today, she knows it by heart. None of the numbers she adds or subtracts help reveal anything.

Kit glances at the glow-in-the-dark hands of the alarm clock: 11:07 PM. She should be tired. How did the girl in the Mayflower get from the ballroom to the storage area off the stairwell? She could've been coaxed out of the ballroom by the killer. Entranced by his good looks and charm. How was this girl fooled? How does the killer know just which buttons to press, to make a girl trust him? How did he know which buttons to press for *this* girl?

And what was her name?

Goddammit.

Kit throws off the blankets and reaches for her robe, scuffs on her slippers. She tries to keep quiet—Dottie is trying to sleep, and Kit is already operating on a goodwill deficit. She goes to the door and finds her handbag, fumbles inside it. The little white business card is at the very bottom, caught on the bag lining.

She gathers up the notepad and pencil from beside her bed, then goes back to the door and leaves the room.

There is a pay phone in the schoolhouse, but it's in the kitchen. Kit goes all the way down to the first floor, pads across the foyer and through the cafeteria in her slippers and robe. A group of girls drinking coffee, on a break in the cafeteria, look at her with amusement before resuming their conversation. Kit knocks at the lintel of the kitchen door to get the attention of a staff member and is shown the location of the staff pay phone: It's in the back of the pantry.

She moves a couple of cans of green beans aside so she can lay her notepad on the pantry shelf. It's not until she lifts the receiver that she realizes she didn't think to bring a nickel. She has to contact the operator and call collect.

Fortunately, Raffi Ramale is a night owl.

23

Sunday morning and Moya is still in her pajamas. She doesn't know if she has the energy to get out of bed and find something to wear.

She will, though. It's what she does: Every morning, she gets up and finds her costume in the armoire, does her hair and makeup, dons her glamorous shield, and steps out to do battle. On the days she's feeling low, she makes herself look particularly good. It's a kind of armor and it's useful, but the effort involved is so damn tiring.

She wishes that calling in sick didn't feel like cowardice.

When a knock comes on the door, the accompanying voice makes her catch her breath.

"Moya, it's me. I need to talk to you." A pause. "Moya, are you still in there?"

The alarm clock reads 7:02 AM.

Maybe, if she's really quiet, Kit will give up.

But Kit persists. "Moya, I know you're inside—I can smell your cigarette smoke. Come on, please open up."

Moya swears sotto voce, stubs out her cigarette, and puts the ashtray on the nightstand. She applauds herself for not glancing at her reflection while passing the armoire—she shouldn't care anymore how she looks in front of Kit. She jerks the tie of her men's dressing gown into a hard knot at her waist and yanks open the door.

Kit walks in and begins speaking without preamble. "The girl at the Mayflower was Veronica Luca. She was twenty years old, and she arrived with a colleague from the War Department, another stenographer. She was killed in the linen room off the stairs—the place where staff usually store tablecloths and napkins and kitchen supplies."

Kit ticks off things on her fingers. She's wearing the peacock-blue utility dress with a cashmere cardigan, and she would look nicely put together, except her hair is a fluffy mess.

"Kit, what are you doing here?" Moya resists the urge to reach out and tuck Kit's hair into place. She crosses her arms against her chest instead.

"Close the door and I'll explain."

"I am not—" Moya cuts herself off when she realizes that the volume of her voice is already rising. This is the last thing she needs everyone to know about, so she closes the door. "Okay, the door is closed. That doesn't mean I want you to explain. I told you that you need to let the murder investigation go—"

"And I understand that," Kit says. "I do. But I'm here for three more days, and I can help with—"

"We don't want you to help. Me and Dottie and Violet will be fine without—"

"I need to *do something.*" Kit throws her hands out. "I can't stop thinking about it. And while I'm still here, I may as well—"

"*No*," Moya says. "Kit, for God's sake, let it go. Why do you even care? You're *leaving*."

"*I've never wanted to leave.*" Kit's face is flushed, her breathing hard. All her words come out clipped. "I know you don't trust me, and that's understandable, but we *had* something, Moya. Something I don't want to say goodbye to. I've spent four years in the Hall, and I never wanted to leave—and I especially don't want to leave *now*."

There's a long silence as they stand there staring at each other. Moya wants to be angry, knows she *should* be angry, but the anger won't come. It's deeply confusing.

Kit smooths a hand over the front of her dress and gathers herself with an effort. "Raffi gave me his number on a business card the night we went to Club Caverns. I...I couldn't sleep last night, so I called him. He gave me a lot of information about Veronica Luca's murder."

"You called Raffi?" Moya finds her voice has gone hoarse.

"Yes." Kit looks up, into Moya's eyes. "I have three days left, and I want to use them to do something good. Three days—that's all. Please give me three days, and after that I swear I'll go quietly. I'll cooperate with anything you want me to do."

"Three days." Moya balls her hands into fists to stop herself from reaching out.

"Yes." Kit's body seems to sway forward, in Moya's direction, but she changes her momentum at the last minute to step toward the armoire. "I need to look at the murder board.

I need to check something. Raffi said there was something left behind at the scene of Veronica Luca's death—a small pink purse. I remember what we noticed at the scene of Libby's murder, in the laundry at the Farms—"

"Libby Armstrong didn't have a purse," Moya says. She has shifted back, and now she watches as Kit pulls the armoire doors open, pushes the clothing to each side.

"That's what *he* took." Kit stands in front of the armoire, scanning the patchworked collection of notes and cards and maps and pictures. She taps a note. "There—I put it down in my report, that Libby's purse was missing."

"So he's left another souvenir at this new murder." Moya finds that, despite herself, she's caught up in the trajectory of Kit's train of thought.

"That's three murders now. And I need to check the records on Dinah." Kit turns to face Moya directly. "And I want to have another meeting. Today, at lunch."

"*Today?*"

"I have an idea, and if I can get a confirmation from Dinah's notes, I'd like to share it with the whole group. Maybe once I'm gone, you can all do something useful with it."

It's really not helpful, Moya thinks, how she turns to total putty whenever Kit looks at her with those sincere, soulful eyes, her whole body radiating fervent determination. But that's Moya's reaction, and unfortunately, she's stuck with it.

Right now, she can only press her lips together and nod her assent.

24

The training book said that the two places where codes are best attacked are at the beginning and at the end, so we always tried those first. And wouldn't you know—it worked.

—OPAL BUKOWSKI

"Talk fast," Violet says, chafing her hands together in their fingerless woolen gloves. "I took the early shift break, so I need to be back in ten minutes."

They're gathered at the stables attached to the old indoor riding arena. It was a walk away, but Moya said they couldn't all gather in the gazebo without attracting attention: The gazebo is close to the schoolhouse and visible from the cottage. The stables, on the other hand, are deeper into the forest, out of sight of the main buildings and the construction zone. Kit can see past the rows of empty stalls to the riding arena entrance. The smell of livestock and old leather lingers, but it's been nearly a year since they sent all the horses away. The building is surrounded by trees, and while the sky higher up is a clear, sunny blue, the air around them is dark and crisp. Kit has her arms crossed against the chill, scuffing the soles of her shoes against the remnants of dried sawdust. Moya stands by the door, bundled in a coat with a draping collar. She's lit another cigarette and looks like she's exhaling plumes of frost as she faces out toward the trees.

Dottie is near the entrance to the old tack room, in a winter skirt with thick stockings and a cream sweater with little decorative red bows that Kit has always disliked. "This is crazy. I don't know why we're all here—"

"We're here because I was given some information about the most recent murder, of Veronica Luca," Kit says. "Libby Armstrong's pink purse was found beside Veronica's body."

Dottie crosses her own arms, echoing Kit's pose. "What does it matter now?"

"It matters because we're not giving up on this," Kit insists. "Even when I go, you three will keep working on this, right?"

"Right," Violet says immediately.

Moya glances at Kit, but only briefly. "Right."

Dottie throws up her hands. "Okay, fine, I guess."

Kit confronts Dottie head-on. "Listen. These murders are bigger than anything going on with *me*. We owe it to the victims—and to every potential victim—to keep going. Do we agree on that or not?"

Dottie's pretty mouth purses, but she nods. "Yes, we agree."

"Good." Kit relaxes a little. "Because we need to get that straight. And I have a theory about the murders that I want to tell you before I go."

"A theory." Dottie still looks unconvinced.

"That's right." Kit shifts on her feet, releasing some tension. "Look, Raffi told me that Libby's purse was found near

Veronica's body, and Moya and I checked the notes to confirm. Then I went back and checked the notes on Dinah's effects, from the hospital. Dinah was given an object, too—but it was so small, we never picked up on it."

Violet's hands still. "What object?"

"A ring." Kit slips the index card she wrote in Moya's room out of her pocket, to read from. "In her effects, there was a small silver ring."

"How do you know it wasn't Dinah's?" Dottie asks.

"Because it was engraved: *Always in my heart MW + DT.*" Kit shows them where she's scrawled the details of the engraving on the card. "*MW*—Margaret Wishart."

"The girl who drowned," Moya says quietly, from her satellite position. She's still turned contemplatively outward.

"I think we can say, pretty conclusively now, that she didn't drown." Kit lets her expression become serious. "And I don't think we'll make any progress on this unless we try a different approach."

"What do you mean?" Violet rubs at her biceps.

"I mean we need to start getting ahead of the killer."

"The man who's killing these girls is smart," Dottie points out. "We knew it would be hard."

"Yes, he's smart," Kit agrees. "We *did* already know that. And we can go over and over the information about the murders. But without a new strategy, we're just reacting, waiting for the next girl to die. That's not right. If we keep playing it like that, more girls die, and we're always going to be two steps behind."

227

"What kind of new strategy did you have in mind?" Moya has stepped closer, her face pale and sharp.

Kit feels herself resonate with Moya's nearness, has to focus on what she's trying to say. "Okay, you all know that the easiest points of entry for any code are the beginning and the end. They're the places most vulnerable to attack." Kit pushes through her heels to stand firm. "Margaret Wishart was killed, but not stabbed. Her ring was the first souvenir. I think Margaret Wishart's murder was the beginning. We need to find out as much as we can about it—I want to go to the place where she was killed."

"What will that do?" Dottie frowns. "She died *months* ago. What do you think will still be there?"

"I don't know," Kit admits. "But it's the place the killer started. We have to start there, too."

Violet sucks on her teeth. "We'd have to catch the bus. I'll need to check the timetable for the bus that goes along Maine Avenue Southwest."

"Can you check it now? Can we go after work?"

Dottie's mouth screws up. "You want to go today?"

"I don't have many todays left," Kit says quietly.

"We go today. This afternoon." Moya pulls her coat around herself. Now she surveys each of them in turn. "Margaret was murdered in January, and Dinah a month later. Libby was killed two weeks ago. He struck again on Friday. He's speeding up. We need to move fast before another girl dies."

25

The golden guess is the learning star
of truth.

—WILLIAM FRIEDMAN

The bus is an old clunker, like every bus Kit has ever been on. Kit stands in the aisle, near the back, and Moya takes a seat close by. There are plenty of other commuters: girls from the Hall, two boys in service uniforms, a couple of matronly women in brown utility dresses with their hair tucked under scarves, marking them as cleaning staff. Kit feels a pang of recognition.

She also gets a sliding sense of dislocation when Violet gets on the bus with everyone else and promptly moves to the rear seats. Dottie settles herself next to Violet without thinking, but Violet frowns at her.

"You can't sit here."

Dottie is oblivious. "But...it's an empty seat."

"These are the segregated seats," Violet hisses, looking sideways, away. "You can't sit here."

Dottie's face screws up, uncomprehending, but she gets up and moves one row forward, to sit beside Moya.

"Better," Violet says, visibly relaxing.

"This is ridiculous," Dottie grumps. "I'm only sitting one seat in front of you. I'm talking to you over the seat!"

"Don't make a scene about it," Violet murmurs. "You'll just make trouble for me."

"Well, fine," Dottie says. "But it's ridiculous."

"Tell that to the Arlington County Board."

"We never did this in Baltimore," Dottie huffs.

"Are you sure about that?" Violet crosses her arms. "Maybe you just never noticed."

"Uh, ladies?" People are glancing their way, so Kit decides to change the subject. She lowers her voice. "We should talk about possible suspects."

Violet raises her eyebrows. "We have possible suspects now?"

"We each talked to people at the Mayflower," Kit reminds her. "So what did we learn?"

"Apart from the obvious." Dottie flicks a glance in Kit's direction.

Kit smothers her sense of guilt. "We haven't pooled our information yet, but the man we're after was there—so who did we talk to?"

Moya has been looking out the window, but she turns back now, eyes clouded in thought. "Of the guests we were introduced to, only a few of them seemed to be on target. John Farrell was one. Bob Martelli. Richard Norton. They're all under thirty-five, well-to-do, handsome, charming."

"And some of them are powerful," Kit notes.

Moya nods. "Raffi's looking into their affiliations, to see if any of them have links to the Bund. Bob Martelli's father is big in tobacco. Richard is well-connected in the War Department."

"Which would put him in a good position to pick out girls," Dottie muses.

"John Farrell was the youngest," Kit adds. "I could see him at a jitterbug dance. Not the others, though."

"Maybe." Moya shrugs. "Dottie, did you get word on anyone?"

Dottie shakes her head. "I was pretty much run off my feet all night, so I didn't get a chance to gossip. But there was a man in the crowd who kept coming over, asking for drinks, giving me compliments...."

"A pest, in other words," Violet says, voice dry.

Dottie grimaces and nods. "He was about twenty-five, good-looking. I managed to get his name—Henry Robinson."

"That's a commonplace name," Kit says, wincing.

"Sure is. But I got his workplace, too. He's with the Securities and Exchange Commission."

"Nice job, Dottie," Kit says admiringly.

Dottie glows for a moment before remembering that she doesn't like Kit anymore and switching to a confused frown.

Kit wants to sigh. She turns to Violet instead. "Did you have any luck at the Mayflower?"

"I spent more time in back-of-house than Dottie," Violet says, nodding. "All the girls I spoke to said to avoid one guy—Charlie Sharpe."

Moya seems intrigued. "Did you get a look at him?"

"Oh, yeah. He came up to me for champagne one time. Tall white guy, a little on the skinny side but kind of a wiry skinny, y'know? Strong. About thirty—he might've been younger—and a very slimy smile. He even tucked his card into my apron."

"Yuck, but great work." Kit finds the information exciting. "Have you still got this card?"

"Right here." Violet takes out her purse and scrounges inside with her neatly gloved fingers. The business card is on heavy cream cardstock, with elegant typography. It reads *Charles Sharpe, MD,* and it has a handwritten phone number.

"He's a doctor?" Kit gets an electric sizzle of excitement. "That would fit very well with what we know—smart, good at planning, good with knives.... Violet, you're a champ."

"I know, right?" Violet grins. "If he falls into our lap like this, I swear I'm gonna crow about it."

"You just said it, though," Moya observes. "If he falls into our lap. You know statistics, so you know the chances of that happening—in a city of nearly six hundred thousand people— are pretty low. I mean, we'll give all these names to Raffi to dig up more info, but realistically, chances are that *none* of the men we spoke to at the Mayflower are the killer."

Kit bites her lip, looks out the window. They've traveled past the Jefferson Memorial and the Tidal Basin, gone along Maine Avenue SW, and now they're turning onto Water Street. There are almost no trees near this side of the Potomac, but the ones that survive have newly rejuvenated branches stretching skyward.

"But he was there," Kit says. "He was *right there*, in the ballroom. Mingling with the guests or lurking around in back-of-house... and he had his equipment with him."

"If the police had stopped and searched him, he'd be in jail right now," Dottie realizes.

Kit nods. "And Veronica Luca would still be alive."

"We're too slow," Violet declares. "We're connecting information too slowly to act on it."

"Not this time," Kit says darkly. "This time we start trying to get ahead of him."

Dottie presses the bell for their stop. The area they pile out onto is windblown and smells briny. Traffic passes, creates a buzz to compete with the wind, but there are fewer private cars and more delivery vans and utility trucks. From where she's standing on the sidewalk, Kit can see a sign for an oyster bar and a drugstore across the street. Farther to the right, a pool hall. Beyond that, a series of rowhouses starts.

"There's traffic enough on the street," Kit notes. "He's damn confident, this guy—the attacks are all in populated places."

Halfway up the next block, a man at a trestle stall is gutting his catch and throwing the fish innards behind him, off the edge of the sidewalk and into the water. Dottie wrinkles her nose at the smell of the pungent breeze. "What was Margaret Wishart doing in a place like this anyway? She can't have been catching the ferry in January."

"Was the ferry running at all?" Kit asks. "We should get a timetable."

"There was no mention in the news report of why she was here," Moya says, "and the ferry still runs short trips across the channel in the winter, to East Potomac Park. But she might not have been on the ferry—she might have come to the seafood market." Moya lifts her chin toward the fisherman and his stall, her loose hair blowing across her throat in the chill wind. She shivers. "God, it's freezing here. Let's move over to the ticket office."

They have to walk down a ways to find the pier 4 ticket office, a small brick building with a gabled roof. The long length of the pier stretches out behind the office, over the water. A marquee-style wooden pavilion covers most of the pier.

The ticket office they're sheltering by has stout iron gates blocking entry on either side. Beyond the pier and its covered waiting pavilion, Kit can see all the way across the channel to the green of the park.

"Folks still fish off the pier," Violet notes. "Maybe not this one, but some of the others."

Kit scans the street-side entrance and the nearest gate. "Can we get down to the waterline from here?"

Moya checks the gate—thoroughly locked—and then cranes her neck to look for a ferry worker. "Nobody seems to be around."

"Sunday," Violet reminds her. "People will mostly be at St. Dominic's."

"Handy for us," Moya says. Kit watches her walk toward the edge of the building.

"Do you know where exactly Margaret Wishart was found?" Violet asks. "Who found her?"

Kit is distracted by the lean lines of Moya's figure beneath the layers of coat and tweed trousers. She has to focus on Violet's question. "The news report only said 'two stevedores'—it didn't give their names. But she was found beneath a pylon close to the water's edge."

Dottie shivers. "She must've been half frozen over."

"Ladies—over here." Moya calls. She's gesturing from the far left corner of the building.

"Oh, she isn't," Dottie breathes.

"Looks like she is." Kit grins. "Come on."

As they approach Moya's spot, Kit discovers that where the brick edge of the pier meets the road, the fence is only braced iron struts, just waist high. Obviously, nobody thought pedestrians would be so foolish as to venture over the fence.

Attached to the brickwork are the rungs of an iron ladder leading straight to the water.

"I'm not going down there," Dottie declares.

"Where's your sense of adventure, Dot?" Moya gives her a bland look before taking off her coat and handing it to Violet. "No, I'm going alone. I'm the only one who had the good sense to wear trousers."

Kit's quite certain that Moya gives her a hot, fleeting glance. Then Moya has slung her legs over the fence and is maneuvering her way onto the ladder.

"Be careful," Kit says automatically, anxious butterflies in her belly as she watches Moya descend.

"Smell nice down there?" Violet calls.

"Lovely." Moya wrinkles her nose, managing to appear both capable and elegant while clinging with both hands to a ladder. Moya's feet stand on another rung about three feet from the lapping gray water. "Yes, the delightful aroma of bilge."

"What can you see?" Kit asks.

"Pylons." Moya looks over her shoulder in the other direction. "There's no bank to speak of—the water goes directly up to the pier, right to the drop-off from the sidewalk."

"So Margaret didn't die here, unless she and the killer struggled in the water."

"Seems doubtful." Violet steps back, looking through the iron gate to the length of the pier. "It would've been easy for him to catch her in the pavilion on the pier, though. Or he could've grabbed her at any point along Water Street, dragged her into a secluded corner, then dumped her body off the sidewalk straight into the channel."

"She would've just floated down until she got caught on something," Dottie says. She shivers.

Kit looks at how close Moya's feet are to the water. "You can come up now."

"Wait," Moya says, and she looks toward the rear of the ticket office, a new note in her voice. She steps up one rung, then stretches her left foot across a gap between the brickwork and the concrete pile beneath the abutment that marks the start of the pier.

"Moya—" Kit starts.

"Almost..." Moya's toes touch, then hold. She's wearing her soft boots, which helps, but it still makes Kit nervous. Then Moya's standing with one foot on a huge rusty bolt in the pile, legs straddling the gap. She quickly slings her hand across to grab an iron cleat on the abutment, probably used for tying off boats. She uses the cleat and the wooden edge of the pier to haul herself up to the walkway in one strong motion.

"Are you crazy?" Violet calls. "Someone could come along! How are you gonna get back?"

But Moya ignores that. She walks swiftly over to an area behind the gabled ticket office, someplace the rest of them can't see.

Kit jogs back to the iron gate, grabbing it with both hands. "Moya, what are you doing?" There's a minute's lull in which she can't see Moya at all. "Moya?"

A flash of movement, then Moya reappears. "Take this."

She locks eyes with Kit, presses something into Kit's hands through the jail-like gate bars. Kit feels Moya's breath on her face. It's the closest she and Moya have been to each other since the night at the Mayflower, and Kit feels the connection like a zap of electricity. They could reach their arms through the bars and hug each other in this moment— but she'll be damned if she only gets to touch Moya with iron bars between them.

"Come back out. Right now," Kit urges. Part of the urgency is concern that Moya will get caught; a larger part is that she wants Moya back within arm's reach.

Moya nods. "Coming now."

She dashes back to the edge of the walkway. Kit moves over hurriedly to where Violet and Dottie watch Moya lever herself down onto the cleat, then lower to the eye bolt. Her booted foot skids once on the bolt, holds. Kit releases a breath.

"Goddammit, she's gonna slip and end up in the water," Dottie mutters.

"She'll be fine," Violet says, the breeze pulling dark curls out of her French roll and dashing them against her face. "And if she falls in the drink, we'll just haul her out and get a cab home."

The bundle in Kit's hands is cold fabric, stiff and greasy to the touch, but she doesn't look at it until Moya has navigated the distance between the bolt and the ladder, climbed up the rungs, and—with Violet's helping hand—scrambled over the fence and back onto the sidewalk.

"Made it." Moya grins, but she's shivering. She takes her coat back from Violet gratefully, then gestures at Kit, who returns the bundle to her as they all gather around.

"What is that?" Dottie asks.

Moya squeezes the cold-stiffened fingers of one hand into a fist, shakes them out. With her other hand, she grips the bundle of dirty sailcloth. "There's an equipment hut behind the ticket house. I saw it when I was looking over the abutment, and I got an idea. Look at this."

She unfolds the waxed, waterproof canvas—and reveals three knives.

Violet sucks in a breath. "Oh my lord."

"I was watching that man doing the gutting over there and thinking of the fish market," Moya says, "and that's when I realized. Margaret Wishart wasn't cut—but her death was the first. And this is where he got the *idea* for the cutting. When he saw tools like these."

"That's a fisherman's knife." Dottie points at a long case knife with a caribou handle. "Papa sells them in the store. You open it out; it's got a little hook sharpener on the pick."

"And that's another fishing knife," Kit notes. "A scaler.

They make them the same in West Virginia, with the cork handle so they float. And that's a fillet knife."

Violet picks the fillet knife out of the bundle. The wooden handle is brown from use, and the leather sheath is long. When she slides it out of the sheath, it emerges with a whisper: eight inches of worn-down steel, razor-sharp.

"Ladies," she says, angling the blade to catch the light, "I think we've just figured out the murder weapon."

26

Well, you don't *have* to understand the
language of the codes you're deciphering. It helps, but it's not necessary.
                                    —BRIGID GLADWELL

"So we've got a weapon," Dottie says. "What else have we got?"

Moya's sitting beside Kit, back on the bus, which is less crowded now. The sun is sinking, and the light coming through the bus windows is pale pinkish-yellow. Violet has taken her county-assigned seat, just behind Kit's shoulder, with Dottie in the seat across the aisle from theirs.

Moya is tired in her bones. Whether it was the excitement of the afternoon, the lateness of the night before, or the emotional exhaustion of the last few days, she doesn't know. But as they travel along Washington Boulevard, she feels the rattle of the bus rocking her into a nap.

Only she can't rest yet. "Okay." She sits up straighter. "He's tall, white, wealthy, good-looking. He's well-connected, if he's going to political parties—but obviously he keeps his personal political affiliations quiet. He's confident—has been from the beginning, it looks like. He has his own car."

"I've been thinking about that," Kit says. "Could he be sharing? I know that a lot of people are now sharing one vehicle and splitting their gas ration."

"It's possible, I guess," Violet says. "But if he's rich and connected, would he need to do that?"

"Fair point."

"We have the four locations where he's struck," Dottie says, picking up the thread. "Can we assume now he's on the west-southwest side? Or at least that's the area he knows well."

"Good thinking." Moya rubs her temple, where a headache is building. "It's all still too vague."

"We've got the contours of the man, but nothing solid," Kit agrees.

"Don't sell it short," Violet reminds her. "We've got a good idea of who he is, what he's done, the weapon he used to do it."

"But we don't really understand why he's doing it, which means we can't get the jump on what he'll do next." Kit smooths her skirt over her knee; Moya hears the pencil calluses on her fingers catch on the fabric. "He's *saying* something with these murders. Sending a message. But what's the message? It feels more like a personal statement than a political one, and I can't figure it out. It's like…I can't understand his language."

Moya shudders. "Do you really want to?"

"To find him? Yes, I do," Kit insists.

Violet lowers her voice, leans in. "Listen, are you a codebreaker or not? You've been breaking Japanese ciphers for months—do you speak Japanese? No. But you know how it works. You can break a foreign language cipher if you know how the letter arrangements in the language behave."

"We have to figure out how his letters behave." Kit cants her head, thinking. "Then we'll understand his language."

"You got it." Violet grins. "Now buck up. Okay, this is my stop. It's been a real pleasure, ladies, even if I am going home smelling like fish."

She waves as she gets off the bus. Out the window, Moya sees electricity poles and a row of slightly worn shop fronts with their awnings flapping. A series of terrace houses are strung along Arlington Boulevard here, at the corner of Glebe Road. Violet has another bus ride before she reaches Lowell Street. She seems a very small figure in a quiet area, and the landscape is darkening, the sun well below the horizon now. . . .

In the shop fronts, newspaper headlines in their wire frames scream "Government Girl Murders: Latest Updates!" The papers are turning the story into a citywide frenzy. As their bus pulls away, Moya realizes with a queasy jolt that they should all start taking more precautions when they're alone.

"Do you think it might be time to go to the police with this?" Dottie asks.

Moya snaps back from staring out the window. "What?"

"I mean, we have a lot of information now," Dottie goes on. "Should we be taking it to the police?"

Kit seems to be considering. "I don't think so."

"Why not?"

"We've got generalities, but nothing specific," Moya suggests. It's warm in the bus: She pulls the collar of her coat away from her neck and rubs her nape. "The police don't like supposition—they need proof."

"We're close," Kit says, "but not close enough."

Dottie blows out a breath. "I guess you're right. I wouldn't believe us." She narrows her eyes at Moya. "I swear, though, if you pull another stunt like the one you did today, I'm disowning you."

Moya thoroughly enjoyed her "stunt"—especially the part where she met Kit at the gate bars. "You're just jealous you didn't get to go down the ladder."

"You made me so nervous!" Dottie laughs and glances over. "Kit, too."

"She was not." Moya gives Kit a look.

"She was," Kit confirms, shrugging. "I can't help it. I'm a worrier."

Dottie snorts, grins at Moya. "We'll both disown you."

"You wouldn't," Moya says in mock horror.

"I would." Dottie tosses her blond curls. "Don't test me."

The easy laugh between them all calms something in Moya's chest. Kit seems more relaxed, and Dottie appears to be thawing. But the knowledge that they've only got a few more days in Kit's company turns Moya's feelings melancholy.

The melancholy stays with her all the way to their stop in front of the Hall, despite Dottie's jokes about smelling like brine. Although she can't help laughing at Kit's suggestion that they all need to use the Lava soap in the schoolhouse laundry. Maybe it's just that she likes to see Kit smiling.

They arrive at the gate, dig for their badges to show the on-duty MP. Moya has a few extra moments to search as he waves through a shiny black Packard with passengers in the rear seat.

"Hey, look." Dottie lifts her chin at the car. "Are those diplomatic plates?"

"Evening, ladies," the MP says, returning to his station. He takes all three badges at once, checks their photographs, and runs his finger down a clipboard.

Moya returns her ID to her pocket, then realizes something is making her nose wrinkle. She lifts a palm and sniffs, makes a face. "You know, I *might* be using the Lava soap when we get inside."

"You ladies can go on through," the MP says. But when they move forward to the gate, he stops Kit with a hand on her arm. "Not you, ma'am."

Moya feels a sudden, swooping sensation in her stomach.

Kit glances at the MP's hand, her expression going still. "Excuse me?"

"You can't go in, ma'am." The MP looks her up and down. "Your security clearance isn't valid."

27

We had a badge, with our picture....
It was a round badge, about an inch
and a half. It was red, and had your
picture on it.
                    —WILMA BERRYMAN

Kit has a disorienting attack of vertigo.

"But this is a mistake," Moya says immediately. "We all work here. We left the grounds together at four thirty this afternoon—"

"No mistake, ma'am." The MP releases Kit's arm to point his finger at the clipboard again. "I've got a green light for Crockford, Dorothy, and Kershaw, Moya. But there's nothing here for Sutherland, Katherine."

Kit rubs her arm and sees Moya draw herself up. In an instant, she is transformed into her steely eyed, glamorous persona. Kit would be impressed if she weren't so terrified.

"Miss Sutherland is one of my girls," Moya says. "I'm her immediate supervisor. Is this a new regulation? When did this happen?"

"I was issued new instructions two hours ago," the MP admits. "Only those with a completed security check can enter."

"By completed security check, you mean the current review." Moya's gaze narrows. "That review is ongoing. Are you telling me that every girl I supervise whose surname falls somewhere below Q on the alphabet is now locked out of this facility?"

"I can't tell you that, ma'am. I don't have all the information about—"

"I want to speak to your warrant officer." Moya's posture is ramrod-straight. Even with her hair tossed and her hands briny, she looks formidable. "This is unacceptable. I want all my girls back in the building, including Miss Sutherland."

"Ma'am, I can get on the phone—"

"You do that," Moya says. Then—somehow playing both roles of castigator and mitigator—she softens her tone. "Look, I'm sure this isn't your mess, but we need to clear this up right now. I'm tired and I'm hungry, and I want to get my girls back home. Call your warrant officer, and let's get this straightened out."

As the MP gives her a relieved-looking nod and turns, walking to the guardhouse to make his call, Moya swings back to Kit.

"Look at me." Her eyes are intent and her voice is low. "You need to look like I'm telling you something reassuring, okay?"

Kit licks her lips and tries to settle the roil in her stomach, compose her face appropriately. "Okay."

"What the heck is going on?" Dottie whispers.

"Listen," Moya says, and Kit can't look away. "Dottie, get your purse—don't make a production out of it. I want you to slip Kit whatever money you have on you. Do it in a relaxed way. If this goes south and Kit has to bolt, at least she'll have some cash."

"Will I have to bolt?" Kit's stomach is full of ash. She drags her gaze from Moya's face, checks the window of the guard-house. She can see the MP, talking into a phone receiver.

"I don't know." Moya exhales a shaky breath. "God help me, I don't know."

"The diplomatic car," Dottie says suddenly. "Do you think that has something to do with all this?"

"Maybe. Have you got your purse?"

"Sure. Of course." Dottie fumbles in her coat pockets, her expression so theatrically neutral that Kit's sure the MP is going to notice. "Kit, I'm gonna turn and face the road. Moya, can you run interference?"

Moya doesn't need to reply; she simply stalks off toward the guardhouse as if she's getting ready to make another ruckus.

Kit's knees are shaky and her fingertips feel stone cold. She steps closer to Dottie, steps in front of her. Dottie's pale-faced, with a blinking blank look that dissolves a little once Kit is standing within arm's reach.

"I don't remember how much I have in my billfold," Dottie whispers. "It might not be enough."

"It doesn't matter," Kit whispers back. *Oh, Dottie.*

Dottie's voice is quavering. "I hope you don't need it. Just take it. Please."

Kit clasps Dottie's hands with her own to make the exchange. From a distance, they will look like two friends sharing encouragement. Along with the folded cash, Dottie's grip conveys warmth and desperate friendship.

She clutches Kit's hands tight. "I'm sorry I was mad. I miss being your friend. Please, God, I hope this isn't goodbye."

"Me too," Kit says. She has to swallow hard to hold back inopportune tears. "Come on, now. We should smile for the MP."

Over Dottie's shoulder, she can see Moya talking to the MP again, her gestures brusque. The ashy feeling in Kit's stomach is strong. *I should be thinking of which way to run.* But her mind has gone completely empty of directions. And now she and Dottie have to move to the side as another car—a black Chrysler—eases toward the gate off Arlington Boulevard.

As the driver's side window is rolled down, Kit recognizes the car. And the driver.

"Hey there, what's going on? What's the holdup?" Emil Ferrars is in shirtsleeves, his jacket on the passenger seat. He leans out the window, eyebrows lifting at the sight of Moya and the MP. "Lord, don't tell me that poor guy is trying to argue with Moya."

"He won't let me in," Kit blurts, then feels her blush climb to her cheeks. *As if Mr. Ferrars needs to know that!*

"He what?" Emil Ferrars grimaces, ducks his head back into the car to kill the engine. Then he gets out, grabbing his jacket. "Did you lose your badge?"

Dottie steps in. "Her badge is fine. But he says her clearance isn't valid, because she hasn't been through the security review."

Mr. Ferrars frowns. "That review is still ongoing."

"That's what Moya said!"

"Okay, I think I know what this is about." He glances toward the guardhouse, back at Dottie. "Will you be okay here for a second? I'm going to see what I can do."

"Oh, that would be..." Dottie seems a little tongue-tied. "That would be wonderful. Thank you so much."

Shrugging on his jacket, Emil Ferrars moves off to join Moya in discussion. It's cold now, and the lights have come on at the gate and in front of the cyclone fences.

"D'you think he'll be able to help?" Dottie asks.

Kit tries to quell the jitter in her knees. "I have no idea."

But clearly something shifts in the conversation, because five minutes later, Emil Ferrars and Moya return. Moya still has her stiff, formal supervisor face on, but there's not so much panic in her eyes.

"It's fine," Mr. Ferrars says with an easy smile. "You're good to go."

"Emil vouched for you," Moya says to Kit. "And we both signed slips to say that you're under our management until you get your full clearance."

"Okay." Kit experiences the relief as a falling sensation. She can't show exactly how relieved she is in front of Emil Ferrars, but she feels sweat break out in her palms. "Okay. Phew."

Dottie is able to express it more vehemently. "Oh, thank God!"

"Now, let's go," Moya says. "It's late, and we should all get in out of the cold."

"Jump in the car," Emil Ferrars offers. "I'll give you ladies a ride up to the schoolhouse."

Inside the Chrysler, it's warmer. Kit's nerves are still jangling, and the adrenaline drop has left her dizzy, so extra warmth is good. She can't talk freely in front of Mr. Ferrars, but Dottie, sitting with her in the rear seat, makes up the shortfall.

"Thank you so much for speaking on Kit's behalf," she says. "I don't know what we would have done if you hadn't come along."

"Well, I'm sure Moya would've handled it okay," Mr. Ferrars says, his cheeks coloring. He focuses on navigating the driveway. "But I couldn't leave you all standing out front of the gate in the dark."

"It was good to have someone else there to back me up," Moya says.

Mr. Ferrars glances in the rearview mirror, wets his lips. "Look, I know what's going on—and you're going to find out anyway, so I might as well tell you. There are some overseas visitors at the Hall. They arrived a few days earlier than expected, so the security review is a little behind."

Overseas visitors—*the English guys*. Kit only barely stops herself from saying it.

Moya looks flabbergasted. "I heard the visit was due. But how come I didn't know about this?"

"Word only came down late this afternoon," Mr. Ferrars says apologetically. "To be honest, we were all caught on the back foot."

"Well, I really appreciate you vouching for me," Kit says.

"No problem." Mr. Ferrars parks in his usual spot, switches off the engine. "But hey—get your clearance! It's going to be impossible to come and go without it for the next week."

"I will," Kit confirms.

"Ladies, let's move," Moya says, opening her door. "Emil, I owe you one."

"Where have I heard that before," he laughs.

"Thank you again," Dottie says as she bundles out of the car.

"You're welcome." Emil Ferrars's dark hair falls over his forehead as he gives her a gentle smile. "Nice to see you again, Miss Crockford. Are you doing okay?"

"I'm good," Dottie says, her expression transforming. "I'm great."

"Dottie, come on," Moya says; then she's hurrying them away to the door that takes them into the schoolhouse.

Kit follows Moya's lead under the stairs and along the hall. "Where are we—"

"Your room," Moya says. Her words are very clipped.

They climb the stairs all the way up to Three. Kit takes enormous comfort in the sight of her own tidy bed: If the situation weren't so urgent, she would want to just fall onto it and go straight to sleep. But that's not possible right now, so she settles for piling Dottie's crumpled money on the nightstand and then sitting on the mattress.

Dottie closes the door with her back. "Oh my god, that was close."

"Too close." *And there's a solution.* It makes Kit's chest tight, but she has to say it. "I... I should go."

"No!"

"No," Moya agrees, stripping her scarf away. She stations herself by the door as Dottie moves to the other bed. "That's a dumb idea and you know it."

Kit gestures beneath the bed. "My bag is packed. I just need to leave on some errand—"

"You can't leave yet."

"Moya, whether I go now or go Wednesday, they're going to find out *who I am*. And with visitors in the Hall—"

"I just signed for you," Moya insists. Her eyes are wide and earnest. "*Please*, Kit. I know you must be scared, but let me figure out what's going on."

Dottie has taken her coat off and dropped onto her bed. "It's the English guys, right?"

"It looks that way," Moya confirms. "But give me a minute. Kit, I mean it. Don't take off until I get more information, okay? Can you wait that long?"

Kit bites her bottom lip. "I can wait."

With a last look, Moya opens the door and walks out. Kit watches the door close behind her. It's very quiet in the room now. "It's crazy for me to stay. It puts all of you in danger by association—"

"Don't you talk like that." Dottie's expression is scathing. Then her shoulders slump, and her whole body seems to soften. "Kit, it feels so *mean*, you leaving. I know it's not your fault, but that's how it feels."

Kit nods, slow and small. "It feels like I'm abandoning you. I know it."

"Wednesday," Dottie says, sighing. "And it's petty to say so, but that's the day before my birthday."

"What?"

"My birthday is Thursday."

"I had no idea." Kit feels Wednesday getting closer every

252

minute. She looks at the familiar interior of the room: the window with its dark green curtains, the towels hanging on the back of the door. Her roommate, whose defining traits are her generosity and her kindness. Sitting opposite each other like this, their knees are nearly touching. Kit doesn't want to cry. "Dottie, I'm so sorry. I'm sorry I didn't tell you who I really was."

Dottie sighs. "You said it's crazy for you to stay? This whole situation is crazy." She tilts her head, curious, and Kit's familiar with that, too. "You were really a maid?"

Kit smiles sadly. "Yep."

"What was it like?"

Kit thinks about how to reply, because no one has ever asked her before. No one asked her if she wanted to become a maid, or what the experience of it was like—not even Katherine asked her. The answer surprises even Kit. "It was a lot like this, to be honest. A life of service. You get used to not letting your own life show at all. You have to be discreet." She ducks her head. "I mean, I've been hiding who I am for the past nine months, but in a lot of ways, I've had four years of training for this role and this job."

Dottie's mouth opens and closes. "That sounds... confining."

"I rebelled, though." Kit quirks her lip. "I got free. Katherine gave me an out, and I took it. Even if I get caught, it will have been worth it. Just to have lived on my own terms for a while."

"You'd be happy?"

"Don't get me wrong, I don't want to be convicted for

treason. But I've had nine months of freedom. Fulfilling work. The chance to use my mind. To serve my country in a way I never would've imagined." Kit clutches the edge of the mattress. "To make friendships I'll never forget. Dottie, can you forgive me?"

Now they are knocking knees, and Dottie is hugging her. Kit has been grateful many times, but this moment feels like a particular gift. Kit hugs Dottie back, and together they reach across the gap as they squeeze tight and hope for the best.

28

We treated the codes like puzzles—like a game. But we knew it wasn't a game.
—BETTY JOHNSON

"Have you tried subtracting a simple additive, *then* chaining?" Opal taps the pencil she's holding against the nail of her thumb.

"We tried using the fourth digit as a sum check, but that wasn't it."

"It could be something obvious, like...a prime number?"

"Um, I don't know. I've tried most of the obvious additives, but I haven't tried single-digit primes." Kit blows a strand of hair away from her face. "Okay, I'll try two, three, five, and seven. After that, I'll pass it on to Brigid to keep going with double digits while I chain the results. Let's see if that gets us anywhere."

Opal shrugs assent, so Kit pulls her notepad closer and flips to a new page. She can subtract with one part of her mind, while the rest of her mind focuses on three other problems.

First problem: Her existence at Arlington Hall is tenuous, and she could be discovered at any moment.

The second problem: The language of a man who kills girls continues to elude her.

And the third problem: Moya is still just out of her grasp. In a few days Kit will be gone, and Moya will be only a memory.

And this is unacceptable.

Kit thinks of the haughty way Moya said it yesterday: *This is unacceptable.* The tone of voice she used is similar to the internal voice in Kit's head, saying that reconciliation and memories are not enough, that Moya is a risk she's willing to take, consequences be damned.

But once word gets out that Kit is an impostor, Moya could be accused of conspiring to cover it up, and those consequences will ruin Moya's future, so the problem is unsolvable.

Kit rubs her closed eyelids with the heels of her hands. When she opens them, there's a rustle as heads turn all over the room, taking in a sight at the door. It's a young man, accompanied by Captain John Cathcart. The two of them are standing just inside the door frame, so you can barely see past them into the hall.

"Uh, excuse me." Captain Cathcart is in his uniform, as usual, his bearing typically upright and polite. His scarred lip twitches as he makes the announcement. "Ladies, can I have your attention, please."

The young man beside him is also tall, but very blond. He's wearing a white shirt with a loose black tie, a dark gray waistcoat, black trousers. A camel-colored greatcoat is slung over his arm, as if he brought it along but found it too warm to wear, which Kit finds surprising because they've had the radiator running all morning to keep off the chill. There's a moment of resounding quiet as all the girls in the room take in how good-looking the young man is.

"Ladies," Captain Cathcart goes on, "this is Mr. Julian Harding. He's visiting the Hall for a few days with some colleagues. We've been asked to show them around and offer every courtesy—which I'm sure you'll all be happy to do."

"Hello," Mr. Julian Harding says. He waves a hand. "Thank you for having me. I'll try not to be a bother."

"Oh Lordy, he *does* sound like Cary Grant," Opal whispers right near Kit's ear.

"No bother at all," Brigid says genially, walking closer to the pair. "But you probably haven't caught us at our best. We're stuck on something right now, so everyone's a little frazzled."

Which is true, Kit notes. All the girls look a little underdone. Opal's hair is coming out of its bun. Carol has slipped off her shoes; she's been padding around in her socks. Most everybody is wearing the clothes they had on yesterday, including Kit, as they match wits with the code on the cards.

"I'm a little frazzled myself." Mr. Harding's pale cheeks go pink. "My brain still thinks I'm in London and it's dinnertime."

Opal grins. "Then come on in—if you're from the future, you might already know the answer to this problem!"

Mr. Harding glances at Captain Cathcart for approval. "I *am* supposed to be observing. . . ."

Captain Cathcart frowns, weighing this up. There's a brief flurry of girls' voices imploring Captain Cathcart to "have a heart!" and "let the poor guy in, Captain!" until he gives his nod. Then Mr. Harding is herded over to the tables, surrounded by milling girls.

"Stand back a little," Brigid admonishes them. "Geez, give the guy some air. It's time to get back to work anyway—come on, ladies."

Opal advances as the other girls retreat and find their chairs. "Hiya, have a seat—yep, any of those seats is fine. Take the one next to Kit."

"Er, thank you." Julian Harding takes a chair by the table, laying his coat over his knee and glancing at the array of girls inside the room. "It's a little cramped in here, isn't it?"

"I'm guessing if you're allowed in, you've seen this kind of setup before."

"Yes," he admits. "We have a similar operation at home."

"Great—that means I don't have to do a lot of explaining," Opal says. "Right now we're working on a new stack of cards, and we're having a heck of a time figuring out the messages."

"And your name is..."

"Opal Jenks—pleased to meetcha. And that's Kit, and you already met Brigid." Opal smiles broadly as they shake hands, before she's interrupted by Edith, holding another card. "You got something, Edie?"

"Nope." Edith sets the card between Kit and Mr. Harding. "I just tried recombining, like you suggested, but I got nothing."

"We figured that recombining might be a long shot," Kit acknowledges. "But we had to try."

"May I see?" Mr. Harding's interest is obviously piqued

by the little blue index cards. "I don't imagine I can suggest anything you haven't already tried, but I'd like to see how you do it."

"Here." Kit shows him the card. "We've all been working on the same two sets of numbers, to see if we can find a break somewhere. But so far we've been stumped."

Mr. Harding frowns at the lines of numbers. "Is there... There's no address line?"

"That's what's got us stumped," Opal says.

"How bizarre..." He reaches for a pencil absently.

For the next half hour, Julian Harding sits at the tables poring over the cards with them. Kit discovers that he is a year older than she is, that he wears reading glasses while he works, and that his waistcoat and pants don't match because his luggage is still in transit. The English contingent arrived faster than expected because their ship got bombed near the Gulf of St. Lawrence, so they completed the trip by air from St. John's in Newfoundland.

"The US Army has a base there, yeah?" Kit pushes a new notepad across the tabletop in his direction.

"Yes, luckily for us." He takes a blue pack of cigarettes out of his waistcoat pocket with his left hand while scribbling down some figures with his right. "Although all the planes smell faintly of fish. Can't complain though, can you? That would be a bit churlish. Have you tried prime numbers on this?"

"We've just started now," Kit says, turning to a fresh page. "Actually, I was supposed to do that."

Mr. Harding lights his smoke—some disgusting dark French

tobacco, from the smell—and taps his pencil against the card. "Might I make a suggestion? Try the number seven. Or possibly eight."

"Why seven and eight?"

"Because the Japanese usually consider them to be lucky numbers."

Kit's eyebrows lift and she looks at Opal, who shrugs. "Okay. Might as well give it a shot."

"We could try the other lucky double digits," Opal says. "Seventy-seven, seventy-eight, eighty-eight."

"What about nine?" Kit suggests.

"No," Mr. Harding says immediately. "Nine is an *unlucky* number. The pronunciation of the Japanese word for *nine* has the same sound as the word for *suffering*. Like *four*—it's pronounced with the same sound as the word for *death*."

"Fair enough. All right, seven and eight—I guess we give it a shot." Newly excited, Kit shoves her old pages of figures off to one side.

She's only written down two lines of digits before there's another disturbance at the door. It's Captain Cathcart again. "Hi—Mr. Harding, you're getting along okay?"

"Splendidly," Harding replies.

"Well, that's great." Cathcart's gaze searches past him. "Uh, Miss Sutherland? You're wanted down in the gymnasium."

Kit feels as if she's just had a bucket of ice water thrown over her. "Pardon?"

Captain Cathcart doesn't seem to notice her frozen expression. "Yep, it's for your security review. Got your papers with you?"

Kit shakes her head, wordless.

"Then it would be a good idea to stop off at your dorm and collect them. You need me to walk you?"

All of Kit's senses have heightened. Cathcart suddenly seems less like a benign presence: His scarred lip lends his face a malevolent cast; his taciturn demeanor seems more sullen than reserved. *And he was at the Mayflower.* It's like she's only just remembered.

"Uh—no," she stammers. "No, thank you, I'll be fine."

Kit rises from the table, her legs wooden. Opal smiles at her encouragingly—Opal got her clearance stamped last week—and it's an effort to make a smile in return. Once Kit leaves the table, Opal and Mr. Harding lean closer together to work on the code, like water rushing in to fill an empty space. Brigid gives Kit a little wave, but no one else notes her departure.

29

You took an oath when you went to work. . . . People were very careful.
—WILMA BERRYMAN

Kit walks on automatic feet to her room. The curtains are open, and the room is cold and bright with sun. *This is an emergency—I should contact someone.* But Dottie is at work somewhere in traffic analysis. Moya is on Four. Violet has a rostered day off.

Kit is alone.

She collects her handbag, with her identity papers tucked inside in their gold envelope. What is she supposed to do? Grab her carpet bag as well, then dash out the door once she gets downstairs? How far will she get? Will they even let her leave the compound?

She has no idea.

Kit sits on the bed. This day was always coming, but she'd set the worry of it aside. *I'll leave before my name is called. . . . I'll be gone by Wednesday, so why think about it. . . .*

Maybe she's always somehow *wanted* to be caught. Maybe a court martial wouldn't be so bad. It's not as if she's been selling state secrets or colluding with the enemy. She's just a girl who's taken on an assumed name. . . .

And a man in Detroit was convicted for giving that

escaped German POW coffee and a sandwich. The jury only deliberated for an hour and a half before sentencing him to death. Everybody is on high alert these days. Every infraction is viewed through the lens of war.

Kit chews at her lip. She doesn't really have a choice. She's here now. This is the moment she was always going to arrive at: just herself, some flimsy paper documents, and a fake name.

She takes a deep, fortifying breath and leaves the room. By the time she reaches One, her toes are numb in her shoes and her hands are shaking. She straightens her collared cardigan and her skirt, hitches her handbag higher to give her fingers something to do. Then she walks through the foyer and the auditorium-cafeteria and opens a large set of double doors.

The old gymnasium isn't a place she's as familiar with, because it was never a huge feature of Katherine's life. Since the War Department took over the school, it's been used for official meetings and classified archives. The floor is still buffed and shiny, as if—at any moment—a bunch of school-girls will come running in to play badminton or practice their waltzing. But there are trestle tables set up now, and filing cabinets, and large maps are tacked to the walls all along the right-hand side.

An MP stands guard near the window. This man does not have a broom handle like the soldier she met the first time she tried to leave Arlington Hall. He carries a rifle, and the letters on his armband are a stark white.

On the left-hand side, farther down, is a chunky rectangular desk with two people sitting behind it, facing an empty chair.

One of the people at the desk waves Kit closer. For a moment, she considers turning around and running, running....Then reason reasserts itself and she heads toward them.

The desk is adorned with paperwork in folders, set with precise symmetry at each corner, and a large blotter. A Bakelite telephone sits in front of a gaunt-looking man who is dressed in black like an undertaker. He has metal-framed spectacles, and his hair is thinning: Kit can see the start of a bald spot at his crown as he leans forward over a set of documents and makes a notation.

The woman behind the desk is the one who waved. She seems entirely ordinary—matronly, almost, in her dark gray serge skirt suit. Her hair is short and rolled into wings that frame her face. She gives Kit an almost-smile. "Miss Sutherland, isn't it? Have a seat."

"Thank you." Kit sits in the empty chair. The room is large; all sounds echo and are magnified. Her tongue is so dry it sticks to the roof of her mouth.

"You've brought your paperwork with you?"

"Oh. I have, yes." Kit fumbles in her handbag and retrieves the gold envelope. Inside, the school reports, the references, the precious birth certificate.

The woman takes the envelope and nods over the documents. She tucks them back into the envelope and adds them to the top of the collection of folders on her side of the desk. Kit wants to know if she will get her envelope back, but she can't unseal her throat to ask.

The woman draws another folder from the stack, opens it, and peruses a report.

"Well, Miss Sutherland, we seem to have almost everything in order. It says here that you are of above-average intelligence and can be depended upon. You are a conscientious, hard-working girl. Your supervisor added a commendation to your character report in December of last year."

"She did?" Kit blinks. Any commendations she received in December were added well before she and Moya had any sort of personal connection, which is warming.

"Yes." The matronly woman makes a notation on the report with a pencil. "She said that you were integral to a breakthrough in process last November, resulting in an improved workflow in your section."

"Oh. Yes." Kit remembers. She had suggested it would be more efficient if each girl in the workroom was allowed to share cards with another girl, to work on a break collaboratively.

"We have your birth record information here. It states that you are a native-born girl, of Anglo-Saxon race and normal appearance."

Kit nods, hoping she is still of "normal appearance." What does that even mean?

"All that remains now is to collect a direct character reference," the woman says. She turns to the gaunt man, who has been silent all this time. "Mr. Timmons, what do we have?"

The man—Mr. Timmons—touches a finger to the bridge of his glasses and glances at Kit as he pulls a piece of paper closer. "We have two telephone numbers, Miss Sutherland. One for a Mr. Leighton Wallace, who is connected to your family as an attorney, and one for a Miss Annabelle Grey, who was the vice principal of the school here, before it was repurposed."

"Oh," Kit says. She feels a cold sweat break out at the nape of her neck.

"Do you have a preference for whom we contact first?"

"Oh." Kit has to swallow hard. "Um. No."

"Then I will contact Mr. Wallace first." Timmons reaches for the receiver of the black telephone in front of him.

Three numbers are dialed, and Timmons waits. Kit hears the small female voice on the other end of the line—the prologue of her doom.

"Long Distance."

"Operator, I'm calling Philadelphia." Timmons adjusts his glasses again. "Baldwin one, two two one five. My number is Main six, nine nine one three."

"Thank you," the operator replies.

While Timmons waits for the call to connect, he reaches into his jacket pocket, finds a pack of cigarettes. He draws one out and lights it with the hand not holding the phone.

"So you've been working with us for nearly ten months," the woman says.

Kit feels faint. She drags her attention away from the tip of Timmons's lit cigarette, her stomach clenched tight with nausea. "Yes. I mean…yes. I guess it has been nearly ten months now."

"And you've enjoyed the work?"

"Yes. Yes, I have."

The first month or two were terrifying, of course—she

was figuring things out and learning to mask herself. But that didn't mean it wasn't also pleasurable, to meet and make new friends, to work with her mind instead of her callused hands, to earn her own money and spend her free time however she wished.

Ten months of living on a distant shore. Of living free.

"Have you had any difficulties with the work? Or have you found any of the cafeteria or dormitory conditions to be inadequate?"

Kit wishes she could listen to the quiet conversation Timmons is having on the phone, instead of having to refocus on the questions the woman is asking her. There is a brooch on the woman's lapel, in the shape of a starburst. A large purple gemstone glitters at its center. Kit tries to ignore the saliva now clogging up her throat, the perspiration condensing in her hairline.

"I've had no problems at all." She forces strength into her weak voice. "It's been wonderful.... It's been the best job I've ever had."

Timmons is still talking on the phone, in a low undertone. His razored eyebrows meet in a frown. He sets his cigarette into a small black ashtray beside his papers so he can pick up his pen and make some notes.

The room swims a little, and Kit wonders if she will topple off the chair.

"There is a note here, saying that you speak conversational French and that you have studied astronomy and some higher mathematics...."

The woman with the starburst brooch talks on. Kit feels

as if she is in a distant zone of existence, somewhere details seem very sharp—the brooch, the cigarette smoke, the patterned grain of the wooden desktop—but her reactions and breathing have slowed almost to zero. She waits for the MP to clap a heavy hand onto her shoulder.

Timmons presses his finger to the hook switch, dials again. Again, the operator connects his call.

"Do you have any hobbies, Miss Sutherland?" the woman asks.

Kit's mind is reeling. "Books. I...I like to read."

"It says here that you're a member of the Crossword Puzzle Appreciation Society in the Hall?"

"Oh. Yes. Yes, that's right."

Timmons sets the phone receiver back into its cradle and collects his cigarette from the ashtray. He passes the notepaper, with his scrawls, sideways to the woman, who looks at it.

"Ah." The woman glances at Kit, back to the paper. "Apparently, Mr. Wallace considers you to be dependable, a loyal citizen of sober habits. He says that you do not take strong drink and that your family is highly respected, with no communist connections, and living in a desirable part of the state."

Kit feels a pain in her chest from lack of oxygen. "I... what?"

"Yes. And Miss Grey has said that you are an intelligent student, with a love of books and classical music. She says that you fought some health problems over the course of your years at Arlington Hall and had the fortitude to overcome them and excel in your studies. She commends your employment with the United States government and considers you an excellent candidate for department work in any capacity."

Kit suddenly finds that she can breathe, and that her first breath is long and unsteady. "I...I'm..." She has to think fast, which is hard to do right now because she is deeply confused. It's also incumbent upon her to look calm and expectant rather than shocked. This involves considerable effort. "I'm very glad to hear that," she replies feebly.

"Yes, that's a very nice reference." The woman tucks the notepaper into the folder to her right, collects Kit's envelope and passes it to her. "You may have these back now."

"Of course... thank you." Kit clutches the envelope.

The woman selects an official-looking form from the folder, signs it, and passes it to her left. The man in the undertaker's suit also signs, then takes an ink pad and a stamp out of the desk drawer. He stamps the form decisively.

The woman now smiles at Kit properly. "Thank you for your time, Miss Sutherland. We've completed your review, the paperwork will be passed on to your superiors, and you'll be able to collect your new pass from the fourth floor later this afternoon, at the conclusion of your shift."

"I..." Kit finds enough spit to lick her lips. *How has this happened?* "Thank you. Thank you very much."

"You can return to your station now."

Kit holds her envelope tight, stiffens her knees, and takes a step away from her chair.

"Miss Sutherland?"

She freezes. *Maybe this is it. Maybe now...*She makes a half turn, to see the woman tilting her head, eyebrows raised.

"Don't forget your handbag, Miss Sutherland."

Of course. Her handbag. Kit steps back, reaches down for the handbag, feels a staggering vertigo as she straightens back up. Will she faint? She has gotten this far, and she will not faint.

She turns and walks for the door. She does not rush, because her legs are still unsteady. She walks past the MP with his rifle until she is at the door, opening it, passing through, closing it.

Then she leans against the door, gasping like she has risen to the water's surface from the sandy floor of the ocean.

Wondering how in God's name she is still here.

30

Working so intensely like that gave
us a real feeling of loyalty to each
other. We all helped each other—there
was a sense that we were all in this
together.

— ROSE OVERTON-MITCHELL

In Moya's room on Monday evening, a celebration.

Four girls sitting around the green baize tabletop, four glasses, four voices, sometimes talking at once, but now Moya has claimed the floor. She's been trying to explain everything to Kit, who's looked shell-shocked since the moment she arrived.

"No, really," Moya says, "the telephone numbers in your file were easy. I just swapped them out for a different set of numbers. And I found out the interview times, so I knew roughly what time they'd make the calls. The real work was done by Dottie and Raffi and Violet."

"I mean, I've known Becky Piedmont since we were *kids*," Dottie says, her cheeks flushed pink and her eyes sparkling. "When she got work at the Telephone Exchange, I threw her a party—which is where she met Joe, and they got married in June last year, so basically I introduced her to her husband, which was neat."

"And she didn't think it was strange, that you wanted

her to redirect phone numbers?" Kit's eyes are huge and her voice sounds fragile. Her whiskey glass sits practically empty; Moya was the one who poured half the glass straight down Kit's throat when she first came to the door in tears. Kit's new character reference—which Moya has read—says she takes no strong drink. But that reference, among other things, is a lie.

"Oh goodness, no, Becky didn't even hesitate." Dottie waves a loose hand. She's already had two brandy and sodas. "In fact, last Christmas, we played this prank—"

"Wait, wait," Violet says. "I have to leave for the bus in five minutes, so I want to say something first." She holds up her glass, which is still half-full of clear soda water, in a toast. "This one's for you, Kit. You gave me the push I needed to put in my college application—"

"You did it?" Kit's mouth drops open. "Ohmigosh, Violet, you did it!"

Violet waves this away. "Yes, I did it, now let me finish. Okay, as I was saying…Kit, I can pretend to be Miss Grey on the phone any day of the week—which was terrifying, by the way, and I'm not afraid to admit that—so long as we get to hang on to you."

"To Violet's college application!" Dottie raises her own glass. "And to keeping Kit!"

"To keeping Kit," Moya echoes. She smiles at them all as they drink—they've taken collegiality to a whole new level with this caper, and she has no regrets. Her room is glowing with warm light from the various lamps, one of which she draped with an orange scarf for extra ambience. "Eight to the Bar" by the Andrews Sisters is boogying out of the Philco, and the mood is festive. She just wishes she could figure out how to put Kit's mind at ease.

Kit's eyes are hot, her face wan. "I don't...I don't know what to say. Do you know how much trouble you'll all get in if anyone finds out what you did?"

"We know," Dottie declares, throwing an arm out, "and we don't care! You're one of us, and code girls look after their own." She hiccups. "I tell you, though, I would have paid real money to hear Raffi's impersonation of Mr. Leighton Wallace on the phone to the examiner."

"Ha! Me too. I wonder if he recorded it for posterity?" Violet tugs her coat on over her button sweater and green skirt, and collects her handbag and gloves.

"Oh God, I hope not." Moya swirls the toffee-colored liquid in her glass. "I don't want any evidence left over for anyone to find. I've swapped the numbers back, so there's nothing in Kit's record. With a little luck, nobody will ever be any the wiser."

"Thank you. All of you." Kit looks at each of them in turn. "I can never repay you. But if there's anything you ever need—"

"We need *you*," Violet reminds her. "We'll never figure out who killed Dinah and the other girls without you. Now you don't have to worry about getting arrested for treason, you can turn your mind to it properly. Look, I've gotta go."

"Thank you so, so much." Kit stands from her chair to grip Violet's forearms and kiss her on the cheek. "I can't even say."

"Oh, get away," Violet says, but she's blushing. "Like I told you, you're much more useful when you're not a maid. Now let me go before I miss my bus."

"Hold on, Violet, I'll walk down with you." Dottie also rises. She's a little silly and loud-voiced from the booze, but not unsteady on her feet as she walks over to grab Moya's ice bucket. "I'm going down to the kitchen for some more ice. D'you gals want anything?"

"No, I'm good," Moya says.

Kit just shakes her head.

"Come on then!" Violet urges.

The two of them exit together, Violet hurrying Dottie along. Now it's just Moya and Kit. Kit collapses back into her chair, as if the removal of ten months' worth of tension has left her boneless. Moya feels light and a little giddy, and she knows it's not from the whiskey—she holds her liquor too well for that. She closes her eyes a moment, enjoying the feeling.

"You could all be court-martialed for conspiracy to commit treason, you know," Kit says softly.

The upbeat tune on the Philco is replaced by Tommy Dorsey's orchestra playing "There Are Such Things," and Kit's words fall into the low, quiet sway of the music.

Moya opens her eyes and nods slowly, regarding her glass. Her elbows are on the table, her forearms and wrists exposed where the sleeves of her black silk robe have slipped down. "You're right. We could be." When she looks over, Kit's gaze is full of wonderment and worry. Her eyes are dark and deep in the lamplight.

"Why did you do such an insane thing?" Kit whispers. "Moya, why would you take such a risk?"

Moya takes a last swallow of whiskey and puts down her glass. "You'd do the same for any of us."

Moya's never thought of herself as a rule breaker: She's a supervisor—she *upholds* the rules. But of course, that's not completely true. There are many ways in which she's broken the accepted order. Many personal wants she's policed and controlled, so she can get by. Many aspects of her life that she's papered over and disguised, too...

Maybe it's time to unbuckle some of her armor, so she can live a real life. Maybe it's time she stopped thinking of those vulnerable parts of herself as weaknesses and turned them into strengths.

Maybe it's time to start breaking a few more rules.

Kit still seems at a loss. "I don't know what to say."

Moya takes in Kit's pale cheeks, the tremble in her bottom lip. Her galaxy of freckles and her scared, hopeful eyes. Moya's filled with a longing so acute it's like an ache.

"You've got a second chance now." Moya swallows hard. "Say you'll use it. That you'll live your life, take chances, dream dreams. Say you'll stop looking over your shoulder. Say you'll stop hiding who you really are."

Say you'll stay. But those are words Moya can't utter, no matter how much she wants to. Maybe Kit will take her new liberty and run. If that's what she decides, then Moya will have to live with it—at least it will be Kit's free choice.

Kit blinks like there's a pressure behind her eyes. "A second chance, huh?"

"Yep."

"And do I get a second chance with you?"

Moya stops breathing for a moment.

She unstoppers her throat to inhale, light-headed with hope. "Kit, you've had a second chance with me since you woke up in the library—"

Then she doesn't speak anymore because Kit has reached out, grabbed a handful of the lapel of Moya's silk robe, cupped Moya's jaw with her other hand, pulled her close enough to kiss fully, softly, ferociously.

Their mouths meld, come apart for breath, meld again. Moya makes a quiet, hitching sigh. Her hand slides limply off the baize and onto Kit's thigh, and she feels, for the first time in forever, as if she has found a place to rest.

31

Kit wraps her arms around herself against the chill breeze waft-
ing through the gazebo. "Okay—Violet, I was thinking about
what you said, about foreign language ciphers. You were totally
right. And I've been racking my brain to figure out how the
letter arrangements in the killer's language behave, but now I
think I've got it. Are you ready? This is who we're looking for."

"Hold on," Dottie says. She and Kit have swapped roles;
Kit has the information, so Dottie is being compiler. She
balances the index card on her knee as she sits on the little
gazebo bench.

Kit called this Tuesday lunch meeting in a hurry, and
nobody had time to walk to the stables. Moya is due back
inside in five minutes and has come without her coat; she is
taking this opportunity to have the world's fastest cigarette.
Violet is sitting beside Dottie, watching Kit as she paces the
boards back and forth.

Dottie finally finds her pencil in the pocket of her skirt.
"Got it, I'm ready."

"Tall, white, wealthy—we know all that stuff." Kit turns and starts back the other way. "It was the personality stuff we were missing. What this man is really like. But I finally figured out that part about how letter arrangements behave—it's his *behavior* that's the key to his personality. It's the language of who he is."

"And if we get an idea of his personality, we can match him up with suspects," Moya says, puffing furiously. "Yep, go."

"We knew he was confident," Kit says, listing things on her fingers, "because he assaults victims in public spaces, in daylight, in the middle of parties. But he also induces them to leave well-populated areas and go with him. That means he's charming—persuasive."

"Someone who uses charisma to coax girls into following him," Violet says, nodding. "And who has the forcefulness to make them stay."

"That's right. He has a dominating personality—most people with his politics like to dominate, intimidate. He intimidates his victims. Being white—in Dinah's case—and wealthy puts him in a good position to exert more influence, too."

"That makes sense."

"He hates women," Kit says firmly. "I don't think he would want to work with women, or be bossed around by them. A man like that would want to work somewhere women are subservient, if they're around at all."

"A place with very few women," Moya suggests. "Or none. The military, a boardroom, some other male-majority industry—"

"What else?" Dottie is scrawling everything down.

"Yes, he's intelligent," Kit goes on. "Yes, he's a planner. But he's also doing more than just planning these murders. He's taking souvenirs, and he's using those souvenirs to play a game with the police. Teasing the police like that... I think it means he's arrogant and controlled. The only evidence he leaves behind is what he's left deliberately. I think that level of self-control means we're looking for an older guy, closer to thirty than twenty."

"That rules out a few of the men from our Mayflower suspect list, like John Farrell," Moya says, grimacing.

"Ruling out is good," Kit says. "That means we're narrowing the range."

"You said Richard Norton is with the War Department," Violet suggests. "That's male-majority."

"But there are a lot of girls working secretarial in that department," Dottie counters. "Same with Securities and Exchange, where Henry Robinson works."

"Bob Martelli is out, too," Kit says. "He's only twenty-one."

"But Charlie Sharpe, MD, fits the profile." Violet gazes off into the trees. "In fact, he fits the profile very well. Tall, wealthy, white, working in a male-majority industry. Doctors have power. And he's arrogant, charming. The way he stuck his card into my pocket that night at the Mayflower..."

"He likes to get his own way," Kit says, thinking about it. "We should ask Raffi to check Sharpe's affiliations."

"It might be him," Moya agrees, but she's shaking her head. "It might be a lot of men. I said we shouldn't get our hopes up that any of the guys we met at the Mayflower were the killer, remember?"

"But the killer was *there*," Kit counters.

"Yes. And so were more than six hundred other people."

"So where do we go with this?" Dottie looks up from her index card, shaking out her pencil hand. "Is now the time to go to the police?"

"I'm not sure." Kit stops pacing to sit on the bench opposite Violet and Dottie. She chews her bottom lip. "We have a profile and a potential suspect, but it's pretty thin."

"We should give it one last shot." Moya grinds her cigarette out with the heel of her shoe and crosses her arms against the breeze. "Even if it's just to find out what the police know."

"And why the details about the symbolic mutilations on the bodies aren't showing up in the newspapers." Violet rubs her biceps in the cold. "You better believe I've noticed *that*. Moya, you said you made contact with Detective Whitty, so you should go back and give him a try."

"I agree," Moya says. "We should go together. How does this afternoon sound?"

Violet looks taken aback. "You want me to come along?"

"Why not?"

Dottie nods vigorously. "You can back each other up."

"Why not…" Violet glances away, thoughtful, before looking back. "Okay. I'll come."

"I'm not convinced you'll get anywhere," Kit says, standing from the bench. "Although I guess it would be good to know what the police have. And at least we can say we tried. But hey, I've gotta get back. I volunteered to take an extra shift, because things are so tight in the workroom and Julian Harding is only here short-term."

They all have to get back—Moya is not on an assigned break, and Violet's colleagues could see her if anyone bothered to look out the window. She disappears in that direction as Dottie and Moya and Kit clump back toward the schoolhouse.

The idea that they have a profile of the killer—a *suspect*, even—but no way to verify it is gnawing at Kit's brain. She's quiet as she hurries back up the stairs with Moya and Dottie, who split off on Three to go to their respective areas. Dottie is returning to traffic analysis. At the door to the workroom, before she heads for the stairs to the fourth floor, Moya brushes Kit's hand.

"Coming down later for a drink?" Moya's expression is bland, but her voice has a fine vibration.

Kit grins, feeling the vibration under her skin. "Absolutely."

That's all they've got time for, and Moya heads for Four as Kit hurries back to her chair. She settles herself and grabs for fresh notepaper.

"Any progress?"

"Nothing yet," Opal replies gloomily. "There's new color cards trickling in, though. Brigid split us into blue cards and yellow cards."

Kit surveys the room. The atmosphere is busy but subdued, each girl hunched over her workstation, focused on her own knotty problem. Julian Harding is sitting in a chair, too, shirtsleeves rolled and reading glasses on, pencil moving. It's still strange to see a man in the room, but he appears to be quite comfortable in this otherwise all-girl space. Harding has disappeared at times, to various meetings with higher-ups and tours of other parts of the facility at Arlington Hall. But something about the puzzle that the girls in the workroom are struggling with seems to keep drawing him back.

Everyone largely ignores Harding now—too busy and concentrating too hard to register his presence—but the girls appreciate that there's another set of hands. He does the same work everyone else is doing. He's currently counting back rows with the pencil in his right hand, a noxious-smelling cigarette slowly burning away in his left.

Kit finds her pencil. "I'm still on blue cards?"

"Yep." Opal waves toward the girls across from them. "Yellow cards are over that side."

They've given up going over the same two messages using different techniques. Now everyone working the blue cards has a stack, and they're throwing everything but the kitchen sink at each individual card, trying to get a hit. Kit gets back to work, checking potential substitutions on the groups of digits that Brigid has already attacked with prime numbers.

Two hours later, Kit is pretty tired of staring at the same sets of numbers. She takes the rubber band off her stack and shuffles them like playing cards. She sorts through the cards, searching for patterns. Then she lays them out on her desk in rows and columns, not sure what she's searching for.

There's nothing. Nothing that she can see. She's been

staring at these cards for days, and nothing is presenting itself.

She rearranges the rows and columns, using the first four-digit code group as a starting point, arranging in ascending order. Then in descending order. Then she tries arranging by point of radio origin. The blue cards look like a memory puzzle in front of her, but there's still nothing.

Julian Harding's voice drifts over. "Find any answers?"

"No." Kit shakes her head without looking at him. "Because I have no idea what I'm looking for."

"What are you arranging them by?"

She tells him. Opal leans back in her chair so Kit can show Harding how some of the code groups seem tantalizingly related—but the connection breaks down on close inspection.

Harding frowns. "These are by point of origin?"

"Yes."

"And they're all on the same frequency."

"Yes."

He rises from his seat, stubs out his most recent cigarette, and comes closer. "What about arranging by date of transmission?"

"Like de-duping?"

"Yes, but I think we're more interested in the thread of the messages than in any duplications."

Kit rearranges the cards on the table, checking the dates. The first date the blue cards began arriving was March twenty-ninth. She starts with that date and manages to get six cards down before she hits a snag. "I'm missing some. Have you got anything from March twenty-ninth?"

Harding sorts through his cards, hands her five. Kit takes away every card that isn't from March twenty-ninth, to make room, and puts those cards in a separate stack. Then she lays out the new cards, before casting around. "Opal, have you got any cards from March twenty-ninth?"

Opal sorts through her own cards, selects three. "You got something?"

"Probably not," Kit admits.

"Worth a try, though."

"Everything's worth a try." Kit is already slotting the cards into place. "I think I'm still missing some."

Opal stands in place and raises her voice. "Ladies, listen up. Anyone got blue cards from March twenty-ninth?"

A rustle through the room, as girls search through their stacks and pluck out the requested cards, hand them over. By the time Kit's assembled every card they have from that date, the collection covers both her workstation and half of Opal's.

"This is all of them?" Opal asks.

Kit nods. "Unless some went to another workroom."

"Not that I know of."

Harding is chewing the end of his pencil. "It's still not there, is it."

"Nope." Kit squeezes the nape of her neck. "It feels right, but it's not quite—"

"Wait." Harding suddenly leans forward over the table. Pencil now stuck behind his ear, he starts rearranging the cards.

Kit frowns, moves closer. "What are you doing?"

"Date of transmission and *time* of transmission." Harding's eyes have an intense glow. "If you take the time of transmission into account and put them in order of receipt…" Harding's long fingers move fast, sliding cards around into the correct position. Opal sweeps a stack of notepaper and a box of rubber bands out of the way as the memory puzzle grows on the table.

"They're all short, sharp messages," Harding says as he slides cards into place. "It's been driving me barmy, that they're all so short. Nothing useful is that short. But maybe, if we put all these short messages together in order, like—"

"Like a jigsaw puzzle," Kit exclaims suddenly. "Not a memory puzzle, a *jigsaw* puzzle."

"So you end up with a series of short messages that combine somehow, although I don't know how they—"

"*There.*" Kit has been counting across the rows, and now she stabs a finger onto the seventh card and then onto the eighth card. "And there. Seven and eight—lucky numbers. They have the same code group at the start of the message."

Opal is leaning closer, too. "And the next three cards have a starting code group that matches." She taps the ninth, tenth, and eleventh cards, points onward, excited.

"A different code?"

"Maybe."

"You're right." Harding leans his hands on the table, both arms straight. "I think that's right. Cards seven and eight are significant. Cards nine and onward are a separate grouping."

"What about the first few cards?" Kit asks. "One to six?"

"They're so short—some are just a single, repeated line. I think they're junk messages."

Opal frowns. "So they're, what, a distraction?"

"Yes." Harding removes his glasses. "Yes. They're like...a scattered diversion."

"So cards seven and eight—"

"They're the real start of the message." Kit feels a thrill course through her. "They have the same code group at the beginning, they're linked, they could be—"

"The address line." Harding looks at her. "Kit, I think you've got it. My god."

"Girl, you did it!" Opal whoops, clutching Kit's shoulder.

Brigid's head lifts across the room. "What? Did you get it?"

Harding nods, grinning. "Yes, I believe so."

"Right on, Kit!"

Other girls are taking notice now, faces creased with relief at the idea there's an end in sight. They cheer and call out, shaking their fists in the air in congratulation. Kit can feel herself blushing.

"We can't celebrate yet." Kit takes a deep, excited breath. "If that's the address line, we still have to break it."

"But now we *have* an address line, thanks to you!" Opal gives her a side-on hug and a fierce grin. "You got a brain on you, Miss Sutherland."

"You really do." Julian Harding stands up properly. His waistcoat is unbuttoned, his hair disheveled, but he's smiling. He shakes her hand. "Well done, Kit. Jolly well done. Good Lord."

Kit remembers something Moya said, what feels like years ago. "It was a group effort."

A voice from the doorway. "Am I interrupting?"

Kit looks over—speak of the devil, Moya is standing there looking sinfully tempting in a black silk blouse and tweed pants. It's the same outfit she was wearing two hours ago, but damn.

Opal, face radiant, replies before Kit can recover her wits. "We think we got a break."

"Really?" Moya's eyebrows lift and she steps over the threshold, gaze arrowing to Kit.

"It's early days, but maybe yeah." Kit can feel herself blushing again.

Harding buttons his waistcoat. "Do Mr. Kullback and the other fellows need me upstairs, Miss Kershaw?"

Moya blinks at him. "Ah, no. I just need to speak to Kit for a moment. About another matter."

"Oh." Kit puts down her pencil and resists the urge to tidy her hair. "Okay—one second."

She hands off the discussion about the best ways to approach the new address line problem to Harding and Opal. Then she follows Moya out into the corridor.

She's just realized that Moya is carrying her trench coat. Kit keeps her expression neutral and her voice low. "What is it?"

"Violet sent me a note." Moya looks down the corridor, back again. "She wants to see us down at the cottage."

"At the cottage?"

Moya nods. "Grab your coat."

32

My god, you should have heard the cheer
go up when we got a pinch!

—EDITH YOUNG

Moya leads Kit out of the schoolhouse via the kitchens, excusing them both to the staff. That pink flush of victory on Kit's cheeks is mighty appealing. It reminds Moya of the way Kit's color heightens after they've been kissing...and she really needs to concentrate more, or she's going to trip on these back stairs.

Out the kitchen rear entrance is the start of a graveled path that cuts across the quad at a diagonal. Moya pulls on her burgundy trench as they go. They pass the wooden park benches and shrubs that were once elegantly shaped and are now a little overgrown—no one has time to tend to the topiary; they're all working too hard.

Bearing left onto another path takes them to the door of a three-story house built of the same stone as the schoolhouse, which used to be where the Head of School lived. Violet holds the white-painted door partially shut with one hand. Through the gap, Moya sees a glimpse of a workroom staffed entirely by Black women in civilian dress, with stylishly rolled hair. They are sitting at separated desks, their heads down, pencils flying. It's a peek into a different world, and Moya has to restrain her curiosity when Violet closes the door fully.

"You made it." Violet tucks her pencil behind her ear.

"Kit's unit got a break," Moya explains. "Things are ramping up."

"Good for you." Violet gives Kit an approving smile. "Actually, we got a break here, too. But that's what I wanted to tell you. We got it from a pinch."

Moya is familiar with pinches. It's when somebody in the field of battle—sometimes an armed team with deliberate intent, sometimes an Allied mole working in enemy intelligence—captures enemy cipher keys or codebooks and passes them on. The value of a pinch is stratospherically high, and they're infrequent; Violet's unit got lucky. The pinch is only useful for as long as the enemy doesn't realize their cipher keys have been intercepted. Once they find out, the codes change again. But for a codebreaker, that window of time can be a lifeline.

Moya knows codebreaking purists who consider a pinch cheating, but those folks can go all the way to hell. This is war. You take whatever advantage you can get. "That's great," she says. "But why did you—"

"It made me think," Violet interrupts. "*That's* how we can catch our killer. We create a pinch. We'd have to seed a little—put the word out that there's a piece of evidence or something around Veronica Luca's murder. Then once the bait is in place, we see if Charlie Sharpe or any of the other suspects fall into the trap."

Kit frowns. "But how would we...ohhh."

Moya nods. Kit has always been a quick study. "Raffi. He could write a new article about the murder at the Mayflower."

"Would he do it?" Violet asks.

"I think so," Moya replies. "Yes. It's already high profile, and the media is eating it up. It's also newsworthy that nobody has solved the murders yet. Raffi can say there's fresh evidence, or even a witness."

"But that's not true. Can he lie in a newspaper article?" Kit asks. "Is that allowed?"

Moya lets her amusement tug at her lips. "He doesn't have to lie. He can hint a lot, without saying anything outright."

Kit's forehead wrinkles. "It's a risk."

"But it's a strategic risk to improve our chances, like A. Randolph's March on Washington—just the threat of it was enough to make a change." Violet shifts in place, excited. "We should do it. If Raffi writes an article saying there's a possible witness report, and if he encourages the public to contact the *Star* with tips or information..."

"Our guy will contact the *Star*." Kit is nodding slowly. "That fits with his personality type. He'll want to know what's going on. He'll want to know if anyone has any real clues. And he's arrogant enough to think he won't ever be suspected or get caught."

Moya feels a flame igniting in her chest. "Which is exactly where he's wrong." She checks her watch. "Violet, it's coming up on three thirty. Do you think Mr. Coffee would release you early, under my supervision? We could get a head start on our trip to the police station; then I can drop you home and call Raffi as soon as I get back."

290

"Maybe." Violet looks excited, energized. "Let me go see."

She whirls back through the crack in the doorway, and once again Moya catches a glimpse of the Black unit, the women hard at work. Why do they need to be separated from the rest of the code girls in the schoolhouse, if their work is the same? It makes not a lick of sense.

"Things are picking up steam, aren't they?"

Moya turns to see Kit gazing abstractedly toward the Hall.

"It's like a feeling in the air...." Kit shivers, as if she's shaking the feeling loose, and looks back. Her gaze wanders over Moya from head to toe, and a smile appears on her face. "You're going to visit Detective Whitty wearing pants?"

Moya snorts, puts a hand on her hip. "He'll have to deal with it."

Kit glances around quickly before stepping in closer. "If you and Violet are going out, I need to get back upstairs— see you tonight for the group meeting?"

"Count on it." Moya manages to sneak a warm handclasp with Kit before she walks off. Kit's skirt hem blows a little wild at the back in the breeze, and Moya smiles to see her go.

Violet appears in the doorway again, clutching a blue gabardine coat. "Mr. Coffee said yes." She looks quietly thrilled. "So we're just marching over to the police station, huh?"

Moya ties her trench in front as they start moving. "We can do our marching in a taxicab, I think. Come on."

But once they're down the driveway and out the watch gate, taxicabs prove harder to find than Moya expected. She and Violet stand on the edge of the curb, and twice Moya raises her arm and watches clearly empty cabs pass them by.

"What the hell." Moya waves again in vain. "Why won't they..."

She turns her head in time to see Violet raising her eyebrows.

"Why won't they stop?" The girl gives her a tired look. "Why do you think?"

"You spend money like everyone else, right?" Moya shakes her head in frustration, drops her arm. Looks at Violet face-on and sighs. "And you're a person, like everyone else. I just find the whole concept baffling."

Violet squints at her. "I've been wondering about that, you know."

What she's been wondering has to wait: At that moment, a cab driver finally takes pity on them and pulls over. Moya slides into the rear seat and provides directions as Violet settles in beside her and tugs the door closed. It's warm and still inside the big Checker cab.

Moya turns on the vinyl seat as the cab pulls away from the curb. "What did you mean, 'you've been wondering'?"

Violet smooths the wool of her coat over her knee. "Well, I mean that you and Kit and Dottie have all seemed comfortable working with me. Right from the start."

"Why wouldn't we be?" But Moya can tell she needs to provide more clarification. She sits back against the seat. "Segregation wasn't really something I thought about, until I came down south. I grew up in New York City, in a mixed

neighborhood. Italians, Irish, Puerto Ricans, Germans...
and, yes, some Black families, too. We all jumbled up
together. Helped each other—the folks in my street, anyway. That's what community is supposed to be about."

"That wasn't Kit's experience, though," Violet points out.
"Or Dottie's."

Moya digs in her trench pocket for her cigarette case.
"Well, it's Dottie's nature to like everyone." She hears her
own voice turn dry. "Although you saw how she was on the
bus. Baltimore's so white, it probably never occurred to Dot
before that conditions might be different for other people.
But she's learning." Finding the hard metal case at last, she
runs a thumb over its surface. "Kit...I think Kit feels like
her own sins were so big, she can't cast judgment on others. And I know she grew up disadvantaged, so she wouldn't
wish disadvantage on anybody."

"That's true." Violet presses her lips. "I guess I wasn't sure
how this would play out. I figured you and Dottie and Kit
might think it was strange, working with a Black girl." She
looks Moya right in the eye. "My mother would be grateful
just to be included. But I'm not from my mother's genera-
tion. I have higher expectations."

Moya holds Violet's gaze. "You're right to have them.
Things need to change."

Violet makes a small smile. "At least if us four girls can
work cooperatively, it's encouraging."

"We're in this together," Moya says firmly. "We have to
support each other. God knows, women of every type have

enough to deal with without adding more garbage to the mix."

"Amen to that," Violet says, and a few minutes later, the cab is drawing up outside the police station.

Moya pays, because she has an allowance for it as a supervisor; then they're both clambering out and tidying their clothes on the sidewalk. The Arlington County station looks imposing, with the tall columns either side of the big heavy door, but Moya has been here before.

Violet gazes up at the building, her expression uncertain. "What do you think the police will say?"

"I have no idea." Moya frowns at the door, wind tugging at her hair. She draws a cigarette out of her case, cocks her hand, and gives Violet her best sardonic look. "But make sure your skirt is straight. Because I guarantee Detective Whitty will notice."

Violet rolls her eyes, and the two of them head for the stairs.

33

The future belongs to those who believe
in the beauty of their dreams.
            —ELEANOR ROOSEVELT

Fresh from a shower, Kit stands at the mirrored door of Dottie's wardrobe, trying not to fuss too much with her hair. She's getting ready to go to Moya's while trying not to look like she's getting ready.

Dottie is in a slip and her robe, sitting on her bed with her hair tied in a scarf. She's painted the nails of one hand a lovely spicy shade of pink, and now she's doing the other hand. Nail polish is in short supply: This bottle is shared by a number of girls on the floor.

Dottie blows on the nail of her ring finger. "So d'you think Raffi will agree to write the article?"

"I don't know." Kit tucks in her white cotton blouse. "But it's probably already something Raffi was going to do anyway."

"Only he wasn't going to imply that Veronica's murder at the Mayflower had a witness," Dottie says, examining her pinkie.

"We just have to trust that Moya's persuaded him to do it." Kit buttons the front of her blouse properly.

Dottie grins as she glosses her final nail. "Moya can be pretty persuasive."

"I'll agree with that." Kit pushes back her hair at the front one last time, then abandons looking at the mirror. "Okay, we'll be talking murder business soon enough—let's change the subject. What are you going to do for your birthday?"

"I don't know." Dottie shrugs and tucks the little brush back into the bottle. She screws on the cap and reclines on her pillows. "Probably nothing much. I couldn't even get a day off this year."

"Well we have to do *something*."

"Maybe we could go to Club Caverns again." Dottie's eyes sparkle as she waves her fingers to dry them thoroughly.

"That was pretty fun," Kit agrees.

Dot makes a rueful face. "I'm kinda broke."

"Me too."

They both snort, then break into laughter.

"So maybe not." Dottie chuckles, before turning her blue eyes on Kit. "Okay, I have a question. What are *you* gonna do, now you don't have to run?"

The whole idea makes Kit stop and think. Tomorrow is Wednesday, the day she was due to have a day off—the day she was due to leave. It still doesn't seem quite believable that she's staying here in the Hall. The concept of having a future is too new. Every time Kit tries to think, plan, consider the subject, it shies away from her. It's like petting a spooked horse; she has to steal up to it gently, come at it sideways. Confronting it head-on like this never seems to work. "I don't know." She tilts her head. "I just assumed I'd keep working, and… things would go back to normal. Whatever that is."

Dottie sits up. "There's still a risk, though."

"There's still a risk." Kit nods. Somehow admitting this

296

is easier than thinking about the future. "There could be another security review, or someone could just decide to dig a little deeper. Howard Lascar could track me down. Some new hire from Pennsylvania might know the Sutherlands.... I don't know. Anything could happen."

"You should be thinking about the future, Kitty-Kat," Dottie says softly.

Kit's new policy is honesty. "I'm . . . not used to doing that. I'm not used to thinking further ahead than next week."

"So start there." Dottie leans forward. "What do you want to do next week?"

Kit looks away, unsure of the answer. She tries to frame it as a joke. "How about what I want to do in an hour? In an hour, I want to be sitting at Moya's card table, listening to the Philco and talking next steps. Come on, you getting ready?"

Dottie leans back again, considering. "Mm . . . I don't think so."

"What do you mean? It's a group meeting—"

"No, it isn't." Dottie shakes her head. "Moya already sent word that Violet can't make it. Her mom needed her home tonight for some kind of family dinner."

"Okay, then it'll be you and me and Moya."

"Well, I already know about Raffi's article from you, and you can give me a report about Moya and Violet's trip to the police." Dottie lifts the blanket from underneath herself so she can tuck in her feet. "So I'm thinking I might take the chance to go to bed early."

"But—"

"It'll be just you and Moya." Dottie smiles as she loosens the scarf over her hair. "Don't you kind of want it like that anyway?"

Kit goes hot, then cold, then hot again. Finds herself sputtering. "Well, I don't know what you—"

"Kit." Dottie settles the scarf on the bedpost. "I'm not shocked, okay? I've been Moya's friend for over two years now. You think I don't know who she likes to date?" She wriggles herself under the covers. "I see how the two of you look at each other, and it makes me happy. I want someone to look at *me* like that one day."

Kit can only stand there, filled with a grateful tenderness. She reaches out a hand to the dresser to steady herself. "Well...okay then."

"While we're on the subject," Dottie says, fluffing her pillows, "what do you think of Emil Ferrars?"

"Mr. Ferrars?" Kit sputters again.

Dottie blushes a little. "He said hello to me in the cafeteria yesterday, and I just got a feeling off him."

"A feeling?"

"You know." Dottie's smile is a private one now.

Kit tries to stop her head from spinning. "Has he done anything more than say hello?"

"Not yet—but I'd kinda like him to." Dottie snuggles into her pillows, grinning. "Go see Moya. Enjoy the music."

"Okay. I...I will." Kit blinks. It's all a little much to take in.

Dottie curls over on her side. "Turn out the light when you go? I'm too tired to wait up."

Kit collects her cardigan and her handbag. She flicks off the light switch, leaving Dottie to her romantic dreams, and lets herself into the corridor.

The schoolhouse has a hushed feeling at this time of

the evening, despite the sounds of the workrooms farther down—the carpet deadens some of the noise. Kit's very aware of the rich colors of the carpet, the dark wood of the dado and the banister, the ornate cornices in the ceiling. She feels very *present*, and a strange sense of gratitude is lingering inside. It carries her all the way downstairs, until she's standing outside the wooden door on Two.

She raises her hand to knock, and suddenly the full import of what Moya said last night comes over her: She doesn't have to hide who she is anymore. She can be Kathleen and still be Kit. She can keep doing the job she loves, that she's good at. And she can fall for Moya, unreservedly....

Kit's hand dips with the thought, her knuckles grazing the wood. Within seconds, the door opens, as if Moya has been waiting and listening for her arrival.

The sound of Jo Stafford singing "Fools Rush In" washes gently out into the corridor. Moya's hair is down, the tie on her black silk blouse loose in front and the collar open. She looks so beautiful that Kit almost can't take it. Behind her, the lamps in the room are warm and low.

"Hey." Moya's smile is relaxed and genuine. She has a soda in one hand, and her expression is no longer professionally formal but soft, tired, happy. Everything about her seems calmed by Kit's presence.

"Hey," Kit says, smiling in return, stepping inside.

I can fall for Moya, unreservedly....

From the way Kit's heart jolts in her chest, she knows she fell long ago.

34

"'*But that depends largely on assistance from the public,' an official said today. 'We implore further witnesses to come forward.' Anyone with information on these horrifying crimes is encouraged to contact the* Washington Star. *Reports and calls will be afforded all professional confidentiality.*" Dottie tosses the newspaper onto the coffee table in the library. Raffi's article has run right beside another piece about working women being harassed on public buses and news about the latest protests over equal wages. "I don't know. The idea that a suspect might call in about the Mayflower murder sounds kinda iffy. Do you really think our guy will contact the paper?"

"Yes," Kit says firmly. "Hearing that there was a witness to Veronica's murder at the Mayflower will claw at him. He'll want to know what's going on. He'll call, even if it's just to snoop for whatever information the *Star* has."

Dottie grimaces. "Which is nothing. They don't *have* any information—it's just stuff Raffi made up."

"The part about the witness, sure." Violet moves the pile

of crossword puzzle books to one side so she can reach a paper bag of cookies. "But the rest is real. The rest is what Raffi got from us."

"What if our guy calls with a fake name?"

"That's a possibility," Violet concedes. "But if he's as arrogant as every Nazi, he won't think anyone will connect him with the crimes. It's like Kit's personality profile suggested— he's planned it all out. Nobody would possibly suspect him, right? I think he'll use his real name. And I think he'll call the *Star*, claiming to be horrified by what happened at the event he attended, and ask what information they already have and if he can help."

"So now what do *we* do?" Dottie asks.

"We wait." Kit dips for her own cookie. It seems a bit sacrilegious to be eating in a library, but Violet has brought a small sack of her mother's home-baked oatmeal macaroons. It's been so long since Kit ate home-baked anything, she's almost forgotten what it's like. "Gosh, Violet, these cookies melt in your mouth. Your mom is an amazing cook."

"She is," Violet acknowledges, cupping her palm under her cookie to catch the crumbs.

"Is that really it?" Dottie makes a face. "We just wait?"

"Well, we know—thanks to Detective Whitty—why the information about the symbolic mutilations hasn't made it into the press. Colonel Corderman asked the police to suppress that detail, for national security reasons." Moya's face is angled down at the collection of folders on her lap. She is not eating cookies. She's smoking and leafing through the top folder with her unoccupied hand. "And Whitty has agreed to pass on information, if they find out anything new. If you think we can believe him."

Violet rolls her eyes. "*I* don't believe him."

"Me either." Moya makes a face. Then she shrugs, raises one of the folders in her lap, and waves it. "So all we can do is wait and examine suspect profiles. Raf compiled information about the Mayflower suspects from the list we gave him. He hasn't dug up everything about political affiliations yet, but he's put these preliminary folders together. Here, take a look."

Moya divides the files so they've got one each, and keeps two for herself. The room is warm with light, a cozy nest safe from the night outside. Curtains are drawn across all but one window; through that gap, Kit can see the black glitter of mounded car roofs in the parking lot. Beyond that, the trees in darkness.

It's Wednesday—the evening of the day Kit was supposed to be escaping. Instead, she's here in this quiet room with her friends. The library is a place she now associates with sorority, as well as respite.

"Kit, you said John Farrell is too young," Violet says, chewing her cookie and checking her file.

"Yes, but we don't know for sure." Kit washes down the last of her macaroon with a sip of water from her glass. "The kind of personality this guy is, it makes sense that he'd be older. But we should keep our options open."

"Well, even if he didn't fit the age profile, it looks like we can rule out Bob Martelli right away," Dottie says, running her fingertip down the top page in her file. "It says here he was in Canada with his father in January."

"Great—elimination is good." Moya glances up at Kit and nods, looks over at Dottie. "Put that one on the couch. We'll make that the discard pile."

"And Richard Norton has an alibi for the night of Dinah's murder," Kit notes, checking her own file. "He was at another event, and apparently a whole lot of people saw him there." She begins to pass the file to Dottie to put on the couch, then pauses. "Should we trust that his alibi is solid? I don't want to overlook someone who might have friends lying for him."

"Let me see." Moya takes the file Kit offers, scans through the relevant page. "No, look—Raffi's got witness statements, and one of the people who saw Norton was Jean Westmore. She's one of the unit managers in Munitions. I'd believe her. She's got no reason to lie."

"Okay, good. Discard it is." Kit nods as that file goes on the dump pile. "That leaves us with John Farrell, Henry Robinson, and Charlie Sharpe."

"I really don't think it's Farrell," Violet says, considering her pages. "He just doesn't seem smart enough. See what you think."

Kit and Dottie lean over to see Violet's file, careful not to upset Violet's water glass on the coffee table. While they're looking, Moya makes a noise.

"What is it?" Kit moves the water glass to a safer location.

"Robinson is still a maybe." Moya blows smoke above their heads and angles her folder's papers. "But look at Sharpe. Lives on the west side. Was definitely at the party in Downtown. Has a history of being sleazy. Medical license."

Violet examines the papers and nods. "He fits the age demographic—he's twenty-eight."

"Then why not a scalpel, or...or some other kind of doctor knife?" Dottie asks. It's a good question, which Kit had not even considered.

"Here." Moya points at a line of typed print. "This might answer that question. He owns a boat."

"He owns a boat?" Violet leans farther to see. "That could place him at or near the docks. And he'd have access to nautical or fishing knives."

"Then that could be him." Dottie has put her half-eaten cookie to one side. "Charlie Sharpe could be our guy!"

"Yes, but...wait. Okay? Wait." Kit tugs at her skirt hem. "We're just drawing some lines of interest for the police. It might be Sharpe—it might be anyone. Let's see if Sharpe calls the *Star*. If he calls the *Star*, then chances are much better that he's the man we're looking for."

Dottie groans. "Oh, for Pete's sake. I know there's nothing more we can do, but it's *killing* me to have to sit on all this information."

"Hold tight," Moya counsels her. "Our time is coming. Raffi's compiling a list of all the men who contact the *Star*, so we can check each of them out. Let's put Sharpe, Robinson, and Farrell in a pile and go through them more later once we've heard back from Raf. There's more we can do."

"What else?" Dottie asks plaintively.

"Well, we still have to find out more about Veronica and Margaret for the murder board," Kit offers.

"Fine. What else?"

"I've contacted Ruth for copies of the autopsy report on Veronica, and for more details about the knife wounds on all the girls," Violet says. "We should confirm whether the wounds were made by a fisherman's knife or a fillet knife, or another type of knife entirely."

"What *else?*" Dottie asks.

"That's it, Dot," Kit says, wishing she sounded soothing. "Now we wait."

"And hope our killer sticks his head up," Violet adds.

"Yep. It's a patience game now," Moya confirms. "We've baited the trap, now we see who bites." She stubs out her cigarette in the standing ashtray beside the arm of her club chair and gives Dottie a wry grin. "So that concludes our Crossword Puzzle Appreciation Society meeting...unless you have any other news to share."

Dottie gives her a look. "Moya..."

"Oh, come on," Moya says. "You know you want to tell."

Dottie blushes. "Okay—fine. I have news. Emil Ferrars asked me out for my birthday."

"Dottie!" Kit says, and then there's a hubbub of voices, which Dottie tries vainly to hush.

She extends her hands. "Okay, settle down. It's not a big deal." But her pink cheeks belie those words.

Kit can't stop grinning. "You said you got a feeling."

Dottie is still blushing furiously. "Well, I thought he was interested, but that maybe he already had an arrangement with some other girl. It turns out he's just shy."

"When did he talk to you?" Violet is leaning forward, rapt.

"This morning after breakfast." Dottie struggles to control

a smile and fails. "I went down to the cafeteria and got the newspapers for Four, then I got my coffee and he got his coffee, and we kinda bumped into each other a little. Then, while we were cleaning up the spill, we got talking."

"Well, that is just the cutest," Violet says, sighing.

"I mentioned that it was my birthday tomorrow, and he just... asked me out." Dottie gives up controlling her smile.

"Where are you gonna go?" Kit sits up straighter, excited for her. "He's taking you to Club Caverns, isn't he?"

"Actually, no," Dottie admits. She snorts and rolls her eyes. "It's silly, because we're both working Thursday and we'll be seeing each other all day. Also, he's run out his gas ration, so we can't drive anywhere—"

"Catch the bus!"

"Wait for me to finish!" Dottie makes a mock frown, before smiling gently. "Look, it's just a birthday, and I didn't want to make a drama out of it anyway. We're going to have a picnic, here on the grounds."

"That's perfectly fine," Violet says approvingly.

"A late afternoon picnic under the trees?" Moya finally succumbs to the lure of the cookies, gestures to Violet to pass her the bag. "Sounds kinda romantic to me."

"You know how these things go. We might hate each other." Dottie doesn't look as though that's an outcome she's seriously considering.

"Where on the grounds will you go?" Kit thinks of the longing in Dottie's voice when she said *I want someone to look at* me *like that one day* and feels thrilled for her. "Have you got a picnic basket? Oh, wait—we could help you set up!"

Moya is nodding. "I can arrange a blanket."

"I can talk to the kitchen staff about food," Violet agrees. "They probably have a basket in the pantry somewhere."

"Well, thank you. And if you want to come with me tomorrow and set things up, I won't say no." Dottie is blushing again, but obviously pleased. "I guess the best places would be the gazebo or the stables?"

"The gazebo is kind of visible," Kit suggests. "The stables are more private. You don't want every girl in the schoolhouse staring at you out the windows."

"Good point." Dot straightens her shirt. "All right, we can talk about it some more tomorrow. Thanks for offering to help me set up."

"You're welcome," Violet says, then winks. "I mean, come on—we need *some* excitement that's not murder- or treason-related!"

"I'll give you some alternative excitement," Dottie retorts. "Julian Harding. He's turning heads all over the Hall."

"I thought you were looking forward to spending time with the English guys," Kit teases.

Dottie shrugs. "I mean, he's cute and all, but it's a major distraction. Every girl in traffic is hoping to catch his eye and arrange a whirlwind courtship."

"That'd be quite a whirlwind," Violet notes, stacking the folders neatly. "The English group are leaving Friday, right?"

"To go to Dayton," Moya confirms. "He'd better not steal any of my girls for some lightweight romance."

Kit shakes her head. "I don't think he's a 'lightweight romance' kind of guy."

"That won't stop everyone from talking about it." Dottie rolls her eyes.

Violet gives her a mischievous look. "You don't wanna throw over Mr. Ferrars and try your luck with Julian Harding?"

"You mean, hitch up with a guy who's not even gonna stick around till the end of the month?" Dottie waves a dismissing hand. "Not a chance."

"Not to mention you'd have to go to England," Moya notes.

"What's wrong with England?" Kit asks.

Moya brushes crumbs off her lap. "People say the food's bad and the weather's worse."

Violet laughs. "You wouldn't care about the weather—you'd just stare at Julian Harding's face all day." She catches Kit's surprised glance. "Yes, I've seen him. Mr. Kullback brought him and the others on a tour of the cottage yesterday."

"You got your sights set on England?" Moya teases.

"Not because of Mr. Harding," Violet scoffs, before her voice and expression both change. "But they say there's Black servicemen in England right now. Soldiering and living free."

Kit raises her eyebrows. "There's no segregation laws in England?"

"Nope." Violet chooses another of her mother's cookies. "Who knows—maybe after this stupid war is over, I'll go check it out."

"Stupid war," Moya echoes.

"Stupid war," Dottie agrees, sighing.

Violet's face is contemplative as she nibbles her cookie. "There are lots of things in the world that are stupid."

35

We typed up in that attic on the fourth
floor, and it was terrible. In winter,
we used to wear all our sweaters just
to stay warm, and in the summer, we'd
broil.

—GINGER PERRY

"So, here's the latest calculations we've done on the address line."

Kit taps her pencil on the sheet of paper. It's Opal's day off, and without her, Kit has been doing the heavy lifting in the workroom on the potential address code break. She and Julian Harding have been sitting together at the table, trying different methods of attack, everything from the typical to the outlandish. They're not there yet, although Harding is tenacious—rather like herself, Kit acknowledges.

The solution feels tantalizingly close, but it's Thursday afternoon, and the sun is sinking through the windows of the workroom. Kit is running out of gas. She's got just enough left in the tank to finish up this shift and then help with the setup for Dottie's picnic date.

She smothers a yawn with the back of her hand. "Mm—sorry. Anyway, I did the transcribing myself and got Betty to check it. All the numbers are solid."

"Do you need a nap, Miss Sutherland?" Julian Harding is looking at her, amused.

"Probably," Kit admits. She stretches her back. "Yesterday was supposed to be my day off, but I took an extra shift. I'm running on coffee and adrenaline right now."

"Did you have to take an extra shift on my account?" Now Harding looks concerned. "I'm very sorry, I didn't mean to—"

"It wasn't your fault, and you don't have to apologize," Kit says. "I made the choice to keep working. We only have you for what's left of today, and we've been making good progress with this code because of your help—I want to see if we can break some of it before you leave."

"That would be a nice parting gift, wouldn't it?" Harding smiles softly. His tie is loosened and his blond hair is messy. He's basically taken on the same air of deshabille that all the girls in the workroom wear.

"Any kind of gift, we'll take it," Kit says. "Miss Caracristi and Miss Berryman and Mr. Ferrars have made headway on some of the other address code groups, thanks to that Burma pinch and the Navy cribs—"

"Miss Caracristi is trying to book-break—completely reconstruct the enemy's codebook—which I find quite incredible," Harding notes. "She's clever enough that she just might get it, too."

"But they can't work *all* the codes. If we can get a few face values for this one, then maybe we can figure it out after you go...."

"And then that would be one less they had to worry about." Harding nods. "And I could go back to England tomorrow feeling like I've been useful in some way, at least."

Kit's eyebrows lift. "You're going back to England? I thought you were all going on to Dayton?"

"That's for the other gentlemen in the group—Mr. Tiltman and Mr. de Grey. They're going to look at some machinery in Dayton. . . ." Harding colors. "I'm not sure how much I can say, but yes, they're going on. I'm going home. I had a telegram yesterday that my father is unwell. Also, my colleagues in the UK need some support."

"I'm sorry to hear about your dad," Kit says. "And it's a shame you can't stay."

Harding rubs the back of his neck. "It seems cruel to have come all this way and only be staying for a handful of days. I wish I had a month. We could break some good codes in a month."

"If we can break *one* code, it will have been worth it," Kit reassures him.

Brigid's voice calls out from the other side of the room. "Kit!"

When Kit looks over, Brigid lifts her chin toward the door. Moya is in the doorway, carrying a stack of reports in manila envelopes. She's wearing the shearling collar jacket with a white shirt and the tweed pants. Her sleeves are pushed up to the elbows, her hair twisted into a loose black bun. She makes looking gorgeous seem effortless. Kit has to restrain a broad smile as Moya walks closer.

"Hello, folks." The glance Moya gives Kit is playful, but she's talking to Harding. "I'm not here to hurry you along, I've just come to steal another one of those French cigarettes you carry around."

"The Gitanes?" Harding looks surprised. He fishes in his trouser pocket. "Here, take the rest of the pack."

"Oh, I can't. I don't mean to—"

"You're not depriving me," Harding points out, passing her the blue packet. "I've got more in my luggage. Plus, I've stocked up on Lucky Strikes while I'm in America, so I'm rather awash in cigarettes right now."

"Well, thanks." Moya accepts the gift with a grateful incline of her head.

"While you're here..." Harding looks between Kit and Moya. "Miss Kershaw, you might be able to help us with something. I'd really like to keep working on this problem we've been tackling for the last few days."

"Are you making any headway?"

"We are," Harding acknowledges. "But I only have another eighteen hours in this country, and it's rather annoying to leave without getting the job done."

"Please don't feel bad," Kit says quickly. "We've done so much since you arrived, and maybe with another hour—"

"Kit, another hour isn't quite going to get us there, and I'm sure you know that," Harding says. "But how would you feel about staying on with me for a few hours more?"

"Staying on?" Kit's surprised. She's done overtime before, but only when the whole workroom contingent was needed to cover a shift.

"I know you're tired," Harding concedes, "so I'm sorry to ask, but it feels very close. With another few hours, we could crack it."

Kit considers. The idea is deeply tempting, she has to admit. "A few more hours?"

"I'm hoping that will give us the time we need." Harding has turned again to Moya. "Would she be able to do that, Miss Kershaw?"

"Maybe." Moya wears an undecided frown. "Kit, are you sure you'd like to stay?"

"I guess. I mean...Yes, I want to make the break." Then Kit realizes what it'll cost. "But oh—Dottie."

Moya squints, shakes her head. "You can't be in two places at once—Dottie will understand. It'll be okay."

"Really?" Kit makes her call. "In that case, yes, I'd like to stay on. I agree with Mr. Harding. I think we're close."

"Can you arrange a place for us to work, Miss Kershaw?" Harding gestures at the bustling interior of the workroom. "Once the shift changes, this area will be used by others. We just need a small space, with a table to spread out the cards."

"I'll figure it out," Moya confirms. Her gaze turns toward Kit. "Can we have a quick chat out in the hall?"

Squeezing between the chairs, past Carol and Brigid and the crammed tables, Kit follows Moya until they're in the quiet end of the corridor.

"What's up?"

"Are you sure you want to keep working?" Moya strokes the side of Kit's arm. "You look beat."

"I'm okay."

313

"Julian Harding gets a ride home tomorrow—he can sleep on the trip. You've got to get up at seven thirty in the morning and go back to work."

"I'm fine," Kit insists. "I promise. And if we manage to break this code, my tomorrow will be a whole lot easier."

"Well, there's no guarantee of that." Moya tugs a French cigarette out of the pack Harding gave her, but doesn't yet light it. "Look, Raffi called to say he's sending us something this afternoon—a list of men who called the *Star* about the article. We're going to meet at my place tonight at eight to go through the information."

"What about Violet?"

"She's staying late. And it'll be after Dottie's date, so she can come, too."

Kit sighs, although she's sure she's doing the right thing. "Damn. I feel bad backing out on Dottie. But this is probably more important."

"Under the circumstances, it is," Moya agrees. "I'll arrange a place for you and Harding to work up on Four, so you don't get disturbed."

"I thought it was packed up there?"

"I'll find you a spot."

The idea of working on the hallowed fourth floor is galvanizing. It's where the real think tank of Arlington Hall is located. Miss Caracristi is there; Mr. Kullback's office is there. . . . It's the nexus of intellect that powers the war efforts all over the building.

And now Kit will be codebreaking there.

314

She doesn't want to seem too excited, but it's an effort.

"Okay, thank you." She lowers her voice. "By the way, if you're going to smoke those cigarettes, I don't know if we can date."

"You'll get used to them." Moya winks before squeezing Kit's hand. "It's freezing up on Four. Don't forget your coat."

36

The complex nature of Enigma was also
its greatest weakness: No letter of the
alphabet could be encoded as itself.
—PROFESSOR JULIAN RANDOLPH HARDING

The "spot" that Moya found for them is, indeed, a spot: It's a tiny bathroom under the fourth-floor eaves, barely large enough for a table and two chairs. Kit can see the places where a partition was hastily installed to separate this bathroom area from the room alongside. The ceiling is at a sharp angle, and if Julian Harding straightens too fast, he'll bang his head on the exposed beams. The bathroom's geography makes no sense: There's a random showerhead above a white-enameled cast-iron tub—littered with deciphered intercepts that haven't yet been filed—along one wall. But there's no sink or faucet anywhere. And Moya was right: It's cold. Kit's glad she's wearing her coat.

At least their table is in front of a window. The glass has been soaped in the middle to prevent glare—and prying eyes, although the only way anyone would be able to see into the fourth-floor window is if they were parachuting past, or maybe standing with a pair of binoculars in the tip-top branches of the trees in the forest near the schoolhouse.

Harding has already unpacked their boxful of cards, plus

notepaper, pencils, and erasers. "Is this enough room to spread out?"

"I think this is all the room they've got for us." Kit turns on the desk lamp and settles in her chair while Harding remains standing. He likes to pace, she's noticed.

As she arranges the cards on the table, a movement out the window catches her attention. Far below, three figures wend their way along the gravel path in the quad, past the woolly topiary shrubs and the cottage, then farther into the trees. Kit sees the brown of Moya's jacket, the flash of Violet's purple skirt. Dottie is in green—it's probably the green dress she wore to Club Caverns. No, that can't be it. It must be her green coat, as the afternoon is getting late and the temperature is cooling.

"People you know?"

"Oh." Kit startles, drags her gaze away. "Yeah. I mean, you know them, too. That's Moya, plus Dottie Crockford from traffic analysis. And another girl, Violet, from the commercial unit."

Harding leans a hand on the window frame and squints at the retreating figures. "Bit late to be going for a ramble, isn't it?"

"Dottie has a date with Mr. Ferrars, from the Hall," Kit explains. "They're picnicking at the old stables."

Harding looks quizzical. "All three of the girls are going on the date?"

"Moya and Violet are going to help Dottie set up the picnic," Kit explains.

"Ah. That's nice of them." Harding polishes his glasses on his sleeve. "You were planning to join them?"

Kit shrugs. "Yeah, but it's okay."

"Then it's doubly nice of you to stay. Also, I know you're weary."

"I'm weary, but I want to work this out."

"Then shall we continue? Let's have a look at that last run of numbers...." Harding shuffles through the papers in his other hand. "Ah, right here."

They work on recovering what Kit suspects are the additives to the code group numbers, and Kit's stomach starts to remind her that dinnertime is close. But it's not just hunger that's making it hard for her to concentrate. Even as the digits on her notepad start to fall into a more understandable pattern, something in her mind just won't stop nagging her.

Only she can't figure out what it is.

"They're quite amazing, you know," Harding notes. "The machines that make the code, I mean."

"Not these codes," Kit points out.

"No," Harding acknowledges, "these are pulled out of code books and tables by enemy radio operators half a world away, in battle, under fire...." He squeezes the bridge of his nose, rubs his eyes beneath his glasses. "But the machine codes are tougher. The sheer number of variables you have to calculate is incredible. And the machines themselves are ingenious."

"You've seen Enigma machines?"

Harding nods, pushes his glasses up into his hair. He's sitting across from her, one leg crossed over the other, his chair set back from the table so he can rest his notepad on his knee.

"We have a couple of recovered ones at Bletchley." He glances away with a quick grimace. "Er, I'm not exactly sure how much you're allowed to know, but I've seen them."

"What are they like?"

"They're so big, about the size of a stenographer's typewriter?" Harding demonstrates with his hands. "When you hit the keys, the internal rotors and gears produce randomized code letters—very efficiently, too. They're precise, clever little bits of work."

Kit watches the way his eyebrows lift. "You admire them."

"I admire the mind that can come up with something so simple and so fiendishly effective." Harding gestures at his notepad, then her own. "Do you have any idea how much brain power has been thrown at figuring out Axis codes? You're one of thousands of people on four continents working to break them. We're even building *other* machines to help decrypt them. It's staggering, really. I just wish all that intelligence and energy were being used for good things, instead of...this." He waves a hand, taking in the room, the intercepts, the war.

"So how do you break Enigma codes?" Kit's tired, but she really wants to know.

"You start by remembering the rules."

She squints. "I didn't know there were rules. You just said the codes were randomly generated."

"They are," Harding admits. "But Enigma always maintains certain standards. For instance, no letter is ever encoded as itself."

Kit remembers that she has heard this, or some rumor like it, before. It tugs at her, this information, in a way she can't quite understand. But if she can keep Julian Harding talking about it, maybe it'll come clear.

"So if you see an *A* in a message...," she prompts.

"Yes," Harding says. "You can be completely certain that your *A* will be any other letter from *B* to *Z*, but it will never actually be an *A*."

He says *zee* in the British way, *zed*. Kit nods to show she's following. "Okay."

"Yes," Harding says, warming to his topic. "It's the only idiosyncrasy in an otherwise very clever disguise."

A very clever disguise... Kit feels her senses prickle.

"But once you know that rule," Harding continues, "it can help you work out how the letter arrangements in an Enigma code behave—"

"Wait," Kit says. "Can you repeat that?"

"I said, it helps you work out how the letter arrangements in the code—"

"Oh my god." A blinding rush of heat, like a bolt of lightning in her nerve endings. It radiates from her chest outward, forcing her posture straight. Kit stares at Julian Harding. "Oh my god. I think I've screwed up."

"I beg your pardon?" Harding frowns at her.

She grabs her notepad and starts scribbling madly.

Harding is leaning forward now. "Kit, what are you doing? Have you thought of a break for—"

"One second. Please stop talking." Kit keeps scrawling. "The letter arrangements. I thought I knew his language. But I didn't know—because he was *disguising* himself. Oh my god, he's completely different—"

"I'm sorry, was it something I said?" Harding looks dumbfounded.

"*Yes.* You talked about how no letter is encoded as itself with Enigma." Kit has jotted it all down in two lists, and now she's adding to them. "I got some of the personality traits completely wrong. I thought our guy was good at charming the victims out of public places—that he was confident and charismatic." She looks at Harding blindly. "But it's not that. It's because they *trust* him. Do you understand? Do you know what that means? It means he's *unthreatening.*"

"I have absolutely no idea what you're talking about," Harding says.

Kit is frantic. "And he *doesn't* work in a male-dominant environment. He works with women *all the time.* He's *subordinate* to women—and he doesn't like it." She grabs Harding's lapel with one hand. "He's a chameleon. He's disguising himself. Do you get it?"

Harding gapes. "I really don't."

"The objects he took from the victims—yes, sure, he's showing off his intelligence to the police, taking trophies, playing a game. But the Nazi symbolism...It was all about throwing the police off the scent. They're looking for a madman, a German sympathizer. But it's just a smokescreen. This man works with the war effort."

"Miss Sutherland—"

"Which means his disguise is deliberate." Kit grips the fabric of Harding's jacket as she stares at the window. "And he's operating on Enigma cipher principles to create his disguise. He's manufactured this whole persona with the evidence to make himself *seem different,* like he's encoding himself in another way to direct attention elsewhere. That means he's..."

"He's what?" Harding seems caught up in her frenzy, even without understanding it.

"Oh no, no, no," Kit whispers, horrified.

"Kit, what is going on—"

She locks eyes with Harding. "He's a codebreaker."

"Kit—"

But Kit has already pushed out of her chair. Now she's pacing in the cramped space between the table and the bathtub. Her words are mostly for herself as she chews at her thumbnail.

"*Think*, Kit." She pushes both hands into the small of her back, looking up at the low ceiling as she turns. "He was definitely at the Mayflower event. He's unthreatening, intelligent, white, wealthy. He owns a car. He fits the profile. And he's one of the only people who would've worked with Enigma codes...."

Harding stands and comes closer. His hands are open but his voice is firm. "Kit, you're obviously distressed by something. And I'd like to help, but you need to tell me *what the hell you're talking about.*"

But she is not listening to him, because it has all come to her in one great tidal wave of understanding. The thing that was dancing in her brain. The thing that was important. The mistake she's made, and what it will cost.

She turns and puts both fists into the lapels of Harding's jacket. Sees a glimpse of her own face—drawn and ghastly pale—in the reflection in the window as she holds on for dear life.

"Moya and Violet never came back from the stables."

37

We always used to prioritize messages in one of three ways: routine, urgent, and absolutely frantic.

—EDITH YOUNG

"I don't know what that means," Harding says helplessly.

Brain churning, Kit realizes she's going to have to make an account. "Okay, let's do this fast. There's been a series of murders in Washington, DC."

"What?" This is not what Harding was expecting.

"All government girls, almost all linked to social events, all of them brutal—horrible. Moya and Dottie and Violet and I are connected because...Look, that doesn't matter. We've been tracking the cases, using codebreaking processes. We've communicated with the police, and we're talking to a reporter."

That gets his attention. "You've been talking to a *journalist*?"

"It's fine. He's a friend, he knows about us....Listen, that's not important, okay? What's important is that Emil Ferrars fits the profile of the killer. And the girls haven't come back from the stables."

"*Emil Ferrars?*" For an intelligent guy, Julian Harding takes a while to catch up. "But he's...he's been critical to the codebreaking efforts here. He's...For God's sake, we want to take him back to England with us!"

"I don't *care* if he's critical to the codebreaking effort!" Kit feels the blood rise in her face. "If he's a rapist and a murderer, I want him *caught*! And none of that matters—we're wasting time!" She grabs his lapels again. "Julian, did you see the girls come back from the forest?"

"I...I don't recall." Harding looks flummoxed. "I don't think so, but I wasn't really looking—"

"Then there's only one thing I can think of to do," Kit says, and she whirls for the door.

Harding startles. "What are you—*Kit*!"

But she's on a roll now, not stopping for anybody. Kit thrusts past him out into the tight corridor on Four, walking briskly along the carpet runner. The space narrows until she's at the very end, outside the door of Emil Ferrars's room.

She tries the knob—locked.

But Kit has navigated every room in the schoolhouse, and she knows all the tricks for getting into them, too. She slips her brand-new laminated Hall pass out of the pocket of her skirt, slides it carefully into the gap between the jamb and the door lock. Jiggles carefully as she turns the knob.

The lock springs open.

"Kit, what do you think you're *doing*?" Julian Harding's furious whisper comes from right behind her shoulder.

She glances back at him. "What does it look like I'm doing? We need proof. I'm jimmying the door to Emil's room to find it."

Harding looks distressed. "Are you out of your *mind*? His clearance level is—"

"Come in or stay out—it's your choice." Kit flicks on the light switch, illuminating the claustrophobically small space where Emil Ferrars resides. There's a single bed in the far left corner, a nightstand with an empty glass, an alarm clock, a desk lamp, a pile of books. The bed is made, the linens pulled tight. A dresser stands along the right wall. There's an armchair—the room's sole luxury—on the right closer to the door. On the seat, a folded copy of a newspaper.

Everything looks so normal.

It might not be him. It might not be him....

"Time to find out," Kit mutters.

Far from being stumped over where to start, she's uniquely fit for this task. She knows what it's like, to live a lie. To conceal things. To conceal the person you really are.

If she were living in this room, where would she hide things?

"Under the bed," she whispers.

She marches to the bed, kneels and gropes with her right hand while her left palm stays firm on the mattress, stabilizing her crouching position. *Floorboards, grit, floorboards...* She stretches farther. *Dust, floorboards...* A rectangular object. Solid, feels like a suitcase. Kit hunts along its length for the handle, finds it, yanks the suitcase out.

It's a small traveling case. Made of some dark brown, molded leather. Nondescript. There's not even an identification tag.

"*Kit*," Harding says in a stage whisper. He's somewhere behind her, probably poking his head in through the door. "We need to get out of here. Someone could come along and—"

"Stop whining at me from the doorway and come inside," Kit says. "I think I've got something."

She hears the creak of door hinges; then Harding is standing beside her, his shadow looming. "It's just a suitcase. Everyone has a suitcase."

"Shh," Kit says, and she finds the snaps on the case with her thumbs, presses down.

The locks make a gunshot snap.

Kit lifts the lid.

There's a pause.

"Oh my god," Harding says. Now he's using his normal voice.

Here is the small pile of newspaper clippings about the murders, fastened with a paper clip. A yellowing, open envelope contains scraps of fabric—pink, black, robin's-egg blue, shimmering gold. In the right-hand corner, a jar with a screw-top lid holds...hair? Kit lifts it up. Yes, it's hair. A leather pouch of some kind—she doesn't want to look in that.

A much-washed hand towel is folded up neatly in the bottom of the case. On top of the hand towel, something incongruous: an earring, drops of gold and jewel-sparkle glittering from the pendant.

"That's what he took from Veronica," Kit whispers.

Most damning of all, attached to the inside lid with leather straps, like the kind you find in a picnic basket...

326

"Is that a knife?" Harding says hoarsely.

"Yes," Kit says. "It's a fisherman's knife—a fillet knife."

She cannot unsee all this. Will never unsee it. But now she has taken it in, she recognizes something. There are gaps in the arrangement here. Spaces. There is space for another hand towel. And there should be gloves—where are the gloves?

There is one more thing, and it is the most important thing. There are *two* sets of leather straps on the inside lid of the suitcase. That means...

Kit feels her breath leave her body in a rush.

She closes the lid of the case, presses the snaps. Shoves the case back under the bed.

"But...That's the *evidence*!" Harding shuffles back as she gets off her knees. "That's all the proof you need to—"

"Yes," Kit says, making for the door. "And if the authorities find it here, they'll know Ferrars is guilty. We leave it."

"But what do we—*Kit!*" Harding is back to stage whispering as he follows her back out to the hallway.

"Out. Now." Kit closes the door behind him. She twists the doorknob carefully to ensure it stays closed. "Come on."

She walks as fast as she can back to the bathroom, Harding trailing behind her. Back in the room, she trots to the table, shoving cards, notes, pencils into a pile. She turns out the contents of her coat pockets onto the wooden tabletop.

"You never answered my question." Harding's face, in the soapy window reflection, is pale and shocked. "What do we do now? We can't just leave that suitcase there and...Do we call the police?"

"No time." Kit's found very little of use in her pockets: a pencil, an index card, her compact, the old ticket stub from the bus trip to the pier. She turns around to Harding. "Do you have a pocketknife?"

"I . . . Yes." He seems to have recovered some of his mental faculties, but his movements are stiff and jerky. He feels in his trouser pockets before grabbing for his greatcoat. He hands her a small knife, the short blade folded into the deer-bone handle. "You're going after them, aren't you?"

"Yep." Kit puts the knife in her coat pocket, along with the pencil and an index card. "Do you have anything else?"

"I don't . . . Let me check. . . ." Harding fumbles in his greatcoat pockets, passes her a collection of items: a hand-kerchief, his cigarette lighter, a small tin of mints. "I don't know if any of that will be useful."

"Thanks." Kit gives back the mints, but adds the other items to her collection.

"I'm going with you." Harding starts buttoning his waist-coat. "I'll help you—"

"Julian." Kit steps closer to him. She puts a hand on his forearm and squeezes. "You're a good guy, Julian Harding. A good guy. I don't know what's gonna happen, but I wanted you to know that."

Harding stills. "Thank you." He squints at her. "You don't want me to come, do you?"

"You'll help me a lot more doing something else," Kit says. For the second time, she takes her brand-new lami-nated Hall pass out of her skirt pocket. She looks at it, then gives it to Harding. "I want you to take this. Go to the MPs on duty. Show them my card and tell them they need to find me in the forest near the old stables."

He looks skeptical. "And they'll, what, just chase after you on my say-so?"

"They will when you tell them this," Kit looks him straight in the eye. "Listen carefully. I'm not who you think I am. That's not my name on that card. My real name is Kathleen Hopper. I took the name 'Kit Sutherland' from my employer, who I worked for as a maid. All my paperwork is fake. My identity is fake. If you tell the MPs—"

"Are you *joking*?" Harding's eyes are bugging out.

"I'm not joking, Julian. I've broken the Espionage Act—"

"You're a *maid*?" Harding thrusts a hand into his hair.

"Julian. *Julian*. Look at me." Kit squeezes his forearm hard again. "Tell the MPs that I'm an impostor, with fake papers, and I'm running loose on the grounds. If you tell them about the murders, about Emil Ferrars, they'll take too long to verify—but this is the one thing that will get them moving fast."

Harding slumps back against the table edge, staring at her. "This is all rather a lot—"

"I know it's a lot. But I'm gonna need backup. You're my best chance of getting it. Do you understand?"

His mouth opens, then he simply nods.

"Good. Thank you." Kit buttons her coat, pats down her pockets. "I wish I had a flashlight. . . . Okay, that's it. Give me two minutes to get out of the schoolhouse, then go straight to the MPs. Don't stop for anybody. If the MPs won't move, you've gotta *make* them move."

"If this is all real, then what you're doing is horribly dangerous," Harding says.

Kit is already heading for the door. She turns to look back. "They're my friends. Dottie and Violet and..." She can't say Moya's name, or she'll lose all her nerve. "They're my best friends."

"I feel awful, letting you go alone," he blurts out.

She makes a watery grin. "Then come after me. And make it snappy."

38

We were always underestimated. That
proved to be a mistake.
                              —BEVERLEY GASKIN

It's normal for girls in the Hall to dash about on errands, but
running would draw attention. Kit doesn't want to draw too
much attention until she's near the stables. Her feet won't
wait, though. A thin, blindingly bright line of fear sizzles
inside her, quickens her strides as she descends from the
fourth floor to the third, hurries through the corridor to the
next set of stairs, her footsteps deadened on the carpet.

*Moya and Dottie and Violet and Emil Ferrars and Violet
and Dottie and Moya and Moya and Moya...*

She grabs for the banister and runs into a wall of khaki.

"Whoa, hey there." Captain Cathcart steadies her with a
hand on her upper arm. "Slow down. I didn't get you, did I?"

"What?" Kit looks up at Cathcart's tanned face, the whit-
ened scar that deforms his lip. He has blue eyes, she realizes.
"I'm sorry I bumped—"

"I didn't get you with my elbow there, did I?" His expression is apologetic. Then concerned. "Are you okay, Miss
Sutherland? You look a little shook up."

"I—I'm fine," she stammers. "You didn't get me."

"Oh. Okay then." Cathcart removes his hand and makes a space for her to pass. "As you were."

I should say something, Kit thinks. Something innocuous and meaningless, designed to deflect. But the game is over. She's played it and played it—now she's had enough.

"Mr. Harding is up on Four," she says suddenly.

Captain Cathcart gives her a look of polite confusion. "Okay...Thanks."

"He needs help," Kit says. "He...he needs help with something, I think."

"Oh. Okay." Cathcart blinks. "Then...I guess I'll go find him."

"You do that," Kit says, and she quickly continues going down.

She marches through the foyer and the large double doors of the cafeteria, then heads for the kitchen to confirm what she already knows in her head and in her gut.

"Hello, excuse me." She knocks on the jamb, until one of the aproned women looks over. "Excuse me. The girls who left with the picnic basket...They haven't come back yet?"

The woman sets down her dish towel and comes closer, wiping her hands on her apron. "You mean young Violet and those other girls? No, ma'am. They're not back yet. It's getting mighty late for a picnic."

"Yes, it is," Kit says, and then, impulsively, "I'm gonna go fetch them back."

The woman raises her eyebrows. "You wanna pass through? The back door here is quicker."

Kit's chin lifts. "Thank you, much oblige."

She passes through the kitchen and the back door. Two stone steps draw her onto the path that leads through the quad to the forest.

Much oblige, she thinks wildly as she crunches fast over the gravel. *I haven't said "much oblige" for ten months.*

Even yesterday, a slipup like that might have meant questions. Things are coming back to her now, though. Old things she thought she'd put to bed.

She can go much faster now she's out of the schoolhouse—she hurries until she enters the tree cover. But it's well past gloaming, the shadows even darker under the white oaks. Kit can't see the uneven ground well enough to put real speed on. Her pace is very brisk, but she's not running like she wants to be.

She has to be sensible: If she trips over a tree root and sprains her ankle, she'll be useless.

Should've brought a flashlight. Should've brought a scarf for my hair. Should've brought a lot of things, goddammit.

She feels in her coat pockets, checking that Julian's knife is still there. The air around her tastes green and cold—the tip of her nose is cold. Her sense of perspective is altered by the lack of light: Trees seem far away, then suddenly rush out of the gloom. The forest has a quiet hum as she heads deeper into the grounds.

Back at the schoolhouse, things will be happening. Julian will be talking to John Cathcart, talking to the MPs, doing what's necessary. Kit wonders if there will be a holdup as they check his claim about her against her paperwork. Will they get the real Mr. Leighton Wallace away from his dinner to explain that Katherine Sutherland is deceased?

Loamy dirt and needles from the loblolly pines cushion the impact of her feet. The breeze crackles against her cheeks as she moves. Abruptly, through the swarming dark under the trees, the glimmering outline of a building—

The stables.

Kit has never been here at night. The wood and whitewash of the stables' exterior is blued in the moonlight. There's the front entrance, the double doors open wide and dark. To the west, a large fenced exercise yard, open to the air. Trees, yes, but not as many trees close by—not as much cover.

She remembers the internal layout. Inside the entrance, the old tack room on the west side, then the stalls: ten in all, five on each side of the center aisle. The aisle leads through to the indoor riding arena.

A memory: Moya blowing smoke as she stands at the door of the stables in her wrap coat. Moya winking at her. Moya's soft cheek, her lilting grin.

Kit clenches her fist against the tree and steadies her breathing. The need to rush forward is strong, very strong, and Kit wrestles with it. Plunging in blindly could be fatal.

She shouldn't walk right in the front entrance. Emil Ferrars knows her, knows the girls—he has likely noticed her absence from the group. The other girls may have told him that she is working elsewhere. Kit shudders to think of how he might have extracted that information.

Breathe. Think about Emil Ferrars.

He is twenty-two years old. He is singularly intelligent. He studied mathematics at Princeton. He is tall and slim and pale, with brown hair. He wears reading glasses. He gets tension headaches.

Now to combine it with what she knows of Emil Ferrars as a killer.

He is a chameleon. He is arrogant, playing a game with the police. Playing a game with all of them. The night she and Moya knocked on his door to go find Dottie at Arlington Farms—*My head just hit the pillow.*

Of course his head just hit the pillow. He'd just come back from murdering Libby Armstrong. Kit clutches the tree trunk. So Ferrars is arrogant. But he conceals the arrogance well; he is cunning. Nothing he does is unplanned.

This, too, has been planned—the knife was missing from the suitcase. The gloves, the hand towel. He was planning to kill Dottie during the picnic. But he didn't bring the golden-drop earring from Veronica Luca. And he has never killed so close to home. What has changed his pattern?

We want to take him back to England with us. Julian said it. That's the trigger—Ferrars is planning to leave for England. He can wash his hands of the government girl killings here and start afresh, with a whole new country to plunder....

Kit's breathing is almost under control now.

Something else she remembers.

Inside the stables, after the horse stalls and before the indoor riding arena, there's a junction. The aisle splits into a T. One side goes west to the exercise yard, and the other side goes east. Doors at each end. Ahead, the arena.

She has to go into the stables. The idea fills her with terror. But it is more terrifying, thinking of what Emil Ferrars might do to Dottie, to Violet, to Moya.

Kit jogs soundlessly, wide to the right of the door, to stay out of the sightline.

Near the entrance lies evidence of the abandoned picnic: A wicker basket sits on a patch of moon-bright ground just inside the stable door. Beside it, a rumpled plaid blanket and two candle lanterns, unlit.

Kit moves between the shadows, hugging the wall. She's right beside the picnic leavings. Dottie's green coat is dumped near the stable door. An uncapped bottle of 7UP lies empty, its contents dribbled onto the ground.

The sound of someone crying. Kit cups her ear against the wall of the stables. More sounds. Some of them make her fists clench. But she thinks she knows, now, where the sounds are coming from.

Time for the trickiest part.

Kit crouches down, then goes lower, onto hands and knees. Her palms connect with grass and old sawdust. The smell of ancient horse manure is strong. Wild clover is growing right up to the hinge of the door. She waits, listens, her skirt hitched to her thighs. If Emil Ferrars catches her creeping in through the front entrance, everything will go to hell.

As she's thinking it, an evening breeze courses through the surrounding trees, leaves rustle....

Now.

She scurries with the rustling sounds, crawling fast through the moon-bright patch at the front entrance, into the safety of shadows in the next empty doorway.

Kit presses herself against the wall. The smell of dry leather and molasses. She's in the tack room.

Farther away, a voice cries out. *"No! Please don't—"*

Dottie. The urge to run toward the voice is like a physical pain. She has to think. She has to do something.

Distract Emil Ferrars. Create a diversion.

Kit searches inside herself for something she can use. She is just a girl. A girl smart enough to unravel Emil Ferrars's web of lies, but a girl all the same. She has no skills except decoding and deception, and those skills are useless now.

She imagines Katherine scolding her. *That's not all you are. You're a girl with a head full of geometry and piano playing and crossword puzzles....*

But Kit knows the truth. She is still the girl from Scott's Run, the girl whose sole talents lie in her duties. *What can a maid do against a homicidal genius from Princeton?* The thought brings tears to her eyes. She dashes at them roughly with the back of her hand. She is all there is. The MPs will come, but maybe not in time. If she has only a maid's skill, a girl's strength, then that will have to be enough.

What are her maid skills?

How to be discreet. To go about her duties unobtrusively. How to mop a floor. How to steam iron. Draw a bath. Lay a tea tray. Light a fire in the grate—

Kit exhales, soft and low.

We fight with what we have, and she knows how she will fight.

39

Now there must have been some feeling
all over that things were going to get
worse.

—WILMA BERRYMAN

Moya's ears are ringing.

The tinnitus is worse, somehow, than the bite of the thin, coarse rope around her wrists and ankles. She can still see and feel her fingers—they're cold from having the circulation cut off, but they're there—and her ankle bones are rubbing together. But the ringing in her ears, like a great peal of bells inside her head, makes concentrated thought impossible. That makes her scared. She needs to be able to think, now more than ever.

"No!" Dottie cries out. "Please don't—"

Emil cuts her off with a slap to the face. Sudden and efficient. He's good at slapping women, this new Emil Ferrars. This version that Moya is trying desperately to adjust to.

"Shut up," he says. His face is expressionless, detached. "You don't get to say no."

He goes back to methodically slicing the buttons off the front of Dottie's dress. Two buttons. Three buttons. Dottie is crying. The satin of her brassiere is exposed.

Moya feels sick. Beside her, Violet is shivering. Her hands

and feet are tied, too. They're huddled together on the ground, sitting on the hard sawdust just before the entrance to the indoor riding arena. The wooden half wall is at their backs. Moya can feel Violet's quaking through the places they're connected, at thigh, bicep, shoulder.

Violet is terrified.

But still gutsy as hell. She screws up her face and screams, "Leave her alone!"

Emil stops what he's doing. Saunters away from Dottie, who stands there, legs trembling, hair disheveled, her dress loose on her shoulders, and her hands tied together.

Dottie moans. Moya understands. If Emil is paying attention to Dottie's friends, he's giving her a temporary reprieve. But it's an awful equation. Awful. There's no way for any of them to win in this equation. Every option is bad.

Oh God, why didn't we work this out sooner?

It happened so damn quickly. Moya and Dottie and Violet had trooped into the forest together. They all set up the picnic: cleared a space free of leaves and branches, laid down the blanket, arranged the basket, the lanterns. Laughed and picked flowers and made jokes.

Then Emil had shown up early. He wasn't supposed to arrive until five thirty. Apart from being early, he'd seemed normal. His dark hair was tousled in the typical way. His brown trousers and white shirt were pressed, and he was wearing a suit jacket, in preparation for his date. Dottie had blushed.

Emil's eyes had lit up when he'd seen her. He'd seemed fine.

"Well, look at all of you," he'd said with a smile.

"Hi, Emil. We were just clearing out." Moya had felt like

339

she was intruding. She and Violet had only meant to help with the setup for the picnic, not be there when the beau arrived. They gathered their coats, preparing to leave.

"Hold on a second," Emil had said. "You don't have to rush off."

"Uh, we kinda do," Violet said, grinning at Dottie. "You kids have fun now."

"Okay, fine." Emil smiled. "I get it. But before you leave— have you seen the baroness's stall?" Emil waved a hand to the inside of the building. "The Baroness Lillian Campbell of New Brunswick sent her daughter to Arlington Hall when it was still a school. She had an exclusive stall set up for her daughter's horse, with a hot water faucet and a bronze feed hopper. There's a plaque and everything. You should see it before you go."

"Can I see?" Dottie asked.

"Sure. Take a look."

He'd gone into the dim interior of the stables, Dottie walking up the center aisle beside him. Violet had looked at Moya and shrugged, then followed.

Moya had wanted to get back to Kit. And she'd desperately wanted a smoke, but she went inside. She figured it couldn't take long.

Distracted by the need for a cigarette, Moya thinks. *Goddammit.*

Dull late-afternoon light filtered through the windows high at the back of each horse stall. Emil had ushered Violet forward to the stall at the far right end of the aisle. He'd grinned, then encouraged Moya herself to go ahead and look.

340

When she'd peered into the stall he indicated, she only had time to say, "I can't see a plaque—" before the world exploded. Her head was slammed against the wooden rail of the stall, her knees kicked out from under her. The sound of Violet's yells had come through a fog of stars and pealing bells.

When Moya resurfaced, she was on the ground, slumped against the wall of the horse stall. Violet's cream sweater was up close. Her purple skirt had ridden up, exposing her knees, and she had a warm hand on Moya's arm.

Moya blinked, and sounds came back on.

"—do it. I'll do it, okay?" Violet was looking up at something. "Just don't hurt Dottie."

Moya followed the line of Violet's gaze, but what she saw made no sense. Emil Ferrars was standing behind Dottie, who was whimpering in her polka-dotted dress. Emil was wearing dark leather gloves. He was holding Dottie's hair back from her neck with one hand, and in his other hand...

A fillet knife, the sharp steel glinting.

"Emil," Moya said. Not a question, more like she was speaking his name to confirm it.

"Hi, Moya," Emil said. He was grinning. He looked at Violet, his grin turning razor-pointed. "This is taking too long."

That's when Moya heard her own voice become questioning. *"Emil?"*

Instead of replying, he had tugged at Dottie's hair. She gasped.

"I have to tie you up," Violet said, by Moya's head. Her voice was quavering. "Moya, listen. I gotta tie your hands. I'm sorry, but I gotta do this."

341

"Yes, you do," Emil said. "Tie her hands, then come over here."

It had all happened with a kind of nightmarish slowness after that. Emil had made Dottie tie Violet. Then he'd made them move out of the stall, into the aisle, and farther along, to the entrance to the riding arena. He'd kept the knife at Dottie's neck. Dottie had been crying. That's when the slapping had started.

How has this happened? Moya found the answer to the question still escaping her. She'd needed to lean on Violet to walk. Her head was pounding, and where she'd rested her forehead against Violet's pale sweater, there was a red stain.

Once all the girls were by the open arena entrance, Emil told them where to sit, or in Dottie's case, stand. They were separated from each other by a space of eight feet that felt like a mile. He'd made Dottie tie Moya and Violet's ankles; then he had tied Dottie's wrists.

And the whole time, Moya had been trying to think past the bells in her head.

How had they not known? How had they been so fooled? By Emil—*Emil*. The quiet guy who put pencils behind his ear and forgot about them. The guy she'd worked with for the last ten months. *Ten months*. The guy whose car she'd ridden in, who she'd round-tabled over codes with on Four, who she'd had coffee with in the cafeteria. The guy with the suspenders. The guy with the headaches. Had he ever really had headaches?

She's sure as hell got one now.

As Dottie stands helpless and moaning, as Emil walks closer, Moya examines his face for any sign of what she missed, but all she can see are his brown eyes, once warm, now glittering with malice.

"Leave her alone," Emil repeats, savoring the words. He squats down and stares at Violet. "Does that mean I should let Dottie be and play with you instead?" He extends his hand with the knife, uses the tip of the blade to flip back a curly strand of Violet's hair. Violet shudders.

Moya is so sick of being afraid. "It means you should walk away, Emil. Just turn around and—"

He moves so fast—the knife tip slides between her lips and she freezes. Emil examines its position dispassionately. It's poised now in the corner of her mouth. Moya feels the steel bite there, making a small split in the delicate skin.

"I am very tired," Emil says quietly, "of listening to girls talk. Do you know that? They talk all day. It's like they don't know how to shut up. Well, I've figured out how to make them shut up. It's very effective. Would you like a demonstration?"

Moya cannot say no. She cannot even shake her head. She can only hold Emil's dark, unending gaze. A warm itch of wet slides from the corner of her mouth down to her chin. She can't wipe it away.

"Can you imagine?" he says. "Month after month of being trapped in that schoolhouse, surrounded by female noise. The gossip and the chatter. The smell of them. Their self-importance. The way they're constantly *there*. The chaos of them—it invades your brain. And they're *everywhere*. In the street. In the office. In the goddamn Pentagon. It's like a fucking plague. A plague of *girls*."

Emil is looking at her with such hate that Moya feels dizzy.

"I'm doing my part," Emil says. "I'm doing my part in the war against it. I'm culling. But you figured that out, didn't you?"

It takes her a moment to realize what he's talking about. This is the killer they've been chasing. But how did he know they were chasing him?

"At first, I thought you'd seen me take Veronica downstairs at the Mayflower," he goes on. "But then when Dottie accepted my invitation for a date, I knew. You figured out some of it, but not all. Not exactly who. That was perfect for me! I knew your identity, but you didn't know mine. *You didn't know mine!*"

Emil grins wider. The tip of the steel in Moya's mouth has a cold, iron flavor. Or maybe that's the taste of her own blood. She's too scared to swallow; the knife might cut further.

"The whole thing is great," Emil says. "I can deal with all of you at once. Up until now, I've been taking a girl here and there. But it's time to try something different—it's time to step up. The only awkward part," Emil reflects sadly, "is that one member of your little gang is missing."

An image of Kit's face, the curve of her smile, stands out in Moya's mind. For the first time, Moya finds herself truly lost. Her vision gets blurry. She doesn't want Emil to say Kit's name, to even *think* about Kit. Moya doesn't want to cry, but the tears come anyway. They sting on her cheeks and on the cut at the corner of her mouth.

Emil leans in, his eyes stark, showing the whites. "So here's what we're going to do. We're going to play here. You said to have fun? I'm going to have a *lot* of fun. Three times the fun, in fact. Then when we're done, I'm going to find your little friend in the Hall, and have fun with her, too."

"How did you know?" Violet asks suddenly.

Her question comes from right beside Moya's face, and Moya stiffens in an effort to avoid startling, to avoid the knife. Then Emil withdraws the knife from her mouth, and Moya gasps. She gasps because the knife is removed, and she gasps because she understands that Violet has asked the question regardless of the danger to herself, with exactly this aim in mind.

Clever, gutsy girl. Moya is shaking with relief and anger both.

"How did I know it was all four of you?" Emil is already standing up. "That was easy."

He walks back to Dottie. She is sobbing quietly. Moya is trembling so much she can hardly breathe, but she feels Violet's bound hands find her own. She clenches Violet's fingers tight.

Emil lifts a hand—not the one with the knife—and strokes Dottie's hair back from her face while she cries. "It was easy, wasn't it, honey? Do you want to tell them how I knew?"

In the ominous quiet, a voice rings out.

"It's because Dottie told you," Kit says.

40

Any man-made code can be broken by a woman.

—AGNES MEYER DRISCOLL

The reaction is immediate; Emil grabs Dottie and spins her so her back is pressed to his front. Dottie yelps. There's a gasp Kit knows is Violet's, but she can't look in her direction now. She focuses on Emil: His shirt is unbuttoned at the neck; the fall of his dark fringe shades his face. Beneath his hair, his eyes are hard, his cheeks like caves. He looks like a shark of the deep. How did she not see this before?

Because he is an impostor, just like you. Because he only allowed you to see him a certain way.

Kit steps out from the shadow of the stall door, into the moonlight, keeping her eyes on Emil, and on the knife at Dottie's waist. Rather than allow Emil a moment to secure his advantage, she continues talking.

"I remember what Dottie said, about the day you asked her out." Kit's throat is dry, but she keeps speaking. "She said she met you in the cafeteria while she was getting coffee and the newspapers. Those would be the newspapers delivered every morning, that are collected and taken up to Four."

"That's right." Emil's hand is digging into Dottie's upper

arm, but his face has regained its focus. "Welcome to our picnic, Miss Sutherland."

Kit ignores that. "One of those newspapers is the *Washington Star.*"

"Kit," Dottie gasps.

Kit keeps her expression completely neutral, despite being furious, blindingly furious at Emil Ferrars, for what he's done. "And you saw the headline, didn't you, Mr. Ferrars? The headline of the article—'Mayflower Murder Witness Comes Forward.'"

She still can't shake that old, ingrained habit: *Mr. Ferrars.* "And Dottie noticed you noticing," Kit goes on. "She reminded you that she'd seen you at the Mayflower that night."

"Kitty, *please,*" Dottie gasps.

Kit can hear her accent—her own, real West Virginia accent—unfurling itself through her words as she speaks. "And because she thought she could trust you, she confided in you. She said that she and Moya Kershaw and Kit Sutherland and Violet DuLac, from the cottage, had been at the Mayflower the night of Veronica Luca's murder. Dottie told you that we were cooperating with the police."

"Ohmigod—*Dottie?*" Moya's faint voice. Kit can't look.

Emil Ferrars offers a cold smile. His eyes are equally cold. "You're very good at working these things out, Miss Sutherland."

Dottie is weeping, her cheeks red and wet. She's talking only to Kit. "I didn't mean to...I didn't know....Oh, Kit, I'm so *sorry.*"

347

For the briefest moment, Kit looks at Dottie, putting every encouraging thought she can muster into that glance. "Dorothy Crockford, don't you dare apologize—you've got nothing to apologize for." She looks back at Emil. "This man made you trust him. That's what he does. He acts sweet and kind and unthreatening, and girls fall for it. We all fell for it. So don't you feel bad, not one bit. It's my fault for not seeing him clearly the first time."

Emil Ferrars's smile vanishes into a sneer. "Do you think you're seeing me clearly now?"

"I know I am." Kit keeps her feet firmly placed, arms loose at her sides. The air from the arena smells dark and cool. The old scent of horses reminds her of the schoolgirls of Arlington Hall. "And I hope you're seeing me clearly, too. You think the English guys are going to take you out of here, away from the mess you're making. You think you've got an advantage—Dottie under your arm, and Moya and Violet there on the floor, and you with the knife. But you're wrong. You don't hold the advantage here. You've read all the signs wrong."

"Have I?" Emil looks positively furious now, condescension dripping from him with every word. "Miss Sutherland, I don't think you know what you're talking about. Girls like you..." He pulls Dottie's hair back, lifts the knife until it's poised at her throat. Kit hears her gasp. Emil's mouth screws up. "I know girls like you. I work with them every day."

Kit holds her ground, hands clenching into fists.

"One Army ID badge and you think you're a soldier. One line of code and you think you're a genius." Emil grins.

It's different from his usual grin—twisted and cruel. But of course, this is his *real* grin. "You think you've got the intelligence to keep up. You think you're battle hardened. Girls playing at soldiers, safe behind front lines.... You're not fighters at all. You give in *every damn time*. So yes, I know girls like you. I've *killed* girls like you."

Kit steps one pace closer. This man does not intimidate her. Emil Ferrars will need to suffer the consequences for the things he's done. She will be the one to deliver those consequences.

"Is that what you think? That you know me?" She shifts so Emil Ferrars can see her eyes clearly. She pours every ounce of scorn and loathing into her gaze. *"You don't know anything about me.* You don't know who I really am. You don't even know my real name."

She sees his smile falter. She steps closer—only three steps from Dottie now.

"Your disguise was good, Emil, but mine was better." Each word she utters rolls through the arena, echoes borne on shadows. She lifts her chin. "Because I am not Kit Sutherland. I am not from Pennsylvania. And I am not like all those girls you know—I am the code you never broke, and I don't play by the rules."

Then the old cans of cleaning fluid and wood varnish and neat's-foot oil that Kit set on fire in the tack room explode in a deafening, incandescent storm.

41

Have you ever fought for something
truly important? I mean, really fought,
with every fiber of your being? That's
what we were doing at Arlington Hall.
                            —BRIGID GLADWELL

There's a *WHOOSH* behind her, and a rush of heat and light, and a number of things happen all at once.

Kit flinches, feels warmth on her shoulders and the backs of her legs. Emil startles harder; his eyes go wide as he ducks, his face glowing with the fire's illumination. His right arm jerks back automatically with the shock. Kit's suddenly huge shadow casts him in crevassed relief.

Dottie turns around and *shoves* him. "Kit, GO!" Dottie yells, but his hold on her arm still snags her.

Moya and Violet are in the corner of Kit's eye as she darts forward to pull Dottie clear. "*KIT!*" Moya cries.

Emil Ferrars has an expression of seething hatred on his face as he lunges toward Kit with the knife. Kit reels back as his arm descends. She staggers; then Dottie's body is in the way.

"Dottie!" Violet yells.

Dottie barrels into Emil, her shoulder colliding with his chin. Emil cries out. He rights himself, grabs Dottie by the hair, shoving his knife hand in near her waist. Dottie arches and lets out a shriek.

"*DOTTIE!*" Kit screams.

But Emil Ferrars is already pushing Dottie away, toward Kit. "*Take* the stupid bitch, then!"

And suddenly Dottie is in Kit's arms—a warm, shocking weight, her body limp and lolling. Kit holds tight, and they fall to the sawdust together as Emil Ferrars turns around and vaults the wooden half wall into the riding arena, sprints for the other side. There's a door there, she knows, only two hundred feet away.

"NO!" Moya yells.

Kit feels heat on her back. Orange light from the fire is flickering all over. Something explodes in the tack room with a pop, and Kit flinches again.

"*Kit,*" Dottie croaks. She is sweaty-faced, her blond curls radiant, her eyes very bright in the firelight. She's clutching at Kit's forearms.

"It's okay," Kit croons. "It's okay, I got you—"

"Kit, *chase him,*" Dottie gasps, squeezing Kit hard. "You need to get him. *Don't let him go.*"

"Kit!" Violet yells. The fire is catching on old harnesses and hay in stalls close by.

Kit slings an arm around Dottie's waist, gets them both up, and pulls her in the other girls' direction. Dottie releases a cry of pain when Kit jerks her forward, which Kit will hear in her head forever.

Moya reaches up with her tied hands. She's still on the ground, so Kit basically pours Dottie onto her lap. "Take her!"

"I've got her," Moya says firmly, then she looks at Kit. "Kit, I—"

Kit crouches down. She and Moya are perfectly eye to eye, and this is the perfect time, so she leans forward swiftly and kisses Moya on the lips. Then she scrambles back up and grabs in her coat pocket for Julian's knife. She flicks the blade open with one hand and attacks the ropes on Violet's wrists until they fall away. The flames behind her sound like hungry demons.

"Give me the knife," Violet cries, and she takes the knife before Kit can reply, slices at her ankle ties. "Moya—"

"Here." Moya holds her wrists out to Violet. All their voices are raised over the crackle of flames. "This building is going up like a torch!"

"Get out of here, all of you!" Kit yells, shedding her coat, balling it up to press on Dottie's wound.

"We'll take care of her," Violet yells back, slashing Moya's ankles free. "Go! You need to move fast if you're gonna catch up to him!" She tosses Kit the knife.

"*Kit,*" Moya says, her pale face limned and glowing. "Go, go."

Nothing can stop Kit from pursuing Emil Ferrars now. She turns and flies through the open entry to the riding arena, following Emil's path.

Her oxfords immediately fill up with sawdust—she kicks them off. She's running, skirt hitched, breath panting. Her stockinged feet slap the floor as she chases after the murderer of four women.

Perspiration clings to her forehead and cheeks. A sharp stitch of pain flares under her ribs; Kit realizes that sitting in the workroom hovering over codes hasn't exactly fitted her well for frantic pursuit. Then her palm slams into the rear door, and she wrenches the handle open and plunges through.

Instantly there's a smell of green sap and a shocking rush of crisp night air. Kit's senses are assailed by the sudden quiet as she moves toward the trees. She holds the deer-bone-handle knife out in front of herself, her hand shaking. Her practically bare soles shrink against the feel of cool grass and dirt underfoot.

The forest at the back of the stables is dark, but not utterly black. There's a brightening flicker on the nearest pines as the fire in the stables gains momentum.

Which way would he go? Back toward the schoolhouse? She's about to turn in that direction when a rustling snap of vegetation makes her swing around fast.

Emil Ferrars grunts as he slashes downward.

Kit feels something like a smack on her own knife arm. Suddenly there is pain, bright and blinding, and she drops Julian's knife and cries out, backs away. Knees caught in her skirt, she stumbles on the tussocks beneath her feet, falls heavily on her tailbone.

Emil is on her in a heartbeat, slamming her back against the dirt. His arm is raised for a second strike.

"You thought you could beat me." His breaths are loud, his expression deranged. He presses her against the ground with the weight of his body. "You thought you could *expose* me, make me run—"

Kit's yell is guttural as she pushes against his knife arm with her hands, her arms, her shoulders—with every muscle

353

she's got. Sticks and pine needles rasp her spine through her clothes as she bucks, but Emil Ferrars has her pinned fast.

"I *knew* you'd chase me," Emil grinds out. His teeth are gritted in a snarl. Sweat from his forehead spatters her like a mist. "So predictable. You think you're so smart. I've fought girls like you—"

"*SHUT UP, SHUT UP!*" Kit screams in his face. The long fillet knife is wavering above her cheek. Her arms are shaking, her right arm smarting and weak.

"You always make the same mistakes!" Emil crows. "You think you can beat the knife. Girls *always* think they can beat the knife. But that never happens. Girls like you don't know—"

There's a sound like a crack of lightning, and Kit screams, and what she doesn't know will remain forever unknown because Emil Ferrars's head suddenly bursts apart on one side. His body follows the same shearing trajectory, and he topples over, off her.

Kit's arms clutch empty air. Her ears are ringing loud. She's aware that something hot and wet is slicking the side of her face, dribbling into her hairline. All she can do is gasp and gasp. She's cold; the ground is hard. Her breath blows steam into the night air.

High above her, past the treetops, the stars are brilliant, their voices singing.

There are other voices.

"Thought he'd shot you, oh my *god*," Julian Harding says, suddenly overhead, his broad tweed-covered shoulder blocking out the stars. Julian is not wearing his spectacles.

He only needs them for reading, Kit remembers.

"Are you all right? Kit, can you hear me?"

"*KIT!*" someone screams; then Julian is abruptly shoved aside and Kit is enveloped in Moya's warmth.

Kit looks up at the sky and feels the press of Moya's breasts against her chest, Moya's sharp elbows and skinny arms and the smell of her, which is sooty and sweet all at once. Kit closes her eyes, curls her arms around Moya's neck.

For a while she just lets Moya hold her, because that is what they both need. She won't cry, because once she starts it will be difficult to stop. Crying can come later. All she wants is to lie here in the dark, on the ground, with her face tucked into the hollow above Moya's collarbone.

"Oh my god, Kit, you're bleeding," Moya says, voice hitching. Then Moya's arms are around her, helping her sit up.

Kit sees Julian Harding, flame-haloed by the stables behind him, kneeling beside them on the grass and looking horrified. "Do you need a handkerchief?" he says. "I have a handkerchief. . . ."

"Yes," Moya says curtly, holding out a hand.

"You already gave me your handkerchief." Kit's voice is croaky. She's surprised it still works. "I used it to light the fire. Your cigarette lighter and your handkerchief—"

"I've got another one," he says. He fishes the white square out of his waistcoat pocket, shakes it out, and gives it to Moya.

"It's like you're made of handkerchiefs." Kit feels feather-light. She endures the tugging and pressure as Moya binds her arm. "Ow."

"We need a medic," Moya says.

"Yes, quite." Julian rubs his face with one hand. He looks like he's in shock. "I can't believe you're—"

He's interrupted by a man in uniform who comes limping fast.

"Miss Sutherland, we need to move you." It's John Cathcart. He's wincing from some pain, which Kit assumes is the old injury in his leg, and he's holding a revolver. "The stables are going up quick—"

There's a creaking sound. Kit realizes they're only a half-dozen yards from a building that has fire crackling out from its roof. She watches the dancing flames for a moment, fascinated.

"All right, folks, come on." Cathcart's voice is authoritative. "At least fifty feet safe distance. Miss Kershaw, can you help Miss Sutherland?" There are other figures moving around nearby, figures in dark uniforms and white helmets; she can see their MP armbands from here.

"Where's Dottie?" Kit asks suddenly. "And Violet?"

"They're okay," Julian says, standing up. "The MPs got them out of the building. Kit, it's all right."

Moya says, "Come on, lean on me."

"You've got a head wound," Kit remembers, slinging her good arm around Moya's waist for support.

"That doesn't matter," Moya demurs. She nuzzles Kit's forehead with her own as she gently urges her to move, before turning her face toward Cathcart. "Captain, where are my girls?"

"Miss DuLac is seeing to Miss Crockford on the other side of the stables," Cathcart says, walking with them. "There's a medic attending. I'm headed there now. Will you stay with Miss Sutherland?"

Moya nods, which is a relief. Kit doesn't think she could physically tear herself away from Moya right now. She's having trouble putting one foot in front of the other.

Cathcart holsters his revolver. "Miss Sutherland, I'm sorry you were put in harm's way. I wasn't near enough to tackle him, and I couldn't see any other course of action—"

"Did you make that shot, Captain?" Part of Kit is tucked against Moya's body and part of her is still floating free.

"Yes, I did, ma'am."

"That was an amazing shot. You saved my life." Kit looks over her shoulder and sees Julian Harding lay his tweed jacket over Emil Ferrars's upper body. "Emil was...He killed four government girls. Margaret Wishart, Dinah Shaw, Libby Armstrong, Veronica Luca...We have evidence, lines of investigation for the police—"

"Miss Sutherland, it's okay," Cathcart says with a grimace. "Mr. Harding already showed me the suitcase."

"Ah." Kit suddenly wants to sit down again. "Moya—"

"Grab her," Cathcart says swiftly.

"I've got her. Walk with me," Moya commands. "Come on, Kit. Over to the tree—no, this tree."

Once they get to the pine tree, Moya sits down with her. They lean against the scratchy trunk and each other, watching the fire consume the stables and light up the night.

Moya wraps Kit's arm again with the blue scarf from the pocket of her shearling jacket. It doesn't hurt so much now. The warmth of the fire feels nice on Kit's face.

A jeep's headlights flash and bounce through the trees. There are MPs talking to Julian Harding at the place where Emil Ferrars died. Kit's gaze flitters to that scene, flitters away. Cathcart limps toward them.

"I knew you'd try to come," Moya whispers into Kit's hair. "God, I was so scared."

Kit doesn't have the heart to tell Moya what's going to happen next.

"They're fine," Cathcart says as he gets closer. His leg is obviously giving him a lot of grief now. "I mean, Miss DuLac is okay. She's with the MPs, giving a statement. Miss Crockford—"

"Is Dottie going to be all right?" Kit swallows hard.

"They've taken her to the hospital—I carried her to the jeep. She's a little more touch and go, but she's strong and the medic said she's got good signs." Cathcart looks toward the burning stables. He shoves at his hair in that way he always does; Kit thinks it's a nervous habit. "Miss Sutherland..."

"It's all right," Kit says. "You can say it."

Moya squints. "Say what?"

Cathcart bites his scarred lip. "Your name's not really Miss Sutherland, is it?"

Moya makes a little sound, a groaning gasp. Kit shakes her head slowly.

"Well, that is...not good." Cathcart winces. He has an air of resignation. "Miss Sutherland, I'm sorry, but I'm obliged to—"

"*Wait*," a voice says, and Julian Harding has jogged closer. He's staring at Cathcart accusingly. "Captain, I thought we talked about this. You said an arrest was your least preferred outcome."

Cathcart tongues his back teeth. "We did. And I did."

"Then don't do this." Julian's sharp cheekbones are accented in the firelight. "Look, I have no influence over the processes of American military justice at all. And I know this is an awkward situation. I'm British, we certainly understand awkward...."

"She lied on her papers," Cathcart says quietly. He glances at Moya. "Other people conspired to conceal her identity—"

"Yes, yes," Julian says impatiently. "She also broke Japanese ciphers crucial to the war effort and exposed a serial rapist and murderer *within your own organization*. John... please don't do this."

Cathcart hesitates. Kit can feel Moya squeezing her hand.

"Listen," Julian says. "I have a suggestion regarding Miss Sutherland's situation. It might save face all round...."

Cathcart pauses, tilts his head. "I'm listening."

Kit is listening, too. She's listening hard.

42

No code is ever completely solved, you know.

—ELIZEBETH FRIEDMAN

It's Friday, late afternoon. The view outside Kit's dorm room window is inviting: the green expanse of lawn, the cherry trees in full leaf, warm sun glittering on the white of the administration cottage. Behind the cottage, glimpses of the construction work, ongoing.

A blue-tailed swallow flits past the window. In the forested area to the left, only a blackened patch of tree line—still smoking—gives away what happened last night.

Kit tucks a final pair of rolled-up stockings into her carpet bag and glances toward the construction area again. Those fresh-painted workrooms will be ready for the influx of new code girls by the end of April. She almost wishes she could stay to see it: All the girls in their skirt suits and summer cardigans, pencils at the ready. All the bright, shining faces, the river of girls, the army of girls flowing to their tables, keen to pit their wits against Japanese signal men hunkered down in the South Pacific who don't even know that Arlington Hall and its cadre of smart girls exist...

"Axis don't stand a chance," Kit whispers, smiling.

"What did you say?"

Kit looks over, filled with relief. "You're awake."

"Yeah, but as soon as I wake up, I feel sleepy again." Dottie's in her bathrobe, her golden hair spread across the mounds of pillows on her bed, her overall complexion very pale. Her face is still soft with tiredness. "Those pills really knock me out. You talking to yourself, Kitty-Kat?"

"Just thinking about the new girls coming in the summer." Kit shakes the nostalgia loose. "Are you sure you're gonna be okay tonight? Maybe you should've stayed in the hospital—"

"Ugh, no way, hospitals are the worst." Dottie grins at Kit's frown. "Don't start on about that again. I'll be fine. Opal's coming before dinner, and the infirmary nurse is coming to take care of me at seven. I've got girls lining up to check in on me—"

"Not to mention a certain captain who's been extremely attentive," Kit notes.

"Well." Dottie makes a movement like she's trying to toss her hair, but stops and grimaces when that proves uncomfortable. "John is a very nice man—"

"*John*, is it now?" Kit smiles.

"He's a very nice man, and don't you smirk at me." Dottie rolls her eyes. "He's just stopping by to say hello, which is a kind thing to do."

"Uh-huh. Very kind."

"He carried me to the ambulance, you know."

"You told me about it already. Twice."

"Well maybe I did." Dottie's gaze wanders sideways. "But I'm not even thinking about stuff like that right now. It's all still...too fresh in my mind...."

"I know, hon," Kit says gently. She sits on the bed and takes Dottie's hand. "And I know it'll take a while. But you remember what I said. There was no fault in anything any of us did. You're a hero, Dot. How you put yourself in front of me—"

"I know." Dottie looks back from the sight of Kit's carpet bag on the opposite bed, squeezes Kit's hand. "But let's not talk about that now. Did you say goodbye to Opal and the girls?"

"I did," Kit says.

"Good. Have you got everything you need? You've got that weird face again...."

"Am I doing the right thing?" Kit asks suddenly.

"Well, it's the only thing you *can* do, hon." Dottie makes a wan grin. "But putting that aside... Yes, Kit. I believe you're doing the right thing. Don't you be scared now. There's nothing to be scared of. Except me," she amends, "if you don't write me regular, like I asked."

"I'll write you," Kit says. "Dot..." She can feel her throat getting thick. "Dottie, I'm going to miss you so."

"I know, Kitty-Kat." Dottie's eyes are shining, too. "But it'll be all right."

A voice comes from the open doorway. "Miss Sutherland? It's getting close to time." Julian Harding is dressed in a traveling suit, his greatcoat over one arm. He's holding a small suitcase in his other hand. "Would you like me to take your luggage downstairs? If you'd like a few more minutes..." His gaze moves to Dottie, propped up in bed. "Hello, Miss Crockford. I hope you're feeling better?"

"Well, sure, Mr. Harding," Dottie calls in reply. "I'm

feeling a lot better now I don't have a knife jammed through my innards, thanks for asking."

"Erm…" Julian still seems uncertain of how to react to American humor sometimes.

Kit saves him from replying. "I'll take my own bag, Julian. Gimme one more minute."

"All right. I'll see you downstairs shortly." He tips the front brim of his fedora in Dottie's direction. "Adieu, Miss Crockford. Best wishes for your recovery."

"Thank you!" Dottie lifts her chin, grinning.

Kit watches Julian depart. "You're a tease."

"Forever and always." Dottie winks. She clasps Kit's hand tight. "Okay, it's time. No long goodbye business, you know I hate that."

"Did Moya already—" Kit starts.

"She did," Dottie confirms. "Now kiss my cheek and go. And make sure to write."

"I will," Kit says, swallowing back tears. She kisses Dottie's soft cheek as instructed. Inhales Dottie's cornflower scent. Presses their foreheads together. "I love you, Dottie Crockford. Be well. Get better."

"I love you, too," Dottie says. "And I will." Her own chin is trembling and her voice is a whisper. "Now get out of here and go live."

Kit nods—it's time. She grabs her jacket. It's the navy traveling jacket with the peplum waist that Katherine left her. Kit slips it on, careful of the bandage over the stitches on her right forearm. She faces the mirror and fixes her blouse under the jacket, straightens her skirt.

"Don't forget your hat," Dottie reminds her.

Kit pins the hat over her rolled hair. She opens her compact and powders her face, covers the red splotches beneath her eyes. Her hand, applying the lipstick, is faintly shaking. She finishes with the makeup and tucks it away in the brown vinyl handbag.

"Gloves, gloves," Dottie says.

"Got 'em." Kit sets her handbag on her right wrist, away from her bandage, hefts the carpet bag by the bamboo handle with her left hand. All her paperwork is inside, plus her wages. She's already tucked ten dollars into her jacket pocket.

"Go well, my friend," Dottie calls from her bed. She kisses her fingers and blows the kiss Kit's way.

"Love you," Kit says. Before she can start crying again, she walks out the door.

Now she's moving, she feels better, but it's still like a part of her soul is being torn in half. Her heels tramp the red carpet to the stairs—she's in a pair of Violet's shoes, because her own oxfords were destroyed in the stables fire.

She has to watch her feet or risk stumbling because her eyes keep tearing up. Every step she takes is a goodbye to the familiar, goodbye to the world she knows.

"Dammit," she whispers. "Come on, now."

"You okay there?" a familiar voice says at the landing on Two. Violet is in a blue skirt and a cream blouse and a forest-green sweater. Her hair is its usual beautiful riot. A brown paper bag dangles from her hand. "Oh, girl," Violet says, shaking her head. "You're going to mess your makeup and you haven't even made it out the door. Take this."

Violet hands Kit the paper bag, hunts in the pockets of her skirt.

"Are these cookies?" Kit says, voice hitching. But she doesn't need to ask; she can smell the cinnamon and oatmeal.

"Here." Violet passes her a Kleenex. "Blot your eyes. Yes, they're cookies from home. You're gonna need something for the trip."

"Oh gosh. You already gave me your shoes...." Kit sets down her carpet bag and tucks the cookie packet into her handbag. She dabs with the Kleenex, not knowing where to look. Her cup is full, and emotions are spilling out of her in a way she can't seem to navigate. "Oh gosh. Violet—"

Violet grabs her for a hug. Kit squeezes tight. Violet's arms are strong and warm. Finally, Kit pushes them both apart.

"You're going to visit me, right?" Kit clutches the Kleenex. "Don't say *I'll see*. Say you'll visit when you can."

"When my term here is done, I'll try to visit," Violet says, nodding. "Don't know how I'll do it, but I'll get there somehow. Come on, let's walk you down. Got your bag?"

"I've got it." Kit lifts her carpet bag again, forcing her feet to move. "Did you talk to Raffi?"

"I did, and I explained as much as I could in a phone call." They stride past the workrooms on Two, making for the stairs to the next level. The sound of typing is a humming chatter. "He wants to meet up and get the details about what happened with Emil Ferrars. I said I still didn't know if I was allowed to speak about it, but I'd see."

"Meet him anyway," Kit suggests. "Go to Club Caverns and dance. Drink a margarita for me."

Violet snorts. "I'll think about it."

"Don't think about it, just do it."

"Maybe I will." Violet holds the banister as they take the stairs down to One.

"Do it for Dinah," Kit says impulsively. She feels as if she has to say everything, too much, in the time they have left. "And say yes to Howard. Talk to Mr. Coffee about it—"

"I've already said yes to Howard," Violet says. "And Mr. Coffee said there might be another job for me. He said there's this place called the NACA, at Langley, that's crying out for Black computers—"

"Oh my god, Violet. That's it." They've reached the parquet on One, and Kit drops her bags, clings to her friend's arms. "That's it. You're doing it."

"I don't know—I really don't." Violet bites her bottom lip, her chin quivering. "But hope's all I've got, and I've got to try."

"You're gonna be amazing." Kit holds Violet's gaze. "Promise me you'll be amazing."

"You know it." Violet's face breaks into a watery grin.

"I know it. And don't back out on me. I want to see you again before this war is over. There's freedom where I'm going—you might like the taste of that."

"I might." Violet swallows, nods. "Okay, that's enough now. You've got to go. I've gotta go back to my shift."

"Better go, then. Did you already see Moya?"

"I did." Violet dives in for one more hug. "Take care, Kit."

Kit holds on for dear life. "You too, Violet. I hope I'll see you soon."

They break apart and Violet turns to go, turns back.

Her smooth brown cheeks are highlighted by the sun, her dimples accenting the curves. She looks at Kit with strange amazement. "We really did it, huh?"

Kit nods. "We really did."

"I guess that means...we can do anything."

Violet smiles, walks away. Kit is aching at so many good-byes. One more goodbye might be the end of her.

The light in the foyer is bright, the grand double doors open. The air smells of spring and warm asphalt, from the driveway outside.

There's the sound of footsteps, and a light touch on Kit's arm.

"Come on," Moya says gently. "The car's waiting."

She looks like a fashion advertisement in a pair of navy wide-leg trousers and a white pin-tucked blouse with navy pumps. Her black hair is rolled to perfection, set off by her fire-engine-red lipstick.

Every time Kit sees Moya, she's stunned all over again. "You look beautiful. Did I tell you that?"

"A couple of times, yeah." Moya smiles gently. There's a graze near her temple, just near her hairline. Aside from that, you'd never know what Moya's been through in the last twenty-four hours.

"If I have to say goodbye to one more person, I'm gonna start bawling."

"Lucky that's the last one, then." Moya collects a red clutch and her burgundy trench coat from the old adminis-tration desk. "Ditch the goodbyes—stick to compliments."

Kit feels like she's going to burst with all this emotion.

"I guess I'll have plenty of time to keep telling you you're beautiful during the trip."

Moya just grins. "I imagine some of my glow will have worn off by then, but knock yourself out."

"That's when I'll switch to telling you how brave and smart you are."

"You cheese." Moya rolls her eyes, but she looks secretly delighted. "Give Julian your bag."

"Yes, I'll take that," Julian Harding says, walking up to collect Kit's carpet bag. "Is this all you're bringing, Miss Sutherland? It feels rather light."

Kit shrugs. "That's all I've got. The rest belongs to someone else."

Moya gives her a soft smile. Julian walks Kit's luggage out to the car, and Kit finds that Moya has taken her hand.

"Ready to stop looking over your shoulder?" Moya's eyes are shining, the light from the open door giving her a radiant halo.

"To avoid a court martial?" Kit laughs and squeezes Moya's hand, brings it to her lips. "So ready. But you said you hate the English weather...."

Moya leans so their foreheads touch, her eyes closing. "If we're together, I'm sure I'll cope."

"Moya." Kit feels her body tremble with these feelings. "I want to live life, take chances, and dream dreams...but only if I can do it with you."

"You got me." Moya straightens and grins, blinking back tears. "You got me good—and that's one code you won't ever have to decipher."

Kit's still smiling as Julian returns, ushers them forward. "This way, ladies."

Kit tears her gaze away from Moya to look at him. "So this airplane we're flying in—"

"Technically, it's a seaplane," Julian says as they walk toward the door.

"He keeps going on about the 'technically' parts," Moya says, tucking Kit's hand into the crook of her elbow. "It's a guy thing."

"That's correct," Julian affirms. "It's certainly a 'guy' thing, to want to know the specifications of the vehicle in which you're traveling thousands of miles through enemy territory."

Moya rolls her eyes again. "It's only taking us to Newfoundland. They're going to row us to the steamer from there."

Kit's eyebrows lift. "They're rowing us?"

"Well," Julian says, "only to the steamer. The seaplane for this first leg is a fixed-wing aircraft capable of taking off and alighting on water."

Kit squints at Moya. "So...it's a flying boat?"

"Yep." Moya catches Kit's eye. "What's so funny?"

Kit shoulders her handbag and looks through the open entrance of Arlington Hall. The outside sun is warm. She's really doing this. She's going to walk out the door and keep on walking.

"Nothing you'd ever believe." Kit smiles at Moya. "But I'll try to explain it to you on the way to England."

AUTHOR'S NOTE

When the publication of *The Killing Code* was announced, a good author friend of mine, Lili Wilkinson, exclaimed, "I always wanted to write a codebreaking-ladies book but couldn't face the research (or the maths) and now Ellie Marney is very kindly writing it so I can just read and enjoy!"— which made me laugh, because she wasn't wrong: There was a LOT of research involved in the making of this book, and if I've made any errors or taken license with details, I hope you'll forgive me.

I would first like to thank all those who granted permissions for the use of quotes by female codebreakers in *The Killing Code*. I'd particularly like to acknowledge Megan Harris, research specialist at the Veterans History Project of the Library of Congress, who provided advice around permissions for quotes by Ann Caracristi; Melissa Davis, from the George C. Marshall Foundation, Lexington, Virginia, for advice around permissions for quotes by Elizebeth Friedman; the National Security Agency for the use of quotes by Wilma Davis (née Berryman) from their Oral History Interview series; and the National Physical Laboratory in the UK for advice around permissions for quotes by Alan Turing. I acknowledge the generosity of HarperCollins for the use of quotes by Agnes Meyer Driscoll (from *And I Was There* by Rear Admiral Edwin Layton et al.).

I also very much appreciate the kind advice of Jason Fagone, author of *The Woman Who Smashed Codes* (Dey Street, 2017).

I have tweaked history a little when describing the first segregated unit of Black cryptologists, which didn't exist until 1944. But William D. Coffee—originally hired as a janitor—organized Black codebreakers and ran the daily operations of that office. He was awarded the Commendation for Meritorious Civilian Service in 1946. The book *Invisible Cryptologists: African-Americans, WWII to 1956* by Jeanette Williams (Center for Cryptologic History, NSA, Series V, Vol. 5, 2001) provided important information about this crucial unit.

I would like to acknowledge the other authors whose tireless work uncovering the secrets of wartime signal intelligence, and the contributions of women during World War II, was so critical to the development of the manuscript. Particular mentions must go to Cindy Gueli, author of *Lipstick Brigade: The Untold True Story of Washington's World War II Government Girls* (Tahoga History Press, 2015); Charlotte Webb, author of *Secret Postings: Bletchley Park to the Pentagon* (Booktower Publishing, 2014); Michael Smith, author of *The Secrets of Station X: How Bletchley Park Codebreakers Helped Win the War* (Biteback Publishing, 2011); Margot Lee Shetterly, author of *Hidden Figures: The American Dream and the Untold Story of the Black Women Mathematicians Who Helped Win the Space Race* (William Morrow & Co., 2016); and Robert Harris, author of *Enigma* (Hutchinson, 1995).

A number of podcasts provided essential details for *The Killing Code*, particularly the *Bletchley Park* podcast and the UCL podcast *Codebreaker: My Top-Secret Codebreaking During*

World War II, a recording of a fantastic speech by the late Captain Raymond C. "Jerry" Roberts. I'd also like to send my love and appreciation to author Kate Armstrong, and her amazing podcast *The Exploress*, for advice and suggestions along the way.

Some people went out of their way to provide assistance— I'd like to acknowledge and give hugs to author Kelly Gardiner, who sourced materials on my behalf from the current Bletchley Park estate and museum. Thanks so much, Kel!

Above all, this book would not exist without Liza Mundy's staggering work of research, *Code Girls: The Untold Story of the American Women Codebreakers of World War II* (Hachette, 2017). When I first read the book, my imagination caught fire. Throughout long months of drafting, I went back to *Code Girls* again and again for inspiration and detail, and I encourage everyone who has an interest in the extraordinary work of women codebreakers to read it.

If you have an interest in codebreaking, see what you can make of this:

```
23  5 12 12  0  4 15 14  5  0 25 15 21  0  1
18  5  0  1  0  8  1 14  4 25  0 12  9 20 20
12  5  0  3 15  4  5  2 18  5  1 11  5 18
```

And if you're *very* clever, give this one a try:

```
GIJV HMXI WYY YBI Y RELNC JSXRVI
AYHCLVCKOCB
```

ACKNOWLEDGMENTS

I'm always so exhausted at the end of writing a book! And this book was particularly tiring, written over long pandemic months while everything seemed to be falling apart. There were a number of false starts and rewrites, but we got there in the end, and I couldn't have done it without a whole cast of friends and supporters.

First thanks should go to my amazing agent, Josh Adams, and the team at Adams Literary, to whom I owe a large debt of gratitude, always. Thank you so much, Josh and Tracey!

Secondly, I'd like to thank my editor, Hallie Tibbetts, who took my story and polished it to an absolutely perfect shine. Hallie, you were right! (About a lot of things, but especially about trusting my writing.) I'd also like to thank Liz Kossnar for taking up the reins so brilliantly and wrangling *The Killing Code* to final publication. Thank you, Liz.

Many thanks to the incredible team at Little, Brown Books for Young Readers—especially to copyediting whiz Vivian Kirklin (sorry about all the ellipses!) and production editor Jake Regier. Gratitude to Sarah Van Bonn and Jennifer So for outstanding proofreading skills. Massive thanks to Bill Grace, Andie Divelbiss, Christie Michel, and Savannah Kennelly from the Little, Brown sales and marketing team, which never gets enough credit, and once again, all love to the incredible Siena Koncsol in publicity. I'd like to make a special note of Charlene Allen, who read this book for authenticity in its portrayals and provided advice on making it better.

I'd like to especially mention my acquiring editor, Hannah Milton, who first read *The Killing Code* and loved it— thank you, Hannah. Sincere best wishes, and good luck on all your adventures.

Thanks, too, to the fabulous folk at Allen & Unwin for bringing *The Killing Code* to Australian and New Zealand readers. All my gratitude to Sophie Splatt, Jodie Webster, Eva Mills, and every member of the publishing and publicity team.

So many readers have written to me or shouted encouragement during the writing of *The Killing Code*—thank you from the bottom of my heart. Special thanks to my newsletter peeps (hi!) and to everyone on social media who has given me a boost when I needed it.

I would hardly write a word without my main crew, the Great Goosemoot, the Council, the House of Progress team—all my love and hugs to Amie, Lili, Nic, Skye, Eliza, Peta, Kate, Liz, and Ebony. Thanks to Jay Kristoff for cheering from the sidelines and to Will Kostakis, who is a total boss. Many hugs should also go to the women of the Vault, especially Fleur, Rachael, and Gab. And I couldn't have dragged myself over the finishing line without C. S. Pacat, who is a true friend and a bloody amazing writer.

Final thanks always go to my family. Big hugs to my sister Lucy as well as Bae, Millie, Frankie, and new lad Ewan. My own kids keep me sane somehow, and with this book, they endured long days when I was bolted to my writing chair—Ben, Alex, Will, and Ned, I hope you know how much I love you.

And to my partner, Geoff—I say it in every book, but it's still true: You, sir, are a prince amongst men.

xxEllie

Christopher Tovo

ELLIE MARNEY

is a *New York Times* bestselling author of crime thrillers, including *The Killing Code, None Shall Sleep, White Night, No Limits,* the Every series, and the Circus Hearts series. Her books have been published in ten countries and optioned for television. She's spent a lifetime researching in mortuaries, interviewing law enforcement officers, talking to autopsy specialists, and asking former spies about how to make explosives from household items, and now she lives quite sedately in southeastern Australia with her family. Ellie invites you to find out more about her and her books at elliemarney.com.